Into The Mist

A LaShaun Rousselle Mystery

Lynn Emery

Lazy River Publishing
Baton Rouge, Louisiana

Lynn Emery, Lazy River Publishing
P.O. Box 74833
Baton Rouge, LA 70874
www.lynnmery.com

Publisher's Note: This is a work of fiction. Names, charac-ters, places, and incidents are a product of the author's imagina-tion. Locales and public names are sometimes used for atmospheric purposes. Any resemblance to actual people, living or dead, or to businesses, companies, events, institutions, or lo-cales is completely coincidental.

.

Into The Mist/ Lynn Emery. -- 1st ed.
ISBN 978-0-9965272-5-5

Dedicated to the strong resourceful Louisiana women of color, past and present. From the nameless enslaved heroines brought from Mother Africa, to those who have made a mark in history, such as Marie Laveau, Henriette DeLille, and Madam C.J. Walker, we are all your daughters.

"Lache pas la patate"
(Don't Give Up)

Chapter 1

At almost six o'clock in the morning, LaShaun and Chase were up, ready for the day. Chase hadn't yet put on his Vermilion Parish Sheriff's uniform. The royal blue shirt with the department logo in gold thread still hung over the door of their bedroom. Instead he wore dark denim jeans with his favorite sweatshirt. LaShaun padded about in fuzzy slippers and her own cotton sweats. Her thick hair was pulled back into a single braid down her back. Despite her work-at-home attire, she wore her favorite small gold hoop earrings.

"What is it with these gloomy days?" Chase muttered as he looked out through the bay window of their breakfast nook. "I'm so ready for spring."

"Well, you'll be waiting a few months yet. We're just digesting Thanksgiving dinner, darlin'. By the way, drag that box of Christmas decorations out of the attic for me." LaShaun continued humming as she fed mangoes, plums and peeled apples into the food processor.

"Yeah, sure." Chase took his empty breakfast plate to the dishwasher and put it in. He leaned against the counter watching her in silence.

"What?" LaShaun said without pausing in her task.

"You really serious about making all of the kid's food," Chase said.

"Stop calling her 'The Kid'. She has a perfectly lovely name. I picked it out myself. Joëlle Renée Broussard. See how it rolls off the tongue." LaShaun smiled. Almost four years after her birth, LaShaun could not help but feel wonder at the little blessing.

"I'm not going to say that mouthful every time I talk to her. Ellie is just fine." Chase poured his second full cup of hot coffee.

"Even your mother complains when you call her 'The Kid'." LaShaun poured the fruit concoction into a jar. She shot him an amused sideways glance. "I think you do it to annoy Queen Bee."

"Nah, I wouldn't deliberately irritate my dear mother. Even if she does take every chance to make snide remarks about you." Chase frowned. "Over a year and she's still tossing attitude about us our way."

❧

LaShaun put the jars of baby food into the refrigerator and closed the door. Wiping her hands on a dishtowel, she faced her husband. "I'm sorry about your mama, babe. I..."

Chase put down his coffee cup and used one long muscular arm to pull LaShaun against his chest. "Don't apologize. My mother's narrow-mindedness is the problem, not you. Everyone knows you're perfect in every way."

"Oh sure they do," LaShaun blurted out with a laugh. She titled her head up to kiss his chin. "The folks who think I'm a wicked voodoo priestess who chops off the heads of chickens under a full moon."

"We do happen to have a freezer full of chicken parts," Chase quipped. He chuckled when she tapped the end of his nose with her forefinger.

LaShaun playfully pushed him away. "Keep your job in law enforcement. Comedy is *not* your calling, Chief Deputy Broussard."

"I should finish up chores around the home-stead before I head off to the substation. The gloomy weather won't help the mood around there." Chase picked up his coffee again.

"Ugly huh?" LaShaun said.

"As only a battle between drug dealers can be." Chase went to the mud room where they kept garden boots, jackets and gloves.

"I saw the morning news on KTL-NBC. That woman is cut up bad they said, in critical condition. I hope she survives to tell y'all what really happened." LaShaun walked closer so she could hear.

"Violent meth head, cycle of abuse that turns deadly. He's on the run." Thumping came as Chase moved items around preparing for his chores.

"Hmm, sounds straight-forward enough."

LaShaun silently said a prayer of safety for her family. She and Chase took great pains to keep the darkness of his work and LaShaun's past brushes with supernatural evil away from their home life. They needed to protect Ellie for as long as possible. Maybe she could have a few years of seeing the world as bright and wonder-ful before... LaShaun shook off the thought of what could lay ahead for her child.

"Hey, babe. We haven't made a decision about the dog yet," LaShaun said, eager to change the subject back to mundane family matters.

"What dog?" Chase called back.

"Don't try it. You agreed that Ellie would enjoy having a pet. Plus, a dog would be great company for us while you work long hours fighting crime." LaShaun poured the baby's ce-real into a pot of boiling water and stirred.

"We've got an alarm system in the house and one outside. Unless you plan on getting a mean junkyard Rottweiler, I don't see the point." Chase strolled back into the kitchen, work gloves tucked into his waistband.

⚜

"Studies show a barking dog is a deterrent to burglars, and what alarm system outside?" LaShaun looked at him.

"Our neighbors. Betty Marchand doesn't miss a thing going on over here, and her husband will pull out his shotgun in a minute. Oh, and he installed a couple of cameras to cover his barn and the back field behind their house. A few animals have been stolen in the past month or so." Chase grabbed a large trash bag from a drawer. He emptied the kitchen garbage bin into it.

"Humph, Xavier, Sr. isn't that jumpy. Besides, only a few chickens wandered off. Nosy Betty had him put up the cameras. You can bet she's scanning our property on the regular." LaShaun waved the large spoon as she talked.

Chase laughed. "Well, you have given her reasons to be... curious."

"Hey, not my fault some crazy cult decided the Rousselle family cemetery is supernatural ground zero." LaShaun gave a snort and went back to stirring.

"Which reminds me, I ran a query a few days ago. The ring leader of Juridicus hasn't surfaced yet."

"Juridicus spread the kind of mayhem and violence y'all dealing with right now. I wonder..." LaShaun squinted ahead as though the tile above her cooktop held clues.

"Meth and some of these other designer drugs cause wild side effects. Some of the crime scenes look like horror movie sets. Jabbing holes in themselves, tearing chunks of flesh out of other people, violent psychotic stuff. Screaming at demons or gargoyles," Chase replied, "nothing supernatural."

"Juridicus has a positive genius for staying invisible."

"Their leader is gone. The rest of the members are either on the run with him, in jail or dead. At least around Vermilion Parish and New Orleans."

LaShaun frowned. "Their headquarters still exist."

"He wasn't charged with a crime, so forget a search warrant. I can't justify the time and expense of doing an extensive search. Dave would have questions I couldn't answer."

Sheriff Dave Godchaux, more politician than lawman, had won election to office just shy of two years ago. He was a nice enough guy, but tended to be a stickler for playing by the rules. He wanted to keep the mayor and others happy. Talk of cults in Vermilion Parish would most definitely not accomplish that goal. Tourists to the lush swamps, grassy prairies and serene bayous didn't care for the idea they might end up as sacrificial offerings.

"Maybe I'll try." LaShaun murmured. She stared into the bubbling rice cereal.

"We shut down his crew, so he's lost his power I figure. I mean, he had those cult members convinced he couldn't be stopped. Now they know better, so they've scattered."

⚜

"They won't give up so easily. Like the old folks say, the devil stays busy." LaShaun jumped when Chase spoke right over her shoulder into her ear.

"No. Don't go looking for their kind of trouble."

"But I could..."

"And you're going to scorch Ellie's cereal," Chase added. He reached around her and turned off the burner beneath the pot. Then he turned LaShaun around until she faced him. "No internet search, no tapping into your fortune teller buddies, no nothing."

"They're not fortune tellers," LaShaun shot back.

"We squashed Juridicus like roaches, okay. They're finished. Let sleeping dogs lie," Chase said firmly.

"Fine. I won't look for Neal Montgomery," LaShaun huffed when Chase's dark Cajun gaze didn't waver, "or anything about the Juridicus crew. You know me too well."

"Exactly." Chase nodded before he turned to his task again. He grabbed the bag.

"Speaking of dogs..."

"Start thinking about what breed you might like. Since you want to research something, look at dogs good around kids," Chase replied as he headed to the back door.

"Smart advice. No wonder I keep you around," LaShaun teased.

❖

"You didn't marry me for my brains, woman. Admit it." Chase winked at her with a saucy half grin.

LaShaun put the spoon back into the pot of cereal. "That turned out to be a bonus, but the rest of the goods did pull me." Before she reached him, Ellie's voice came from the baby monitor on the granite counter top.

"You've got a hungry kid to feed, and I've got house chores." Chase laughed at the scowl LaShaun gave him. "Hey, you wanted a regular family life. Welcome to reality."

She gave a melodramatic sigh. "Romance is on the backburner. Go on. Hey, check the propane tank level while you're at it."

"Wow, you went from seductress to drill sergeant real fast." Chase gave her a sharp salute.

Ellie's baby voice got louder through the monitor. Her soft whining threatened to erupt into a full-fledged howl. LaShaun moved quickly to pour cereal into the warm bowl. Then she poured juice into a cup with a built-in straw. Ellie's fussing became more insistent with each passing second.

"I may be the sergeant, but we all know who the general is running this show," LaShaun murmured.

She gave the high chair one final swipe with a clean damp cloth, then headed for Ellie's room. LaShaun smiled as she looked ahead to her usual morning routine. The scent of baby

⚜

lotion mixed with the smell of food cooking. Having a regular life suited her just fine.

As she got closer to Ellie's room LaShaun felt the familiar prickle along her arms. The physical sensation acted as her biological alarm system. Ellie's voice had gone from irritable to light chatter. She spoke, paused and babbled again. The sounds came through the open nursery door just opposite the master bedroom.

"Ba-ba, weee. Mama come."

Caution won over LaShaun's mother instinct to call out to her. Being part of the Rousselle bloodline meant life would be different for Ellie. Yet surely they had more time. It couldn't be this early. LaShaun paused, then hurried her steps down the hallway.

"Mama is here."

Dressed in her pink pajama onesie, Ellie stood holding onto the rails of her white toddler bed. Chase's father had customized it by painting baby animals on the headboard and footboards. Ellie wore a calm expression as she pointed to a corner. LaShaun scanned the room from the doorway. Nothing out of place. Then LaShaun saw movement out of the corner of one eye. She glanced sharply and gasped. Curtains of pale yellow and green strips billowed softly out from the window.

"I didn't leave this cracked last night, did I? Maybe daddy opened it this morning. The heat did work overtime last night." LaShaun chattered over Ellie's baby talk in an attempt to reassure herself. She shut the window with a firm thud. "That had to be it."

"Daddy out." Ellie pointed to the window as though countering her mother's argument. "My Daddy." Ellie continued a sing-song repetition about her daddy. Then she clapped her hands.

"Who were you talking to, hmmm? Who was my Joëlle Renée talking to so early in the morning?" LaShaun crossed to the bed and picked Ellie up.

"Ma-ma-ma," Ellie murmured. Then her cute face twisted into distress. "Hungry, mama."

"Yes, yes. We're going to get some yummy into that tummy right now. Here we go to the kitchen for breakfast."

LaShaun heard water running from their master bedroom. Chase's baritone voice hummed along with the radio as he cleaned up. She started to ask him about the window, but Ellie's fussing returned full force, so LaShaun continued on to the kitchen. Twenty minutes later, Ellie had eaten her cereal and happily sucked from her juice cup. When Chase appeared, she dropped it with a delighted squeal. Her little arms reached out for him.

"There's my girl looking pretty as ever. Ellie boo-boo, daddy's sweetheart." Chase picked her up, kissed her plump cheek, and grinned at her.

"Don't shake her or you'll be changing shirts," LaShaun put leftover cereal in a sealed container.

⚜

"We can still sing about the baby rabbits, squirrels and possums." Chase launched them into Cajun French lyrics of a children's song.

LaShaun enjoyed watching him gently sway around the kitchen with Ellie trying to sing along. They had agreed to speak Louisiana Cajun and Creole French often to let Ellie pick up the language. After a few minutes, he finished to Ellie's applause. He put her back in the high chair. Ellie seemed to know the show was over. She went back to sucking juice. Between sips Ellie would chant "mama" and "daddy" softly. Chase smiled at her, love shining from his dark eyes.

"She's a beautiful little miracle, isn't she?"

"Yes, she truly is," LaShaun agreed. Then she thought back to the nursery scene. "And she'll be sneezing if you keep leaving the window open."

"Who me? Not that I remember. It did get too warm in here last night, so maybe I did."

"Like how big a crack, quarter of an inch, half an inch, or more?" LaShaun said, working to force a casual tone.

Chase faced LaShaun with both hands on his hips. "You sure gettin' picky. We got a rule now on how much to crack her window? I can be trusted with my baby girl."

"I didn't mean... Oh stop." LaShaun snapped a kitchen towel at him with a grin.

"Hey, she's a Broussard; she's made of hardy stuff, right, Ellie?" Chase said to the toddler.

⚜

Still sucking juice, she waved at him as if agreeing.

"Oh so it's two against one," LaShaun protested.

Chase took a call on his cell phone. He talked for five minutes then hung up. LaShaun recognized his "on-duty" expression, though the fact that he wasn't frowning indicated nothing serious had happened. She hoped.

"Time to go Broussard ladies." Chase went to retrieve his duty belt and gun from the large hall closet. He returned moments later with his coat and a dark olive felt hat.

"Nothing too bad, huh?"

"Nah, nothing to worry about. Not compared to the stuff we been through. Glad that's behind us." Chase crossed to Ellie, gave her a quick kiss and then kissed LaShaun on the cheek. "I should be home on time this afternoon. 'The good Lord willing and the creek don't rise' as Grandmére Jeanne used to say."

"Bye, honey." LaShaun waved at him, but Chase's attention was on his cell phone again and the job.

"Just you and me, Ellie. What shall we do? Mais oui, Un chien, ma petite fille." (Yes, a dog my little girl)

"Ma," Ellie said with enthusiasm.

LaShaun gazed out the window to the woods on her property. "We need a special dog for you."

⚜

****

The next morning, LaShaun bundled Ellie into a jacket with matching overalls. The skies had cleared, and the temperature warmed to the mid-fifties. She drove down Rougon Road until she got to Highway 82. Thirty miles later, she turned onto Old Sugar Mill Road. Just as Miss Rose had instructed. A small lane branched off about two miles west. Another ten minutes brought her to the gravel drive with a large mailbox shaped like a horse. The rear end held the opening for mail.

"And I thought Miss Rose was exaggerating," LaShaun said to Ellie. She glanced in the rearview mirror to find the baby wide awake and taking in the sights.

"Horse, le chev." Ellie pointed

"Le cheval," LaShaun corrected. Ellie repeated the word sounding closer to the correct French pronunciation. "Good girl. Let's not discuss which end of the horse is facing us."

LaShaun drove her bronze Subaru Forrester along the crushed gravel, grateful she hadn't washed the SUV yet. Mud puddles splashed as she hit a couple of small holes. She spotted a circular driveway that curved in front of a cottage style home. A familiar black Ford Explorer was already parked there. Justine Dupart Tullier, one half of the quirky twins LaShaun had grown close to, waved as LaShaun parked beside the Explorer. Justine and Pauline had joined forces with Rose Fontenot a few months before to help LaShaun fight Juridicus. The three older women introduced LaShaun to an organization of others with preternatural gifts.

"Told you it was easy to find. Just sounds complicated. Didn't take you long to get here either." Justine blew Ellie a kiss. "Oh, she's a doll. My second daughter is expecting her first. I hope it's a girl. Got three grandsons already. I love them to death, but they're all mud and sweaty kisses. How I'd just love to shop for pretty dresses."

"Hi Justine." LaShaun smiled as the middle-aged woman chattered along in true down home southern style. "You're looking good. How's your sister?"

"Grumpy as always. Here, let me lighten the load." Justine whisked Ellie away from LaShaun. She cooed and cuddled the baby.

"She's a bit fussy around people she doesn't know..."

LaShaun waited for the usual squawking that preceded loud bawling when strangers touched Ellie. Instead the toddler blinked rapidly as she looked around the scene and then up at Justine. She studied the unfamiliar face, then looked at her mother. When LaShaun smiled encouragement, Ellie smacked her lips and grinned at Justine.

"First time we meet and we're friends already. Baby knows Aunt Teen is on her side. Now let's go look at the puppies, eh?" Justine nodded toward the house.

⚜

"Well, I guess we will," LaShaun said as she followed Justine.

A tall café au lait man emerged from the house. His bushy light gray beard came down the front of a red plaid flannel shirt. He radiated a strong aura of quiet royalty that startled LaShaun. She stood still for a moment adjusting to the effect. After a moment, Justine noticed LaShaun had stopped. She faced her. Ellie had grown quiet as well.

"LaShaun, this is Mathieu Baptiste." Justine dipped her head to the man. "Morning Mathieu. Thanks for inviting us."

"Nice to meet you." LaShaun willed her feet to move toward him, and she extended a hand. His firm cool grip startled her a second time.

"Good meeting you, LaShaun. I knew your grandfather you know . . . and your grandmother," Mathieu added after a pause.

LaShaun felt drawn to Mathieu in a disturbing, but not totally unpleasant way. When he let go, LaShaun almost gasped. Then the sensation retreated. He reined in the power, which meant he had control. She also noticed the pause before he mentioned Monmon Odette, which told her a story was behind it. His calm hazel-eyed gaze communicated he could read her as well.

"I've never met anyone who knew Papa Rousselle," was all LaShaun could think to say. Her mind worked to process the flood of information absorbed with so few words.

Mathieu's smile transformed into an ordinary grandfatherly type. "We were good friends. One day I'll tell you stories of us hunting together as boys. But today we find a puppy for the little one."

"Le cheva," Ellie chirped.

"Oui, mon Cherie," Mathieu replied promptly. "You have your pick, little princess. This way, this way."

He waved them to follow as he set off down a path around the cottage. About fifty yards behind the house stood a smaller cottage. What would have been the front porch had been fitted with black metal bars. Divided into four sections, open archways led to rooms. Dogs of various sizes and colors yapped at the sight of them. Mathieu led them to the large fenced in area behind it.

"That is one fancy dog house," LaShaun murmured to Justine.

Justine laughed at Ellie's wide-eyed expression as she looked at the dogs. "They're fine le chien, eh Cherie?"

"Yes, I do love my dogs. But the finer touches are my wife's doing. She insisted on those planters. Very particular, like most nurses."

"She still works, a public health clinic in Abbeville," Justine put in.

"I have to say, it impresses my customers." Mathieu whistled and several dogs trotted up to the fence, tails wagging. He opened a gate and left them as he talked. "I only keep a few: seven, twelve at most."

⚜

"Seven is the symbol of completeness from the Bible. Twelve means power and authority," Justine whispered.

When Ellie babbled, Justine smiled at her before handing the baby to LaShaun. She joined Mathieu in the enclosure. LaShaun watched as Mathieu spoke with affection to each dog in turn. Some barked, others trotted around him and Justine in circles. LaShaun admired their healthy coats. The dogs seemed to know they were on display. They jockeyed for position, eager to be noticed.

"They're all so lovely. I'm having a hard time choosing," LaShaun said.

Mathieu continued to pet the dogs as he spoke over his shoulder. "Ah, Ellie will know."

"I hardly think Ellie can select a dog," LaShaun said with a laugh. She walked along the fence eyeing the dogs. "We don't want a young puppy of course, too much work with a baby already. Maybe one nine months to one-year-old. Of course then I'd have to train him, or her."

"No, you don't understand," Mathieu replied. He turned to face LaShaun with a sober expression. "Your little girl must choose, as he will be her protector."

"She'll recognize a connection to the dog," Justine added.

"You're not joking." LaShaun stared from Mathieu to Justine.

❧

"Come, they'll be gentle with her. Step in-side so she can take a closer look." Mathieu beckoned to LaShaun.

LaShaun gazed at the dogs who answered with barks and wagging tails. Though the gate was open, none of the dogs tried to escape. Something about the scene struck her as odd. The dogs quieted as if they sensed her hesita-tion. None of them approached her as she stepped into the enclosure. Ellie babbled point-ing to one dog and then another. She laughed. After a few seconds the dogs resumed running and jumping around. One, a soft gray color, trotted over to them. Justine stopped petting a brown and gray spotted hound to join them.

"Ah, such soulful eyes," Justine said, "yet playful, too."

The dog gave a soft huff, not quite a bark, and made a lap around them as if to prove her point. He bounded while Ellie clapped her soft chubby hands in approval.

"He is beautiful," LaShaun agreed. She mused on the strangeness of waiting for an in-fant to decide on a pet. "How—"

"Eleven months next week. He's a mixed Great Weimar, a mix of Great Dane and Wei-maraner," Mathieu said promptly.

"What's his name?" LaShaun warmed to the dog as she watched him.

"Ask Joëlle Renée," Mathieu replied.

"Okay now, c'mon. Ellie knows maybe twen-ty words. She is not going to name a dog.

❧

Granted she does seem to like him more than the others..." LaShaun's voice trailed away.

She studied Ellie's expression. The baby hadn't taken her gaze from the gray dog for several minutes. Ellie waved an arm and the dog trotted over to her. LaShaun jumped when he reared up to place two paws on her waist. He presented his muzzle to Ellie. She gazed at the dog, then giggled.

"Bo."

Mathieu beamed at Ellie. "Well, that's it then. Her new dog is Beau, a male by the way. I have his papers. All in order with shots. Wonderful choice, ma petite."

LaShaun blinked rapidly as he bustled off rubbing his hands together. All she could catch of what he said was something about the paperwork and feeding him. She looked down at Beau and then at Justine. Beau yawned and sat down as if taking a break now that the formalities had wrapped up.

"What just happened?" LaShaun gazed ahead as Mathieu disappeared through the back door of his house.

"You have a new pet. Pauline and Rose will be impressed when I tell them. You've made a fine, fine choice my child. Yes, indeed."

"Justine, the dog..."

"Beau," Justine broke in.

"He's almost a year old, so how can we simply change its name? You don't think she picked a name because she blurted out a sound." LaShaun kissed the soft dark curls on top of Ellie's head. Then she pulled the hood up to protect her from the cool morning air.

"As I said, Ellie is connected to him and he will respond. And she didn't give him a new name. Ellie called him by name." Justine laughed at LaShaun's baffled expression.

"Beau, mama." Ellie reached down just as Beau lifted his muzzle again to be petted.

Justine tilted her head to one side as she looked at LaShaun. "Well?"

"Wait until Chase hears about this adventure." LaShaun grinned at Justine.

"After all he's seen, I doubt he'll bat an eye," Justine joked.

"Come to my office, ladies," Mathieu yelled from his back door. "To my office so we can finish. Yes, yes."

LaShaun waited while Justine closed the gate, though it hardly seemed necessary. Indeed, once inside, Mathieu assured them they could have left it open. He let the dogs run free regularly in the open meadows of his land. They always returned.

"This is their home," he said with a wide smile when LaShaun remarked on it. "Now these are his papers. I put a bag of food in your Subaru. I put one seat down, hope you don't mind. No, no happy to do it. I have plenty, a storage shed full of fifty pound bags."

Fifteen minutes later, Beau sat next to Ellie in her car seat. LaShaun and Justine stood saying their goodbyes to Mathieu. When his phone rang, he scurried off to conduct more business.

⚜

Beau jumped into the back of the SUV. Then he lay down, head on both large paws. He and Ellie seemed content to wait while the adults finished visiting.

"We'll be in touch for a meeting, Rose, Pauline and me. You should get a babysitter for Ellie. Some things she should not hear just yet." Justine nodded with a thoughtful frown.

"Um, okay." LaShaun studied her. "You have more to tell me?"

"Unfortunately, yes." Justine's solemn expression gave way to a lighter one. "But today the sun is shining, and Ellie has a new best friend. So, we celebrate the little joys."

LaShaun hugged Justine and thanked her for the help. Justine tooted the horn of her Explorer before driving off. With one last wave to her, LaShaun got into the Forrester. Beau lifted his head as though giving her the all clear sign. She turned on the radio to soft music. Ellie hummed along in off key baby fashion. Though she started the SUV, LaShaun paused to look over the registration and health documents Mathieu had provided. LaShaun read the first few lines and then stopped.

"Male puppy born to Lady M on December 27, 2015. Named... Beau on January 2nd." LaShaun looked from the papers to Ellie, who smiled at her before turning to pet Beau on the nose.

⚜

Chapter 2

That evening Beau greeted Chase when he got home later than usual from work. LaShaun had alerted him via text messages throughout the day, so he wasn't surprised. She'd bought supplies and even got Beau listed with the local vet. Beau lay in his doggie bed half dozing as they ate dinner.

"He's a good lookin' dog, I gotta admit," Chase said between chews. He drank from his water glass and sighed. "I like that he's quiet. After the day I've had..."

"Beau is just about perfect." LaShaun waved to Beau, who lifted his head once then settled back again.

"Give him a few days and we'll see how well behaved he is," Chase retorted. He stabbed his fork into more beef.

"Sure, like most males, they're on their best behavior during the honeymoon. Once they get comfortable the real guy comes out." LaShaun grinned at Chase.

"I get the feeling we ain't talking about the dog anymore. Watch it, lady." Chase pointed his fork at her. "This is some good beef stir-fry. Who needs takeout when I got you at home?"

"You're welcome. Fresh veggies, noodles and the right ingredients are key. And yes, I'm going to make sure we eat more organic foods. Including you, Beau." LaShaun nodded to the pooch, who gave a low woof.

Chase ate the last tender morsel of beef. After draining his water glass, he rose and walked over to Beau. He kneeled to scratch behind one of Beau's ears. "So now I've got both my girls talking to the family pet and spoiling him. Organic chow and this fancy dog sofa. You've seduced my women, boy. I'm kinda jealous."

"We have plenty of love to go around in this family," LaShaun teased. She began clearing the table.

"He's pretty big. Beau is gonna eat us into debt the older he gets." Chase rubbed Beau's smooth gray coat.

"Ellie chose him so he's just right." LaShaun put away leftovers.

Chase walked to the kitchen. He washed his hands before helping her. Then he started loading the dishwasher. "So you're telling me Ellie chose this dog over all the others."

⚜

"I wanted her to feel comfortable with any pet I chose of course. If she'd been scared or nervous, then no point in getting her a dog, right?" LaShaun packed up a lunch for Chase to take the next day. She included an egg roll as a little something extra.

"Tell me everything." Chase turned on the dishwasher then leaned against the counter, arms crossed.

"I don't know what you mean."

"The magical twins suggested a specific dog breeder, so there must be some hocus-pocus involved. Beau looks like a normal dog to me, but then, you looked like a normal woman when we first met." Chase dodged the potholder LaShaun tossed at his head and caught it mid-air.

"Keep it up, Broussard, and you'll go into work with a bandage on your noggin." LaShaun shook a finger at him, then sighed when he crossed his arms again. "Okay, okay. Monsieur Mathieu Baptiste is Justine's fourth cousin. He has a way with animals, an intuitive kind of bond. Also his dogs aren't spooked by paranormal vibes. They're more likely to protect us when we have to battle evil spirits."

"Promise to never say stuff like that in front of my boss."

"Everybody within twenty-five miles of Beau Chene thinks I hold regular séances." LaShaun laughed, but stopped when she noticed Chase was serious. She raised her right hand. "I solemnly swear to avoid referring to any and all supernatural phenomena in close proximity to Sheriff Godchaux."

"Thank you."

"Look, since ancient times, dogs have been regarded as protectors from evil. In Mesopotamia, Sumer, and Egypt dogs were companions to the gods. They protected homes from enemies. So..." LaShaun's voice trailed off.

"Here we go." Chase pulled a large hand over his face.

"Adam and Eve were farmers after the fall, so were their sons. They used dogs to protect the herds. In Jewish tradition, Abel's dog stayed with him for days even after his brother Cain murdered him. Legends say certain bloodlines are those first herd of dogs." LaShaun shrugged as Chase continued to stare at her. "What?"

"Let me just get this straight. Your support group for psychics have dogs descended from Abel's dog, the Biblical Abel." Chase blinked at her. Beau made a couple of soft woofs. He pointed to Beau. "You stay out of this."

"Stop calling us a support group for psychics like it's a disease or something. Anyway, they have a name, TEA, LLC."

"You're kidding, they formed a corporation? What's TEA stand for?"

LaShaun smiled. "Third Eye Association. Third eye means being able to see beyond the senses, and more than just psychics. Like Mr. Baptiste, some have extraordinary gifts that don't involve the dead or supernatural."

⚜

"I'm officially in my own version of the world of wizards." Chase hung his head, eyes closed. Then he looked up at LaShaun again.

"We're not 'sorcerers, but we have gifts. We use ours to fight 'the dark side'." LaShaun pitched her voice low to imitate a movie villain.

"Does Ellie have paranormal ability?"

"Would it bother you if she did? Of course there was no way to be sure, or that she'd show signs at such a young age," LaShaun said softly and glanced in the direction of the nursery.

"What signs?"

"It could be just a coincidence... But she named our dog." LaShaun cleared her throat as Chase walked up to her.

"'Scuse me?" Chase frowned.

"She pointed at him and said 'Bo'. So at first I thought, hey, she makes up names and stuff all the time. But Mr. Baptiste and Justine looked pleased, and then afterward, I read on the registration papers that he was named Beau a few days after birth."

Chase's expression relaxed. "You got it right the first time. I'll bet she was going boo, bo, ba-ba the whole time. Anything else?"

LaShaun decided not to mention the open window in Ellie's room, or how she seemed to be having a conversation with someone. Or something. "No..."

"I'm not saying it would be a bad thing for her to take after her mama." Chase pulled LaShaun into her arms. "After all, you're pretty damn amazing. But let's not read into normal baby talk."

LaShaun smiled at him. "We did have a pretty typical day afterward. The usual fussing for her food, getting most of it on herself and the floor. Oh, and I brought Beau to her play date with your sister Katie's twins. He's so good with children."

"What did I say? You're the average work-at-home mama." Chase kissed her forehead and then yawned. "Let's follow Ellie's lead and hit the bed."

"You said something about after the day you had. Not more killings I hope," LaShaun replied.

Chase finished tidying up the counter top as he spoke. "Not here, just over the line in Acadia Parish off Highway 13. But it could be related. One of their deputies is coming down to sit in on the court hearing and talk to me. I don't' know why they want to drive all this way. With phones, emails and even video conferencing, they could save time and gas."

"Hmm, sometimes face-to-face is best, even with all our technology. The human touch is still important." LaShaun thought of Justine's parting words about meeting with her, Miss Rose and Pauline.

"Yeah, maybe. I just hope—" Chase stopped when the ringing of his cell phone cut into their conversation. "Hello. Yeah, MJ, I figured you weren't calling just to say hello. When? Right."

⚜

He hung up, no trace of fatigue in his move-ments.

"Our warm bed is waiting." LaShaun wrapped both arms around his waist as she walked behind him.

"A law officer's work is 24-7, darlin'. You know not to wait up." Chase patted her hands at his waist.

"Ellie and Beau wore me out, so not likely. Can you tell me?" LaShaun let go but followed him to their bedroom.

"You'll sleep better not hearing the details. I'm going for a quick look-see, so I shouldn't be gone long."

Beau trotted in to join LaShaun as she watched him get dressed. Chase kicked off his house moccasins and put on warm wool socks against the cold December night air. His dark brown boots went on after. He pulled on a den-im shirt first, then a pullover sweater. Last, he slipped into his brown suede jacket and felt hat.

LaShaun cupped his face. "You're the best lookin' cop in the state." Then she kissed him.

"You could be right," Chase said, checking himself in the mirror. He chuckled when she gave him a playful swat on the shoulder. "Hey, Beau. I'm counting on you to guard the home front."

"We'll be just fine."

"Put on the alarm as usual. I've already checked the perimeter." Chase spoke in his take charge, on-duty tone.

"You make it sound like we're in a war zone," LaShaun quipped.

"Sometimes it feels like it." Chase retrieved his duty belt. With a last kiss he was out the door.

As LaShaun locked it behind him, the land-line phone rang. The antique clock down the hall chimed a quarter to ten. "Hello."

"La maison est en mauvaise ordre, allons la réparer," came a throaty female response. (The house is in bad shape, let's repair it)

****

"But you told Chase you wouldn't go looking for evidence that Montgomery or his cult is operating again." Savannah squinted at LaShaun across the table. "I'm an old married lady compared to you and—"

"We're the same age," LaShaun replied promptly. "And you've known me long enough to realize lectures go over my head."

"Keeping secrets, even with the best of intentions, is a seriously bad idea," Savannah finished despite LaShaun's squint of annoyance.

The two friends sat at a small café table in a corner of the St. Julien family shop on Main Street in Beau Chene. Savannah St. Julien Honoré's law office was two blocks away. Her father, Antoine, sold handmade carved wooden figurines. Other Louisiana artists sold their paintings, stoneware and sculptures there also.

⚜

Lagniappe also sold pastries and candy made by Savannah's aunt, a famed Vermilion Parish cook. Decked out for Christmas, the shop had been a tourist and local favorite for over twenty years.

"Hmm, your Tante Marie's banana nut muffins can't be beat." LaShaun nibbled a morsel and washed it down with café au lait. "As usual, I'll share what you find out with Chase, but only if there's anything to know."

"And your promise?"

LaShaun sighed and sat back against the café chair back. "Let me have this rare mom's day out in peace. It's like I'm on the witness stand and you're the prosecutor."

"Humph."

"Look, I promised Chase *I* wouldn't search. You, on the other hand, weren't part of the deal." LaShaun picked up her mug again. "So let's skip the 'I'm trying to keep you out of trouble again' speech."

"It's never worked anyway," Savannah shot back. "Try not to become a murder suspect this time."

"So funny. Now what did you find out?"

Savannah gave a resigned sigh. "Down the rabbit hole we go. I came up empty on the Juridicus ring leader. Far as I can tell, Montgomery isn't practicing law in this country."

"He could have gone abroad. He wasn't charged with a crime, so there's no reason he couldn't leave the US." LaShaun gazed through

❧

the shop window without seeing the quaint small town scene outside.

"True. We know Juridicus had international ties, lawyers all over the world representing some of the worst of the worst. I still can't believe it. Lawyers and judges dressed in black robes and chanting incantations. Whew," Savannah said.

"You didn't tell me some of them were judges," LaShaun blurted out. Then she lowered her voice when a couple of customers glanced their way.

"Sure, let the entire town know we're stirring your magical pot again," Savannah mumbled. She smiled and waved at Tante Marie, who worked the counter. The older woman lifted an eyebrow, but went back to chatting with two customers.

"Don't be so dramatic. So we've got people with even more power in Juridicus. Bad news." LaShaun heard Miss Rose's late night phrase echo.

"Juridicus members still have meetings at their headquarters in New Orleans. I'm surprised they've got the nerve after that mess with Montgomery being tied to a murder," Savannah said.

"Why not? Juridicus was never mentioned. As far as anyone else knows, a group of crazy folks took their role playing too far." LaShaun drummed her fingers on the glass table top.

⚜

"Well, his influential buddies no doubt helped. Including Philip Trosclair." Savannah said his name quietly.

LaShaun grunted at the mention of the member of that rich, powerful old Vermilion Parish family. "Their influence in Louisiana is like the roots of a two-hundred year old oak tree. Thick, deep and wide."

"But it's not just the Trosclair clan. Juridi-cus' members list reads like a Who's Who of old New Orleans families. I dug deep, so you owe me."

"I'll buy you another round of beignets," LaShaun teased.

"Big spender. The word Juridicus means a day of court or justice. The group's website has been updated in the last six months at least. Very impressive. Their mission statement talks about seeking justice for the underdog. Not just the poor, but those who are wrongly accused. Lots of high-minded twaddle about changing the world for the better, making the justice sys-tem work to get the right results, etc."

"Yeah, and?"

"They've formed a non-profit as a separate division from the core group called HOPE. Le-gal pros take up cases. The non-profit arm helps the accused and their families with social services, housing, financial assistance, even finds them jobs. That includes folks getting out of prison."

⚜

"Sounds wonderful. Too bad they're a bunch of demon loving sadists bent on world domination," LaShaun murmured quietly.

"Now who's being dramatic?" Savannah raised a palm when LaShaun started to object. "Granted they got up to some creepy cult crap. But you broke up their party. You know the only good thing about crazies up to no good? They do insane stuff that gets them noticed by law enforcement eventually."

"Yes, but look at the damage they do in the meantime. A few members with no direct visible ties go to jail. Juridicus is free to continue operations. How many cases of killers have they been repping?" LaShaun looked at Savannah with a frown.

"There's no pattern, if that's what you're asking. Even if we tried, their attorney members are practicing just like the rest of us. Some are in law firms, while others have private practices. They take cases from the Justice Project, or get assigned by courts in capital cases." Savannah shrugged and then drank the last of her latte.

"The fact that they're mostly defending serial killers, wouldn't stand out. Nobody ever claimed the devil or his minions were dumb," LaShaun replied softly. "I've got to find a way of forcing them into the open."

"Look, like all good Catholics, I know there are demons, spirits, saints and angels. Montgomery and his posse may be impressive, but..." Savannah gazed at LaShaun.

⚜

"Yes, I do believe they're trying to usher in a new world order." LaShaun glanced around to make sure the other three tables were empty. Then she leaned forward. "Evil and chaos chip away at social order. To most folks it looks random, but there's method to the chaos."

"You talk like those folks who march around shouting the end is near. Not to mention those apocalyptic sects," Savannah replied.

LaShaun sat back with a laugh. "Relax. I'm not about to take a group into the mountains to wait for the end of times."

"Glad to hear it," Savannah joked. Then she got serious again. "Your crime right here is related?"

"Maybe not. Then again." LaShaun raised an eyebrow.

"Lord." Savannah bit her lower lip.

"Cheer up. All I've got is theory." LaShaun smiled at her friend. "We have enough humans behaving badly to make me think they must be devils."

"I could write a book, but I won't. Client-attorney privilege. Even in my civil practice, the vindictiveness and double-crossing leaves even jaded me breathless at times." Savannah gave a shudder. "Let's talk about mundane stuff, like kids. So Ellie is spending quality time with her grandmother. Progress, eh?"

"Speaking of witches," LaShaun replied dryly.

Savannah choked on the last chunk of beignet she'd just put in her mouth. After a few coughs, she took a breath. "Girl, don't."

She and LaShaun laughed hard. LaShaun pretended to pound her on the back. Savannah coughed more as they both giggled uncontrollably for several minutes. Tante Marie came over with two glasses of water and put them on the table. Tante Marie planted her hands on both of her generous hips. Even after six children, she still had her hour glass figure, though with more curves. At sixty-seven she looked good in the red sweater and dark blue corduroy jeans. She gazed at them as they both drank.

"You two better not be plotting confusion. *Again.*"

"No, ma'am," LaShaun and Savannah said together. Then they laughed more.

"Uh-huh, like I believe you." Tante Marie's dark eyes narrowed. "At least leave the town standing once you're through."

"For sure." LaShaun grinned at her and winked.

"We don't start trouble, but we finish it. Hey, that could be our slogan." Savannah tapped LaShaun's shoulder.

"Give me strength. Kiss your little one for me, LaShaun." Tante Marie waved a hand at them as she went to greet two new customers.

"Will do," LaShaun called after her. She looked at Savannah. "I don't think we have much credibility with her."

⚜

"Bad track records. Anyway, back to the other Mrs. Broussard."

LaShaun grimaced. "Katie and Sharon took Ellie to see her. Chase will pick up Ellie in another hour or so. It's a compromise."

"You have to bridge that gap some kinda way. The holidays will be miserable otherwise, and Ellie will begin to sense it."

"Yeah, I don't want her to think she has to choose sides in a family feud, but Queen Bee doesn't make it easy. I could deal with her. As long as she doesn't treat Ellie like an outcast. The second either Chase or I think that's happening, we'll step in." LaShaun nodded.

"In the meantime, you keep your distance when possible." Savannah shrugged. "Not ideal, but workable."

"At least Elizabeth is mostly on her best behavior when we do have family gatherings. Though I'm not looking forward to the big Broussard Christmas. They go all out with dinner on Christmas Eve, then we go to Mass, back home to bed, and get up to open presents the next day." LaShaun gave a groan.

"Lord, sounds exhausting."

"It is. Chase's sisters think it's time to retire the tradition. Katie has the twins, plus her six year-old. Sharon says it's too much work trying to satisfy her parents and her in-laws. Even Elaine, the good, loyal daughter agrees. So the Broussard siblings suggest we just have Christmas Eve dinner early at their parents'

home and then everyone go to their respective homes." LaShaun sighed. "Thank God, too."

"Oh-oh, you're going to be blamed." Savannah pointed to LaShaun.

LaShaun rolled her eyes. "I don't care. A few months of her pouting will be worth it in the long run."

"Yeah, you marry the guy and his *family*. All we can do is make the best of it." Savannah shrugged again.

"Sure, says the woman with perfect in-laws."

"I did catch a break. Although one of his sisters tends to be bossy. Luckily she lives in Dallas." Savannah grinned. "Distance makes for harmony."

"But I work to get along because of Ellie. The things we do for our kids." LaShaun smiled at the thought of Ellie.

"Including not looking for crazed cult members. Don't poke the hornet's nest."

LaShaun's sunny mood clouded over. The memory of curtains floating and Ellie babbling to someone, or something, gave her a chill. "Trouble can come even when you're not looking for it. Closing your eyes to the signs is dangerous."

****

Saturday morning dawned into a beautiful day for December. In typical Louisiana fashion,

the weather warmed up to the sixties after being cold for over a week. LaShaun kissed Chase
goodbye to leave him and Ellie for a father
daughter day. He'd laughingly assured her he
could take care of their toddler, so she set off to
Mouton Cove and the home of Rose Fontenot.
The drive helped LaShaun clear her thoughts
on recent events. When she pulled up to Miss
Rose's sprawling ranch home, Pauline waved to
her from the front porch.

"You got a good man. He spends times with
his baby girl." Tall and slim like her twin, Pauline nodded with approval.

LaShaun laughed. Typical for Miss Rose
and the twins. None of the usual greetings or
chit-chat. They gave their opinions on what
they already knew. A relief with other psychics
since they had to curb the habit with the non-
gifted, meaning over ninety percent of the population. She gave Pauline a peck on the cheek.

"Good morning. I followed instructions and
didn't eat breakfast, which means..."

Pauline clapped her hands together. "You're
ready to eat. Rose just put the andouille sausage on the grill."

Miss Rose and Justine hardly paused in
their spirited discussion of a local election as
they greeted LaShaun. She happily fixed a
plate for herself and poured rich, dark coffee in
a mug. As the three older women continued debating, LaShaun took the edge off her hunger.
She savored enjoying the fluffy biscuits made
even better with honey from a nearby farm.

"I don't trust any of 'em," Justine said to finish her argument.

"Just because she got fancy friends and family in positions of authority doesn't mean she's crooked," Pauline said.

"Sometimes things are just what they seem. So LaShaun, what have you found out?" Miss Rose said. She and the twins waited while LaShaun washed down some of her food with coffee.

"I haven't found any evidence that Montgomery and Juridicus are trying to revive another malevolent force."

"Me neither." Miss Rose frowned.

"Good. We whipped up on 'em, so they're off licking their wounds." Justine bit into a slice of sausage and continued between chews.

"We know from experience they're skilled at working behind the scenes. What looks like a series of unrelated events is a complex plan" Miss Rose gazed over her reading glasses.

"Wheels within wheels," Pauline said.

"We don't know they're doing anything, Rose." Justine blinked when Pauline scowled at her. "I'm not being naïve. But... we forced them underground, which means they can't do as much damage."

"Or they're biding their time. Let's keep looking," Pauline said. "So we can't find Montgomery or his girlfriend."

"Probably dumped her once she stopped being useful." Justine focused on breakfast again.

⚜

"What about Juridicus and their sister organizations?" Miss Rose looked at LaShaun.

"My friend says they're still representing some of the most heinous killers around," LaShaun went on before Miss Rose could speak, "which is no different from lawyers all over the country and the world."

"Ironic. We suspect them of trying to break both kinds of law, man and God's. But on the surface, it looks like they're after justice." Pauline waved a hand with an expression of disgust.

"Plenty of folks go to prison for crimes they didn't do. Social activists love them." Justine shook a fork at them, a slice of sausage on the end of it. Then she put the morsel in her mouth.

"Not to mention Juridicus has never been implicated in wrongdoing, or criminal activity," LaShaun added. "They even have a non-profit now serving families of the accused, but also kids in the community."

"We should find out more about it, dig beneath the surface." Miss Rose left the table and came back with her laptop.

"Hey, let's at least finish breakfast," Justine protested as she poured more coffee in her mug from a carafe.

"You've had two biscuits and three pieces of sausage. At that rate you won't be finished with breakfast until lunch," Miss Rose shot back. "It's almost ten o'clock already."

"Not yet nine thirty." Justine squinted at her long-time friend. "Don't exaggerate."

"I agree. We shouldn't waste time." Pauline looked at LaShaun. "Tell me about the morning with your little one. She was in the room talking, the window was open."

"I didn't see or sense anything, and Ellie talks a blue streak all the time. Well, what passes for talking anyway." LaShaun forced a laugh to fight off the unease in her stomach. Pauline's intense scrutiny didn't help.

Pauline took both LaShaun's hands in hers. "Describe colors, sounds. Be exact."

LaShaun glanced at Justine who nodded at her to comply. Pauline closed her eyes. LaShaun began to talk and after a few moments lost herself in the memory of that morning. As she did so, her senses became heightened. She drifted from Miss Rose's breakfast table to her own home. After a few moments, LaShaun opened her eyes. She didn't remember closing them but obviously had at some point.

"What happened?" LaShaun felt panic rising.

"Ellie is safe, child." Miss Rose put a hand on LaShaun's arm. "Tell her Pauline."

Pauline let go of LaShaun's hands. "She is."

"For now." Justine gave them all a solemn nod.

"For now?" LaShaun repeated. Two simple words that took on an ominous meaning.

⚜

"There's no immediate danger, but..." Pauline heaved a deep sigh. "Feelers going out
searching for something."

"The open window?" Justine's eyebrows
scrunched together in thought.

"Possible. Children can sometimes see entities even in day time that adult sensitives
can't. Of course we all grow out of it. I used to
talk to an African ancestor all the time until I
turned four. Still miss that old man." Pauline
looked at her twin with a brief smile. Then she
grew serious again.

"So you think Ellie saw a spirit. My God,
she talked to this *thing*." LaShaun gripped the
edge of the table.

"The presence was weak. That's all I can
say right now." Pauline rested against the chair
back.

"I'll reach out to a couple of friends in the
New Orleans TEA. See if they have anything
remarkable to report." Justine stood and put an
arm around LaShaun's shoulder. "Don't assume the worst. Could have been some passing
spirit just visiting with your little one. Nothing
malicious at all, right, Pauline?"

Her sister blinked rapidly as she seemed to
pull back to Miss Rose's kitchen. "Happens all
the time, sure. There are benign spirits around
us"

"Then I have to find out which kind is trying to establish a connection to my child,"
LaShaun said, her voice shaking. "I don't like
the idea of either one talking to Ellie."

⚜

"Ah, you won't have a choice. Any more than you did. Her training must begin. We'll teach you," Miss Rose added quickly when LaShaun frowned.

"Even at her age there are things we can do and practice with her. Trust me, she'll understand. Just like she understood with Beau. Justine, you'll need those books we have for children. You know the ones. They look like Sunday School lessons."

"Yes, but they're not for children Ellie's age." Justine took out her iPad mini, pulled out a stylus and started making notes.

"Yes, she can't read yet. Can she?" Pauline turned to LaShaun.

"Single words like dog, cat, cow. Y'all are serious?"

"We'll have to improvise then. Use more pictures. Maybe flash cards," Miss Rose replied in a mild tone.

"Easy enough to do," Justine said without taking her gaze from the computer.

"Magical lessons for our baby. Chase is going to love this." LaShaun couldn't begin to fathom how to start such a conversation.

Coffin."

Chapter 3

LaShaun spent the rest of the weekend enjoying her family. She didn't want to darken such a bright time with talk of spirits reaching out to Ellie. By Monday, LaShaun had convinced herself there was nothing to worry about. All it took was a single text message to wreck that notion.

Ellie gurgled happily around a fist full of grits. She loved the warm cereal, though she got more on her face than in her mouth. Chase stood in the den before the television finishing up his second cup of coffee and watching the news. LaShaun hummed a tune as she began the task of cleaning up the baby and her high chair. When she glanced over, Chase frowned at his cell phone instead of looking at the television. He strode over to her, cell phone held out.

"We're going to need a sitter."

Two hours and three more urgent texts later from Chief Deputy Arceneaux, LaShaun followed Chase's truck. They headed to the Vermilion Parish Sheriff's substation near Cow Island, a small unincorporated community. Chase would be staying at work, so LaShaun drove her SUV instead of riding with him. They'd had only a few minutes to talk between calling around to arrange childcare, getting dressed and feeding Beau. They'd had to find a babysitter willing to take on a fussy toddler and a dog at the last minute. Tall order. Beau made it clear he would not leave Ellie's side. Despite grumbling from Chase, LaShaun's instinct told her to follow Beau's lead. Azalei, LaShaun's mouthy trouble-maker cousin, stepped up to the plate. Unemployed again because of her attitude and sharp tongue, Azalei arrived at their home with a girlfriend in tow. LaShaun had detailed written instructions by that time.

Chase parked his Dodge Ram truck in his reserved space and waited for LaShaun at the door for employees only. "I can't believe you let Azalei keep Ellie. Weren't you the one always telling me she's no good?"

"Azalei has changed, well mostly. She's great with kids. For money of course. Her problem is getting along with adults." LaShaun grabbed Chase's arm as they walked quickly through reception and toward Sheriff God-

❖

chaux's office. "I don't know what a crime has to do with me."

"Me either," Chase replied low with a frown. He glanced around as they walked as if searching for a clue.

MJ met them halfway down the hall before they went to the sheriff's office. Tall and strong, Myrtle Jeanne Arceneaux had been the first female African-American Vermilion Parish Deputy. Guts, brains, and dogged determination led her to become Sheriff Godchaux's Chief Deputy. She looked the part in black slacks, matching jacket, and a crisp striped shirt. MJ's grim expression eased as she gave LaShaun a brief hug. After LaShaun helped with several unusual problems in the past, she and LaShaun forged a friendship.

"Morning you two. Way to start a Monday, huh?" MJ said.

"At least we had a wonderful weekend." LaShaun sighed. Being summoned by Sheriff Godchaux meant the good times were over.

"What the hell is this about?" Chase lowered his voice when a group of deputies and civilians passed them.

"Best let the boss explain. Oh, and the FBI has been called, but they're only consulting at this point. On standby in case we need them or this case crosses state lines." MJ opened the glass door of Sheriff Godchaux's office cutting off Chase's next question.

Detective Mark Anderson stood when they entered. He moved to stand next to the sheriff's polished wood desk. His only greeting was a crisp nod designed to include all three of the newcomers. Dave Godchaux raked thick fingers through his iron gray hair as he looked up from the computer screen.

"Give us a minute, Det. Anderson," Dave said.

After a few seconds, the younger man headed for the door. "Yes, sir."

When the door shut quietly with a firm thud, Dave blew out a puff of air. "Mornin' Mrs. Broussard. I hear the baby is growing up fast."

"She is. Seems like yesterday I brought her home from the hospital."

LaShaun smiled as she sat down next to Chase. MJ remained standing, as if nervous energy made sitting uncomfortable. Dave sighed again, ruffled through papers on his desk and looked at the computer screen again. He seemed to consider how to begin.

"We got a kidnapping, little girl, six years old. She was playing in the yard outside their house, a trailer home in that park off Slater Road." Dave looked down at a sheet of paper. "Name of Clover Leaf Estates. The mother looked for her. She was gone." Dave crossed his arms across his broad chest and sat back.

"That was yesterday around lunchtime," MJ said. "The mother came in this morning to report it."

Chase raised an eyebrow. "Wait a minute. A six year old goes missing in the middle of the day, and her mother waits until the next morning to report it?"

"And why wasn't the child in school?" LaShaun added.

"We've had a few calls to the trailer park, Chase. Domestic disputes that turn violent, drug raids, the usual. Last week our deputies chased a couple of car burglary theft suspects down Slater Road to guess where?"

"Clover Leaf Estates. Fancy name," Chase replied.

"The land owner tried to build a subdivision but went bust back in 2008. So being an enterprising sort, he opened a trailer park instead. Started off not so bad, but it's gone down in the last six years." Dave waved a hand. Then he slid a photo across his desk. "Anyway, the little girl's name is Dina Menard."

"Her mother is twenty-five and has three other kids all younger than Dina. And you're right, Dina should have been in school. The mother has an open child welfare case. Dina misses school a lot." MJ held up a second photo. A woman with dirty blonde hair and watery blue eyes stared vacantly at nothing. "Her mother, Sherry Bradford. The father is Dylan Menard. They lived together off and on. Dylan has a history of abusing her."

"And an arrest history going back to when he was a juvenile. I know, because I picked him up a couple of times. The Menard extended family is trouble." Dave scowled.

⚜

Chase glanced from MJ to Dave. "Didn't we bust a drug ring and put three of them away?"

"Yeah, in 2011. Dylan's father, one older brother and an aunt. The aunt served fifteen months. The other two are out as well," MJ replied.

"So you're thinking maybe Dina's disappearance is related to the family's drug business?" Chase asked.

"At this point it could be anything. Sherry isn't an attentive mother by any stretch of imagination. She's supposedly in a drug treatment program. But maybe she's back with Menard and using again. The other wrinkle is Sherry has a brother who's a registered sex offender. He lives a mile down the way." MJ crossed her arms. "He's in the lobby playing the part of the concerned uncle."

"So you've got a rich pool of suspects. Why are we here? No scratch that, why is my wife here?" Chase looked from Sheriff Godchaux to MJ and back to his boss again.

Sheriff Godchaux studied LaShaun before he answered. "The mother insisted on talking to you."

"Far as I know, we've never met," LaShaun replied to the unasked question in the sheriff's dark gaze.

"Maybe you're related or something. Could be she's heard of..." Chase stopped when his boss raised a hand.

"Sherry and the Menards are white," the sheriff said.

⚜

"I'm white along with the rest of my family, but Ellie is my baby. Lots of families have mixed extended kin, even if they don't want to claim 'em." Chase crossed his arms.

"There aren't any Menards or Bradfords related to the Rousselle family. I'd know, Chase," LaShaun said. "I don't understand how she even knows to ask for me."

"Are you joking? You've been involved in three high profile murder cases in this parish. With full media hoopla I might add. Who doesn't know about you and the hocus-pocus stuff." Dave pulled a meaty hand over his face and sighed. "Miss Bradford isn't charged with a crime. She can ask to speak to or be represented by anyone she likes. She chose you."

"Sherry won't speak to the child welfare case worker or the lawyer family court assigned to represent her. She insists on talking to you. Alone." MJ raised both eyebrows at LaShaun.

Det. Anderson appeared at the door and entered when Dave nodded it was okay. "Tommy Bradford is kicking up a fuss. I handled him. He's a real low life."

Chase covered LaShaun's hand with his and looked at her. "You don't have to talk to the woman. Let the detective assigned explain—"

"Mark tried, for almost two hours," MJ broke in. "She answered his questions for the most part. But now she only wants to talk to LaShaun."

"Something weird about all this, babe." Chase squeezed LaShaun's hand.

"Every time LaShaun is involved, things are weird," Sheriff Godchaux retorted. "So what else is new? Look, the mother isn't too stable based on her history alone. I get that. But the damn clock is ticking and a little girl needs to be found."

"An Amber Alert has been issued. Dave's partner is working to get billboard's up with Dina's picture if we don't find her in the next couple of days or so." MJ gazed at Chase and then LaShaun.

"We're not sitting around waiting for your wife to wave her hands and work some kinda magic, Broussard. Uniforms are out interviewing witnesses. Her lowlife uncle is at the top of the list." Dave's mouth turned down in a sour expression.

MJ shot a glance at their boss. "But we're not jumping to conclusions yet, right? Even if we don't like sexual offenders."

"Yeah, yeah. We need solid leads. If the mother hasn't told us everything, then you can help," Dave said to LaShaun.

She stood. "I agree. Take me to her."

"Ok, I'm out voted. I sure as hell don't want my family dragged into a criminal investigation with folks like the Menards. They're a mean bunch, and they hold grudges. Just saying for the record in case things go sideways." Chase stood.

"From what I recall, your wife can handle herself in tricky situations," Dave replied dryly.

⚜

"Thanks, Sheriff." LaShaun gave him a half smile.

"Yeah, well..." Chase squinted at her.

"I'm going to talk to a distraught woman, mother to mother. Totally different from those other times. We're in the middle of a sheriff's station. Nothing will happen." LaShaun tapped Chase's hefty bicep.

His only response was a grunt of cynicism. LaShaun knew his thoughts as if he'd spoken aloud. Chase and Sheriff Godchaux remained in his office. She followed MJ to the interview room deeper into the station's interior. Det. Anderson disappeared for a few seconds and returned carrying a cup.

"Not sure this is a good idea. I could get more out of her if we don't give in to her demands I think." Det. Anderson shot a side glance at LaShaun and then back to his boss.

MJ gazed at him with an impassive expression. "Let's do whatever it takes to bring this child home safe, okay?"

"Of course," Det. Anderson said after a beat of hesitation. He opened the door, nodded to the two women and then followed. "Here's some water, Miss Bradford. You asked for Mrs. Broussard, so here she is."

Sherry brushed strands of limp hair back from her forehead as she blinked at LaShaun. Dark circles under her eyes stood out starkly from her pale skin. "You look taller and younger than I thought you'd be."

LaShaun smiled at her. "Could be the boots, two inch heels. I don't' know about looking younger though. I've probably aged since my little one started walking. Chasing her around is exhausting."

"Kids are hard. Not that I don't love mine. But there's always so much to do, and they're screaming for food or about a toy." Sherry closed her eyes. "Never stops."

"I'm sure you're doing your best, Miss Bradford." LaShaun sat across from her.

"I am, though them social workers don't believe me. I tried finishing school at the community college. But then I got pregnant with my second baby. Illegal immigrants keep takin' all the jobs, so it's hard to find work." Sherry's eyes narrowed as she twisted her hands together.

"I see."

LaShaun didn't bother to argue with the woman's racist statement. Vermilion Parish has little to no problem with illegals, but facts wouldn't persuade Sherry's thinking. She needed someone to blame.

"Tell us anything you might have left out about that day or the night of Dina's disappearance," Det. Anderson said.

"I need to talk to you alone." Sherry glanced at Det. Anderson and MJ. "And don't listen in. I don't want them to find out."

"What?" Det. Anderson took a step toward her. "Who are you talking about?"

MJ put a restraining hand on Anderson's arm. "Sherry, if you know or even suspect who has Dina, you need to tell us."

"Maybe they're watching, but they might just think you're visiting your husband or friends in here." Sherry spoke low as if to herself. "Don't know, but I have to try."

"We don't have time for games. Explain what's going on if you care about your kid," Det. Anderson barked. "Or maybe you did something to her."

"I do care about my kids," Sherry shouted. "Everybody keeps saying I don't, but I do my best. You don't know what it's like. You look at me like I'm nothin' but trailer trash, but I try so hard. I don't get help from their no good daddies. Why don't you blame them, huh?"

"Of course you're doing all you can," LaShaun cut in sharply to head off another reply from Det. Anderson.

"I told you I wanted to talk to her alone." Sherry swiped away tears from her face.

"We're leaving. Det. Anderson." MJ yanked open the door, jerked a nod for him to go first, and waited. When the tall man stomped out, the door shut behind them softly.

LaShaun turned back to Sherry. "You grew up poor. Your parents have a lot of problems, so they were no help. Then you met Dylan, and he was nice at first, but y'all partied too much. Even so, you got off the drugs when you got pregnant the first time, right? With Dina I mean."

⚜

Sherry heaved a few breaths before regaining a small measure of composure. "Yeah. Dylan ain't a bad person, not really. I, uh, got back on drugs then we broke up. He didn't get too mad when I got pregnant for some other guy, my second baby Nathan. Not that first time. I had a miscarriage after that, and then... I swore my youngest was his. I'm sure he is." She stuck out her chin as if daring LaShaun to question her.

"Okay, so Dylan tries his best, but he keeps getting arrested, and you're doing drugs again."

"I have a few beers once in a while. I got a right to relax with all I got on me." Sherry frowned at LaShaun. "What do you know about it... with your fancy life? You people got it good."

LaShaun let the "you people" remark slide because of a missing child. Otherwise she would have set the woman straight with the quickness. Instead she counted to ten and leaned forward with an expression of empathy.

"You're under a lot of stress on a good day, and now Dina is missing. I get it. So these people you mentioned, they don't want you talking to me." LaShaun felt waves of fear coming from Sherry.

"Old Mrs. Vincent down the road from me says you can see things. Tell things, like you just did with me. Knew my parents and everything before we even talked. You got to come to my house." Sherry sprang to her feet. "We got to go now."

❖

LaShaun stood. "The police will need to—"

"I told them all I know. None of them can help me with this. Come on, let's go. Mrs. Vincent says you will know what to do or find another voodoo woman who can help." Sherry grabbed a dirty imitation leather handbag from the back of her chair.

"Sherry, calm down."

"They've got Dina, I'm sure of it. That Det. Anderson don't know what he's talkin' about. My brother didn't take my girl. Tommy wouldn't put a finger on her. He got that charge because he was seventeen and his girlfriend was almost fifteen. She got scared when her mama caught them together. We're wasting time." Sherry's words tumbled out in a rush as she grabbed LaShaun by both arms. "You got to come to my house right now."

LaShaun looked into Sherry's wild glazed eyes. Try as she might, LaShaun couldn't summon enough psychic energy to push past the muddle of strong emotions. Regret mixed with guilt and craving for drugs. Despite what the young woman had said, Sherry hadn't been telling the whole truth about her drinking, or drug use.

"Not until you tell me why," LaShaun said.

"The symbols. All over the walls. They say you can read the signs. Maybe the ones what took Dina will bring her back, if you go to them." Sherry heaved in great gulps of air.

****

Forty-five minutes later they stood in the rundown single-wide trailer Sherry and her kids called home. One of about fifteen trailers in the park, the interior looked as dreary as the outside. At least the three main mini-streets of the trailer park were blacktopped. At some point the property owner had kept the site fairly decent. Those days were gone. Some of the yards were nicer than others. Sherry's wasn't one of them.

Anderson suggested, and Chase agreed, that Sherry should stay in the cruiser with a female deputy. So she sat outside while LaShaun, Chase and Det. Anderson entered the trailer. LaShaun stood in the open door taking in the whole picture. Anderson went down the hallway to the small bedrooms. Chase stayed quiet as he looked around the kitchen and cluttered living room.

"This is a bunch of bull," Det. Anderson said when he rejoined them in the main living area. Then he directed his raised voice at Chase's back. "Sherry Bradford knows more than she's letting on. She put this crap on the wall to throw us off."

"Maybe. Forensic analysis might give us some clues." Chase sighed. "Listen, I agree with you about the mother, but if we discredit her outlandish story, then we'll have a lead on what she's up to. Agreed?"

⚜

Det. Anderson grunted then grimaced at the mess around them. He kicked a pile of dirty laundry out of his way. "Yeah, whatever. We should charge the woman with violating public health laws. This place is disgusting."

LaShaun tuned out Anderson's complaints. She heard the male voices as faint background noise. Her focus was on the strange symbols, but not reading them. LaShaun gave up on that effort fast. She didn't recognize the writing, so trying to decipher the message would waste time. Still she stared at them hard. Then she stepped close to the wall and sniffed.

"Don't touch it. At least not without gloves," Chase said over her shoulder.

"Cinnamon," LaShaun said, cloves and something else I can't quite figure out. Maybe ethanol."

"Damn, you've got one sensitive nose." Chase started to say more, but moved off when Anderson beckoned to him.

LaShaun stood back from the wall again. She continued taking pictures with her cell phone. Then she texted them to Miss Rose and the twins. Three walls had neat lines of the script. There was obvious order and method to the characters. A message obviously. For Sherry or LaShaun?

"Okay, let's bring in Ms. Bradford," Chase said to Anderson. "Maybe she'll tell us about this."

"If we can believe a damn thing she says." Anderson gave a snort as he marched out.

⚜

"He's not a bad guy, just impatient," Chase said before LaShaun could form her comment.

"What's his story?" LaShaun turned to the dark lettering to snap another photo.

"Worked in St. Bernard Parish for a while. After that he went to Jefferson Parish Sheriff's Office. Good arrests record, though some say he bends the rules." Chase went to the door and started out.

"So he got himself in trouble in Jefferson Parish. Stepped on big enough toes that he decided moving way out to Vermilion Parish was a good idea." LaShaun didn't turn around as she spoke.

"You got all that just from me saying—"

"Why else would an ambitious law officer leave a major urban area to work way out in the country?" LaShaun texted the last picture to her friends. Almost immediately her phone started vibrating as they replied.

"Dave wouldn't have hired him if he thought the guy was dirty." Chase broke off and stepped away from the door.

Seconds later, Sherry walked in followed by Anderson. The female deputy brought up the rear, fanning her face. Sherry blushed as she took a few more steps.

"I didn't have a chance to clean up the last few days. The kids... they're always into something and I stay tired." Sherry started to pick up a toy truck, but Dave blocked her.

❖

"Don't touch or move anything until we say so. Explain this," Anderson rumbled and waved a hand at the walls.

"I, uh, I went out last night. The kids were sound asleep, and Miz Thibaut next door promised to check on them every hour or so. Um, my friend's car broke down so I got back late." Sherry twisted her hands together. Her words tumbled out with more explanations, or rather excuses.

LaShaun studied her as she spoke. She felt an urge to question how she could leave a four, three and one-year-old alone. Instead she pressed her lips together. Sherry no doubt knew the deputy or Det. Anderson would question her neighbors. Still the young mother tried to offer a less damning account of her actions.

"What time?" LaShaun said before Det. Anderson could speak.

"Maybe one o'clock this morning. Like I said, took a while for our other friend to come get us." Sherry was fidgeting with the collar of her dark green jacket.

"And that's when you saw the writing?" Chase made a circuit of the wall to stare at it again.

"No. I mean I don't think so. I was kinda tired when I got in. I fell asleep on the couch." Sherry pointed to the brown sofa made of imitation suede.

"Tired. Yeah." Anderson crossed his arms and gazed at her hard.

❧

"I mighta had a few too many beers. But I wasn't driving," Sherry put in quickly. "I woke up and saw all this on the walls. Then I remembered Dina hadn't come home, so I called my cousin. She lives down the lane." Sherry pointed to the window as if they could see her cousin's trailer. Then she slowly lowered her arm.

"Dina would go there to play and stay overnight?" LaShaun glanced at Anderson, hoping to head him off from turning bad cop. Sherry might stop talking.

"That's right. Dina loves my cousin's little girl. She nine, but she doesn't mind Dina following her around. I mean, everybody around here's always been nice to us. I got family right down the lane. I didn't think…" Sherry's voice died away so that her last words seemed to evaporate in the air.

"To recap your story, you went out to party when you didn't even know where your six-year-old kid was, left your three youngest here alone, got back drunk after one in the morning, woke up, saw the writing and decided something was wrong." Det. Anderson pressed his lips together.

Sherry flinched. "I didn't leave until almost ten, so really it wasn't all that long."

"Uh-huh." Anderson put on his sunglasses and looked away from her.

Sherry faced LaShaun. "They say you'll know. Tell me what this says. Where's my girl?"

⚜

"I don't recognize these letters, Sherry," LaShaun replied. She read regret in the woman's eyes.

"We'll have to do some more research," Chase added. "Det. Anderson, take a set of pictures for the department. Work with Deputy Wilcox to scrape samples of the ink off. We'll send it to the state police lab for analysis."

Det. Anderson hissed low. "Right. We'll track down who decided to be an artist in the middle of the night."

"It wasn't me. Tante Alice and grandmamma says it's evil. If that's true, then they got my Dina and no tellin' what they done to her by now." Sherry's voice rose to a hysterical whine. "It don't take long to hurt a little girl."

At Chase's signal, the female deputy stepped forward and took her by the arm. Their voices faded as Sherry allowed the deputy to lead her away. "C'mon, ma'am. I'll take you over to your mama's house like you said. Let's pack a few things."

LaShaun turned to Chase. "Where are the other children?"

"The middle child's father picked him up. The other two are with Sherry's mama. DCFS hasn't made a decision on removing the three youngest yet."

The Louisiana Department of Child and Family Services, notoriously understaffed and underfunded, might well be leaving the children with relatives. At least Sherry wouldn't be left alone with them in the short-term. Chase pulled LaShaun aside so that they were across from the action in the dining area. Anderson continued taking pictures yards away. A second deputy helped him. Both carried evidence bags and collection tools.

"Your phone keeps buzzing like a trapped wasp. What's up?" Chase said low. He watched her read text messages from Miss Rose, Justine and Pauline for several moments.

"They don't know either, but they're working on finding out."

"But you said the writing is in letters." Chase frowned at the walls.

LaShaun scrolled to the photos of the writing on her phone. She gazed at them as she talked, "Yes, an alphabet. They're arranged to be sentences I think, not pictures telling a story. But I'm sure no authority on arcane languages. I've only studied a few like the Enochian Language, the Rune of Othalan, and a few others."

"Naturally it couldn't be something simple. No, we got the Rune of Whatsit." Chase let go of a long sigh.

"The Rune of Whatsit?" LaShaun grinned at him.

"Do me a favor. Keep that language of the ancients talk between us for now. You know what kind of ink that is because you sniffed it." Chase nodded toward the writing on the nearest wall.

"Yes..." LaShaun pursed her lips together. Then she cleared her throat.

⚜

"That was your cue to give me an answer, LaShaun." Chase nudged her. When Det. Anderson glanced their way, he waved and put on a neutral expression.

"I don't think you're going to like the answer, babe." LaShaun smiled at the other officers. She turned her back to them as if studying another part of the room.

"Let me think. We got a missing child, demonic scribbles on the wall, a drugged out mother, and a Cajun mafia family. Honey, I already don't like a damn thing about this case."

"I never said the writing was demonic or satanic, but from the smell, I'd say the writing was done with Bat's Blood Ink."

"Are you freakin' kidding me?" Chase blurted out. When Anderson jerked around to stare at him. "Nothing, it's nothing. Just keep collecting evidence."

"Think calm thoughts. Let me take a few samples from the wall. Our TEA might have someone who can analyze them. I'll wait until your guys are through then discreetly scrape a bit off." LaShaun patted her distressed lawman husband's arm. "Hey, I could be wrong. Maybe it's nothing but a marker, and some kids thought vandalism would be funny."

Chase glanced to his left, and LaShaun followed his gaze. A photo of Dina, her small heart-shaped face framed by honey smiled at the world.

"And the missing kid? I sure as hell ain't laughing about that."

"No, me either. We're going to find Dina and make sure she stays safe from now on." LaShaun's hands tightened into fists.

Chapter 4

The next day passed with no new clues as to what the message on Sherry's walls meant. Yet what weighed on LaShaun's mind wasn't that mystery, but the location and well-being of a little girl. She saw the image of Dina's sweet face when she closed her eyes at night. Sometimes her hazel eyes melded into Ellie's dark brown gaze to stare back at her. A child's voice calling for her mama woke her up one night. A nightmare that sent her racing down the hallway to Ellie's room. Her hands shook as she smoothed the blanket over the still sleeping baby. Even though it was midnight, she called Rose Fontenot. The older woman didn't get angry or in fact seem surprised to hear from LaShaun. Miss Rose agreed they needed to meet, and then added a terse, "Now get back to bed."

At six am, Chase stood close to LaShaun drinking his morning coffee. "I'm worried about you, babe. Bad dreams mean you're letting my case get to you. I know how you feel. Every deputy is a parent or uncle, or aunt. We deal with murder, beatings, and all kinds of stuff that make you feel just plain dirty at the end of a shift. But when it comes to kids..."

"I can't see her, Chase. Not one vision of Dina."

LaShaun kept her voice low. Chase followed her gaze to their daughter. Ellie bounced around happily in the play pen Chase's father had designed for her. His way of emphasizing he didn't disapprove of their marriage like his wife. A lively tune came from the television, a children's show featuring a big blue dog.

"You always tell me there's no on and off switch. It comes and goes, right?" Chase rubbed her back with one hand.

"Yeah, more like scanning for a radio station. Most of the time all I get is static or voices I can't make out. *You* always tell me that the first forty-eight hours are critical. Where could she be?" LaShaun went back to washing dishes by hand. The busy work helped steady her nerves.

Chase put down his empty mug. "The kitchen is spotless. I bet you cleaned the rest of the house before I got up this morning."

❧

LaShaun sighed as she wiped her hands with a paper towel. "I didn't vacuum though. Didn't want to wake you two. The dusting is done. I organized your desk in the library."

"Gee thanks. Now I can have fun trying to find my stuff," Chase teased. "And you vacuumed yesterday."

"Maybe I'll get something done outside before everyone gets here. Savoie's is delivering lunch by eleven thirty." LaShaun glanced at the wall clock. "I've got plenty of—"

"There's nothing to do outside. No leaves to rake. No weeds to pull. Mr. Earl keeps your family's cemetery real tidy. Flowers put out and everything," he added. "He's coming today in fact."

Earl Gray, a retired groundskeeper and amateur historian, had volunteered. He not only wanted to keep busy, but the Rousselle family history intrigued him. He'd gone to school with LaShaun's uncles. Even so, Chase and LaShaun insisted on paying him. Mr. Earl, a devout southern Baptist, also happened to believe in the supernatural. He kept an eye out for any signs of unusual activity.

"Fine. Maybe the attic can use a good cleaning," LaShaun said. She laughed at the face Chase made at her. "I'm kidding, okay? I won't wipe, scrub or organize anything else. Promise."

"Thank the Lord. Took me fifteen minutes to figure out where you 'organized' my shaving lotion and deodorant in the bathroom." Chase

⚜

finished stacking the plates on a shelf and closed the cabinet door.

LaShaun grew serious again. "What can you tell me that won't violate department policy?"

"Tommy Bradford has been arrested three times on sex related charges, including one charge of indecent behavior with a minor." Chase frowned.

"Damn, not good."

"Yeah. He made a lot of noise the other day, but now we can't find him. Nothing raises the suspicion of cops like a guy disappearing before we can interview him. I got a bad feeling about it."

"What does Sherry say?" LaShaun looked at him.

"Backs their mama's story. Claims Tommy went on a fishing trip with some buddies." Chase snorted. "We strongly suggested they tell him to get his ass back here."

"Right, call his cell or text him. Easy enough." LaShaun went over to pick up a toy Ellie tossed out of her play pen.

"His mama came up with weak excuses."

"They have a history with the police. Not telling you everything is probably second nature and makes sense to them. His mother probably sees Tommy as a victim. Not saying I agree," LaShaun added quickly at Chase's grimace. She wiped off the yellow ball before tossing it into the play pen again.

⚜

"You'd think they'd have the good sense to know this is different. The child could be in danger. The longer she's gone..." He tapped a fist against one thigh.

"Yeah." LaShaun didn't need him to finish the thought. "Well, whisper a prayer that we come up with something."

"Ah yes. The fortune tellers will plug into the ether, gather the collective forces of crystal balls everywhere." Chase raised his hands in surrender when LaShaun squinted at him. "Need something to lighten my mood."

"More like we're going to plug into our Wi-Fi. Miss Rose contacted a linguistics professor. Yes, we have academics in our network."

"Wow." Chase touched the fingertips of one hand to his temple.

"We also have at least two physicists and an astronomer. You'd be surprised at the range of professionals   available   as   consultants." LaShaun grinned at him.

"No, I wouldn't. If cats started raining down, I wouldn't blink these days." Chase gave a grunt as he pulled out his cell phone.

"We only use that in case of mouse emergencies," LaShaun replied with a giggle.

"I think you're only half joking." Chase started to say more, but stopped as he read the text on the screen. "I better get a move on. We have a search warrant for Tommy's house. A neighbor swears he had a little girl over there three days ago."

⚜

LaShaun crossed to him quickly. "I can't be-lieve Sherry would lie knowing, or even if she suspected, her brother is responsible."

Chase gazed at her with a grave face. "I've seen a lot of evil covered up in families."

LaShaun shivered. When Chase hugged her goodbye, at least some of the chill faded. She smiled as he gave Ellie her usual goodbye tick-les and kisses. For the next two hours, she swung between putting on jolly face for Ellie and worrying about Dina. Despite her promise, LaShaun did go outside with Ellie on one hip. Her excuse would be that they took a walk since the weather had turned out so fine. In-deed the sunshine and blue skies made the mid-December day seem like spring. Pulling Ellie along in a bright red wagon, they took a path from the edge of the backyard through the trees. Beau trotted alongside. A brisk ten mi-nute walk brought them to the Rousselle-LeGrange family cemetery. Stone markers dat-ed to the early 1800s with some worn smooth by the decades. Mr. Earl speculated that even earlier graves had sunken long ago into the woods.

As they approached, the figure of a sturdy man in his early sixties appeared above the brush. Then the way cleared to reveal the new iron fence around the gravesite. Mr. Earl wore a long-sleeved blue work shirt and matching pants, boots and a straw hat. He waved at them but bent to continue pulling weeds.

❧

"Y'all enjoying the nice day, huh? Little ones gets rowdy if they cooped up to much. Need to have space to run and play." As usual, Mr. Earl started the conversation as if they'd already been talking.

"Yes sir. How you doing, and how is Miss Joyce?" LaShaun replied.

She glanced down to check, but Ellie seemed unaware of the bumping-along progress of the wagon. Her favorite baby doll claimed her attention. Beau went to Mr. Earl, accepted a pat on the head, and then nosed around the grass. From time to time, Beau lifted his head to gaze at Ellie, then he'd continue exploring.

Mr. Earl straightened. "She's fine, just fine. Still working part-time. See, that's why I married a younger woman. She can support me now that I'm layin' around doing nothin'." He grinned at his own joke. Mrs. Gray was only six years younger.

"You're a planner alright. You need anything?" LaShaun ran a hand over the nearest gravestone, the one with her grandmother's name on it.

"Nah, got all the tools I need. Chase might need to go ahead and buy pellets for the fire ants. But we got time." Mr. Earl wiped his face with a bandana then took a drink of water from a bottle clipped to his belt.

"I'll let him know."

LaShaun smiled at him as she strolled around. She rubbed Beau's back with affection when he approached. The dog gave a soft bark

⚜

then raced around in circles. Ellie rewarded his performance by clapping her hands.

Mr. Earl picked up a garden hoe and chopped at stubborn crabgrass. "Life been quiet?"

"Sorta kinda."

He stopped, took more water and gazed off into tangled vines and brush. "Uh-huh. I heard some talk about what's going on down Slater Road. Something about Satanic symbols."

LaShaun made a circuit around a nearby grave. Soft grass cushioned her steps. "Folks coming up with their own theories already."

"You know they gonna talk. Missing child, strange messages. No telling what wild stories will come out next." Mr. Earl shrugged as he chuckled.

"Wait until they find out I was there," LaShaun retorted.

"Oh they already know. Those sage, holly and dandelions look pretty, but they ain't for show." Mr. Earl gave a sharp nod. The herbs he'd planted had protective qualities against spirits or demons according to local legends. "Don't you worry. Ain't no strangers been out this way."

"Thank you, sir." LaShaun crossed to him. She gave him a quick peck on the cheek.

"You're welcome, child. Don't look now, but somebody is trying to get away." Mr. Earl pointed.

Ellie had climbed from the wagon and started off on her own to look around. Beau

tagged along. He'd nudge her in a different direction if she tried to go too far. Ellie fussed at
him when he did so. Beau would bark back, and
the toddler would go where he wanted.

LaShaun laughed at their battle of wills.
"She won't get far."

"Almost like that dog and her talking to
each other. Kids and their pets. I thought when
our five got grown, the zoo at my house would
disappear. Nope. Joyce got two dogs, a cat, and
a parrot. Says they're for the grandkids." Mr.
Earl's deep laughter rumbled.

LaShaun nodded as he continued making
jokes about his wife and her devotion to their
pets. Yet she watched Ellie and Beau. The bond
between them had grown strong in such a short
period of time. Ellie didn't treat Beau like a toy
at all like most young children. She did indeed
seem to communicate with him. Even more curious, Beau responded as if he understood. If
Chase hadn't noticed, he would soon. LaShaun
had been skeptical even though she trusted the
twins. Still, her own gift confirmed that Beau
was no ordinary house pet. LaShaun wondered
what Chase's reaction would be. Their love was
strong, but she'd introduced so much supernatural drama into his life. Chase's mother had
opposed their marriage, so Chase didn't talk to
her often. When they did visit, tension kept
their conversation superficial. LaShaun's fa-
ther-in-law practically visited them in secret to
avoid conflict at home. Would things get better

or worse? Mr. Earl's gruff basso voice cut through her thoughts.

"Grandchildren can calm a lot of troubled waters," Mr. Earl said. "Me and Earl, Jr. used to butt heads, got hot some times. But long as we don't try to tell them how to raise their own kids, things stay just fine."

LaShaun gazed at him. "Mr. Earl, have you turned into a mind reader?"

"Nah. Just ramblin' on." Mr. Earl grinned at her. His "rambling on" was his subtle way of giving advice or getting information without asking too many questions. "I'm nothin' but a dusty old ordinary deacon at Rosewood Baptist Church. I don't have the gift of prophesy. Though I do know my Bible scriptures. Yes, I do."

"You're a bible scholar is what you are, Mr. Earl. You can answer the most puzzling questions for me. I might have to call on you one of these days." LaShaun looped an arm through his. They walked toward the open gate Ellie and Beau had gone through seconds before.

"Any time. Any time at all. Joyce will be grateful you get me out from under foot at home." Mr. Earl gave a hardy laugh.

"I'll just bet." LaShaun laughed with him.

She scooped up Ellie. They exchanged affectionate farewells with Mr. Earl and headed back to the house. Thirty minutes later, the delivery van from Savoie's catering arrived. LaShaun got busy setting up lunch for her and four others. Miss Rose, as usual, arrived early

⚜

and insisted on helping. LaShaun managed to feed Ellie, play with her off and on, and prepare for her guests. Ellie tried to keep her eyes open, but soon she yawned her way to an afternoon nap. By twelve-thirty, the guests arrived with the twins at the head of the group.

"Hey, girl," Justine called out gaily.

Her twin Pauline waited for a Ford Escape to unload two occupants. Both carried leather satchels. She gestured to them. "Y'all got here right on time. Told you it wasn't hard to find."

"GPS gets the credit," the tall thin white man replied. He wore a tweed jacket over blue jeans. His cap matched the jacket. Thick white hair stuck out from the edges of his cap.

"Yes, thank goodness. Until he gave up male pride and relied on technology, he got lost more times than I care to remember," the short woman next to him replied with a grin.

"LaShaun, this is Daniel Rayford, professor of anthropology at Northwestern U. in Natchitoches, his lovely companion Shelia St. Denis. Shelia of the Coushatta Tribe, a member of the panther clan." Pauline beamed at them. "I can still publicly claim them both as friends despite their shady pasts."

"Only because we know *your* even shadier secrets," Shelia shot back. All three laughed.

"Hello everyone. Enough small talk. I'm hungry." Justine turned sharply and headed for the kitchen door. "I sure hope you gonna feed us before we get down to business."

"Yes, ma'am." LaShaun laughed.

⚜

Soon LaShaun's five guests had settled into eating hot ham, turkey, or beef po-boys; Creole style coleslaw and sweet tea. The conversation about paranormal phenomena was lively. Daniel's gift was remote viewing, the ability to see scenes, people and events across distances. Shelia could sense supernatural entities in real time or traces left behind once gone.

Anyone listening would have concluded that LaShaun hosted a gathering of middle-aged jokesters. LaShaun enjoyed their banter. By the time she served dessert, tiny sweet potato pies for each, LaShaun felt like she'd known Daniel and Shelia for years. LaShaun started clearing the table. Despite her protest, the others joined in. Daniel took the large garbage bag filled with paper plates and more outside to the trash bin. When leftovers were wrapped and put away, all six sat around the table.

"We should get together more often," Shelia said. She sipped coffee.

"Yes," Justine added and smacked her lips. "Lunch was wonderful. Hit the spot."

"I thought you met regularly," LaShaun replied.

"Too busy," Shelia said. "I do the bookkeeping at three of the tribe's businesses."

"I'm still teaching," Daniel added. He heaved a sigh. "Vow of poverty. That's why I'm an old man still working."

❖

"Poo, you love teaching. And sixty-two isn't old. At least that's what I tell myself," Pauline quipped.

"Well, you have a couple of more years before you find out. Amazing how you make one birthday, and suddenly everything hurts." Daniel laughed. The others agreed, laughing with him.

"Seriously though, it would be nice to be social instead of always dealing with trouble." Shelia's words sobered the other four older adults.

"Yes, speaking of which..." Miss Rose nodded to LaShaun.

"Y'all get settled in the family room area while I do a quick check on Ellie."

Miss Rose herded her friends across the open floor plan to LaShaun's den while she was gone. After making sure Ellie was still asleep and comfortable, LaShaun rejoined them and set up her tablet for a video conference. She connected it to the sixty-two inch flat screen wall television for easy viewing.

"Sandy said she won't be free until two," Miss Rose said. Dr. Sandra Portier was a professor in the Humanities department at Rice University in Houston, Texas, her specialty being linguistics.

"Okay, then we have roughly fifteen minutes to catch up on what we know." Daniel went from a genial avuncular type to serious investigator. He gazed from Rose to LaShaun and back again over his bifocals.

⚜

"We don't have much. Dina Menard went missing almost five days ago. No signs of her." LaShaun grimaced at the grim sound of her last sentence.

"Father ruled out?" Shelia leaned forward.

"Not completely, but he doesn't appear to be involved. The police are looking for one uncle, a registered sex offender," Miss Rose put in.

"Hmmm. Send me his particulars. I'll try to get a feel for him." Daniel made notes on a pad he'd taken from his well-used leather satchel. "Be even better if I had something he owned."

"Now how do we pull off getting our hands on his property? It can be small like a keychain or..." Justine looked at LaShaun. "Sherry Bradford asked for you."

"She's also not telling the whole truth and protecting her brother." LaShaun gazed ahead as though she could see her. "I seriously doubt she'll hand over anything he owns."

Pauline nodded slowly. "She and her family obviously believe in supernatural, or Miss Bradford wouldn't have asked LaShaun to get involved. Which means she knows about gris-gris and such."

"And I'm not going to steal something from his house," LaShaun said quickly when Justine started to speak.

"Damn, that's the problem hanging with a bunch of psychics." Justine crossed her arms.

"Okay, I have an idea which is true. We want to find out who took the child, so ruling him out fast would help. Let's hope she trusts me enough to go for it."

"Too iffy. Then she won't trust you either and cut you off," Miss Rose replied.

"I agree. Let me start with the information I have on the brother." Daniel put down the notepad and pulled out a tablet. "I'll text you if I need a hot popper."

That's his term for something personal from the subject," Shelia explained to LaShaun.

"I came up with that no matter what Miguel says. Poser." Daniel gave a grunt.

"Yes, yes, we know." Shelia turned to LaShaun again. "Miguel Sanchez in San Jose made the term 'hot popper' popular in our Twitter group."

"All because I was late to the party when it came to social media," Daniel grumbled.

"Back on task." Miss Rose shot them a glance as she tapped the keyboard of her laptop.

Daniel waved a hand. "Fine. Anyway, if I get a good view, maybe you won't have to go risk alienating your one good family source."

"Yeah. If Sherry Bradford is hiding something, putting her on guard too early in the game could complicate our task," Justine said.

"Hey, are you guys ready?" Dr. Portier spoke from her office at the university. A bookshelf behind her served as a frame. Her dark red hair made her pale skin even more striking. Reading glasses dangled from a chain around her neck. She waved.

"The gang's all here." Miss Rose waved back.

"Nice to meet you LaShaun." Dr. Portier smiled.

"Same here." LaShaun smiled back and sat on the ottoman in her den.

"So, Rose, I looked at the material you sent last night. I have to tell you it's super intriguing. Reminds me of early Assyrian writings on the one hand. Then I thought, no. This is a unique variation of Sumerian cuneiform. Of course, Sumerian writing did change over time. For example, at first the figures were from top to bottom. Then around 3000 BCE, it went from left to right. But this is... Well I'm not sure... Fascinating." Dr. Portier put on her reading glasses. Then she held up her tablet computer to gaze at the screen in admiration.

"Thanks for the lecture on ancient doodles, Sandy. Skip to the part where you know what this is." Justine glanced at her sister and lowered her voice. "She'll go on for a half hour if you let her."

"No, I won't Justine. I have another class in twenty-five. You could do with more studies to expand your horizons." Dr. Portier looked at her tablet again.

"I like my horizons just fine, thank you," Justine retorted.

"Okay, you two. Stay on the subject." Miss Rose shot Justine a warning look.

"The writing, Sandy." Daniel glanced at Justine with a wry grin.

⚜

"I don't recognize it. As I said, I see traces that could be clues, but I'm going to need to do some research."

"This is a message we think. It's written in Bat's Blood ink." Miss Rose frowned as if that detail worried her even more.

"You wanted me to see it with no context at first. Am I right?" Sandy took off her reading glasses and gazed at them through her desktop computer screen.

Miss Rose nodded. "I thought you might get some reading just from seeing the message."

"Of course it might mean nothing." Daniel crossed his arms.

Sandy's eyes lit up behind her reading glasses. The tapping of her fingers on a keyboard came through the speakers. "You could be right, Daniel."

"Hell, maybe they're just nonsense scribbles from some dabbler in the dark arts. You know the types. Make up their own lore and legends." Justine looked around at her colleagues.

Pauline nodded. "I remember this wannabe cult leader in Arizona. He didn't have much formal education but had a genius for manipulating vulnerable people. He created his own language, even wrote a short book using it."

Told his followers that it was an ancient Native American message and convinced them it was real... that he'd lived over a million years ago. What a load of bull." Shelia rolled her eyes.

❧

Daniel stood and walked closer to the television. "Well, Sandy?"

"No, there is order to the symbols or alphabet. I'll need time."

There was barking from the interior of the house, so LaShaun put off asking the questions she had. "I'll be back in a minute. Beau must want to be let out."

Shelia held up a palm. Then she stood, dumping her small tablet computer and other contents from her lap onto the floor. "Who is here?"

LaShaun stared at her in confusion. "I don't—"

"Shh." Pauline put a finger to her lips.

All five of the TEA members stood quiet, watching, and waiting. The barking stopped. An itching tingle crawled up LaShaun's arms, a signal. Shelia's question clanged in her mind like a warning bell. LaShaun dashed down the hallway to Ellie's room before the others could react. Beau stood frozen at the foot of Ellie's bed gazing at the open window. The bright fabric of the curtains plastered the window pane, as if a powerful wind had sucked it outward. Ellie stood just as still as Beau, her wide-eyed gaze at the window. Then she looked at LaShaun and pointed to it.

"No, mama. No." Ellie's sweet face screwed up until she let out a tiny sob.

"Oh my God." LaShaun rushed to scoop her up into a firm embrace. "Baby had a bad dream that's all. Mama's here. Everything is fine."

❖

Miss Rose and the others came into the room. They moved around quietly. Ellie's soft cries turned into wailing as she came fully awake. LaShaun didn't notice the TEA members in the room at first. After ten minutes, Ellie's sobs softened into sniffles. LaShaun hummed the tune Chase sang to Ellie. After another five minutes, the toddler grew quiet. She gazed up at LaShaun with a soft smile.

"I'm through here. Let's go back to the den," Shelia told the others quietly.

"Okay." LaShaun started to follow with Ellie still in her arms.

Justine and Pauline flanked LaShaun, hands on her shoulders. "She's safe," they said in unison. The twins acted in perfect concert when they operated in the supernatural.

"But..." LaShaun glanced down at Ellie, who was stretching a chubby arm to pet Beau.

"My Bo-bo."

Ellie giggled when Beau replied by rearing on his hind legs, paws on LaShaun's waist.

Only then did LaShaun realize the curtains had been pulled back inside, and the window was closed. Dried herbs dusted the sill.

"Do what you'd normally do when she wakes from her nap," Justine said.

"Children need the familiarity of routine, so she won't be frightened even more. Calmly." Pauline's composed tone matched her expression.

Only because of her trust in them did LaShaun resist her instinct to cling tightly to

❖

Ellie. Instead she took Ellie to the corner of the kitchen with her play pen and put her down. The open floor plan allowed her to see Ellie, the only reason LaShaun let go of her. Then she joined the others in the den. Yet even as she walked, LaShaun kept her eyes on Ellie. Beau trotted over to his dog bed not far from the play pen and laid down. His head propped on huge paws, Beau seemed relaxed.

"What the hell just happened?" LaShaun hissed low.

"An entity tried to enter the house. Whatever form it took was strong but not enough. You have protections around the house." Shelia didn't ask but stated the fact.

"How did you—" LaShaun gaped at her.

"Rose told me a bit about the Rousselle family history. If you're grandmother taught you half of what she knew, then precautions are in place. I'm guessing she and your ancestors planted rosemary, dandelions and other protections long ago." Shelia glanced at Miss Rose, who nodded confirmation.

"I didn't feel anything." LaShaun looked at Ellie as another chill took hold.

"Shelia is extraordinary when it comes to sensing spirits. Most of us get a hint compared to her gift for feeling their presence." Miss Rose turned off the television. "Sandy went to class after I explained. I'll text her the details."

LaShaun fought off the urge to cry in frustration. "I thought I could keep my child, my family, safe."

⚜

"You can't do it alone, dear." Pauline put an arm around LaShaun.

"Never works. That's why we have the Third Eye Association." Justine spoke in a brisk to-the-point manner. She waved at her twin's frown of censure. "Hey, she needs the raw truth."

"Indelicately put but no less accurate," Daniel said.

"So we have two problems. A missing child and..." Miss Rose's voice trailed off.

"Some *thing* tried to breach LaShaun's stronghold," Justine finished.

"And are the two related?" Daniel rubbed his bearded jaw with one hand.

Shelia faced LaShaun. "The good news is your defenses blunted the efforts. This spirit, whatever form it takes, only established a weak connection. From what Rose told us, Ellie may have helped fend it off. Beau gave the alarm to wake her."

"At such a young age, gifted children sleep quite soundly. Their preternatural abilities burn up a lot of energy. Just like other activities for a baby. That's why they need naps. Her abilities are dormant when she's asleep." Miss Rose looked at the other women.

"Thank the Lord for naps. Saved my sanity many a day when my three were young," Pauline agreed.

"Ellie and Beau are two assets, but Ellie is too young to train just yet." Miss Rose spoke to the twins instead of LaShaun.

"We usually don't recommend before age six at least, but we've got a credible threat," Justine replied.

"What do you mean?" LaShaun covered her mouth with both hands.

"Justine, you should try choosing your words more carefully," Pauline snapped.

"Umm, right. Sorry. But look, we can assume that this whatever has evil intent. Am I right? Not news to LaShaun." Justine turned to LaShaun.

LaShaun lowered her arms, her hands balled into fists. "She's right. Don't tip toe around me. I've fought this battle before."

"And won." Miss Rose placed a hand on the small of her back.

Justine grasped one of LaShaun's hands. "You've got us, too."

"All of us," Daniel said.

"I'll check outside." Shelia picked up her belongings from the floor. She put the other items in her satchel but held onto her mini-tablet computer.

"I can show you around while at least one of you stays with Ellie." LaShaun started for one of her jackets hanging on a hook near the kitchen door. She stopped when Shelia pulled her back.

"I'll find my way." Shelia's brisk steps took her out the door and down the steps.

"How does she know where to go?" LaShaun watched Shelia move with self-assurance.

⚜

"Like I said, Shelia is one of six in the world. Fortunately, four are in TEA." Miss Rose tapped away on the keys of her laptop as she spoke.

"Shelia can not only sense the paranormal when it's present, but she can pick up residue left behind. Even years later. In fact, she can almost tell what month or day of the week. Of the six, she's the superstar." Justine gave a proud smile as her gaze followed their friend. "I'm going to observe. Fascinating to watch."

"I'll look up invading malevolent spirits in the TEA online database." Pauline took out her cell phone and walked away.

"How does she do it?" LaShaun asked Miss Rose because Justine had scurried to catch up with Shelia.

Miss Rose smiled in understanding. LaShaun hadn't asked for an explanation of Shelia's ability. None of them fully understood paranormal forces. Rather, LaShaun's question was about Shelia's method, the mechanics of how she used her gifts.

"She pulls inward, goes still. We followed you, but Shelia stayed behind. Always the same, she becomes rooted to the spot. She calls it casting her net wide and slowly pulling it in. Then she moved close to the center or source, depending on the situation. The center is what pulls the entity in. The source is where the supernatural energy originates. In this case, she quickly determined the center was key." Miss Rose went about tidying up the den as she

❧

spoke. She patted one last throw pillow on the sofa and straightened.

"I agree with Justine. I'd very much like to see her in action one day," LaShaun said.

"Instinct tells me you'll get a chance soon." Miss Rose gazed out the window.

"Let's figure out if what happened here is connected to Dina's kidnapping." LaShaun rubbed her arms hard at the cold that crept through her.

"Your Ellie may have protected not just herself, but all of us today. She's a powerful one." Miss Rose had transferred her thoughtful gaze from outside to Ellie.

"Now we have to find out what she protected us from to stop it." LaShaun swallowed hard against the lump of terror in her throat.

Chapter 5

The next day, Pauline teamed up with Mr. Earl to plant more shrubs around the property. What the twins and Miss Rose called a psychokinetic fence. Chase, arms crossed, stared out of the kitchen window. He'd come home for lunch on what should have been his day off. He wouldn't, or rather couldn't, rest at home with a missing child case unsolved.

"My mother would have a fit over this," he said, nodding due east where Mr. Earl moved back and forth planting.

"Like we care what Queen Elizabeth thinks." LaShaun grinned at him, but his stone face didn't change. She cleared her throat and continued folding laundry. "Do you?"

"She's my mother, you know. I can't just write her off."

"I never asked you to."

LaShaun stomped down the hall with the basket of clean clothes. Her first stop was Ellie's room. Instead of napping, Ellie sat in bed talking to her stuffed doll. LaShaun eased her down and put the doll next to her on the pillow. Before LaShaun made it to the door, Ellie had popped up again. Accepting Ellie wasn't sleepy, LaShaun took the toddler to her play pen in the kitchen.

"She has her faults," Chase said, continuing on the subject. "Sure she can be stubborn at times."

"Add dictatorial, interfering, judgmental," LaShaun snapped back, "and let's not forget bigoted."

"Maybe you could work harder not to be so defensive." Chase didn't turn around.

"Don't try to push this all on me." LaShaun's voice volume began to rise. She stopped when Ellie stopped playing to stare at her.

Chase faced her with a frown. "Mama's no different from a lot of people around town, LaShaun. Of course she was uneasy when she met you after years of gossip about the Rousselle family and then the two cases that involved you."

"Oh, so it's my family's fault, too." LaShaun glared back at him, eyes narrowed. Why don't I go over there now and apologize for being me. While I'm at it, maybe I should apologize for

❦

Ellie. She's got those notorious Rousselle genes, too."

"LaShaun." Chase raised a finger.

"Spit it out. What's really bothering you? Our life isn't white picket fence all-American enough?" LaShaun paced around the den picking up toys thrown about by Ellie and Beau. The stress of the past few days added to taking care of a small child and dog while Chase worked long hours. It pushed her nerves to the limit.

"Well it would be nice for once, just once, if I didn't have wizards and ghost-whisperers mixed up in my case or my life for that matter. I've got to explain all the damn time when my mother…" Chase chopped off his words. "You don't come close to understanding."

"I get it. You're tired of defending me to Elizabeth and some of your other precious relatives. Now you'll have to tell her Ellie isn't like all her other grandchildren." LaShaun threw stuffed animals and chew toys into the brightly painted toy box. She shut the lid with a loud thump.

"What are you talking about? What's wrong with Ellie?" Chase pulled LaShaun back into the den before she could leave.

"The same thing that's 'wrong' with me, Chase."

"I didn't mean it the way it sounds," Chase protested.

⚜

"Joëlle Renée, my first born, *my daughter,* has psychic abilities. Now go tell your precious mother that!"

"Your daughter?" Chase shouted, then quickly lowered his voice. "Ellie is my daughter, too. Of course I'm concerned about her well-being."

"It's not a disease. You're worried about upsetting Queen Bee and the rest of your bigoted, small-minded family. Tell you what, we'll hide Ellie in the car next time we visit. I wouldn't want you to be too 'concerned', you know?" LaShaun looked up into his dark eyes ablaze with suppressed fury.

"Don't ever suggest I'm ashamed of our child, LaShaun. Just don't."

Before LaShaun could toss back the verbal bomb on the tip of her tongue, his cell phone rang. Their house phone rang at the same time. They separated like two prize fighters at the ring of the bell to answer. Chase stood talking into the phone. LaShaun grabbed the cordless handset from the granite top of the kitchen island.

"Yeah." LaShaun listened, her mind still half on the fiery argument. Five seconds later she got off the phone.

"They want us both at a crime scene." Chase shoved the phone back into the leather case clipped to his belt.

"MJ just told me the same thing. I can't simply pack up Ellie and run off." LaShaun raked fingers through her tangled hair. "Not to mention I need to get dressed. Where am I going to find a babysitter?"

"Wait a minute." Chase strode off, cell phone to his ear, and then returned. "I can take her over to my folks. They're home. Dad says it's no problem. He's at home wrapping the kids' Christmas presents, but he can lock them up in the spare room."

"A whole bedroom? Your parents agreed not to load up the kids with toys." LaShaun went to the play pen and picked up Ellie.

"I didn't say he had them stacked to the ceiling for cryin' out loud. Don't jump to assumptions just because it's my family." Chase followed her toward the hallway.

"Better check to make sure your mother is okay with keeping Ellie. I mean, she's part Rousselle." LaShaun gave a snort.

"Wait a minute, that remark is way over the line. My mother..." Chase pulled a hand over his face. "We can't have this discussion now and not in front of the baby. Okay, the last few days have been rough. The strain is getting to us both. Let's just stop, not say anymore."

LaShaun stared past him as Ellie wiggled in her arms. She heard the note of warning in his deep voice. Insults hurled at his close-knit family were bad enough. But she'd questioned how he felt about their little girl. Chase's words also held an unspoken plea to avoid saying even worse things to each other, which made LaShaun wonder about his mother's influence, about their marriage. What more did he have to say about his secret thoughts? Maybe Chase had miscalculated how much his family's disapproval of her would matter. To say the Broussard extended family were close was an understatement. Like most in south Louisiana, family meant everything. Did Chase blame LaShaun for causing cracks in that bond? Still, he was right. Now wasn't the time.

"Fine. I'll get ready." LaShaun stopped when Chase touched her arm.

"I'll dress Ellie since I'm good to go." Chase held out his arms and Ellie promptly leaned out. He took her from LaShaun. "I'll bet you want to wear your favorite overalls with the pink pony."

He walked away to Ellie's bedroom without waiting for LaShaun to react. His voice, tender and affectionate, came down the hallway. Ellie's answering babbles sounded excited to have her daddy dressing her, an unusual event. LaShaun went to their bedroom to dress with guilt about her angry outburst going along for the ride. Then she reminded herself that Chase had hinted at his resentment, and her anger sparked again. Minutes later, LaShaun met up with Chase and Ellie at the back door. She had her cell phone and tablet just in case she needed to do research or make notes.

Chase looked at her. "We're going to—"

"MJ texted me the address. I have it on my GPS." LaShaun kissed Ellie's smooth cheek before heading through the door.

"I'll meet you there then."

LaShaun waved a hand without looking back. She got into her SUV, revved the engine and drove away. Five minutes later, the hands-free in her car beeped, and she answered a call to her cell phone.

"I assume you're on the way," MJ started without a greeting.

"You do realize I'm a mother with a young child, right?" LaShaun snapped irritably. "Local law enforcement is always dragging me about silly ghost stuff but think nothing of calling me up last minute."

"Whoa, somebody woke up today with a bee in her ass. Sorry, didn't mean to cuss in front of the baby." MJ's throaty voice came through the SUV's speakers.

"Chase is dropping her off at his parents' house."

"Okay, um, see you in minute then."

"Yeah."

LaShaun tapped the button harder than necessary to end the connection, her mind still on the argument with Chase. What bothered her most were the things they hadn't said. The heavy sensation in her chest told her they were moving closer to saying them. And then what?

Ten minutes later, she arrived at the crime scene—Tommy Bradford's house. Sherry and her mother stood outside. LaShaun could hear their wailing sobs as she pulled her SUV behind a sheriff's department cruiser. Arliss Bradford, dressed in an over-sized t-shirt over dirty pink sweat pants, spoke in a voice made gruff by years of smoking.

"We told y'all he didn't have nothin' to do with Dina disappearing. Now go find out who hurt my Tommy."

"You told us Tommy was off fishing, so what was he doing at home?" MJ replied, her voice quiet but firm.

"Well, you can see for yourself he musta come home. While y'all standin' around askin' dumb questions, the same people what killed him might have my baby." Sherry waved her arms around like a pinwheel of distress.

"We have to collect evidence so we can figure out who did this and why. I don't get what you think this has to do with Dina's kidnapping."

MJ continued her insistent pursuit of getting information with more questions. But Sherry and her mother became more emotional and less coherent the longer they talked. Their voices blended together in a mixture of angry shouts. LaShaun used their distraction to avoid being pulled into the storm of recriminations. With permission from another deputy, she put disposal booties over her shoes. She entered the small house where Tommy sometimes lived with his girlfriend. The more or less neat interior contrasted with the way they'd found Sherry's trailer. A blue vase stuffed with yellow plastic daisies lay knocked over on the small coffee table. Pictures of more flowers and kittens dotted the walls. A dead body lay splayed

⚜

out on the cheap throw rug. Tommy Bradford could have been mistaken for having passed out drunk except for the blood on what was left of his face. LaShaun took a step back.

"Strange, huh? Like somebody just dumped him here as an afterthought." Det. Anderson looked around the room once. Then glanced at LaShaun. "Step outside a minute."

"I'm okay." LaShaun willed her gaze away from the dead man.

"I doubt it. Not unless you regularly stare at bodies in bloody crime scenes. C'mon. Some deep breaths of air will help." Anderson gestured for LaShaun to walk ahead of him.

"Maybe for a minute or two." LaShaun followed a deputy taking bags of evidence through the kitchen and out of the back door. "Who found him?"

"Nosy neighbor. She says all kinds of comings and goings been happening since they moved in. Well, since the girlfriend moved here, Brenda or Kris, they had two or three kids. Claims she reported to our station; thinks they were selling drugs." Anderson stopped after they'd walked a few feet. "I'll check to see if we have anything in the system."

LaShaun followed his advice. After a few breaths, she focused on Anderson's words. "So Tommy Bradford might have been selling drugs. But where is Brenda or whatever her name is?"

"The neighbor says they were always fighting, so maybe she took off. But we haven't

❖

checked to see if clothes are missing. You haven't asked why we got you out here." Anderson looked at LaShaun.

"More writing is my guess."

"You're psychic, so I figured you'd know." He shrugged when LaShaun squinted at him from behind her sunglasses. "Just sayin'."

LaShaun sensed no antagonism from the man, just disbelief. Det. Anderson, like most law officers, trusted what he saw, heard, and could verify; hopefully enough to satisfy a court system and put away bad guys. In that way he reminded her of Chase.

"Yeah, well I wish it worked that neatly, Det. Anderson. I can't flip a switch and know stuff. My life would be way easier if I could." LaShaun turned when she heard Chase's voice coming from inside the house. "Anyway, you were about to tell me why you called the local voodoo woman to a murder scene."

Det. Anderson laughed. "In New Orleans all that stuff is mostly for the tourists."

"Not here. Not in many parts of south Louisiana either," LaShaun replied quietly.

His smile faded. "Nothing but an excuse for doing dirt. The devil made me do it. Anyway, more writing found here. This time a message was left on paper. Part of it burned. Can you take going back inside?"

"Sure."

"Good. We don't want to move it until all photos are taken. It's on the dinette table." Det.

Anderson waved for LaShaun to proceed with him back into the house.

Chase met them at the door. "The body has been moved. You feeling okay?"

"Yeah, just fine." LaShaun brushed past him. She took off her sunglasses. "Show me the writing, Det. Anderson."

"What writing?" Chase followed them.

"Another message. This time on loose leaf paper." He led them to the small eat-in section of the kitchen. He stood back while a deputy took more photographs.

"We'll be out of the way soon. Then you can bag this," Chase said to the deputy.

"No rush. We've got other items to collect anyway." The deputy clicked four more pictures from different angles and left.

LaShaun bent forward to read while taking care not to touch or disturb the sheets of note paper. "Hmm, a combination of symbols and words this time. Part of this is a wish spell. The belief is burning it will make your wish come true."

"Wishing for what?" Chase stood on the op-posite end of the round table.

"For success, but I can't read it all. The rest is destroyed. Maybe the pieces in the ashtray can be analyzed." LaShaun straightened and examined the kitchen. White and black candles lay on the counter along with a box of matches.

"Sherry and her mama are hiding some-thing. I say haul their asses to the stations and get them to talk." Det. Anderson scowled at the interior of the house as if offended by it.

"Or make them even less cooperative," Chase said.

"Sherry said something about Tommy's murder being linked to Dina's disappearance. I have to say Det. Anderson could have a point. None of it makes sense. Questioning them at length could be helpful." LaShaun made a circle of the room as she talked. She tingled at leftover psychic energy in the place. A bitter scent lingered.

"Well, since the mind reader agrees, then I'm even more certain," Anderson joked.

LaShaun grinned at him. "I have no idea what they're going to say, but it can't hurt."

Det. Anderson turned to Chase since he was chief of criminal investigations. "I'm going to get started."

"Your case," Chase said with a curt nod. He faced LaShaun. "Since when did you two become chummy?"

"Det. Anderson seems to have decided I'm not a total nut job. That hardly qualifies as us being best buds." LaShaun walked away from him.

"MJ says he asked for you, so I suppose you're his go-to consultant now. Anderson will have a whole new set of voodoo jokes going around the department." Chase followed closely behind LaShaun. When she spun to confront him, he stopped short.

❖

"So you have another complaint. In addition to dealing with your family, I make you a joke with the rest of law enforcement."

"That's not what I said." Chase broke off when one of two deputies collecting evidence waved to get his attention.

"We're finished here. Heading out," the deputy collecting evidence said.

"Got ya. Thanks." Chase waited until the two deputies left the house.

"Yeah, but that's pretty much what you meant. You got a problem, then deal with it on your own." LaShaun crossed her arms.

Chase stared at her as he tapped a fist against one muscled thigh. "Not here, not now."

"Whenever you're ready," LaShaun retorted. They faced each other in silence.

"Uh, is there an issue I need to know about?" MJ spoke from the open door way. When neither spoke, she walked into the compact living room. "Anderson has taken Sherry and Arliss to the station for questioning. You might want to be there to observe, Chase. Patrols will check to make sure the scene isn't disturbed. The landlord is on her way over to lock up."

"Great idea. Get going, Chase."

LaShaun put on her sunglasses and walked away before he could answer. She didn't look at him as he marched past to his department SUV. MJ walked up to stand beside her. LaShaun studied the outside of the house. Peeling faded yellow paint struggled to project an

❖

inviting picture. Despite the pictures and attempts, it all felt wrong. MJ shot a sideways glance at her, but LaShaun spoke first to head off questions.

"Any leads on how this ties in with Dina's disappearance?"

"Lots of theories, guesswork only. We're trying to find out more about the girlfriend." MJ put both hands on her hips. "Maybe Tommy and her were in it together or with a gang. Dina's father is dealing drugs, flush with cash. Could be they wanted money."

"Taking his own niece for ransom? Seems kinda heartless." LaShaun took a step toward the house as if closing the distance would yield clues. Nothing.

"Yeah, well warm family feelings run low in that crowd. Drugs, alcohol, and domestic violence don't help. Goes back at least a couple of generations from what I hear," MJ said.

"Ah yes, the blessing and curse of small town gossip. You get the whole story, but probably not the right one." LaShaun raised an eyebrow.

"In this case we've got police calls, court records and the memories of old cops like Sheriff Triche." MJ smiled at the mention of her former boss and mentor. Sheriff Triche had served Vermilion Parish for over thirty years before retiring.

"Sounds like this girlfriend is a bit of a mystery. Make sure it's not just small town suspi-

cion of a newcomer though." LaShaun looked at
MJ.

"Yeah. Speaking of family tension—"

"I'll do more research on the writing. Text
me copies of the photos. The spell might give us
more clues." LaShaun smiled at MJ and waved.
"Better go pick up Ellie. No telling when Chase
will get home."

"Right. Right. LaShaun, don't let this case
push you and Chase apart. Police work is
rough, and in your situation with you both being pulled in... Well, it's just like a pressure
cooker turned up way too high. You know?"

"Doesn't help, but that's not the real source
of the problem. I'll call you when I know more
about those spells."

"Okay, and call if you need to talk or anything else. Hey, no judgement here, okay? Just
a listening ear."

"I know. Thanks." LaShaun gave MJ a pat
on the back. Then she got in her SUV and
headed off.

****

Glowing red numbers showed it was eleven-
thirty that night. LaShaun lay on her side staring at the digital clock display on the
nightstand. Chase hadn't called, but that
wasn't a surprise. He was probably still tied up
following the loose threads of the case. Or he
was still pissed and just didn't feel like giving

her an update. Either way, his absence bothered LaShaun. Not that he hadn't called. She'd
grown used to the irregular hours and schedule
of a law officer, especially the head of a division. As the Chief of Investigations, Chase put
in even more hours than the officers under his
command at times. No, the lump of unease
lodged in LaShaun's chest had a different
source. Not only were things bad between
them, but she feared their clashes would only
get worse. And she had no idea how to stop the
downward slide.

Giving up at last on the effort to doze off,
LaShaun admitted that she couldn't shut off
her mind, so she sat on the edge of the bed. The
quiet of country living surrounded their home.
She'd lived in Los Angeles for almost ten years,
and at first, coming back to Beau Chene took
adjustment. In the city, lights flashed, glared
and pulsated continuously. The absence of
noise in comparison still struck her. And the
dark... Out from town where she lived, houses
sat separated by acres. Each stood in pools of
light from lamp posts. Quiet. Too quiet.
LaShaun stood. She listened. Then she moved
down the hall quickly to the nursery. LaShaun
entered the room. Ellie looked peaceful, asleep
on her tummy. By contrast, Beau looked alert.

"You can't sleep either, huh?"

She scratched behind one of Beau's ears.
The dog stood at the window looking out. Then
he reared up and planted his paws on the sill.
LaShaun felt rather than heard the low growl

❧

vibrating beneath his smooth coat. His entire body seemed to generate a steady buzz. Her arms tingled as her third eye opened. She pushed away the interference from anxieties about her marriage.

"Show me what you see, boy. What's going on?" LaShaun whispered.

Beau didn't move. And she knew. He wasn't supposed to, not from Ellie's side. LaShaun reached out beyond the bright circle from their security lamp outside. Movement. A shadow kept to the shadows cast by trees. A force pushed against a force. She glanced down realizing Beau projected a buffer. No ordinary dog for sure. Reassured he could hold down the house, LaShaun patted his back.

"Good job, boy. Stay while I take a look around."

LaShaun went to her bedroom. She dressed in seconds, including sturdy waterproof boots. She wore insulated undergarments under a soft cotton flannel shirt and jeans. Her jacket had enough pockets to carry necessaries. It had three inner pockets and two deeper outer pockets. She slipped a palm-sized .380 into one pocket. Next, she clipped a leather knife case to the waistband of her jeans. Armed, LaShaun went down the hallway toward the back door. She paused long enough to turn off the alarm system. Then she reset it to give her a few seconds to go out. With one last glance back at the house, she went down the steps. Nothing looked out of place on the back porch. LaShaun followed her instincts around the kitchen, past the den and to the outside walls of the bedrooms. A curtain twitched and Beau's head appeared in Ellie's window. Then he withdrew.

LaShaun turned to face the woods. Oak, ash and maple trees she knew well loomed up to the sky. The chilly night air pressed in on her, but she didn't feel the cold. At least not from the forty-degree temperature. LaShaun set off for the forest at the edge of her neatly clipped yard. She kept out of the light. As she got closer to the thick wooded area, LaShaun drew the knife. A deeper slice of darkness moved to her left. LaShaun went still.

"Since you know we're here, tiptoeing through the underbrush seems a bit unnecessary," a husky voice spoke.

"Who are you and what do you want?" LaShaun held her arms out. Her right hand held the gun, the left her knife.

"We never expected our task to be easy. You're an able opponent. But your husband? He's not so sure about all of the... hocus pocus I think he calls it. You're alone."

Female, LaShaun thought. Trying to mask the telltale identity clue, but definitely female. "Oh, yeah. Well, girlfriend, you need to stop relying on women's intuition because yours is way off. I'm definitely not alone."

The speaker gave a short hiss. After a few beats of silence, "I can't help but notice you're out here by yourself. Detective Broussard is working late again."

⚜

"If you're feeling so confident, come closer. Into the light so we can have a nice chat. If you visit at a decent hour I might fix us some coffee and beignets." LaShaun took two steps to her left. "I'll shoot your friend if he moves. Even half an inch will earn him a bullet."

LaShaun's senses, all five and extras, operated at full power. Two more figures circled around. They moved with skill, making little noise. Only the faintest swish of leaves, of air being displaced gave them away.

"We don't want to draw any attention. The last thing you need right now is more gossip. Am I right?" The husky voice purred like a cat sure she held the upper hand.

"My gun won't make much noise. Same for my knife, very sharp. Of course screams of pain might get a little loud." LaShaun couldn't tell if any of the figures moved toward the house. Panic punched through her. She had to concentrate.

"To hell with chatting," a gruff voice called out. A figure shot forward.

LaShaun anticipated the attack. She jumped to her right to avoid a kick. When the figure whirled around, LaShaun sliced up and connected with a torso. Then she parried, sliced again. The man dropped to his knees with a series of shocked gasps. Her silver blade would inflict damage on human and supernatural opponents. With him disabled for the moment, LaShaun slammed her weighed boot into his kneecap. Then she quickly ran into the light. Husky voice didn't follow.

"C'mon, let's get properly introduced," LaShaun shouted.

"Oh we will. Never doubt that we'll meet again." The figure seemed to slowly meld into the surrounding darkness as she spoke.

LaShaun started to follow when the security alarm went off. The horn's blare cut through the night. She spun around with one thought, get to Ellie. Two floodlights connected to the system emitted pulsating strobes. They served as beacons for responding law enforcement or firemen. The noise and flashing lights made the house easy to find in the dark rural countryside. LaShaun reached the house and found the back door still locked. Her mind sharpened, she steadied her hands. Forget the keys. Instead she slapped the numbers pad to gain fast access. LaShaun pulled on the door only to curse in frustration. Seconds later three clicks signaled the locking bars had slid back. She yanked open the door, kicked it aside, and stumbled in.

"Ellie? Beau?"

No sound came to reassure her. The interior lights had gone out, but emergency lamps provided illumination as LaShaun ran. Her boots pounded against the hardwood floors. LaShaun skidded on something wet and almost fell. She stayed on her feet by grabbing the door jamb. Beau made low growling sounds as he bent over what looked like a pile of clothes at first.

⚜

With enormous will, LaShaun resisted the urge to run to Ellie's bed. Instead she focused her kinetic energy outward until sweat stung her eyes. Seconds later the lamp flicked on. A bundle lay in Ellie's bed. Heart hammering, LaShaun held her breath as she pulled away the blanket covered with pink elephants. Ellie still lay on her stomach sleeping.

"Merci le bon dieu," LaShaun whispered, her voice hoarse with relief.

She continued a prayer of thanksgiving Monmon Odette had taught her years ago. Satisfied that Ellie rested unharmed, LaShaun turned to examine the dog. Beau's sides heaved from heavy breathing. He lifted his large head. Blood covered his muzzle and matted his sleek fur. Blinking as though he noticed LaShaun for the first time, Beau barked furiously and circled the heap on the floor.

"Okay, boy. We're okay. Stand down."

LaShaun glanced around quickly to make sure no one or nothing had followed her into the room at least. She still held her knife out as she turned in a circle. Beau went to Ellie's bed and took up a defensive stance. He let out low guttural snarls as if warning potential threats. LaShaun stood over the unmoving body. She used one hand to tug it over while her knife hand remained ready to strike. A gurgled gasp made LaShaun step away fast, but it seemed obvious the person couldn't move. More blood stained the wool rug. Only then did LaShaun register the keening sound of sirens. She still stood staring down at the woman when Chase came into the room, gun drawn.

Chapter 6

One hour later, LaShaun sat at the breakfast table. She held Ellie in her lap. Chase had wrapped a chenille throw from the den around them both. Ellie blinked at the activity around them sleepily. She took turns staring up at her mother, at Beau still covered in blood, and the strange people in her house. Yet she didn't cry or seem distressed. Instead Ellie rested her head against LaShaun's breasts, a thumb in her mouth. MJ stood a few feet away talking to a rattled Chase. He kept his voice low, but panic radiated from every gesture.

"Damn it, I should have been here tonight." Chase looked at LaShaun, then turned away.

❖

"Go check on the guys processing the room, alright. Just go," MJ said.

She turned her back to LaShaun as she continued talking to Chase quietly. She pulled Chase along until they disappeared. Moments later MJ came back. Another deputy stopped her before she reached LaShaun. Then Sheriff Godchaux arrived. He and MJ approached after a brief exchange.

"Sorry y'all had to go through this, LaShaun. The most important thing is you and the baby are safe, right?" Dave wore a grave expression. He placed a hand on LaShaun's shoulder. When she nodded, he patted her and then strode off.

"You don't mind if I..."

"I don't recognize the woman," LaShaun cut her off. "Yes, I know you need to ask me questions that can't wait. I'm okay."

MJ pulled another chair out and sat next to her. "You counted three people?"

"Yeah, but there could have been four. A woman did most of the talking like she was in charge. I couldn't see her face. At least one of the other two was a guy. I could tell from his voice and build. The third was..." LaShaun glanced over at Beau. "I need to clean him up. Ellie hasn't noticed the blood yet, but... I don't want her to get upset."

"Beau let me examine him all over without making a peep, not one growl. He isn't hurt. It's all her blood." MJ gazed at Beau.

❖

"You have a way with animals, almost a psychic connection," LaShaun murmured, her gaze on the hallway as people came and went from her home.

"They know I'm not scared is all. Nothing magical. We don't need another psychic running around here tonight," MJ quipped.

"Is that your opinion, or what Chase says?" LaShaun pulled Ellie closer against her body.

"You love each other like crazy." MJ leaned forward. "The strain is testing y'all. Every marriage goes through it."

"Like yours." LaShaun looked at MJ, divorced for ten years.

"Humph, if I'd been paying attention, I would have seen Gentry wasn't in it for the long haul. But Chase? No, girl. He's going to hold on for dear life."

"He doesn't say it, but he misses going to all the big family gatherings like he used to. Maybe some of the talk is starting to make sense to him." LaShaun looked down at Ellie and sighed. "I don't want him to stay just because of her. What an empty life that would be for all of us."

"Stop talking like that, LaShaun. Chase is human, sure he is. He's been dealing with the pressure for almost four years of—"

"Being with me and the baggage I bring." LaShaun swallowed against the bitter lump in her throat.

"No, don't start down that road," MJ said sharply. She sat forward. "Look, police officers

⚜

are more affected by cases involving kids than they let on. Even before we become parents, those investigations are like a kick in the gut with a steel-toe boot. Add to that Chase is worried that a crazy cult is focused on you again, and now Ellie is in the mix. He's scared for both of you."

"And I have no idea what to do about it, MJ, or what I can say to him. I can't stop being who I am. I can't undo my family history." LaShaun's voice trembled with the effort to hold back tears. She took in deep breaths and let them out.

"You think he didn't know the whole story? Girl, please. This is Beau Chene. If I sneeze in the morning, by noon everybody is calling to offer cold remedies. But he's here, which means something." MJ glanced to her right. She stood as Sheriff Godchaux and Chase entered the kitchen.

"Does it?" LaShaun studied her husband's drawn expression. The furrows of apprehension on his forehead didn't ease when he looked at Ellie resting in her lap.

MJ started to answer, but stopped when Chase strode up to them. Their boss followed close behind with another deputy. "Ellie is made of tough stuff. I think she slept through the whole thing. Even now she's still relaxed. She knows her daddy and mama got things in hand."

Chase gave a short nod without looking at LaShaun. "We didn't find anyone outside, but

⚜

there's blood on the grass. I found a couple of signs somebody came up through the woods. We can check them out when it gets light."

"Sure. I'll go see to the sites being secured," MJ said.

"I can do it." Chase started to leave, but Sheriff Godchaux grabbed his arm.

"We'll handle things from here." The sheriff gazed at Chase in silence before he left.

LaShaun stared out of the window into the dark. Flashes of white went off as a deputy took pictures. Others moved around roping off areas with yellow crime scene tape. Silence thick with tension stretched between them for several minutes. Chase cleared his throat several times before he spoke.

"So you're okay." Chase tapped a fist against his thigh.

"Gee, thanks for asking, three hours after I fought off insane ninjas and found a body at the foot of our daughter's crib." LaShaun still did not look at him.

"Drop the sarcasm, okay." Chase sat in the chair MJ had vacated. "This? This is what I was worried would happen."

"And how exactly did you expect me to anticipate and stop it, Chase? Please, I'll take all suggestions from a seasoned lawman," LaShaun snapped. Ellie stirred as if she could sense the anger crackling between her parents. Her lids fluttered, but she settled again into steady breathing.

LaShaun exhaled slowly. She tried to will the bad vibes away so Ellie wouldn't pick up on them. "Okay, I'm sorry for that last crack. But still, it's a fair question. What do you want from me?"

"Calling 911 when intruders show up would be a good damn start." Chase frowned at her. Then he also breathed in and out. "When the security system app on my phone beeped... all kinds of nightmare scenarios went through my mind. That was a helluva long drive to get here."

"Exactly. Deputies are spread out all over Vermilion Parish. You were miles away. How long would I have been waiting? Meanwhile those people would have gained the advantage. I did what I thought was right." LaShaun stroked Ellie's thatch of thick dark curls. By the way his jaw clenched, LaShaun could tell Chase saw the logic. Yet he couldn't concede the point and admit it.

"Well, what's done is done," he muttered.

"Humph." LaShaun shot a heated glance his way and looked off again.

"Not a body," Chase said after a beat.

"What?"

"The woman isn't dead. An ambulance took her to the hospital. She's in bad shape, but still alive." Chase rubbed his hands together. He started to say more when his cell phone went off. "Damn."

"Who is it?" LaShaun watched his frown deepen as he read the caller ID display.

⚜

"Mom." Chase answered the call, but stood and walked away to talk to Elizabeth Broussard. Moments later he came back.

"What did you tell her?" LaShaun bit back the urge to use one of her nicknames: Queen Elizabeth or Miss Queen Bee.

"That everyone's fine and not to worry." Chase paced to the window, gazed out at his colleagues and then sat again. "Look, I shouldn't have snapped at you earlier. The Dina Menard case is nerve-racking enough, but putting you in the bull's eye of some wacko has me on edge. But that's not an excuse for taking it out on you."

"We took vows to be a team, always have each other's back." LaShaun bit her lower lip. She swiped at her eyes to keep tears from falling.

"Yeah. Now more than ever." Chase reached out and adjusted the blanket to cover more of Ellie's back.

LaShaun lifted her chin and gazed at him. "Truce then."

"We need more than a truce. Like I said, we should talk. Ceasing hostility is a start though." Chase returned her gaze.

"Spoken like a true military vet," LaShaun replied with a slight smile.

"Habit." Chase's taut expression eased not quite into a smile. He leaned forward to rest his forehead against hers. "I love you hard."

"I love you back, Deputy Broussard."

⚜

Chase sat straight when a deputy walked by followed by MJ. When they were gone he said, "The woman had no ID on her. Not surprising. White female, about five feet seven?"

"Nothing about her looked familiar, but then blood covered her face. What's her condition?" LaShaun looked at him.

"Critical. Beau went for her throat like he was trained to kill. She lost a lot of blood." Chase studied Beau as he spoke.

"He's safe around Ellie, if that's what you're thinking. Beau isn't a typical guard dog, Chase."

"A ghostbuster on four legs, huh?"

LaShaun sighed with relief at his half-smile. There was no anger in his response. "He'll attack if she's threatened, and obviously his training is to take no prisoners."

Chase's smiled hardened. "I'm good with that when it comes to our daughter."

"There's something else. Ellie can sort of communicate with Beau. They understand each other. But I don't get why she slept through all the racket. I mean, this woman broke into the house, the alarm went off, Beau barked like crazy, but she didn't even turn over." LaShaun whispered as if afraid the sleeping child would hear her.

"Well, her daddy goes out like a ton of bricks when he's tired." Chase rubbed Ellie's back with a smile full of love.

⚜

"No, it's more than her being tired after a day playing." LaShaun turned the puzzle over in her mind.

"Maybe the members of your psychic sorority can give a clue," Chase said with a laugh.

"You're right. Miss Rose and the twins have children who inherited gifts."

"Next thing you're going to tell me there's a Facebook group to exchange tips between mommies with psychic kids." Chase started to laugh again but stopped. He gaped at LaShaun's raised eyebrow. "You're joking."

"TEA members are all ages and at all stages of life. So, yes, a group of mothers do exchange tips. I'm not a member, but maybe I should join." LaShaun winked at him.

Chase brushed back a tendril of LaShaun's tussled hair. "Sure you didn't get hurt?"

"Nah, they didn't even land two good licks on me. I got the moves, Broussard."

"I know, but if anything happened to either of you." Chase blinked hard as he looked away.

"We're fine, baby. And we're going to make sure Ellie stays safe."

"We damn sure will."

LaShaun squeezed his shoulder. "So, I'm guessing this woman is in no shape to give us any answers."

"They rushed her into surgery. She's got damage to her neck and esophagus, bites all over. Beau did a job taking her down." Chase nodded to Beau, who continued to doze as if knowing he could relax.

⚜

"But you should be able to identify her from fingerprints or even motor vehicle photo records."

"Already in motion. A deputy followed the ambulance to the hospital. He'll take a photo once they clean her up." Chase stood when MJ walked over to them still scrolling through messages on her cell phone. "I was just telling LaShaun we're working on getting an ID for the perp left behind."

"Mystery solved. Wait a minute." MJ shook her head. "This case."

"Really?" Chase looked at the phone screen that MJ held up. "Don't know her."

"We found Tommy Bradford's missing girlfriend." MJ's eyes narrowed.

"You mean..." Chase blinked at MJ then back at the photo on the phone.

"One of their cousins works at the Vermilion Parish Hospital. She was in the ER when they brought her in. Of course we gotta confirm."

"What in the seven levels of hell is going on?" Chase's dark brows pulled together in a frown.

"This case is getting complicated for sure." MJ cast a glance at LaShaun and then the photo again.

"Wheels within wheels," LaShaun murmured, quoting a favorite saying of the Dupart twins.

❧

****

The next day LaShaun welcomed the group back to her home. All insisted on meeting fast. Miss Rose and the twins arrived together in Justine's SUV. LaShaun wasn't encouraged by the matching grim sets of expressions the three women wore. After terse greetings, Justine set about opening the video conference app on her laptop. They connected it to the big screen smart TV in LaShaun's den. Daniel Rayford, Shelia, and Sandy Portier appeared in three smaller windows.

LaShaun would not even think of leaving Ellie with anyone, not even family. She wanted her child close by, so Ellie sat in her play pen. Though surrounded by toys, the toddler seemed more interested in watching the adults. Beau sat nearby placidly gnawing on a big rawhide chew bone.

"Well everybody, the last few hours have been interesting to say the least," Daniel began. The others nodded.

"The only good news, and I use the word good loosely, is the news reports are sensationalized," Pauline said. She exchanged a glance with her twin.

"The sheriff's department public information officer spoke to the news directors at two local television stations. He reported it as only a burglary." LaShaun blew out a long breath.

"Nurses cut off her clothing at the hospital, so her all black clothing didn't draw attention. Yet—," Justine put in.

"Somebody breaks into the home of a high level deputy sheriff, and that kind of talk is going to get around. So I figure we have a small window of opportunity before the media wises up." Miss Rose looked around at her colleagues.

"Hey, there is more good news. Our closest neighbors happen to be out of town for the holidays. Mrs. Marchand is better at spreading gossip than any twenty-four-seven news channel," LaShaun said with a grin.

"Yes, but reporters are going to start digging. A woman is in the hospital, no identity, and they'll find out who lives at this address," Daniel rumbled. "You can't keep these things quiet in today's high speed communications world."

"Our adversaries know their attempt failed." Miss Rose shot a worried glance at Ellie. "We must anticipate how they'll respond."

"Maybe they'll back off, even give up. Wait, hear me out," Dr. Portier said quickly, raising her voice to drown out their objections. "Going after a high risk target could be more of a problem than they need right now."

"Sandy, that brings us to the key questions. What did they hope to accomplish? We don't know if they came to deliver a message, intimidate or take something," Miss Rose said.

LaShaun crossed her arms tightly as if cold. "Three attempts to get to Ellie. Two were

⚜

through psychic means. When those attempts didn't work, they decided on a direct approach."

Miss Rose nodded with a grave expression. "Agreed. But you're a valuable target on your own. You've also pretty much wrecked Juridicus."

"What about the dagger?" Justine asked. She glanced at Miss Rose first and then her twin.

"Oh?" Shelia St. Denis leaned forward with interest.

"Right, we haven't told you that. LaShaun inherited an artifact, a dagger which..."

"It's a knife, not a dagger," Pauline broke in.

"Same thing, sister." Justine waved a hand.

"No it isn't. A knife has one sharp edge, while a dagger has a double sharp edge. *Ours* is a dagger. LaShaun has an ancient Mayan knife." Pauline wore a look of irritation. "You should know better, Justine. We've talked about this a hundred times."

"They're both silver, they both get the job done," Justine retorted. "She likes picky details. I'm more concerned with the results."

"Not silver, Damascus steel. For crying out loud, Justine. Pay attention," Pauline snapped.

"Hey, grandfather willed it to you, and you've been jealously hiding it for twenty years. Forgive me for not knowing all about the damn thing." Justine squinted at her.

"You pitched a hissy fit, so stop pretending you didn't care I got it." Pauline waved a finger.

⚜

"Wait a minute, you own a dagger made of Damascus steel? What era?" Daniel's eyes lit up.

"I'd love to see it and LaShaun's Mayan knife. This is fascinating, not that I'm into weapons as a rule," Shelia added.

Pauline perked up. "Grandfather inherited it from his grandfather. It dates to the six-teenth century Turkish empire of—"

"Save the history lesson for another day. Please." Justine poked her sister in the side with an elbow. Pauline scowled back.

"Justine is right," Miss Rose said quickly to head off one of their sibling arguments. "The Rousselle family history is well known in our circles. Juridicus has most certainly done more homework on them."

"For sure. Especially since LaShaun used her knife against them. No doubt they'd love to get their hands on it," Pauline said.

"How'd the woman get in?" Daniel asked.

"She broke a window in Ellie's bedroom. Our system has glass break detectors, so it went off," LaShaun replied.

Shelia scribbled notes as she talked. "Makes sense. Go through a child's room figur-ing she's less of a threat."

"LaShaun also has family journals, at least two rosaries over a hundred years old, and more. This house is a treasure of items the cult would love to get their hands on." Justine waved her arms.

⚜

"Well we have to narrow down exactly what they want," Miss Rose said with a grimace.

"And why," Dr. Portier added.

Silence stretched as the five TEA members pondered the points made. LaShaun couldn't contain her nervous energy anymore. She excused herself to check on Ellie. While in the kitchen, she prepared a tray with coffee and pastries for her friends. Ellie fussed until LaShaun broke off a small corner of one lemon tart and gave it to her. Excited voices pulled her back to the family room where the group sat.

"Tell me you've had a break through. I'm ready for real good news, no air quotes or qualifications." LaShaun sat down on her leather ottoman.

"We finally have a start, thanks to my smart older sister." Pauline snickered when Justine shot a sour look at her.

"By six seconds, and everyone says I look younger than you," Justine retorted.

"Nobody says that, girl. Who you kiddin'?"

"Stop acting like you're still thirteen. I swear." Miss Rose rolled her eyes. "Okay, we still have lots of question marks hanging over our heads, but..." She looked at the TV and smiled.

Daniel cleared his throat. "The TEA has made a number of technological advances in the past, I'd say ten years. Recently our X, Y, and Z Chapter developed an app that looks for patterns of troubling activity. Very impressive stuff."

"X, Y, and Z?" LaShaun blinked at them.

"Generations X, Y, and Z. Young people who have grown up in this new mass communication and digital age. Not that us boomers can't hang when it comes to techie stuff," Justine said.

"But we finally acknowledged they're more comfortable and skilled at writing code, developing apps and more," Miss Rose said. "That was a battle. Egos fell like mighty oaks."

"Hmm, who wants to admit they're not just old, but out of step?" Shelia covered her mouth to stifle a laugh.

"Yeah, yeah. You're part of the under fifty crowd. Bite me, youngster." Dr. Portier grinned at her friend.

"If we can get back to the point..." Miss Rose gave her colleagues a look of annoyance.

"Ahem, right. We can look for a pattern and develop a profile to give us clues. Now we have a definite reference point, Vermilion Parish." Daniel tapped on a mini tablet computer as he talked. I'm messaging Ian McDermott now. He's the app developer and contact to initiate a work order."

"Narrow it to Beau Chene," LaShaun said.

"Just a second." Daniel wore a wide grin a few seconds later. "Even better, they've updated the app so that they can narrow coordinates to geo coordinates. I told him to start wide and

window. They're going to pull o

next time."

"So, we bring out th

tapped on his tablet c

"Herbs won't cut it.

"Clearing my

prayers, protecti

opened her o

scrolling th

Justi

ly. Bea

tenti

"We don't have clear evidence that the crimes are linked." Miss Rose gripped LaShaun's shoulder to reassure her.

"May I also point out that these folks managed to get past our precautions? Another important piece of data." Shelia leaned forward again toward the camera. "These are not rookies, folks dabbling in the occult for thrills."

"More evidence that Juridicus operatives might be in play. Another thing, they knew LaShaun was outside and probably knew Chase wasn't home. Why pick Ellie's window unless..." Pauline looked to Miss Rose.

"Let's not jump to conclusions," Miss Rose said.

LaShaun clasped her hands together. "Pauline's right. She didn't randomly choose Ellie's

⚜

ut all the stops

big guns." Daniel
mputer as he talked.

schedule. I have binding
on prayers and more." Shelia
wn android tablet and started
ough notes.

e went to Beau and scratched his bel-
u rolled on his back and enjoyed her at-
on. "What a good boy, yes you are."

"I can come this morning and be finished
before your husband gets home. Nothing will
look odd to him or your neighbors, so don't worry." Shelia continued to make notes as she
talked.

"I just sent you a few suggestions," Daniel
added

"Thanks, Danny." Shelia grinned at him before she went back to making notes.

LaShaun stood. "Christmas is less than two
weeks away, and I haven't decorated."

Justine crossed to her. "Perfect. We'll do it
today then. Holly all over the windows, the
doors and on the barn."

"Sister, you may be a pain sometimes, but
you're a brilliant one." Pauline beamed at her
twin.

"Holly, one of the most potent protections
against evil spirits and demons." Shelia quoted
as if from a well-practiced lecture.

⚜

"TEA members own a local nursery. We can get fresh wreaths and garlands here from Lafayette in minutes," Miss Rose said to Shelia.

"I'm already on it, Rose." Shelia nodded to her. "Just sent the order to Joe and Christine. I'm only a few minutes away from them, so I'll bring what we need."

Miss Rose turned to Dr. Portier. "Sandy, what about the writing?"

Dr. Portier looked away from the camera. "Some of the pictographs are Sumerian, or close. It has similarities to the Assyrian alphabet, but it's not an exact match. I'm waiting to hear from a pal in California, Dr. Farrah Bakir."

"Thanks for the tutorial on what it's *not*, Sandy. How's about we figure out what it is? Sheesh, academics." Justine smacked her lips.

"Ignoring you, Justine," Sandy replied mildly. "I was about to add that we're very close to cracking this code, or whatever it is."

"At least the house will be decked out for Christmas in high style, El," LaShaun said. Their confidence and teasing helped soothe her jangled nerves.

Miss Rose stood beside LaShaun and put an arm around her shoulders. "We're going to figure this out and make sure you, Ellie and even stubborn Chase stay safe."

"I know, Miss Rose. Don't forget Beau," LaShaun said. The dog padded across the hardwood floor to her as if answering a call.

❖

She rubbed his large head. "Who's protecting Dina?"

Chapter 7

The next few hours were surreal. Shelia arrived as promised, her SUV loaded with the tools of her trade. A truck from Green Thumb Nursery pulled in right behind her. A cheerful dark haired young man, a member of the Coushatta tribe also, hopped out. Muscular with tanned skin, he looked no older than twenty-five. He gave everyone a quick hello before he got to work. His job was to plant three holly shrubs at key points as instructed by Shelia. LaShaun wondered what Shelia's colleagues at the Louisiana DMV would say if they knew her other profession, warding off demons and evil ghosts.

"What will we tell your husband if he comes home?" Shelia raised an eyebrow at LaShaun.

"Chase won't be home for lunch. I wouldn't be surprised if he's gone until tomorrow. He's determined to find out if the burglary at our place is connected to Dina's kidnapping." LaShaun helped Shelia string a lovely garland along the railing of the back porch. Then they strung holly on the windows.

"Yeah, it's personal now. So when he does get home…" Shelia hung one of the dozen holly wreaths on Ellie's bedroom window.

"I'll tell him I went all out to make this Christmas special. I don't want Ellie's holiday to have a dark cloud over it. She'll have to face the hard realities of the world soon enough. I'd like her childhood to be as normal as possible."

"Not like yours. Sorry, we haven't been gossiping. Key members of the team have to know background when we're assigned to a case." Shelia wore an apologetic smile.

"That's okay." LaShaun sighed. "Yeah, I want Ellie's early years to be a lot happier than mine were."

They worked on in silence. LaShaun's mind turned to thoughts of her troubled mother as her hands stayed busy. Francine had the wild side of Monmon Odette with none of the self-control. She'd died too young as a result. Drinking, drugs and the wrong men. Monmon Odette had stepped in to raise her favorite granddaughter. Yet Monmon Odette had let bitterness about Francine's misspent life sour her outlook. Though LaShaun had some happy memories, it appeared the Rousselle and

❖

LeGrange family legacy of tragedy hung over them all. People around Beau Chene whispered history would continue to repeat itself. LaShaun would not let those whispers become Ellie's fate.

Shelia placed the last large wreath on LaShaun's front door. She slapped dust from the legs of her denim overalls, then stood back to admire her technique. "Perfect. Anyone passing will think you have the most Christmas spirit for ten square miles."

"The house looks beautiful."

LaShaun had to admit, the greenery fit right in with the season. They walked back around the house and entered the kitchen. A small Christmas tree sat in one corner. Ellie clutched her favorite doll as she stared at the blinking lights. A larger one was in their living room. The young man stood from his kneeling position.

"Don't tell me you've finished planting outside already," LaShaun said to him.

"Yes, ma'am. I'll leave the big tree for the family to have fun dressing up." He winked at Ellie, gave Beau a pat and headed for the back door.

"I'm about done, so I'll be out in a minute," Shelia called after him. "Ah, the advantages of youth. I remember having that much energy twenty years ago."

"As if you're old," LaShaun quipped. Then she gazed at Ellie and Beau. The two of them behaved as if nothing out of the ordinary had

❖

happened only a day ago. If only that were true.

"Only God knows the outcome, LaShaun. History is not destiny," Shelia said firmly.

LaShaun turned to her. "I hope you've developed the ability to tell the future along with that skill of sensing spirits."

Shelia smiled. "Nah, but I have a few years on you. Your past isn't your destiny. Listen to me. I'm sounding like my grandmother more and more."

"Yes, I hear Monmon Odette coming out of my mouth these days when I'm talking to Ellie. I could sure use her wisdom now." LaShaun felt the familiar nostalgia when she thought of or spoke about her grandmother.

"They live in us and even through us, LaShaun. I only met her once or twice. She was a force. I'm sure she left you a nice arsenal to deal with the world." Shelia made the sign of the cross. "And most important of all, don't forget le bon Dieu."

"Oui." LaShaun smiled at her.

"I know Juridicus is out there putting something nasty in motion, but I have faith that we'll beat them back like always. Now I better get going. My bosses are understanding, but I have to show up now and then."

"Thanks for everything. One of these days, I'll return the favor." LaShaun hugged Shelia.

"Oh don't doubt I'll holler for help when my time comes."

❧

LaShaun followed her outside. After exchanging goodbyes with Shelia and her helper, LaShaun stood watching them drive away. When she turned, Mrs. Marchand stood at the edge of the field that separated their land. The woman craned her neck as she examined LaShaun's house.

"Hi neighbor. Finally got your Christmas finery up I see. Even with professionals to help."

"Morning. We've been so busy that we just got around to it. Thankfully Ellie is still too young to notice mama and daddy are way behind everyone else." LaShaun made to go inside, but Mrs. Marchand took the opening to keep talking.

"Oh my Lord, yes. With all the commotion of somebody breaking in... Beau Chene used to be a peaceful little town. Now every time I turn around they're fishing dead bodies out the bayou or reporting some crime." Mrs. Marchand closed the distance between them as she talked. Dressed in jeans and high top rubber boots, she looked like the typical modern farm woman.

"Yes, times have changed." LaShaun gave her a noncommittal smile.

"Makes me check twice before I walk outside to feed the animals or go to the horse barn. Like that woman they found in your house. Thank the good Lord y'all caught her. Have they figured out who she is?" Mrs. Marchand's dark eyes sparkled with anticipation of getting firsthand inside news.

"Chase doesn't tell me anymore than they release to the public. He and the sheriff are very cautious when it comes to on-going investigations," LaShaun said.

"Breaking into *your* house of all places. Why everyone knows..." Mrs. Marchand blinked rapidly. "What I mean to say is, folks got enough sense not to mess with the Rousselles. Er, I mean—"

"Thanks for stopping by, Mrs. Marchand. Bye, bye." LaShaun waved farewell. She then cocked an eyebrow at the woman and waited.

"Um, sure. I was on my way to the barn to..." Mrs. Marchand stammered on a few more minutes as LaShaun turned away, then yelled, "Nice talking to you."

LaShaun went back inside and let out the giggles she'd held in. "Ellie, our neighbor is worth a good laugh every now and then. What would Mrs. Marchand think if she knew Beau can smell ghosts and goblins?"

"Beau," Ellie blurted out with gusto. Then she shook her chubby fist at her mother.

"I swear you're fussing at me not to say that too loud." LaShaun studied her daughter with her head to one side. "Honestly, that's a stretch even in this family."

The phone rang just as Ellie seemed to answer her, though the baby babble was indecipherable. Beau let out two short barks as if backing up his little person. Still shaking her head and laughing, LaShaun went to the phone. Her good humor had evaporated by the time she hung up.

****

LaShaun arrived at the main Sheriff's Department Headquarters two hours later. The shiny new building sat a mile from downtown Abbeville, the parish seat. Located inside the Vermilion Parish Courthouse Annex, the newer building had been built to match the paint and style of the older historic structure across the street. Once again she'd had to find a babysitter fast. One of Savannah's twin girls, Daija, had decided to help out with filing at her mother's law office in town. LaShaun had dropped off a delighted Ellie after profuse apologies. They'd waved her away and set about making the toddler the center of attention, the main reason Ellie adored her Auntie Savannah and the twins.

LaShaun went from the light-hearted encounter with her friend who'd become like family, to the murky atmosphere of crime. For once, the bustle at the Sheriff's headquarters seemed subdued. There wasn't the usual banter between the officers as they carried out serious duties. Even the civilian employees went about their work with sober expressions. LaShaun didn't have to ask why.

"Good morning," LaShaun said as Chase approached. "Nice to see you, Deputy Broussard."

Chase pecked her on the cheek and led her down a hall to Chief Godchaux's office. "Sorry about the long hours, babe. But you know…"

"Every day that goes by means Dina might not survive." LaShaun shivered at the thought. Still the familiar tingle didn't spread up her arms.

"She could already be dead. Or almost as bad, alive and being sold for sex. Sometimes I hate humanity." Chase opened the door for her.

Sheriff Godchaux, MJ and Det. Anderson looked at them when they walked in. Det. Anderson had an angry set to his square jaw. MJ glared at him before looking at LaShaun again. Sheriff Godchaux marched to his desk and sat down heavily.

"Okay, I'm the subject of an argument." LaShaun sat down and crossed her legs. "I could use a cup of coffee if I'm going to be in trouble again."

The sheriff reached over to pour coffee from a carafe on the table near his desk. He handed LaShaun a foam cup. "You're not in trouble."

"You know more about the woman who broke into my house." LaShaun took a sip of coffee and waited. Anderson stared at a point on the wall. MJ looked at them all in turn.

"Look, I told Savannah this wouldn't take long. So somebody start explaining, or I'm out of here."

⚜

"Kris Evans moved in with Tommy about eight months ago. She has two kids. From what we can find out, she moved here from somewhere in California." Chase paced as he talked.

"She also has a record of drug arrests, disorderly conduct... no felonies. But she's a bit of a mystery before she showed up in San Jose," MJ said.

"I don't understand. You said somewhere in California, but you know she was in San Jose." LaShaun gazed at MJ. The tingle in her body started small, a signal that the story was about to get interesting.

"Her last arrest was in San Jose, but that was in 2011. We're not sure where she's been since then. She did have two arrests in New Orleans in 2004. Then she vanished, resurfaced in California." Det. Anderson looked around. "Look, let's get to the point."

"Stand down detective," Sheriff Godchaux snapped. "I'm still in charge around here."

"Sir." Det. Anderson went back to silent dissatisfaction. He crossed his arms and glared at the wall again.

"Actually, I agree with Det. Anderson. Why am I here?" LaShaun looked from MJ to the sheriff for answers.

Sheriff Godchaux heaved out a long breath. "The Evans woman's cell phone had pictures of items in your home she was going to take, and—"

"Thank God, a typical burglary. She wasn't after my child." LaShaun started to smile, but stopped at the frowns on the other four faces. "There's more."

"To hell with it, reprimand me. A kid's life is on the line. The pictures are of a bunch of voodoo spooky stuff you own. So what are you involved with that led nut job devil worshippers to show up?" Det. Anderson said.

"Careful Mark." Chase faced him with a scowl.

"Enough." Sheriff Godchaux stood to make his point. Anderson gave a grunt, but went silent again. "LaShaun, she also had a photo of you and Ellie. Looks like it was taken on the street in Beau Chene. It's dated August 2016."

"So they've been tracking you," MJ said.

LaShaun uncrossed her legs and put the cup of coffee down. "They?"

"Kris Evans still can't talk, but she's stable. We got in touch with her brother in Georgia. They say she joined a cult or Goth group about two years ago. She'd been into that kind of thing back in high school. They pretty much shunned her, didn't want her around their two kids," MJ said.

"So you think I'm involved somehow?" LaShaun said to Det. Anderson.

"That's bull. My wife—"

The sheriff raised a palm. "Calm down, Broussard."

"Calm down my ass. LaShaun has helped this department resolve at least three high profile murder cases. This is the thanks she gets?"

Chase flexed his hands, opening and closing them into fists.

"Yeah, she always seems to be at the center of something creepy that ends with a pile of dead bodies. Coincidence? Now we have a group of freaks snatching kids and prowling around your property. I don't give a damn about politics. I intend to get answers." Det. Anderson spoke in a level, cold voice.

"You're way out of line, Anderson," MJ blurted.

"I follow the evidence," Det. Anderson shot back.

"Everybody back off," Sheriff Godchaux shouted.

"You're going to stand there and let him accuse us of a cover-up?" Chase stabbed a finger at Anderson.

"Face it, Broussard. Your wife got herself involved in something shady. Now it's blown back on your family. From what I hear, you've got a serious blind spot on this stuff." Det. Anderson let both arms hang to his sides.

"So part of your investigative technique is to rely on gossip instead of facts? Oh that's just great." Chase took a step toward him, but MJ got between them.

"Take it down a few notches guys. We're drawing a crowd." MJ nodded to the glass wall that gave the sheriff a view of the report writing room. Several uniformed deputies stood frozen in place. Seconds later they got busy when they realized the group had noticed them staring.

Chase and Anderson glared at each other like wrestlers on opposite sides of the ring. Anderson blinked first. He waved a hand and turned away. Sheriff Godchaux thumped a fist on his desk as he frowned at them both. MJ hissed out the breath she'd held in.

LaShaun broke into the tense stand-off. "I'd think the same as Det. Anderson if I was in his shoes. We've lived with these cases in Vermilion Parish, so we know them from the inside. All three of you had suspicions about me at one time or another."

"She's got a point." Sheriff Godchaux rubbed his chin.

"Yeah." MJ looked at Chase. He didn't say anything. "Let's take a step back and talk this through."

"Okay, so what do you know?" LaShaun reached up and patted Chase's arm. He relaxed visibly, but wouldn't look at Anderson.

"Things are getting more strange, if that's possible," MJ retorted. "Evans has a boy age ten and a girl age twelve. Her brother and sister-in-law were stunned. They didn't know she had kids. They haven't seen her in at least twelve years."

"Then it makes sense. They didn't keep in touch, she got on with her life." LaShaun shrugged.

"Except we can't find a record she gave birth. We do know that she worked at a day-

❖

care at one point in San Jose, and she did volunteer work with foster children. But no kids have been reported missing," Anderson said.

"So she's been hiding them and home schooling them?" LaShaun's tingle came back.

"No, they're in school here. Well, we think they were." MJ looked at the sheriff.

"We can't find 'em. May be with some of her friends. We're waiting on a court order to get their school files. Birth and immunization records should give us some clues even before she wakes up," Sheriff Godchaux said.

"If she wakes up. Your dog really did a number on her. Takes protecting your kid seriously. I should get one for my family," Det. Anderson said with a grunt.

"Hold on. So you don't know where this woman has been, how she ended up with kids, and where the kids are now. Are you even sure they exist?" LaShaun looked around at the group of law officers.

MJ sat on the edge of the sheriff's desk. "Oh yeah, they're definitely not phantom kids. Maybe they were kidnapped."

"Could explain all the missing pieces. A lot of this mumbo jumbo stuff might be just window dressing," Det. Anderson said.

"To throw us off the trail of the real crime? Seems like a lot of trouble to go through. Most criminals aren't that creative, or smart." Chase frowned in concentration.

⚜

"Did you figure out that weird message somebody left at two crime scenes?" MJ looked at LaShaun.

"A linguistics expert is working on it. She thinks it's a hybrid ancient language. She's working on finding the key to translate both." LaShaun shrugged at the set of frowns facing her. "Translating an unknown language takes time."

Sheriff Godchaux raised a thick eyebrow at LaShaun. "I don't like civilians having inside knowledge about an open case."

"She only know what's been reported in the news," LaShaun countered.

"This is bayou country. Talk of voodoo and devil spirits was bound to get out," MJ said with a grimace.

"Oh, just great." Det. Anderson gave a snort of disgust. "So you've got a group of crystal ball gazers working on a major case? Sure, makes sense way out here in superstition land."

"No crystal balls, Det. Anderson. Professor Portier has access to the best research re-sources around. We're using databases, apps, and our years of experience. You know, sort of like the police?" LaShaun smiled when his face flushed pink.

"Yeah, Anderson. Even way out here in no-where-ville we use computers and our brains." Sheriff Godchaux glared at Det. Anderson until the big man cleared his throat and looked away. The sheriff was about to go on when his phone rang. He barked into the phone, "Now what?"

The sheriff grabbed a yellow legal pad and made notes. Det. Anderson stared at the door as if debating whether or not to leave. MJ watched their boss with a worried expression. Chase clutched LaShaun's arm and pulled her aside.

"No telling how long I'll end up working. Just a warning." Chase pressed his lips together before he spoke. "I want you both safe, so no investigating strange noises. The deputy assigned to that part of the parish will be making frequent checks."

"Thanks. Chase we..." LaShaun glanced at his colleagues.

"I'll always pick your side, no matter what my mother or anyone else thinks," Chase said softly. "I shouldn't have let what she said get to me."

LaShaun moved closer to him until their bodies touched. Chase looped an arm around her waist. "I'll be careful. Between me, Beau, and Mr. Marchand's shotgun, I think we'll be okay."

"Don't forget all the supernatural defenses your pals installed. Yeah, I noticed." Chase's dark eyes twinkled.

"You've been hanging with psychics too long, Deputy Broussard." LaShaun grinned up at him. She tamed the urge to kiss him hard right there in front of his hardened co-workers.

⚜

"I'll get out of the way so y'all can figure this thing out."

"Kiss Ellie for me. Show her my picture so she won't forget what daddy looks like." Chase walked LaShaun to the door and opened it.

Sheriff Godchaux dropped his phone handset into the cradle. "Where do you two think you're going? We're not done by a long shot."

LaShaun turned around. "Sheriff, I don't know anything about Kris Evans, her kids, or why she was in our home. I'll trust the professionals to solve those puzzles."

"You may not know Kris Evans, but she knows *you*. She's awake, weak, but definitely conscious. Not only is she talking in a kind of code nobody understands, but she's saying your name." Sheriff Godchaux stood. "I want you over at that hospital. We need answers. If your friend can't keep Ellie, I'll have Anderson babysit if necessary."

"Wait, what?" Det. Anderson blurted out, mouth hanging open.

"We needs answers. The woman might die any minute," Sheriff Godchaux barked.

"Relax detective. I'm sure Savannah can hang on another couple of hours." LaShaun suppressed a laugh at the look of shock the burly man wore.

"I don't like any of this," Chase muttered.

"Let's go." Sheriff Godchaux marched past them all, a clear signal debate was not an option.

⚜

Twenty minutes later Chase, LaShaun and the sheriff arrived at Vermilion Parish General Hospital. MJ stayed behind at the station. Since Savannah agreed to keep Ellie longer, a relieved Det. Anderson went off to follow more leads. The doctor had insisted on meeting with them before they were allowed to question his patient. They sat in a small conference room on the first floor. Dr. Wilkinson's name was em‑broidered in blue on his white coat. His short cut red hair contrasted with his pale white skin. LaShaun mused he must not be out in the sun much playing golf with the other doctors.

"Doctor, we realize you're concerned about Miss Evans, but we've got a missing six‑year‑old and a murder on our hands. This woman is connected to both." Sheriff Godchaux gazed at the doctor steadily.

"Of course I'm willing to cooperate, but not at the risk of this woman's life. Her well‑being has to be my first priority." The doctor wore a taut frown. "That said, it appears a brief visit is necessary."

"And we appreciate your understanding how urgent it is that we talk to Ms. Evans," Chase put in.

"You have ten minutes only. She's stable, but still extremely fragile. Her wounds are sig‑nificant." Dr. Wilkinson looked at LaShaun.

Chase stood. "Thanks, doc. Take us to her now."

"Fine." Dr. Wilkinson stood and led them to the elevator.

⚜

Curious glances followed them as they made their way to the wing where Kris Evans was being treated. The critical care section had semi-private rooms. To accommodate the sheriff's department, she was the only occupant in Room 333. Conversation died away as they passed the busy clinical station.

"Remember, she's still a very sick person. No matter what she allegedly did—"

"We get it, doc. Trust me," Sheriff Godchaux interrupted. "Stand by in case we need you."

Dr. Wilkinson grimaced at him. "But you said you'd be careful."

"And we will. Ten minutes, like we agreed."

Sheriff Godchaux pushed past him and opened the door wide. Chase also nodded at Dr. Wilkinson as he walked by. LaShaun lingered behind the two men. Anger radiated from the doctor like heat waves from sizzling pavement in the summer.

"We'll do our best not get her upset, Dr. Wilkinson," LaShaun said, then ducked in and let the door whisk close behind her.

"He's pissed," Chase said quietly.

"No matter what she's done, I don't want to harm her," LaShaun said. She faced the sheriff.

"Calm down. The doctor might not be happy I pulled strings, but the clinical team met and agreed a short Q&A wouldn't hurt. Seeing you might calm her down. I mean she's saying your name. The woman's been really agitated from what I hear."

⚜

"Really?" LaShaun turned back to study her.

Kris Evans lay beneath crisp white sheets. A blanket lay folded halfway down to give extra warmth to her legs. A gauze bandage wrapped around her neck. Sutures had been used to close a gash on her left check. Straps tied to the railing on either side of the bed kept her wrists restrained. She stirred as if she sensed a change in the room's atmosphere when they came in. Her eyes fluttered open, and her gaze wandered around the room. Then she focused on LaShaun.

LaShaun stepped forward. "You asked for me, but we've never met before you broke into my house."

"Hmmm."

Kris Evans seemed to strain against the bandages around her throat to speak. Then a flood of raspy phrases came out. Her head moved from side to side.

"What the hell?" Sheriff Godchaux pulled back and stared at the woman.

"She's speaking gibberish." LaShaun moved close to the bed. She leaned over until her ear was only inches from Kris Evans's mouth.

"Gibberish is right. We won't get anything out of her, damn it," Sheriff Godchaux huffed.

Dr. Wilkinson had come in while they were distracted. "Excuse me, but my patient is a human being, not just your suspect."

"Your patient was injured while committing a felony, Dr. Wilkinson. Like it or not she's a

❖

suspect," Sheriff Godchaux snapped. "We definitely want her to recover, doctor. So we can get some answers."

"We're almost done, Dr. Wilkinson." Chase stepped between the two men, his voice conciliatory.

LaShaun had her cell phone out recording the stream of sounds coming from Kris Evans. "Our expert might get some sense out of what she's saying."

"What's she doing?" Dr. Wilkinson moved around Chase to stand on the opposite side of the hospital bed. "Maybe Ms. Evans needs an attorney present."

"You're her doctor, not her lawyer." Sheriff Godchaux raised a forefinger and started to say more, but Chase interrupted.

"We didn't ask her questions. Ms. Evans started talking on her own," Chase put in.

"She's in critical condition and heavily sedated, so Ms. Evans can't give informed consent." Dr. Wilkinson raised his arm, pulled back his sleeve and looked at his expensive wristwatch. "Your ten minutes just expired."

Sheriff Godchaux glared at the doctor. "I don't think you fully appreciate the seriousness of—"

"He's right, sheriff. Ms. Evans is out of it, and we can't even understand what she's saying. We should let the doctor and his staff continue their treatment. The faster she recovers, the better it will be for our investigation." Chase raised an eyebrow at his irate boss.

❖

"Fine. But my office must be notified of any change in her medical status. Is that understood?" Sheriff Godchaux continued to stare down the doctor.

"Yes." Dr. Wilkinson crossed his arms.

"I have what I need," LaShaun said low to Chase. "Thank you, Dr. Wilkinson."

"Yes, thanks," Chase held out a hand. The doctor hesitated a few seconds before shaking it. "We apologize for any disruption in your routine."

LaShaun left the room first. She slipped her phone into the pocket of her jacket as she left. She waited in the hallway while Chase had a whispered exchange with Sheriff Godchaux. Fuming, he strode out with Chase right behind him. Once they were in the parking lot, Sheriff Godchaux let loose.

"I'm going to talk to the hospital CEO about Dr. Wilkinson. He's a sanctimonious..." Sheriff Godchaux huffed in anger.

"The man is doing his job, boss. Besides, he's right. Any decent lawyer could argue Kris Evans has diminished capacity. No way could she consent to giving a statement," Chase replied.

"That gobbledygook isn't a statement," Sheriff Godchaux muttered.

"Yes, it is. She was speaking a coded language." LaShaun held up her cell phone. "And I intend to figure out what she was saying."

⚜

Chapter 8

Chase stood holding Ellie in the crook of one arm in Savannah's law office. The sheriff had merely waved when Chase told him he was talking a break after hours of work. He would go right back but wanted to see Ellie. Dealing with the gritty side of life wore down cops of all kinds. His family was a touchstone to the good things in life.

"A language. You sure? Gobbledygook sounds pretty accurate to me." Chase bounced Ellie while she grinned at him in adoration.

Savannah tilted her head to one side as they all listened to the recording a second time. "I agree. Don't know what the heck she's saying."

"Any language sounds like gibberish if you don't speak it. People create secret written and spoken languages all the time. This sounds familiar. I already forwarded it to the TEA." LaShaun turned off the recording and dropped the phone in her pocket. She lifted the tote bag to her shoulder. "Now come to mama. Back to our regularly scheduled programing. It's almost lunch and nap time for you."

"I'm hungry. What about you baby girl?" Chase grinned at Ellie.

"Dada." Ellie patted his right cheek with a small hand.

"Yeah, she'll agree with anything her daddy says." LaShaun gave an exaggerated sigh.

"We'll have a nice family lunch at the diner. No talk of secret languages, cults, or crime. I'm buying." Chase winked at LaShaun.

"Goes without saying," LaShaun wise-cracked.

They exchanged goodbyes with Savannah, her daughter, and Savannah's legal secretary and made their way to Anna's Kitchen. The café was busy even though it was only eleven thirty in the morning. True to his word, Chase talked about anything but work. LaShaun felt a weight lift as they behaved like a normal young family. Ellie of course made a small mess of her kid's meal. Both parents took turns cleaning her up and tucking napkins around her neck to keep her outfit clean. By the time they parted, tension from their earlier arguments seemed forgotten. Chase gave them both hugs and kisses before he drove off in his department issued SUV.

⚜

"Look." Ellie pointed to a large green wreath hung from a lamppost on Main Street.

"Yes. We're going to have a great Christmas honey bun." LaShaun smiled at the picturesque downtown decked out in holiday finery.

****

For the new days, the festive mood held. Mostly. Christmas with Chase's family came off without a hitch. LaShaun wondered how many warning lectures her mother-in-law had gotten. Mr. Broussard and Chase's four siblings kept shooting significant looks at the elder Mrs. Broussard. When Queen Elizabeth came close to making loaded comments, Mr. Broussard cut her off with skill. One of Chase's sisters would deftly re-direct the conversation flow. Laughing children and presents helped them all have a merry Christmas. A week later, LaShaun and Chase opted to have a quiet New Year's celebration away from the extended Broussard family. Instead, they danced to eighties tunes and sipped champagne to candlelight at home.

The first week of the new year roared in with cold, windy weather. They even got a few flakes of sleet. Gray clouds hung heavy for several days, mirroring the return of gloomy thoughts about missing Dina Menard. Though he hadn't mentioned the case, Chase had worked during the holidays. LaShaun knew his thoughts never went far from the grim reality of what might have happened to her.

Ten days into the new year, LaShaun had a video conference with her friends from the TEA. Dr. Portier displayed a slideshow with her findings. LaShaun sat at her breakfast table staring at the screen of her laptop. Miss Rose and the others were presumably doing the same in their homes. LaShaun took distracted sips from the mug of hot cocoa as she studied the scribbles.

Dr. Portier's voice came through the speakers suddenly. "Sorry for the interruptions before we could even get started. My dean is a workaholic. Happy New Year everyone." Voices from the others returned the greeting.

"It would be even happier if that child had been found," Miss Rose said.

"Amen," Justine and Pauline said together.

"To that end, let's get right to it. What have you learned, Sandy?" Shelia appeared in a small window in the corner of the video conference display. The others stayed invisible, giving most of the screen to the slides.

"Well, none of this tells us where the poor little girl is. Sorry for that. But these messages lead us down an extremely intriguing path." Dr. Portier paused. The silence dragged on as suspense built.

"Spill it, Sandy. Geez!" Justine finally blurted out.

"Sorry, guys. I wasn't being dramatic, just organizing the notes on my computer. Ah, here we go. Dr. Bakir and two other members of the TEA identified the writing. This is the infamous Jairo language. My best guess? Kris Evans used the spoken version." Dr. Portier's image popped onto the screen.

"Oh my," Daniel Rayford breathed. "That's not good."

"One of you clue the rest of us in. Start with who the hell Jairo is. Please and thank you," Justine blurted out.

"And why is he and his language bad news?" Pauline added.

"Not a who, a what," Daniel replied. "An eleventh century Saxon monk named Randolphus Gywnek claimed to have received divine visions from an angel. This angel dictated a true accounting of the slaying of Abel and other events in the Bible. When Randolphus woke up, he wrote down these so-called accurate tales in a language he created. Well, he said this is a language from a warrior group of angels."

"Which he called the Jairo Sacred Script. After the angel. The name Jairo translates as one who enlightens," Dr. Portier broke in to explain.

"According to Randolphus, Cain was justified in killing his brother. Even more, the angel Jairo claimed that Satan was trying to impose divine order and was the good guy. God set loose destruction in the world. He was expelled from the church, and then formed his own philosophy," Daniel said.

"Pooh, never heard of him or an angel called Jairo." Justine scowled into the web camera.

"Well as you can imagine, he and his followers caused quite a stir. They were considered heretics, blasphemers. Some accounts allege that the Templar Knights assassinated many of the followers of this Jairo Sacred Script movement. Rumors persisted right into the sixteenth century that they weren't destroyed, just went deep underground," Dr. Portier said.

Pauline's image popped onto the screen in a tiny window in one corner of the display. "Great. Now what does this message say, and how did a single mother on the bayou end up with it on her wall?"

"I can partially answer your question." Dr. Portier controlled a pointer to follow the symbols on her slide. "This first line says, 'We are the sacred ones who will restore the right order. Defy us and perish. Your children will lead the way.' I don't like the sound of that last bit."

"Okay, a member of this movement, started in eleventh century England, is in south Louisiana and kidnapped a six-year-old? Okay, I'm not going to be the one to present such a theory to the police. Count me out." Justine gave a gruff laugh.

"Me either," LaShaun said quietly. "Here is what I propose. A cult has some crazy idea that taking kids will somehow restore the true divine order of the world. There's good news in this though."

"Which is?" Shelia frowned at them all.

⚜

"They need Dina, so she's still alive." LaShaun let out a slow breath.

"You hope. But why take her in the first place?" Daniel stroked his chin as if that would help him think.

Miss Rose spoke up. "Most of the time, those who are chosen or even sacrificed supposedly have some unique quality. Children are pure, innocent."

"So find out if there is anything unusual about Dina. Focus on the victim, and figure out what makes her valuable. Her mother seems to trust me. I will talk to family members, neighbors, and Dina's teachers." LaShaun said.

"Good. But don't sign off just yet. I have the bad news. Our contacts ran the facts I sent them in the app. We've found three other cases with strange writing left behind after a disappearance. That's in the US alone. Six worldwide so far. We're trying to get copies of those messages to see if they fit. As you can imagine, that will take some doing," Miss Rose said.

"Exactly. TEA is good, but we don't have members in every police force worldwide. Now *that* would be a real accomplishment," Pauline put in. "Rose and I will keep working on gathering more details on the other missing child cases."

"See if the children have any characteristics in common. I'll call Sherry and her mother today." LaShaun got up and grabbed her cell phone from the kitchen counter.

⚜

"How does Juridicus fit into all this? That's what I'd like to know." Shelia's question caused them all to pause.

"An offshoot of the Jairo movement maybe?" Justine looked at her sister.

"The word Juridicus is related to the administration of justice. They're trying to restore true order to the universe. Makes sense." LaShaun sat back down to face the laptop again so they could see her.

Justine hissed and rolled her eyes. "Yeah, if you're crazy as a wild pig on crystal meth."

"Lord be with us in the fight." Miss Rose made the sign of the cross, followed by the twins.

"Ensi-swat-il," LaShaun murmured. (Amen)

****

That afternoon, LaShaun spent a frustrating two hours talking to Sherry, her mother and several other relatives. Before, they'd been more cooperative with her than with Chase and Det. Anderson. That was not unexpected given their history with law enforcement. Not anymore. The Bradford clan were guarded, closing ranks to protect their secrets. By the time Chase came home from work, LaShaun could not hide her bad mood. Still she tried not to let her irritation spill over onto him. They sat at dinner: bowls of steaming shrimp and corn soup, salad, and French bread warm from the oven. Ellie slurped up her dessert having finished her own meal earlier. She greedily licked banana pudding from her fingers.

"You might as well tell me what's wrong. Did my mother call?" Chase dipped a piece of bread into his bowl and chewed on it.

"Hmm? Oh no, I haven't heard from her since Christmas." LaShaun waved a hand.

"And a few months could go by until you do," Chase joked.

"Uh-uh, I'm not going there." LaShaun squinted at him when he gave her an impish grin. Then she went back to stirring her soup.

Chase finished off his bowl, patted his stomach and sat back. "Babe, the soup is double delicious. Now what's up?"

"You're finally away from the grind of dealing with bad people and things." LaShaun started to pick up their bowls and leave the table. His large hand on her forearm stopped her.

Chase pushed her back into her chair. He got up and loaded the dishwasher and put away the leftover soup in a container. Ellie grinned in approval as he used a warm, wet cloth to wipe her face clean. LaShaun tried protesting he'd had a hard day on the job, but Chase ignored her. In minutes the kitchen had been cleared of dinner and Ellie placed in her play pen. Beau dosed near her on his dog bed. Chase took LaShaun by the hand and led her to the family room. They sat on the sofa.

⚜

"You should have some hours of peace. A warm shower and snoozing in front of the television are what you need," LaShaun said.

"No. I need to know what's bothering my wife." Chase cocked his head to one side and waited.

With a long sigh as an introduction, LaShaun told him about the Jairo Sacred Text and the rest of her day. Chase's frown deepened the longer she talked. LaShaun couldn't tell if he was annoyed, suspicious or puzzled. More than likely all three at various points of her narrative.

"I thought Sherry was frantic for us to find Dina. Now it seems like she's..." LaShaun threw up both hands.

"Hiding something? Yeah, the minute we started asking about her brother. I tell you something else, a few cousins and neighbors claim Sherry let Dina stay with Tommy and his new girlfriend. I'm surprised DCFS didn't step in. Tommy wasn't supposed to have kids living in his home. Violation of his parole." Chase grunted. "I don't get these folks."

"Because they didn't know. Sherry could lose all of her kids, and Tommy would go to prison again," LaShaun said. "No wonder they're not talking so much now."

"State police picked up a couple of cousins on drug charges. The family business is about to be shut down. But none of that should trump a missing kid." Chase sat forward, elbows on

❧

both knees. "If Ellie was missing, I'd turn the world upside down until I got her back safe."

"I need to talk to Sherry face to face. Do you mind if I go alone? Bad enough she doesn't trust me now. If you, Det. Anderson, or MJ come, I might not have any chance with her." LaShaun massaged his shoulders to ease the tension from them.

"One concerned mother reaching out to another. That's how I'll spin it if Anderson finds out." Chase flexed under her attention. "That feels good. You know how to bend me to your will, woman."

LaShaun laughed. "Hey, tell them I went even after you told me not to, if it helps. Besides, I have no other motive than to get my hands on one fine Cajun."

"Oh yeah? Let's put baby girl to sleep, and you can get more than your hands on me." Chase pulled a giggling LaShaun into his lap.

They made out on the sofa like teenagers. Chase nibbled on her neck as he put his large hands under her sweater to rub both breasts. LaShaun straddled him. Both moaned as they kissed and caressed themselves into a heat. Beau gave a low bark.

"I think he's reminding us we have responsibilities before we get too far," LaShaun murmured close to Chase's ear. She pulled the lobe gently between her teeth.

Chase groaned deep in his throat. "Lord, please let Ellie fall asleep fast."

⚜

LaShaun slapped his chest lightly. Both struggled to tamp down their lust as they got up from the sofa. Ellie sat hugging her doll, eyelids fluttering as she fought against them closing. Chase let out a soft, "Yes!" LaShaun laughed as she lifted Ellie into her arms. Moments later, after a warm bath and few minutes of rocking, Ellie gave in to slumber. Beau curled up on the soft rug in front of her bed. He seemed to give LaShaun approval to leave. LaShaun went to the master bedroom where she rocked her husband to sleep in a very different way.

****

The next afternoon, Chase came home on time at the Sheriff's insistence. He'd convinced Chase that burning himself out wouldn't do the victims or his family any good. So he stayed home with Ellie while LaShaun followed her own leads, but not without a safety lecture and reminders not to let her guard down with the Bradfords. Progress, since Chase conceded that LaShaun could handle herself with the two women.

LaShaun arrived at Arliss Bradford's house where Sherry was staying. They'd finally agreed to meet with LaShaun. After a brief exchange of terse greetings, LaShaun sat at a cheap dinette table across from Sherry and her mother. She swallowed the hard words that threatened to spill from her brain and past her lips. Arliss Bradford's kitchen had dirty dishes piled up. Two overflowing ashtrays leaked old cigarette butts onto the cluttered counter surrounding the full sink.

"Look, you can tell me what's going on, or you can talk to Det. Anderson." LaShaun leaned back in the rickety chair. "It's your choice. The department is only willing to keep me involved because you asked for me, Sherry. But I gotta tell ya, Anderson's patience is getting short."

"You're working for the sheriff now. Figures," Arliss hissed. She lit a cigarette.

"No, I don't work for the sheriff. Okay, fine. You don't want me involved. I'll leave." LaShaun stood.

"Your husband and his cop buddies want to put me in jail." Sherry gave LaShaun a head to toe glance. "Think y'all better than me."

"If Deputy Broussard wanted you in jail, you would be," LaShaun replied mildly.

"Sherry's at home because they got no evidence, girlie. Otherwise she'd be sittin' in the parish jail. We ain't stupid," Arliss countered. She grimaced at LaShaun through a cloud of smoke.

"True, but acting like you don't know anything isn't helping. Det. Anderson found out you let Dina stay with Tommy and his girlfriend, Sherry. You knew he wasn't supposed to be around kids for at least the year left on his probation."

⚜

"Tommy wasn't no sicko like they made him out to be. That girl led him on. My son was a good boy." Arliss swiped tears from her face. "Y'all the reason he's dead, spreadin' lies about him."

"Yeah, somebody believes he done something to Dina and..." Sherry's voice trailed off as she patted her mother on the back.

"Like maybe Dina's father figured out Tommy and Kris were involved in her disappearance?" LaShaun raised an eyebrow at them both.

"I never said no such thing. For somebody that ain't a cop, you sure act like one." Sherry gave LaShaun a sour look. "I thought you would understand. Folks always sayin' and thinkin' the worst about us."

"I told you better. We could have called Sister Mary to read those signs. Everybody knows she can tell fortunes." Arliss blew her nose into a dingy dishtowel.

"Sister Mary has been arrested five times for conning people out of money." LaShaun pulled out her keyring. "But hey, go right ahead. Let her take a shot at figuring out where Dina is. Goodbye and good luck." LaShaun walked to the back door leading to the small carport. She opened it.

"Wait," Sherry blurted.

"Let her go. We don't need her kind messin' in our business anyways." Arliss squinted at LaShaun.

⚜

"She's the only one that's got the sight, mama. What if Kris knows something?" Sherry muttered.

Arliss slapped Sherry's arm away. "You better not be saying your brother hurt Dina. My Tommy—"

"Hell, Tommy had his ways, mama. We all know what he done," a male voice broke in.

A tall man with deep brown hair stood in the opening that led to the living room.

LaShaun studied him up close and finally saw the resemblance. The man looked like an older version of Tommy Bradford. Yet from his pressed work clothes and bearing, he'd done better in life. She nodded to him.

"My brother George," Sherry said.

"Hello, I'm—"

"A Rousselle. I can't believe y'all call in some so-called voodoo woman. Downright ridiculous." George Bradford ignored LaShaun and focused on his mother instead.

"You didn't see the writing on my wall. Dina just gone like she never even existed. Now you tell me that's not strange," Sherry replied.

"Strange is knowing Tommy had a problem and letting him around your kids. The boy always been off, getting into one scrap after another. When y'all gonna clean up and change the way you live?" George stared at his mother.

"He was your brother, George. You got no family loyalty. Just because you went to that school and got a big job at the plant, married one of them uppity Tullier sisters," Arliss spat.

❖

"Yeah, but who came through to pay for most of his funeral? You didn't mind calling me for money," George replied mildly. He entered the kitchen but didn't sit. "I hope Tommy didn't have anything to do with Dina going missing, but face facts. He might have."

"You just mad because I wouldn't let you take my kids," Sherry shouted.

"And maybe if Heather and me had taken 'em, Dina would be safe living a decent life," George said. He waved a hand.

"She's so perfect, but she can't have her own baby. Well you can't have mine." Sherry stood and advanced on him. "Maybe your precious wife snatched my Dina."

George jabbed a forefinger a few inches from her nose. "Don't be a bigger fool than you already are, Sherry. Want something better than what we had growing up."

His sister spun to face LaShaun. "Investigate them! Him and his wife done called the child welfare people on me twice. I should have thought of this before. They're hidin' my little girl." Sherry hiccupped between angry sobs.

George sidestepped Sherry's attempts to shove him. "See? This is why I don't come around y'all anymore. Living and acting like trailer park trash."

"Stop it or I'll call the sheriff's station, which won't look good for any of you," LaShaun said loudly over their shouts. Her threat brought them up short.

⚜

Arliss pulled Sherry back from George. "Sit down. He ain't worth the trouble."

"I'm leaving. Nothing has changed around here." George stomped off.

"Yeah, go back to that your fancy subdivision and that empty house with no kids in it," Sherry shouted after him.

George stopped and faced them again. He looked at his mother. "This is the thanks I get for bailing you people out time and time again.

"And don't you love lording it over us, throwing it in our faces every damn chance you get," Arliss replied.

"Excuse me for wanting more than jail, beer and bingo night, mama." George looked at LaShaun. "You can tell Sheriff Godchaux to come visit my house anytime. We got nothing to hide. And by the way, mama. We're gonna pick up our baby next week. That's right. The adoption of our little boy came through. Me and Heather don't have to steal a kid." He left without looking back.

"I still say you need to go search his place. I don't trust his snooty wife," Sherry said.

"The detective checked out all family members and other leads, which is how they knew about Tommy. If they had reason to think George was involved, you'd know it." LaShaun buttoned her jacket in anticipation of the cold January day. "Y'all need to do some serious thinking. Hiding stuff from the law isn't going to help you or Dina."

⚜

"They wasted time lookin' at Tommy. That's why Dina ain't home yet," Arliss retorted.

"The writing. What does it mean?" Sherry broke in before her mother could continue her tirade.

"Nothing about where Dina is or who took her," LaShaun replied.

"But you know what it says though. Now who's hiding something?" Arliss yanked on Sherry's shoulder. "What'd I tell ya, huh?"

"We had it translated, but it doesn't make sense. Something about the world coming to an end or changing, and the children being the cause. Was Kris and Tommy into any kind of group with strange beliefs that you know of?" LaShaun spoke to Sherry.

Sherry blinked rapidly. "What? No, nothing like that. Mama, do you know?"

"Hell no. He's not here to defend himself, so you gonna pin it on Tommy. Get outta my house and don't bother to come back." Arliss waved an arm at LaShaun as if shooing her out.

LaShaun ignored her theatrics. "Sherry, you're more intent on defending your brother than finding Dina. If it looks suspicious to me, then imagine what Sheriff Godchaux and Det. Anderson are thinking."

"I do want my baby back. All they did was babysit her a few times." Sherry twisted her hands together and looked at her mother. She shrank away at the frown that twisted Arliss's lined face.

⚜

"No, they didn't. I kept the kid. Sherry just so upset that she don't remember right. Dina would play over there. I always knew where she was," Arliss drawled, and then puffed on her cigarette.

"Y'all didn't know much about Kris, and Tommy wasn't supposed to be around minors. But you let Dina go over there. Hear how that sounds?" LaShaun stared hard at Sherry.

"I had things to do and..." Sherry stuttered and then went silent.

"Kris broke into my house. Strange behavior when her boyfriend has been murdered. We can't find her kids either. We're not even sure where she's been for the past ten years or so," LaShaun pressed.

"Then she's not the girl we thought we knew," Arliss blurted out before Sherry could speak. She shot her daughter another sharp frown, then looked at LaShaun again. "I guess the sheriff and his men better get on their job to find my grandbaby."

LaShaun stood. "Okay. But let me assure you, Det. Anderson and Sheriff Godchaux will gladly charge you with obstruction of justice. They're really good at finding out the truth."

Arliss stood. "You ain't the police, so don't talk big."

"You called me for a reason, Sherry. Anything else happens or you need to talk, give me a call." LaShaun pulled one of Chase's business cards from the pocket of her jacket. She wrote her cell number on the back of it.

⚜

"She won't be talkin' to you no more. If she's gonna call anybody, it's gone be a lawyer," Arliss snapped.

"Sherry is a grown woman and can make her own decisions." LaShaun's gaze narrowed at the older woman until she looked away. She held out the card.

Sherry stared at the card. Then she took it without looking at her mother. "Thanks. I know you're trying to help," she said low, and flinched when her mother snorted in anger.

"I said get out." Arliss stabbed a forefinger at the backdoor.

LaShaun gave Sherry a reassuring nod. Then she faced Arliss with a stony expression. "You heard about my grandmother, Odette Rousselle? She, taught me all she knew. Don't think I won't find out what's been going on, Arliss."

Arliss backed away like a crawfish on the run until her amble butt hit the kitchen cabinet. Her mouth worked, but no sound came out. Sherry gasped and clutched her thin neck. Her gaze darted from LaShaun to her mother and back again. LaShaun didn't wait for them to speak. She strode out, slamming the cheap aluminum door behind her. A strong January wind blew hard, rattling the storm door and windows. As she walked the few yards to her SUV, LaShaun worked to control her anger. Moments later, she sat behind the wheel. She glanced up as she turned the ignition to see Sherry standing in the door. The woman wanted to talk, but fear held her back. But fear of what? Or maybe who.

LaShaun drove through the now dusky overcast countryside toward home. She thought about her own mother. Like Sherry, being a mother took a backseat to her own demons. Monmon Odette had stepped in to nurture LaShaun. In contrast, Arliss didn't appear to be supportive at all. In fact, the woman terrorized Sherry into silence.

As her Subaru Forrester rolled along Highway 82, the weather matched her gloomy mood. Tiny droplets from a thick fog dotted on her windshield. Four or five clumps of houses appeared every few miles. In between, she drove past fields and pastures. LaShaun turned on the radio. She picked up KROF, a talk station in Abbeville. Sheriff Godchaux's deep voice boomed through the speakers, causing her to jump.

"Those are just rumors, Nick. Currently, none of the family members of the little girl are active suspects," he said.

"Reports are that her uncle, Tommy Bradford, served time for sexual offenses involving underage females. He turns up dead. Y'all think he had something to do with it? I mean folks hear stories of human trafficking, and it's got to have parents around Beau Chene on edge," the radio interviewer said.

"We haven't had any arrests for human trafficking in Vermilion Parish for the past year or so. I want to assure the public that there is no evidence of such crimes involved in this case. My deputies have several promising leads that they're following up on right now." Sheriff Godchaux broke in before the interviewer could. "The Vermilion Parish Sheriff's Department has allocated heavy resources to find Dina Bradford."

"I'm sure you have, but what about talk that a voodoo cult is right here in our parish? The longer she's missing, the colder the trail gets. Isn't that right? If there's a conspiracy—"

"Nothing found indicates strangers are involved," Sheriff Godchaux interrupted again.

"So you do think the family is part of this?" a female host spoke up.

"I didn't say that. All I can speak to is what we know as of this hour of the investigation," Sheriff Godchaux said with force.

"No disrespect for our fine law enforcement professionals, Sheriff, but doesn't sound like you know a whole lot," Nick, the male talk show host, put in.

"Well that's not going so well," LaShaun murmured.

She turned down the sound as Sheriff Godchaux sought to recover. She glanced around. The weather seemed to agree with her grim assessment. Although it was only four o'clock, a cloudy sky along with the fog made it seem later. Visibility had reduced in the last few minutes. Her low beam headlights did little to illuminate the road. LaShaun reduced speed to forty miles per hour. Suddenly an object ap-

⚜

peared ahead. She jammed the brake pedal holding her breath. The SUV slowed to a stop. The object melted into the grass of a prairie to LaShaun's left. She jerked the gear shift into park, hit the emergency blinkers and got out. Every inch of LaShaun's skin lit up with the itching tingle. Flattened wet scrub grass marked a track. She followed it a few yards through heavy mist until she reached a tiny figure. LaShaun breathed hard as her heart hammered in her chest.

"Dina, don't run from me. I'm going to take you to your mama." LaShaun stood still, afraid the child would indeed run from a stranger.

The child shook her head hard until her matted blonde hair flew out. "No, no. Please don't make me go back to her, to them."

Chapter 9

"No, I don't want to come nowhere. Just give us Dina so we can leave. I told Sherry she was a fool to get that Rousselle woman mixed up in our business." Arliss Bradford shouted over MJ's attempts to calm her. "While y'all was trying to blame my son, she had Dina all the time. You tell Dave Godchaux I know a cover-up when I smell one."

Four hours later, LaShaun sat listening to her rant as she sipped coffee in Chase's office. A Department of Child and Family Services caseworker had arrived with dry, clean clothes for Dina. She'd brought a clinical social worker with her to interview the child. Arliss's voice went down to a still outraged mumble in the background. Seconds later, it faded. LaShaun took a deep breath then finished the last of the

❖

bitter brew. She stood when Chase came in, Ellie on his hip. The toddler immediately reached
for LaShaun.

"I couldn't find a sitter so I brought her
with me," Chase said as he allowed Ellie to
scramble from his arms into LaShaun's.

"Of course. Who can plan for me stumbling
on a child in the middle of nowhere?" LaShaun
kissed Ellie's cheek. The warmth from her little
body felt good. "Poor baby. Imagine her wandering out there alone, lost."

"Volunteers from three parishes searched
that area. Where's she been, and how did she
get out there?" Chase sat on the edge of his
desk.

Det. Anderson pushed through the half
open office door without knocking. His partner,
Ken Tullier, followed and shut the door hard.
"Those are some great questions we intend to
ask Mrs. Broussard."

Chase stood between him. "Just what the
hell does that mean, Mark?"

"Mighty strange she happens across a kid
half the parish been looking for and didn't even
find a trace. Now her mama is missing. You
know where she is, Mrs. Broussard?" Det. Tullier's thick Cajun accent made the accusation
sound like casual conversation. His stony expression didn't match the tone.

"Of course not," LaShaun replied.

"That's a bunch of bull..." Chase cut off his
rant after a side glance at little Ellie, who
watched wide-eyed.

⚜

"Maybe we was too close to the truth. Tracking down this voodoo-hoodoo angle. So you and your people decided snatching a little white girl was a really bad idea. Best to let her go." Anderson raised an eyebrow at Chase.

LaShaun held her breath as tense silence stretched. Chase's eyes narrowed, his chest rising and falling as he breathed hard. Detectives Anderson and Tullier seemed content to let the moment simmer. Both detectives studied LaShaun and Chase, obviously looking for reactions. LaShaun jumped when Chase started laughing. MJ pushed through the door forcing Tullier to step aside.

"Child services will keep Dina." MJ broke off from further updates when she picked up the charged vibes. "There a problem in here?"

"Go ahead guys. Tell MJ your brilliant theory. They think LaShaun kidnapped Dina Bradford for some voodoo ritual, but then she panicked and pretended to find her. Please lay out the evidence." Chase gave another harsh laugh. Then he put a protective arm around LaShaun's shoulders.

MJ faced the two detectives. "He's joking, right?"

Tullier exchanged a glance with Anderson before speaking. Then he gave a grunt. "Mrs. Broussard has been involved in, no make that a suspect in, a number of incidents. Most of them dealt with weird goings-on. Now a kid goes missing, the mother asks for her, and we only have her word for it that this Evans woman broke into her house. Maybe they were all in it together and had a falling out."

"Must have been a lucky break for you when Sherry asked for you," Anderson said to LaShaun. "You could get inside information on our investigation."

"Either you've both lost your minds, or you have a truckload of hard evidence to back up this allegation. Now which is it?"

Anderson looked at Tullier before he spoke. Then he gazed at MJ. "The Evans woman came to. She said, 'The Rousselle woman knows,' or something like that."

"Or something like that? You're not even sure what she mumbled. Stop right there." MJ held up a palm when Tullier opened his mouth. "I talked to the nurse who was in the room with you when Evans started rambling. According to him, not much of it made sense."

"We can pull together more facts," Anderson replied with heat.

"What facts other than gossip and prejudice?" MJ shot back when neither Anderson nor Tullier answered immediately. She sucked in a deep breath and let it out as the two men glared down at her. "Yeah, that's what I thought. I suggest you do some real police work instead of listening to cooked up fantasy tales about voodoo women."

"Too bad Tommy Bradford can't talk, huh?" Anderson looked at LaShaun. Then he walked out.

❧

"Real police work means following up no matter where the clues lead you, friends or not," Tullier said mildly. He strode through the open door and shut it behind him.

Chase started after him. "I'm going to—"

"No, you're not." MJ put a hand on his chest and pushed him hard. Despite the difference in their heights and size, MJ caused him to step back.

"Brawling with your fellow officers won't help, honey," LaShaun said. "Besides, I'd have questions if I were in their shoes. My past doesn't help."

"Mama." Ellie patted LaShaun's face with a grin, as if she was in on the joke about her mother's infamous backstory.

"You've done nothing but try to help. Stupid back country superstition and bigotry," Chase blurted out. He raked long fingers through his thick dark hair.

LaShaun had the sense Chase wasn't only talking about his colleagues. Her mother-in-law hadn't moved one inch toward accepting LaShaun. She moved closer to him until they stood side by side. Ellie reached out and grabbed the collar of his shirt. His frown eased a bit as he closed his large hand over her tiny one.

"We'll get at the truth and show them all." LaShaun gave him a light kiss on one cheek.

"I hate you have to put up with their kind of crap." Chase pulled LaShaun closer. "You, too, MJ."

⚜

"We never get used to it, but we do learn to keep going. Besides, being successful and happy drives the suckers crazy." MJ put on a sideways grin.

Chase grunted. "All well and good, but I'm going to pound the first chump that tries to insult my baby girl."

"Baba," Ellie blurted out. Her chubby fist seemed to make a karate chop.

LaShaun chuckled as Ellie wore a frown that matched her father's serious expression. "I have a feeling Ellie will be able to handle herself."

MJ was about to answer when a commotion outside distracted them all. Bumping and yelling came from the direction of the open duty room. Then tinkle of glass breaking came next. MJ and Chase headed out at the same time. Chase waved LaShaun back.

"Stay here with the door closed," he called over his shoulder.

"Right. Better idea," LaShaun murmured. She looked at Ellie, who appeared just as eager to find out what was going on.

"Dada?" Ellie jumped in her mother's arms.

"You heard your father. We have orders to stay put."

Still LaShaun went out into the hallway and stretched in an effort to see around the corners. The sounds of a scuffle died away about ten minutes later. At the sound of footsteps, she scuttled back into the room and closed the door fast. She stood across from it when Chase and MJ came back.

"And I thought things couldn't get any crazier." Chase muttered curse words, then stopped when LaShaun frowned at him and nodded to Ellie. "Sorry."

"Now what?" LaShaun looked to MJ for answers.

"Dina's daddy snatched up Sherry and beat her within an inch of her life. The police brought him in. He didn't come quietly." MJ's brow wrinkled at the turn of events.

"No wonder Dina doesn't want to go home," LaShaun said.

MJ looked at Chase. "That's not the worst."

"I don't see how…" LaShaun's voice trailed off as she gazed at her husband. His face twisted into a scowl like she'd never seen before.

Chase appeared to work hard on getting the words out, "Dylan claims Sherry and her family sold Dina."

****

The next day, Miss Rose, Pauline and Justine wore mirror image frowns as they sat sipping hot Louisiana dark roast from cups. The gloomy topic they discussed with LaShaun contrasted with Miss Rose's airy kitchen accented in bright yellow, green and turquoise blue. Ellie squealed with delight as she played with Miss Rose's grandchildren. Yet the sound of children laughing in the next room didn't lighten the atmosphere.

"This is a dark, dark business y'all. Weighs heavy on the soul thinking about it," Pauline said.

"Dark and deep. A mother and grandmother selling their child..." Justine slapped a palm on the table top. "Makes me want to hit somebody."

"I know," LaShaun replied softly. "I've been swinging between sadness and anger since MJ told me."

"So Dylan is convinced that Sherry let her brother molest Dina and sell her away. But is it true?" Miss Rose glanced around at the others.

"Maybe not. The boy been sampling his daddy's product. Meth makes folks crazy. They come up with all kinds of freaky paranoid thoughts.." Justine's tone implied she wanted badly to find reasons to discount the horror.

"Dylan was high when they arrested him. It took five big strong deputies to bring him under control. But let's look at the facts. Kris Evans has children that, so far, the state police or sheriff can't track. Where did she get them? She hooks up with Tommy and his niece goes missing."

"Yeah." Pauline huffed in disgust.

Miss Rose sat straight and consulted her laptop. "We have some answers. Our team in California did a skip trace on Kris. She adopted the girl in 2009 and the boy in 2010."

❧

"I didn't know adoption records were public anywhere," LaShaun said and blinked at Miss Rose.

The older woman smiled. "They're not. We've got TEA members positioned in some of the most useful places like state DMVs around the country and vital records offices."

"Or we developed 'consultants' who can help us, those who understand that evil goes beyond the natural world," Pauline added with a nod.

"This Evans woman became a solid citizen despite her past of petty crimes. She first became a foster parent, then she adopts these two children. But we know she has a history of active cult membership." Justine crossed her arms.

"Any indicators she's joined up with Juridicus?" LaShaun leaned over to gaze at Miss Rose's laptop screen.

"She lived in New Orleans for six years between 1999 and 2005. She evacuated ahead of Hurricane Katrina. That's when she landed in California the second time. She got a job in a daycare center, later as a teacher's aide in public schools." Miss Rose read off the bullet points.

"So it's entirely possible she got involved with Juridicus, which is headquartered in New Orleans," LaShaun replied.

"Unfortunately, we have no way to confirm she did. Juridicus wasn't on our New Orleans team's radar back then. Who knew a group of high powered lawyers was a cover for a cult?"

❧

Miss Rose shrugged. "But she did hang out with uptown types. She attended the same balls and social functions their leaders did. Our New Orleans team put boots on the ground and interviewed people who knew her."

"We've got good people for sure." Pauline nodded.

"Wait, just got an instant message." Miss Rose adjusted her reading glasses as she stared at the screen. "Humph, Evans did volunteer work for The Justice Project. Seems she helped organize some of their charity projects for children in low rent housing developments."

"There's the connection then." Justine gave a satisfied nod.

They all refreshed their cups of coffee as they sat wrapped in their own thoughts. Miss Rose went into her spacious family room, turned play room for the day, when the kids got too quiet in her opinion. Pauline absently started clearing up. Justine paced. Then they all were seated again. LaShaun spoke first.

"Something's not right. This woman led a carefree life of petty crime, drugs and heavy metal rock. Suddenly she's all maternal? And why is Juridicus so civic-minded about families?" LaShaun looked around at her friends.

"They don't do anything unless it fits their agenda," Pauline said with a grimace.

"Exactly. So what are they up to?" LaShaun heaved a sigh.

"Here's the report from our Data Analytics and Informatics Department. Lots of technical

❧

blah-blah-blah about algorithms, multi-branched recursion, and more stuff that us regular humans can't fathom." Miss Rose kept reading. "Ah, now we get to the part in English. Oh damn."

"Rose, we're dying here. Spit it out," Justine said as she waved her arms around.

"We keep track of people with paranormal abilities, especially children. Many of us suffer in isolation thinking we're crazy or worse—possessed by the devil. So we gather and sort through reports of paranormal events, lots of nonsense or scams, you know. Anyway, about seven children of various ages that we had in the database have gone missing in the past twenty-four months." Miss Rose took off her eyeglasses and let out a long whistle.

LaShaun frowned. "Why didn't TEA see this pattern before now?"

"We don't spy on them. Unless they need us, we don't interfere in their lives. They're entitled to privacy after all," Miss Rose replied.

"And anyway, TEA is good, but we don't have the resources to track hundreds or thousands of people. Even if we wanted to," Pauline added.

"Yeah, some of them don't want any part of being 'special'. Others get totally freaked out," Justine added.

"Still, something should have tipped us off with all this fancy technology we have," Pauline said.

Miss Rose put her readers on again. "These incidents are scattered. Three children are in the US: One in Indiana, two from Florida. One child is in England, another in Jamaica and a boy in Croatia. The fourth one was in Panama. Let's see. The kid from Indiana just turned twelve. He's listed as a runaway. So is the young girl in Florida. She's fifteen. Says here her mother reported that she took off with her seventeen-year-old boyfriend to parts unknown."

"Hmm. Without context it doesn't look on the surface to be a pattern," Pauline said.

"Wait, was Dina in that database?" LaShaun asked.

"I just instant messaged Jennifer, one of the team members. She says no." Miss Rose sat back in her chair.

"I've got an idea."

LaShaun pulled out her cell phone and called MJ. Just then the kids came barreling in, five voices calling out questions and giggling. She went into Miss Rose's laundry room away from the noise and hustle. Minutes later, she had answers but waited until she and Miss Rose were able to herd the kids to the family room again. With a popular movie playing and fruit for snacks, they settled down.

"You followed a hunch," Justine said when LaShaun returned to the kitchen.

"Dina is considered a special needs student. She was identified by early screening at the local public health clinic. At first, she developed milestones slowly. Then she rapidly started to advance. When she was five a psychiatrist at the Children's Hospital Clinic in Lafayette gave her a rule out diagnosis of childhood psychosis but also said she might have Asperger's Syndrome. She seemed obsessed with talking to ghosts. Once she started school, what they called her symptoms went into remission."

"Hmm, she might not have been discovered by our team for a long time. We don't have someone in the Vermilion Parish schools since I retired from teaching." Miss Rose adjusted her eyeglasses.

Pauline focused her keen gaze on LaShaun. "Well we'll fix that quick, but back to LaShaun. What else did you find out?"

"That's about it, but sounds like Dina is a medium. Her 'symptoms' of so-called mental illness are really her ability to communicate with spirits." LaShaun sat down. She drummed her fingertips on the green and white stripped table cloth. "Let's assume Juridicus is involved."

"Solid assumption if you ask me," Justine said with a grimace of anger.

"Agreed," her twin sister replied.

"And assume that they're involved in the disappearance of the other children. All of whom have psychic abilities. We know that for a fact because they're in the TEA's database. For at least five years past, Juridicus tried to use killers who also had paranormal gifts. The plan didn't work so well. So now they're improving on it, using children. But why? They haven't given their lives to evil." LaShaun squinted as if it would help her see clearly.

Miss Rose sat down heavily. "Children can be molded, influenced. The children have something else in common, weak or non-existent family support."

"So they're all from poor homes with troubled families. Awful," Justine said.

"No, the two oldest are from an upper middle-class background. But apparently his parents were caught up in doing their own thing. The seventeen-year-old mostly raised himself. Same thing for the girl in Florida. Nice well-to-do families on the surface, but there's serious trouble at home. An older sister reported their mother has been physically abusive and hooked on prescription meds." Miss Rose looked at her friends. "Cults, like gangs, offer love and support to those who feel emotionally isolated, unloved."

"...a sense of belonging. Dina didn't want to go home." LaShaun looked at Miss Rose.

"But she ran away from her abductors," Justine replied.

LaShaun took a deep breath and closed her eyes. She blocked out background noises. The muffled sounds from the movie in the next room receded. The chirping of sparrows outside slowly faded away. She called up the mental image of Dina dressed in denim pants, a pink shirt and a matching denim jacket. The child smiled at LaShaun then darted off down a

⚜

misty path. Objects flashed by as LaShaun followed her. Time slipped away. The sensation of something bumping against LaShaun's thigh brought her back to Miss Rose's kitchen.

"Mama, say bye-bye to the pictures." Satisfied LaShaun was okay, she smiled and raced to the family room.

"Well cut off my legs and call me shorty," Justine breathed. She gaped at her twin and Miss Rose in turn.

"Did I just see that baby girl come call her mama back from channeling a vision? My Lord. Rose, we should get Ellie tested soon." Pauline blinked at Miss Rose.

Miss Rose waved at the twins. "Never mind that right now. LaShaun?"

"They didn't get the chance to send Dina to wherever they're keeping the other children. I didn't see it all, but I think Kris and the other two that came to my house are in trouble with their bosses. They didn't follow orders." LaShaun rubbed her forehead to order the retro-cognition images and sounds. "Okay, I think Kris was supposed to deliver Dina. But they decided to break into my house first."

"To find out more information," Pauline said.

"Or snatch Ellie," Justine replied in a grim tone. "Think about it. Two high value children in one swoop. I'll bet she told her bosses that you have a child. It's no great leap to figure out Ellie would be an extraordinarily gifted child. Her bloodline guaranteed it."

"But Chase..." LaShaun's voice trailed off.

Pauline looked around at the other older women then at LaShaun. "Honey, we traced his family history. At least two ancestors had psychic skills."

LaShaun glared at her. "You've been investigating us?"

"Calm down. One of TEA's functions is to protect us. We can't do that blindly. You come from an extraordinary lineage. I posited that Chase's family might have contained some gifts as well," Miss Rose said, her voice even despite LaShaun's outrage.

"And she was right," Justine said.

"LaShaun, you have more than one paranormal ability. That sets you apart from seventy-five percent of us. You have precognition to a limited extent, and retro-cognition. You can generate heat, maybe even electrical current. Some in the TEA feel like you might have even more abilities that are latent." Pauline spoke with intensity.

"So you can imagine if we're this interested in your progeny..." Justine's dark eyebrows went up.

Miss Rose studied LaShaun for several seconds. "Then our opponents have done their homework as well. The TEA can't be caught sleeping on any possibilities. Not that any of us could have stopped them from researching your genealogies."

"I'm starting to wonder if the TEA is just as sinister as Juridicus." LaShaun stood and went to the window. "When did our lives become open season? It's like we're lab mice."

After a few moments, Miss Rose stood and went to her. "The TEA is over a hundred-sixty years old. Odette provided the TEA with information, as did your great-grandmother and great-grandfather. Your family has been on record for at least three generations. As has mine."

"And ours," the twins said together. They looked at each other and smiled.

"Trust and believe that the TEA is an instrument of good. They've disrupted too many evil plans to count, and saved lives. We live as normally as possible. Look at us. We all have families, jobs and friends. We also have others who understand us and can come to our aid in ways most can't."

LaShaun turned to face Miss Rose. The wisdom etched on the seventy-seven-year old's face proved her words. Monmon Odette would not have made sure LaShaun met her and the twins if they were not to be trusted. No doubt Monmon Odette foresaw her future descendants would need to be safeguarded.

"You're right. But I won't tell Chase what the TEA knows about us, his family, just yet. I... he..." LaShaun sighed.

"I understand, of course," Miss Rose said quietly. She gave LaShaun a brief hug and then sat down again.

"Now we know that at least one cult tied to demonic service is trying to build their own

❧

TEA of gifted. But for very different reasons," Pauline said.

"But what reasons?" Justine picked up the last beignet on a Lazy Susan and munched on it absently, brow furrowed.

"Juridicus is just one arm of the main organization Correct?" LaShaun looked to Miss Rose who nodded.

"Worldwide they're known as Legion, but they've been good at keeping it secret. We found out about fifteen years ago with a lot of hard work. There is power in calling the true name of an enemy. A name gives the true meaning and purpose to a thing or person." Miss Rose's contralto voice dipped with gravity.

"The TEA knows a lot more about Legion than they like. They're big," Justine said.

"We are legion," Pauline said softly.

"Mark 5:9," LaShaun added. She remembered one of many lessons her grandmother had taught her. How to survive contact with demons wasn't typically covered in Sunday school for kids.

"Their mission is to spread chaos, disrupt daily life, and generally cause misery. Great." Justine gave a snort.

LaShaun gazed at the three older women as they all contemplated the adversary they faced. "More than that. Much more. Legion wants to rule mankind, to bring an end to all hope and faith. They want an apocalyptic war so that evil wins the final victory."

⚜

****

That night, Chase's somber mood matched how LaShaun felt. She tried to think of ways to explain what her TEA concluded was happening. But she couldn't find words that would make a feet-planted-firmly-on-the-ground cop take her serious. Yes, Chase was a Cajun Louisiana boy. He knew all of the legends passed down over generations. Despite seeing strange things, even accepting that LaShaun had extra senses, Chase believed in logic.

They went through their evening ritual mostly for Ellie. Keeping to her schedule would give their little girl the security she needed. Chase volunteered to give Ellie her bath after dinner. LaShaun cleaned up the kitchen to the wonderful sounds of splashing water and squeals of joy floating down the hall. An hour later Chase strolled back to join her in the family room. He seemed more relaxed.

"I hope most of the water didn't end up on the floor," LaShaun teased. "You look pretty dry."

Chase grinned as he tugged on the long sleeve olive green T-shirt he wore. "I put on a dry shirt."

LaShaun went in to give Ellie a goodnight kiss and then returned. Chase came in with two mugs of hot cocoa and sat on the sofa next to her. They watched television in silence and sipped the rich hot liquid. The evening news came on. A pretty young brunette led with the top story, an update on Dina's kidnapping. Then she moved on to the Tommy Bradford murder investigation. Chase sighed and rubbed his eyes.

"Are you going to..." LaShaun bit her lip and squeezed his muscular thigh.

"We might as well talk about the cases. I can't shut it off. Can you?"

"Now you're psychic," LaShaun quipped. Then she got serious again. "Was Dina molested?"

"Not penetrated. But that doesn't mean she wasn't molested in some other way. We examined Tommy Bradford's Internet activity. He belonged to a group of pedophiles who exchanged pictures. I won't give you the stomach turning details." Chase winced as if in pain.

"You don't have to." LaShaun didn't need imagination to fill in the disturbing picture.

"We've got the State Police Crime Lab examining trace evidence from Tommy Bradford's murder scene. I'm betting something from Dylan will show up. If not at the house, then on Tommy's body. Tommy put up a fight from what the coroner in Lafayette told us. But that will take time."

"You're trying to get Dylan to confess." LaShaun hit the mute button to block out the blaring used car commercial on the television.

"Saves time, and we might not get hard evidence to convince the DA to even charge him. But Dylan's been around the justice system more than a few times. He asked for his lawyer real quick."

"Which means you had to stop the interrogation." LaShaun drank from her mug. "Check the abandoned house where he had Sherry. Maybe he used it to hold Tommy, too."

"There's no sign that Tommy's body was moved though," Chase replied. He rubbed his jaw. He took out his department issued smart phone. "But I'll email the lab to test blood samples found and compare them to Tommy. Couldn't hurt."

LaShaun sat silent as he worked. Not surprisingly, Chase ended up getting more updates and sending additional instructions to the other investigators. Twenty minutes later, he was still exchanging information with his colleagues. Finally, he put his phone away.

"Seems the Bradford and Menard families did drug business together. Narcotics thinks they supplied drugs brought up from Mexico, supplemented their homegrown meth labs. But they exported some of their product to other states."

"Which made Tommy's betrayal even worse. But does Dylan Menard seem like a family type of guy? Not from what I've heard about him." LaShaun looked at Chase.

"In his world, you can't let people think folks can mess with you or your kin without serious consequences. But honestly, I watched Dylan talk about Dina. The guy was genuinely emotional a couple of times, broke down almost."

After a time, LaShaun spoke again. "I need to talk to Sherry and Kris Evans, Chase," LaShaun said.

"I'm not sure Dave will agree given the situation now. I know damn sure Anderson will object, and in some very colorful language." Chase grunted.

"Sheriff Godchaux will agree, and so will Det. Anderson once they hear what The TEA has found out about Kris Evans."

"Oh hell," Chase murmured.

"Something like that," LaShaun said with no trace of humor at the grim joke.

⚜

Chapter 10

The next morning, while Chase continued the murder investigation, LaShaun went to the hospital to interview Sherry and Kris Evans. LaShaun was wrong in her predictions, and Chase was on target. Det. Anderson wasn't on board with her talking to Sherry or Kris Evans. With great effort he'd kept his temper in check, but only because of their boss. Dave Godchaux could play the good old down home boy when needed, yet when it came to the running of the Sheriff's Department, he turned tougher than alligator hide. He expected his people to work as a team, even if they had to clench their teeth to do it.

"Sir, I want to once again voice how bad an idea this is. We've had enough interference from outside the department to muddy this damn, er, the investigation already." Det. Anderson's face went stiff with the effort to restrain himself.

"And once again, I'll tell you those objections have been noted. Doctor, let's go." Dave glanced at the physician for both women.

Dr. Wilkinson gazed back at the sheriff. He seemed to guess his objections wouldn't be met with any more success. He nodded and led them to Sherry's room. "Her condition has improved at least. The other patient is also stable."

"Thank you," Sheriff Godchaux replied tersely. "Come on, LaShaun."

"Wait, only two of you should go in. I don't want her overwhelmed with law enforcement around her hospital bed." Dr. Wilkinson frowned at the group, which included Chase, Anderson, his partner and MJ. He gestured, and a female nurse stood next to LaShaun.

"Good point. Just me and LaShaun will go in," Sheriff Godchaux said.

"But boss..." Det. Anderson stopped at the look the sheriff gave him. Then he held both palms up in capitulation

"And Nurse Jackson," Dr. Wilkinson put in.

Sheriff Godchaux didn't answer the doctor. He gave Anderson one last scowl before he pushed through the large door. Inside, Sherry Bradford gazed at them wide-eyed, blinking rapidly. Black sutures held together a large cut near her scalp. A neatly shaved section of her bleached blonde hair had been cut away. The

⚜

sheriff stood looking down at her like a stern father figure. LaShaun decided to let him take the lead for the moment. After a while, Sherry's bottom lip quivered. A single tear slid down her left cheek.

"Dylan is lying. I didn't sell my little girl to nobody. You don't know how hard it is. My car kept breaking down. You know how hard it is with little kids and no car? There's always something you gotta get from the store, or the social worker bitchin' about me not takin' em to some clinic. My rent was two months behind." Sherry blubbered until she became incoherent.

The sheriff's glare didn't soften. "We're gonna find out about Kris Evans, what her and Tommy got up to. You want us to know your side, then tell me the truth."

"Kris takes good care of her kids. She understands what's wrong with Dina, and she... Her little girl is special, too. Dina loved goin' over there." Sherry pulled tissues out of a nearby box on the rolling table. She wiped her face hard. When she looked at them again, a defiant frown had replaced the sad face. "You got no right to judge me."

"Kris Evans blew into town less than a year ago, somebody you didn't even know. Then you exchanged cash for your child. I'm counting up all the laws you broke right now. Selling a child is bad enough, but selling her into sex slavery is lower than low, girl." Sheriff Godchaux stabbed a finger at her.

Sherry sat bolt straight away from the pillows. "That's a lie! I never did, Kris swore to me they wouldn't touch her that way."

LaShaun tugged on Sheriff Godchaux's shirt sleeve. When he gave a slight nod, she moved close to the bed. "Listen, as a new mother, I know how rough it is. Children can be so demanding. I have one. It's non-stop. They need something every minute. And you have three."

"Humph, what do you know about it? A big strong husband comes home to you every night. A man you can count on. Dylan talking shit now, but where is he day in and out? Seems like I'm cleaning up baby vomit and diapers twenty-four seven." Sherry blew her nose and threw the tissues on the floor. She glared when the nurse frowned disapproval.

"Your babies didn't ask to come into this world. You laid up and got them. Now you complain because they're here. Well look in the mirror, girl. You're who's to blame." Sheriff Godchaux drew up as if about to go into a full rant, but he stopped when LaShaun raised a palm.

"Maybe you could give us ladies a minute to talk?"

LaShaun gestured to the door. The sheriff glanced at her, at Sherry and then left the room. The nurse said nothing but quietly put on disposable gloves and cleaned up tissues around the bed. Though she continued to frown, the efficient woman said nothing.

⚜

"He's a self-righteous bag of fart wind. Daddy said so when he ran for sheriff," Sherry blurted out before the door whisked shut behind Sheriff Godchaux. She wore a smirk as if satisfied he'd heard her putdown.

"You always listen to what your daddy and Tommy tell you." LaShaun pulled up a chair and sat down.

"Tommy ain't... he wasn't but a few years older than me. Him and my daddy just alike." Sherry picked at a loose thread on the white hospital blanket covering the bed.

"People say your daddy is a hard man, and Tommy—"

"Ain't nobody's business what happens in our family," Sherry snapped.

LaShaun studied Sherry. "I've been the subject of gossip most of my life, so I understand."

"Yeah, except your grandmamma left you lots of money. We still poor as dirt." Sherry stuck her bottom lip out. She darted a side look at LaShaun and then stared at the wall.

"My family worked hard to make it. I know yours does, too. I'm not gonna lie to you. It doesn't look good right now, Sherry, with Tommy's history and what we know about Kris." LaShaun shrugged.

Sherry looked at her sharply. "What about Kris?"

"She has a criminal record, mostly petty stuff," LaShaun added when Sherry snorted. "But still, you know those two kids aren't hers?"

⚜

"Yeah, she told me. Which proves she's a good person. Kris didn't have to take on that load. She wants the best for those kids," Sherry shot back. "With all your money and fancy husband, you wouldn't know anything about us."

"So she could help you out with money and take Dina off your hands," LaShaun said, brushing off the hostile swipe.

"Dina throws temper tantrums every hour seems like. Something strange about that child. Gives me chills the way she looks at me sometimes." Sherry blinked at them. "Kris and her get along great though."

"She understood Dina in a way you didn't. That makes sense." LaShaun worked to sound empathetic.

"Kris takes good care of her kids. I wouldn't have agreed if she didn't. I saw how she kept house, and dressed them all nice." Sherry let her head fall back on the pillow. "What's the big deal? People let their kids stay with a relative all the time."

LaShaun decided not to point out that her brother was a sex offender, and Sherry hardly knew his girlfriend. "That was good of her to reach out, give you relief from taking care of four kids on your own. Where did she get all this money though? Kris must have had a pretty decent job."

"She had money her parents left her. She even set Tommy and Daddy up in business." Sherry lifted her chin.

⚜

"What kind of business?" LaShaun knew Tommy had few skills and little education, their father even less.

Sherry shifted in the bed. She fidgeted with tissues in her hand. "My throat is dry and scratchy."

"Here you go." The nurse appeared from the position she'd taken up in a corner. She poured water into a cup, handed it to Sherry and then retreated again.

"You were about to tell me about Tommy's business," LaShaun prodded.

"Um, hunting and fishing guide. Taking tourists on boats in the swamp. Stuff like that." Sherry waved a hand in the air, a vague gesture that reinforced how false her reply sounded.

"Hmm, I see." LaShaun raised her eyebrows at Sherry.

Sherry sat up again, plumping the pillows behind her. "I'm not stupid. That good cop, bad cop bull is obvious."

"Except you know I'm not a cop," LaShaun replied mildly. "I'm trying to help you. I've been on the wrong end of the law a few times myself."

"I heard. You pulled a cop into your bed, got him to make legal. Smart move." Sherry wore a sly smile.

LaShaun chose to ignore the wisecrack. Instead she leaned forward, elbows on both knees. "When Dina disappeared, you asked to talk to me for a reason. Something Kris or Tommy did scared you."

Sherry's grin vanished, and the guarded expression returned. "Oh yeah?"

"You know what I think?" LaShaun let a few beats pass. She pressed on when Sherry avoided her gaze. "You got freaked out by them or their friends. Maybe it was the writing, or you asked to see Dina and kept getting excuses. Both?"

"I don't know what you're talkin' about." Sherry seemed to study the pattern of threads in the blanket with much interest.

"You started to wonder about Kris, where she gets all that money, and why she was so interested in Dina," LaShaun replied.

"You can think up all kinds of stuff, doesn't mean a thing. Anyway, I can get help even with Kris beat up in the hospital. My little boy is starting to act weird like Dina." Sherry looked at LaShaun, chin lifted. "Not that it's any of your business."

"You still don't know what the writing on the wall of your house said. Maybe they're lying to you, Sherry. We found a message like it next to your brother's body.

"Oh Lord, no." Sherry's eyes widened with terror. One hand covered her mouth as if to keep a scream from getting out.

"Who contacted you after Kris got hurt breaking into my house?" LaShaun leaned forward even more.

❖

The hospital door swung open with a whooshing sound. A woman strode in. She wore a leather jacket over a navy blue suit. "Don't answer, Ms. Bradford. I'm assuming Ms. Bradford and Ms. Evans have been informed of their rights."

Sheriff Godchaux and Det. Anderson came on her heels fast. The sheriff stepped around her first. He looked at the woman. "Ms. Bradford hasn't been charged. She's voluntarily helping us find out what happened to her daughter."

"And far as I know, she didn't ask for a lawyer. So where did you come from?" Anderson gave her an up and down glance.

The woman ignored him and spoke to the sheriff. "Felicia Benoit, attorney representing Ms. Bradford and Ms. Evans for now."

"Isn't that a possible conflict of interest?" LaShaun put in.

Benoit swung her sharp gaze to LaShaun. "And you are?"

"LaShaun Rousselle Broussard. Ms. Bradford asked to speak to me."

"Yes, at the beginning of the investigation into her daughter's disappearance. *Before* she became a suspect," Ms. Benoit retorted. She turned to Sherry. "I'm advising you to not answer any more questions."

"Yes, ma'am." Sherry gave Sheriff Godchaux a smug half-smile.

Sheriff Godchaux's face flushed red. "You've just advised your client against her own best interest. She has the chance to give us clues that could help figure out who took Dina. Cooperating could protect her other children as well."

"So you threatened to take her children, and call this interrogation 'voluntary'. Right." Ms. Benoit gave them all a side-eye. Then she looked at Sherry again. "I'm already talking to DCFS about custody issues. Don't worry. The pressure tactics won't work. They have no solid legal basis to take your children away."

"You better find out more facts before you make promises, lady," Det. Anderson retorted. He spun around and strode out.

"This interview is over. Oh, and don't bother going to Ms. Evans's room either. I've spoken to Dr. Wilkinson. She's in no shape to give consent to incriminate herself," Ms. Benoit said in a cool voice.

"She'll be talking to us sooner or later, Ms. Benoit. I can assure you of that. Kris Evans was caught committing a felony." Sheriff Godchaux turned to LaShaun. "Let's get out of here. I need some fresh air."

LaShaun gave the two women a slight smile and nod before she followed him into the hallway. The hospital door whisked shut cutting them off from Sherry and her new lawyer. Sheriff Godchaux huffed in frustration a few times. Dr. Wilkinson appeared from around a corner.

⚜

"Sheriff, I suspect you're probably not too happy with the way things are going right now," Dr. Wilkinson said quietly.

"We'll push on and get at the damn truth in spite of the bull crap being thrown in our faces," Sheriff Godchaux barked. Several nurses in the nearby clinical hub stared at them in frank curiosity.

"Come with me, please."

The doctor touched the sheriff's elbow and started off down the hallway. LaShaun and the sheriff followed him. He opened a door marked "Consultation Room".

Once the doctor closed the door, Sheriff Godchaux blew out a breath. "What's this about doctor?"

Dr. Wilkinson took off his glasses, cleaned them with a small cloth from his pocket, and put them back on. "Ms. Evans was seriously injured, that's true. But she's making good progress. I think another day of rest and she'll be able to answer questions. I just told Ms. Benoit the same thing. I wanted you to know as well."

"Well that's something at least," the sheriff said, his frown still in place.

"Look, Sheriff Godchaux, My job is treating patients. I have to be as neutral as possible when it comes to their wellbeing: ethically and morally."

"Yes, yes." Sheriff Godchaux waved a hand at him.

"Of course, Dr. Wilkinson. We wouldn't expect you to do anything else," LaShaun put in,

❖

her tone softer than the vibe Sheriff Godchaux was giving off.

"Ms. Benoit reminded me, unnecessarily, about doctor-patient privilege. So I can't tell you anything either woman has said to me." Dr. Wilkinson gazed steadily at LaShaun.

"I see." LaShaun reached out to him with all of her senses. "If Ms. Evans is afraid, you should at least tell Sheriff Godchaux so he can arrange security."

"Has she been threatened? By who?" Sheriff Godchaux said gruffly.

"She startles at the least sound or sudden move, and the nurses report she becomes even more agitated after midnight for some reason," Dr. Wilkinson said.

"He can't repeat anything she's said while she's on strong pain meds. Ms. Benoit would jump all over any such statements," LaShaun said, a hand on Sheriff Godchaux's shoulder.

"Right." Sheriff Godchaux rubbed his jaw.

"Not to mention get me in serious trouble with the Louisiana Board of Medical Examiners." Dr. Wilkinson winced as if imagining that dire reality.

"We have one security staff person. Cliff works evenings after he leaves his other job at Home Depot. One of your deputies works part-time for us," Dr. Wilkinson said.

"I'll talk to him and assign another deputy to assist. Tell Ms. Benoit it's out of an abundance of caution. Her buddies from the other night might get scared she'll talk." Sheriff Godchaux gave a crisp nod. The deep furrows in his forehead relaxed as he took some measure of control.

"Thank you. I'm sure Ms. Benoit will be asking. She doesn't miss much." Dr. Wilkinson pursed his thin lips.

LaShaun picked up on Dr. Wilkinson's unease about Felicia Benoit. "Is there anything else you can tell us?"

"Ms. Benoit had a lot of questions about the routine here, and security." Dr. Wilkinson gave a nervous laugh. "You're going to think I'm letting my imagination go wild."

Sheriff Godchaux grunted. "With the stuff I've seen on these two cases so far, nothing you say will sound weird."

"I guess I shouldn't let the news reports about coded cult messages or local rumors affect me, but I got a funny feeling. I wasn't sure if she was concerned about her clients' safety, or trying to find out about the hospital layout and security for another reason." Dr. Wilkinson laughed again. "Sounds even more paranoid now that I've said it out loud."

"I'm gonna find out more about Ms. Benoit, and who's paying her," Sheriff Godchaux said.

"You must have read my mind, Sheriff Godchaux," LaShaun quipped. She had indeed planned to ask Savannah to check out Felicia Benoit.

"Don't start with me, LaShaun," Sheriff Godchaux retorted.

⚜

****

After leaving the hospital, LaShaun picked up Ellie from her Aunt Shirl's house. Despite a rocky family history, Aunt Shirl and LaShaun had developed a relationship. Ellie seemed to have brought LaShaun closer to the Rousselle clan, though they were a volatile lot. Aunt Shirl and LaShaun's cousin Azalei willingly babysat Ellie when they could.

Three and half hours later, after errands, stopping for gas, then lunch and checking on the house, they sat in MJ's office. Beau was along for the ride. He curled up in a corner, but seemed tuned in to the human conversation.

The Vermilion Parish Sheriff's Department headquarters included a modern annex that had been added fifteen years before. MJ enjoyed a nice view of the landscaped grounds surrounding the historic courthouse next door. Late afternoon sunshine slanted through the window to the left of MJ's desk. The overcast chilly morning had finally given way to a more pleasant afternoon.

Ellie rested in MJ's lap. After a while, she tickled the toddler under her chin. Ellie giggled but didn't move from lying comfortably against her godmother's tummy. "I think someone is ready for an afternoon nap."

"She went out like a little lightbulb while we ran the streets. Didn't even wake up the three times I took her out of the car seat."

LaShaun smiled when Ellie's only reply was a big yawn. She clutched her stuffed rabbit.

MJ's expression turned serious. "They were able to find a foster home for all three of the Bradford kids. The same family that got them before had openings. At least they'll be with familiar people and together."

"You heard Sherry has a new lawyer by now, right?"

"Oh yeah, in the most colorful language Dave could come up with," MJ joked, then got serious again. "Felicia Benoit isn't with the public defender's office. I checked."

"So we don't know who's paying her to represent Sherry and Kris Evans."

"That's not confidential information, but we, meaning the Sheriff's Department, can't make Ms. Benoit or her firm tell us." MJ looked at LaShaun.

"Correction, we don't know right this minute. But we will." LaShaun winked at her. She stood and picked up Ellie. "Now we gotta move. For once mama is going to be the good housekeeper and fix a home cooked dinner."

"Bye little butter bean." MJ planted a kiss on Ellie's cheek.

"Toodles," Ellie blurted out and waved.

LaShaun and MJ exchanged a look then burst out laughing at the same time. LaShaun finally got control and wiped tears from her eyes. Beau bounced up, tail wagging.

⚜

"Girl, don't even ask me where she learned that. I'm going to guess my crazy cousin Azalei though."

Ten minutes later, they were on the road when LaShaun's cell phone rang. The caller ID flashed Pauline's name. She used the blue tooth hands-free in her Forrester to answer. "Hey Pauline and Justine."

"How did you know we were together?" Justine said.

"Seriously, you two are joined at the hip," LaShaun teased. "Now what's up?"

Pauline came back on. "News on the missing kids. Can you talk?"

LaShaun glanced into the rearview mirror. Ellie had dozed off again in the car seat. Beau's large head perched on the seat back as if protecting her while she slept. "Yeah, nothing too graphic. I'm in the car with Ellie."

"No worries. We can fill in gruesome details later. The TEA thinks they know a headquarters where Juridicus and Legion have the kids. That's the good news," Justine said.

"The bad news is looks like it's a complex right outside the Mexican city of Matamoros," Pauline put in, her voice heavy with concern. "A real danger spot according to the US State Department. In fact, the entire state of Tamaulipas, where Matamoros is located, is on the department's travel warning list."

"A hotbed of drug gangs. High homicide rate, too," Justine added.

"Getting intel will be difficult, and of course that's what they intended. Can I hold out hope TEA has contacts in Matamoros or anywhere in Mexico?" LaShaun glanced in the mirror at Ellie again. A black Chevy Tahoe continued to follow her.

"We do, but it won't be easy. Paranoid is Legion's middle name," Justine quipped. "We'll get back to you."

"Are you okay? I'm getting some bad vibes about your trip home." Pauline's voice went low through the speakers. Her psychic gift was psychometry, gaining information by concentrating on objects.

"Think I'm being followed. Or maybe all this talk about Legion and its long reach has me paranoid like them." LaShaun's breathing sped up. "Okay, they turned off on Sugar Mill Road."

"Maybe we better stay on the line."

The twins spoke at the same time, something they did when worried or combining their psychic efforts. LaShaun was about to reply when the transmission crackled, breaking up their words so that she couldn't understand them. A gray van whizzed by going in the opposite direction. The sky had grown overcast again, making the afternoon look darker than usual. She glanced at the clock display. Four-thirty. Darkness came early in mid-January. LaShaun pressed the gas pedal until her speed eased up ten miles over the limit. She debated what to do as a heavy mist rolled across the pastures on both sides of the Forrester. Beau sat alert on his hind legs.

"We won't go home in case we're being followed. Let's visit the Marchands instead. Xavier and his shotgun will come in handy. Agreed?"

LaShaun glanced at Beau in the rearview mirror. He woofed as if giving approval. Then she hit the speed dial feature on her steering wheel. Chase picked up on the second ring.

"I'm on Choate Road. I think I'm being followed," LaShaun said while he was still saying hello.

"Damn it. I'm a good..." Chase breathed hard into the speaker. "Fifteen minutes away at our Kaplan substation. Are you near a house?"

"No, I'm headed to Xavier's place. He and his youngest son stay locked and loaded, bless their gun toting hearts." LaShaun felt a prickle of heat when headlights appeared in the fog behind her. "The black Tahoe is back."

"Slow down, let them pass and call out the plate number. I'm on the radio to the station nearest you." Chase's voice was tight with worry. "Is Ellie with you or still at the babysitter's?"

"She's with me." LaShaun's voice broke. "Chase, if they're after her..."

"You're fading. I'm on my way." The sound of his vehicle door slamming shut and his engine gunning drowned out his words.

⚜

"You can't make it in time. I'll have to figure out what to do." LaShaun gripped the
wheel. She knew the countryside better than
them. At least she hoped so. She might lose
them if she drove across an open field.

"Let them think you haven't made them yet.
Maybe they'll pass to keep up the ruse. I want
that plate number. Please, LaShaun. No warri-
or woman moves right now."

"Okay. Okay."

LaShaun took deep breaths. She risked a
glance at Ellie. The toddler, now wide awake,
blinked back at her and strained forward to
look out the window. Beau growled deep in his
throat. The Tahoe waited for a red compact car
to pass on the two lane highway, then sped
around LaShaun's Forrester as if passing.
Tinted windows obscured a clear view of the
occupants, but LaShaun made out one figure
only. The driver. Then the gray van appeared
behind her.

"LaShaun?" Chase's voice broke up so she
couldn't hear much of what he said.

"Texas plate BCF X349," LaShaun managed
to get out, but the connection had gone dead.
She pushed down the urge to scream.

"Mama, mama."

Ellie's sweet voice rattled her even more.
LaShaun panted a few times before she could
find her voice. "We're going to be fine, sweetie.
Nothing is going to happen."

The Tahoe's tail lights flashed when it
stopped, forcing LaShaun to hit the brakes. She

⚜

jerked the steering wheel to the left and cleared the left rear bumper of the Tahoe by inches. The Forrester bounced as she hit bumps on the unpaved shoulder. Then she aimed the SUV away from the road going southwest. If she kept going, LaShaun knew she'd reconnect with Highway 82, the way home. But she couldn't go there. Instead she'd take a mile-long detour to the Marchand place. Another ten agonizing minutes. Two blasts of a vehicle horn made her jump and Ellie cry out. Then her engine shut down and died. The SUV rolled about twenty feet before it stopped in the middle of a prairie with high grass. Two circles of light approached from the north, another set from the east. The Tahoe and the gray Dodge van approached like large predators stalking their next meal. LaShaun fought to control her racing thoughts. Weapons. She fumbled to get the locked glove compartment open. Then she grabbed the Smith and Wesson .38 special.

"Sènyœr, ekoute mon priyèr," LaShaun murmured. (Lord, hear my prayer)

She continued in the Creole French Monmon Odette had taught her, a request for both strength and divine protection. Viscous haze streamed in through the air vents, as if the fog outside intended to fill the SUV's interior. LaShaun's words stirred the moisture, causing her breath to appear as the air grew cold. Ellie's voice seemed to echo far away. The need to get Ellie out of the Forrester seized her. LaShaun shuddered as she kicked her door

open. She aimed the .38, but saw only the headlights. She swung around, first left then right,
desperate to find a target. Then LaShaun
turned to open the back door so she could reach
Ellie.

"We're not going to hurt your girl, Mrs.
Broussard. She's a precious treasure. We'll protect her until she's ready to assume her rightful
place." The female voice floated through the fog
from several directions.

LaShaun didn't answer. Instead she raised
her voice, calling on the spirits of warrior angels and saints as Monmon Odette had taught
her for dire situations. Laughter rang out
around her. The fog swirled in menacing patterns. Grotesque faces, twisted into fierce gri-
maces, closed in. LaShaun stumbled, feeling as
if she'd entered another world. She couldn't
make out anything familiar. Suddenly she
couldn't find the SUV, though it should have
been only inches away. Her skin felt clammy as
droplets of moisture formed on her hands. A
chill took hold until her teeth chattered.

"Prayer won't help you. Give us the child
and be rewarded," a male voice shouted, impatient, angry, unlike the female speaker.

"Go to hell," LaShaun shouted. Knowing
they felt unsure of their chances calmed her,
but only a little.

The female laughed. "Been there and back."

"Screw this game. I'm taking the kid and—"

LaShaun fired at the threat, and a sharp
yelp followed. Shuffling noises in the grass to

❖

her left made LaShaun wheel sharply and fired twice more. Loud thumps near the headlights signaled at least two people had returned to the van or Tahoe. Maybe both. Sirens cut through the thick atmosphere. Her entire body felt heavy, but LaShaun forced her legs to move. Her entire body shook as her chilled damp clothes clung to her. The gray haze thickened, making her progress even slower. She got to her SUV, heaving in deep breaths. Oily air seemed to fill her lungs.

"Mama's here, Ellie."

A low keening whine, not human, answered. LaShaun clawed at the handle. When she finally got the door open, she found only an empty car seat and blood. Her screams ricocheted inside the Forrester, amplified by a dense mist that moved like a living thing.

⚜

Chapter 11

"**Y**ou left her alone, LaShaun. Why the hell did you leave Ellie alone?" Chase paced as he talked. "You should have been at home. I can't believe you wouldn't just back off and let us handle the investigation."

"You brought me into this case," LaShaun replied, her voice shaking.

MJ grabbed him by one arm and put her face close to his. "Stop it. Now."

Chase jerked free of her grasp, but said no more. He walked away from MJ and LaShaun. MJ gazed at LaShaun. She seemed about to speak, but then changed her mind. Instead she left to talk to one of her officers.

LaShaun sat wrapped in a blanket provided by a deputy. Still she shivered. Cold gripped her down to the bone, into her very soul. Ellie's gone. Those words banged around in her head

⚜

like a painful drumbeat. She fought to think her way through a migraine headache brought on by terror and guilt. Nausea surged and she felt light-headed.

MJ strode around, taking charge to secure the crime scene. Two Louisiana State Police troopers and three Vermilion Parish deputies went about collecting evidence. Det. Anderson pulled up ten minutes later, a blue light flashing on his dashboard. He went to Chase and they talked for a time. Suddenly Chase pushed past him, got into his cruiser and took off. Anderson walked over to LaShaun. MJ joined them.

"He insisted on going out to look for them," Anderson said. He rubbed his jaw with one hand. "Let's see if they contact y'all with a ransom demand."

"They're not after money. They wanted Ellie, and because of me, they got her." LaShaun's throat felt raw as she forced out the words.

"Nothing that happened is your fault," MJ said with force. She glared a challenge at Anderson, who held up both palms.

"I agree. If what you say is true, they've been waiting for the right opportunity. Short of locking you and your kid up for the duration, you did all you could," Anderson replied evenly. "But why do they want your daughter?"

LaShaun fought for control and lost. She sobbed softly. MJ's hand on her shoulder offered meager comfort. After a few moments, she wiped away tears with a wad of tissues

⚜

provided by an emergency medical technician. The EMT waited patiently for MJ's permission to take LaShaun off to be examined by a doctor. Both the sheriff and MJ had insisted, overruling LaShaun's objections.

"We're going to turn Vermilion Parish upside down to get her back, Mrs. Broussard." Det. Anderson's voice rumbled.

When she looked up into his eyes, LaShaun was startled. She'd never paid attention before. Anderson's eyes were dark blue. The intensity in them, along with the assurance in his tone, helped steady her.

"Thank you. The writing left at Sherry's house and found where Tommy Bradford was murdered led us to a cult. They think my daughter has paranormal abilities that can be used for some purpose. What we don't know." LaShaun swallowed against a lump of fear in her throat.

"Who is the *we* you're talking about?" Anderson glanced from LaShaun to MJ, who said nothing.

"A group of colleagues who also have paranormal gifts. We do research and monitor groups who try to use the supernatural to commit crimes or spread chaos." LaShaun looked up at him. "I know that sounds like a bunch of bull to you."

"Look, if the ghost of Marie Laveau popped from behind a bush, I'd take her help right about now. What I believe doesn't matter. If these folks think that stuff is true, we can track

⚜

known members where they hang out and rattle some cages until we get answers." Anderson glanced around as though ready to start the hunt.

"Which is why I just emailed you notes on what we know about Juridicus so far." MJ held up her mini-tablet computer in her hand. Then she stuck it back into her Sheriff's Department jacket.

"What about..." LaShaun couldn't bear to finish. She wanted to ask questions, but the possible answers terrified her.

"We're pretty sure the blood in your vehicle is from Beau. He put up a fight trying to keep them from taking Ellie. The vet we called took him away. She said he'll need surgery. Some SOB cut him up real bad." MJ sat next to LaShaun and put an arm around her shoulder. "You go with Tim here and get checked out."

"I feel like I should be doing something. And I'm fine." LaShaun's protest sounded feeble even to her own ears.

"No, you're not. Make sure you haven't been injured or even given a drug. You seemed dazed when we got here. You need to be at your best to help us find Ellie, right?" MJ squeezed LaShaun as she spoke.

LaShaun looked into the night. Floodlights positioned by deputies formed halos of illumination in the fog. "What about Chase?"

"I'll talk him down. I can trace him easy with the GPS in his cruiser and reach him by radio," MJ replied, her voice soft. "Listen, don't

⚜

pay attention to anything he said earlier. You know that was shock talking."

"Yeah." LaShaun couldn't manage to say more. Her gut told her something quite different.

"He loves you and Ellie so hard. I know this is tearing him up inside. I'll talk to him. He'll feel better if he knows you're okay. Both of you tearing around in circles won't help us at all. Go with Tim to get examined." MJ stood and gestured to the EMT.

"C'mon, ma'am. This is just a precaution. Dr. Daniels is waiting for us at the ER. I'm betting you won't be there longer than an hour or so. No visible injuries, no bruises that I can see. Your breathing is good."

The EMT helped LaShaun into the back of his emergency vehicle as he spoke. A female tech got her to lie down on the stretcher. Despite the circumstances, moments later, LaShaun drifted into oblivion. Her waking nightmare transitioned into a sleeping one as vile creatures clutched at her and Ellie in her dreams.

****

Three hours later, LaShaun sat in a bed of the Vermilion Parish Hospital ER dressed in a hospital gown. Savannah and her cousin Azalei argued. A nurse bustled in to shush them, but they ignored the beleaguered young woman.

"She's coming to my house. I already checked her place, made sure the alarm was set. The security lights are working just fine. Since I have keys, I'll make sure they have food in the house later." Savannah squinted at Azalei.

"Family is just what the doctored ordered right now. Tante Shirl and my mama will make sure LaShaun has everything she needs. Tante Shirl has her spare room all ready for you, LaShaun. And you know she's got a fine house.

Katie, one of Chase's three sisters, pulled back the curtain separating LaShaun from other patients in the ER. She wrapped LaShaun in a tight hug. "Oh LaShaun, everything is going to be alright."

Adrianna, married to Chase's older brother, appeared as well. "We drove over here like crazy soon as we heard."

"She's coming home with us, the Rousselles. Especially since you folks seem to think this is all her fault. She needs loving support, not accusations. I heard what your brother said to her. I mean who the hell talks to a grieving mother like that anyway? Yeah, we all know what the Broussards think of *us*." Azalei punctuated her pronouncements with a sneer.

"Now you wait one minute—" Katie's face went pink as she glared at Azalei.

"No she didn't just insult us considering her rap sheet," Adrianna shot back. "Yeah, baby. I know all about you." She spat a stream of Spanish that didn't sound complimentary.

⚜

"Come on y'all. This isn't helping one bit. Might be better if she came home with me. No drama at my house," Savannah said. Her response brought on protests from both sides.

A tall nurse the color of milk chocolate stepped into the enclosure. "Hey, one person stays. Everybody else out. I'm *not* having this nonsense in my ER. And yes, I'm the HNIC around here tonight. Head Nurse In Charge."

"I didn't start the commotion. Talk to these two." Azalei sniffed, and pointed to Katie and Adrianna.

"I don't care who started it. I'm finishing it right now. Choose who you want to stay, and it better be somebody that can keep quiet," the nurse clipped as she looked at the three quarreling women.

At that moment Miss Rose came up. "LaShaun, we need to talk."

"Dang, it's like the Superdome during a Saints game up in here," the nurse grumbled. "Well, Mrs. Broussard, which one stays?"

LaShaun swallowed hard and looked into Miss Rose's smooth brown face. Tears came back at the expression of maternal understanding. She reached out and Miss Rose moved around the nurse to hug LaShaun.

"Lache pa la patate," Miss Rose whispered. (Don't give up)

"We have a winner. You three, out." The nurse herded Azalei, Katie and Adrianna like they were troublesome sheep.

Savannah followed but turned back to LaShaun. "Call me if you need anything. I can find out information on that lawyer."

"Okay." LaShaun gave her a faint smile of gratitude that faltered and melted away quickly. Then the white cotton curtain around the ER bed closed. "Miss Rose, I put Ellie in danger. Chase was right all along. I know his mother has already said as much to him and everyone else."

"Where is he?" Miss Rose frowned and sat on the edge of the bed, still holding LaShaun's hands.

LaShaun rubbed her forehead. "Somewhere, out looking for Ellie and the people who took her. He won't answer my calls or texts."

"This kinda thing puts a marriage to an awful test. If he loves you, and you love him, then you'll lean on each other instead of claw each other to pieces. Either way, you were raised to make a way outta no way. We gonna find your baby. But don't lose your husband along the way." Miss Rose heaved a deep sigh.

LaShaun shrugged the blanket from around her shoulders. She felt stiff, but otherwise fine as she stood. "That's up to Chase, not just me. I can't live my life apologizing for who and what I am, Miss Rose. But I have to put that aside for now."

"Your vows before God and man, and to the child He gave you..."

"I take our vows seriously, but Ellie has to come first. Let's go get my child."

⚜

LaShaun picked up the plastic bags that contained her clothes. Fatigue fell away as she hurriedly dressed. By the time she had on her ankle boots, Miss Rose had informed the nurse they were leaving. The woman talked to the ER doctor, but both agreed LaShaun didn't need to stay overnight. She had no head wounds and no signs of internal injuries that indicated they should observe her for a period of time. So thirty minutes later, they were in Miss Rose's steel gray Chevy truck on the highway. Their first stop was LaShaun's house, so she could pack a few things, which included her laptop. Though she tried not to, LaShaun ended up standing in Ellie's room crying for a good five minutes. She broke down again when she went to the family room and looked at Beau's empty dog bed.

"I lost them both." LaShaun covered her face with both hands.

"No, cher. You didn't do anything wrong. Focus on the real villains." Miss Rose stood in front of LaShaun. She shoved a box of tissues at her. "Clean up your face, fix your mind, and let's get to work."

An hour later, they were at Miss Rose's house in her den. A fire burned bright in the fireplace. Cups of hot chocolate sat on the polished teak cocktail table. Sandwiches on a platter were untouched. Her husband's paternal attention enfolded LaShaun like a soft cotton quilt of support. The yawing hole in her belly didn't ease, but minute by minute, she drew strength from the older couple. Pauline and Justine arrived at close to midnight.

Pauline, dressed in a flowing skirt and suede boots, looked like she hadn't been roused out of bed in the middle of the night. Her deep red sweater matched the swirling pattern in the skirt perfectly. She stopped tapping the keys of Miss Rose's laptop to speak.

"Okay, so we can't get to LaShaun's SUV for a minute. Daniel could definitely pick up signs from that," she said, referring to Daniel's gift for getting information from objects.

"I haven't gotten any messages from beyond," Pauline put in, speaking like a typical movie medium who talks to spirits.

"The sheriff's department will be processing my Forrester for quite some time. But that doesn't matter." LaShaun glanced at the three women in turn. "Remote viewers?"

"Child, please. The TEA has a variety of gifted at our disposal. They're working as we speak." Justine's eyes lit up as she looked at the screen again. "How I love WiFi and technology. We're blessed with all kinds of resources."

"Except they haven't stopped Legion from snatching children," LaShaun hissed. She squeezed her eyes shut. "Sorry, I didn't mean..."

"It's okay," Justine replied softly, her face solemn.

Pauline leaned forward from her place in a stuffed chair. "LaShaun, we have a group of telepaths working with our data team. They're trying to establish a connection with the children."

"Yes. We managed to collect belongings from all of the children in the last few days. Don't ask how," Justine added quickly.

"I don't care if y'all broke in a dozen houses if it helps find Ellie," LaShaun said. "Chase is the one interested in following rules, not me." A sharp pang reminded her that that was just one of their differences now.

"Ahem, anyway, back to the telepaths. We called on some young people. I mean these millennials, or whatever the new generations are called today, speak the same language," Justine said.

"Yes, and they'll relate to the kids better than us old folks," Pauline quipped.

"Speak for yourself. Fifty is the new thirty, gurl." Justine patted her braided natural hair. She did indeed look a good ten years younger than her age.

"You're fifty-six," her sister shot back, then giggled when Justine glared at her.

Miss Rose rolled her eyes and ignored their catty exchange. "Okay, I have information on the compound in Matamoros. Including an aerial photo, though it's not very clear." She held up the ten-inch tablet so they all could see.

Her husband, Pierre, had been mostly silent and observing. He put on reading glasses as he crossed the room. "One main building and five outbuildings. Could be dorms like military barracks. Those look like two barns. I see a fenced area. Maybe they have horses and other livestock."

"Pierre worked in an Army intelligence unit back in the day," Miss Rose put in. She smiled with pride.

"I was an All Source Intelligence Aviator to be specific. Haven't flown anything more than a crop duster in years though. I even got licensed to fly helicopters in 'Nam." Mr. Fontenot peered at the image. "Big operation. I'll bet they have all terrain vehicles, too."

"Why? Matamoros is a bustling city with a growing economy. I don't see why they'd want to venture out into the wild country. Drug cartels operate in that area." LaShaun stared hard at the photo, despite knowing it wasn't a real time image.

"They've been in Matamoros for a long time. At least two TEA sources found evidence that Legion's roots in the area go back to the Civil War," Miss Rose said. She used the tablet's case to prop it up to allow easy viewing for all.

Justine blinked at the image. "Wow, seriously? I knew we'd been tracking them for about twenty-five years, but didn't realize they had that kind of history."

"Evil goes back thousands of years. You think Satan came up with organizing his minions in the nineties?" Miss Rose quipped.

"Well the Devil doesn't pop in personally to have committee meetings," Justine replied with

⚜

a grin. "I didn't think women and men bent on chaos could agree on much."

Pauline grimaced. "They manage quite well, unfortunately for the rest of us."

"So does The TEA have solid info that Ellie and the other children are kept there?" LaShaun mentally began listing what she needed to travel.

"Don't rush out to pack and book a flight," Miss Rose said quickly, clearly reading LaShaun's intent.

"I'm trying not to go insane just sitting around *talking* while my baby is in danger from a bunch of fanatics. God only knows what they plan to do to her," LaShaun cried and jumped to her feet. She paced in a circle.

Pauline stood, her eyes wide and glassy. "Exactly, cher. God does know."

Pauline's throaty pronouncement made the rest of them freeze in place. LaShaun gasped at the sharp spike of electric tingling that shot through her body. The other worldly look on her face signaled her paranormal ability of divination had kicked in. She went to the carved wooden cross hanging on Miss. Rose's wall. As she fingered the polished mahogany, Pauline recited words in a mixture of Louisiana Creole French and Latin.

"Shush, nobody move for a minute," her twin whispered.

Justine spoke so low LaShaun thought she'd imagined hearing her at first. The kitchen and everything around them became indis-

⚜

tinct. A low melodic humming sound began softly, increased and then died away. Then as though someone had snapped their fingers, the room sharpened into focus again.

"What the..." Miss Rose rubbed her eyes, put on her glasses and looked around.

"Whoa." LaShaun blinked her way to the solid world again.

Justine walked over to Pauline, but didn't touch her. "Sister, that was intense. Where did you go?"

Pauline stood with her back to them all. Then she turned around with her eyes closed. She massaged her temples and then looked at them. "They are impatient with the pace of their plans."

Miss Rose stood. "Legion."

Pauline nodded. "You remember we've tracked Juridicus for the past year or more. Wars, murder, the rise in terrorist attacks that kill the innocent and more all seem like child's play to them. They're tired of causing what they call minor incidents."

"Minor my butt," Justine blurted. "People are killed, sometimes tortured. Whole villages destroyed. Serial killers stalking people to keep them tied up, and then kill them, and they call it minor?"

"Hush," Miss Rose said, cutting into her tirade. "Go on Pauline."

"They've been performing rituals to receive messages from what they call their 'dark savior'. They want to be rescued from the vile world where there is too much cloyingly sweet sentimentality." Pauline turned to her twin. "Of course we know what they want, for Satan to rule. But they're not in contact with him, but one of his favorite imps. I'm not sure they realize that though. Some argue these signs come from the dark savior."

"That's crazy," Justine said. She pressed her lips closed when Miss Rose shot a sharp look in her direction.

"Maybe we can use that dissention to our advantage. Stop them from raining more evil onto the world," Miss Rose said.

LaShaun cut in. "I don't care about their plans. I want my child back, and I don't care who or what I have to slash, slice, or dice to get her."

"But cher, they're connected. There is a reason they are collecting these children," Justine said.

Pauline nodded. "Yes, not clear but Justine is on the right track. I need to get in touch with the TEA, share this information. We have to put all the pieces together to get a full picture. I feel it."

"I'll open the secure cloud so you can video chat with the Strategy Section. That's the division that looks at the information gathered and decides on action steps. All very organized," Justine explained to LaShaun as she grabbed Pauline's tablet computer.

"But we're no closer to finding Ellie. More than likely she's in Matamoros, right? Makes

⚜

sense. They're across the border, out of reach of American law enforcement."

"Not entirely. Mexican authorities coordinate closely with our government because of the violent drug cartels, not to mention the issue of illegal immigration," Miss Rose put in. She sat down again and started tapping away on her computer. "I'm guessing they have the children in a more remote location."

"Which makes getting them harder and more dangerous," Justine said with a frown.

"Exactly, so I think—" Miss Rose stopped at the sound of the doorbell.

LaShaun went to answer, but knew who was on the other side already. Chase's distinct tall, muscular profile shadowed through the beveled glass of the large front door. When she opened it, LaShaun's breath caught in her throat. Dark circles gave his face a hollowed out expression. Chase didn't smile, only nodded as a greeting and walked past her. She closed the door against the chilly January morning.

"Hello everyone. LaShaun, let's talk a minute." Chase didn't look at her as he spoke.

Miss Rose spoke up before LaShaun could get out an angry retort. "I brewed fresh hot coffee for us. Have one of these sandwiches. Made with farm fresh turkey breast or ham. My brother-in-law has the best meats for miles around and the ribbons to prove it."

"No thanks, ma'am." Chase stood stiffly. He darted on a brief glance at Miss Rose before looking away again.

❖

"You haven't had much to eat lately. Your energy is getting low, which means you won't be able to think as clear or take decisive action," Justine said with authority ringing in her soprano voice.

Chase opened his mouth, but he closed it again when Justine walked up to him. "Coffee would be fine, but I can't stay long."

"You need protein. Fix him a nice po-boy, something hot," Justine instructed.

"Right, a hot turkey and gravy sandwich dressed with fresh lettuce and tomatoes. He likes spicy mustard, and I've got some of the best Creole brand around." Miss Rose hurried toward the kitchen.

"Wait, I can't hang around waiting for a meal. I've got to leave," Chase said with force. He stared hard at LaShaun.

"Listen to me, we're on the same side in this thing. Look at me." Justine's voice went high and sharp with the demand. When Chase finally faced her, she lifted an eyebrow. "If you collapse physically, you're no good to Ellie. Eat."

"Won't take but a couple of minutes." Miss Rose hurried off to the kitchen.

"We'll help," Pauline said. She grabbed her sister's elbow and guided her out.

Justine pointed a forefinger at Chase. "Don't you leave."

Chase watched as Pauline marched her sister from the den, murmuring to her. Then he rubbed his chin. "Your friends sure get bossy."

⚜

"I managed to force down a couple of bites from a sandwich just so Justine would shut up." LaShaun crossed her arms. "What have you found out?"

"There's a connection between Tommy's murder and the kidnappings, but not what we thought at first. The Bradford and Menard families have been working together in the drug trade." Chase rubbed his eyes hard.

"Justine is right. You look like you're about to pass out any minute. Sit down." LaShaun pointed to a chair.

"Just for a second." Chase sank down onto a leather recliner, but sat on the edge.

"Y'all already knew both families did some minor drug dealing, if destroying lives can be minor," LaShaun said, remembering the earlier conversation about Legion.

"No, this is more organized. Sherry's daddy, Tommy and Dylan might be slick in their own way, but they're not king pin material. About eight months ago, they started a more sophisticated distribution scheme. They've got customers in Baton Rouge, Alexandria, New Orleans." Chase sighed. "Taking their lowlife business to the next level."

"Which was about the same time Tommy hooked up with Kris Evans." LaShaun sat down on the large matching leather sofa.

"Yeah, but she was charged with petty drug possession and theft based on her record. I don't see her suddenly getting into the big leagues." Chase tried to suppress a yawn and

⚜

failed. The smell of food floated in and he seemed to relax.

"She might if she's part of a bigger organization now. The TEA traced her activity. We're pretty sure she became a Juridicus member, and they're just a small cog in a bigger outfit called Legion."

"A cult again. Damn." Chase slapped a closed fist against the leather arm of the chair.

"Remember, Kris Evans has a history of getting involved in those kinds of groups. Turns out Dina has psychic ability, too. And TEA has identified seven other children that have gone missing, all with paranormal gifts." LaShaun leaned forward as she spoke.

"So Ellie was targeted because of you," Chase said softly, "and the Rousselle family legacy."

"Chase, I..." LaShaun swallowed hard.

"I knew who you were, all about your family history. But this." Chase fell back into the chair. The soft cushion seemed to exhale as he did so. He closed his eyes.

"We can talk about how we can move forward later, only *after* we get Ellie back safe," LaShaun said.

His eyes flew open. "I'll find Ellie. Nobody is going to stop me."

"We'll find her working together," LaShaun shot back, her voice hard as granite.

"Yeah." Chase gave a curt nod.

"Don't worry. I won't tell M.J., Dave or Anderson about the TEA or the supernatural angle. We'll just waste time debating whether it's real or not." LaShaun waved a hand.

"We sure as hell agree on that," Chase replied wearily.

"Here you go, Chief Detective Broussard." Miss Rose pushed a rolling cart loaded with food into the den.

For the next twenty minutes the three older women coaxed, scolded, and bargained with Chase until he finished half of a hot smoked turkey po-boy seasoned with rich gravy. He ended up wolfing down a plate of dinner fries once he got started because the food was that good. Then he downed a glass of sweet tea and stood, still wiping his mouth with a napkin.

"Thanks for the quick meal, but I gotta go. I do feel better, have to admit." He broke off when his work cell phone in a case clipped to his belt buzzed an alert. He read the text on the screen. "Like I said, the Menard and Bradford families have been importing drugs. They've got a connection in Brownsville, Texas."

"Did you say Brownsville?" Miss Rose glanced at Justine and Pauline.

"That's right across the border from Matamoros where Legion has its compound," LaShaun said as she stood as well.

"The TEA identified what we think is a base of operations in Mexico. We have an aerial photo," Miss Rose added.

"Humph, no coincidence. We've got too many threads leading back to Legion." Justine

❧

glanced at her twin, and Pauline nodded solemn agreement.

"Wait a damn minute." Chase spun to face LaShaun. "You might know where Ellie is and you weren't going to tell me?"

Miss Rose shot to her feet and got between them. "We only found out yesterday right before Ellie disappeared. Listen, this is no time to fight each other. Calm—"

"She didn't *disappear* as you call it. She was taken by force because of some cult ass crazy shit you and your friends stirred up." Chase spat the words at LaShaun without looking at the other women.

Justine rose and planted fists on both hips. "Now you just hold up, sport."

"I was attacked, had to answer questions so your deputies and detectives could gather evidence. We're doing everything we can to put together facts." LaShaun felt shaken in the face of his rage as she spoke.

"Facts? More like smoke, mirrors, and magic tricks. We need solid leads. Not mumbo jumbo. I'm not going to waste valuable time listening to wacko conspiracy theories. We're talking about drugs and human trafficking." Chase snatched his jacket draped across the sofa. "I'm sticking to the *real* world to get my daughter."

LaShaun grabbed his arm, digging her fingernails through the fabric of his cotton shirt. "Don't you dare suggest I haven't done anything to find our child. I carried her in my body,

⚜

held her close, loved her more than my own life."

"Then do a better job of protecting her from all this supernatural bullshit." Chase peeled her fingers free of his arm.

"Stop fighting each other," Miss Rose shouted. "This isn't the time to tear apart, but to draw closer."

Chase glared at her, and then glanced around at all of the women. "I'll tear up, burn down, explode whatever is necessary to save Ellie."

"At the expense of your love for LaShaun? You'll destroy the life you've built together?" Miss Rose said, her voice lower.

"I can't deal with... I'm going. Now." Chase went around LaShaun as he strode out.

"Son," Miss Rose started after him.

Pauline stopped her with a hand on her arm. "Let him go, Rose. He's in too much pain to hear you. Taking action is the best remedy for him."

"She's right. I don't want to see any more of my husband for a while," LaShaun blurted out. Then she started to cry despite not wanting to more than anything. She worked to pull herself together. "I agree with Chase on one thing. Standing around here is worse than useless. Every minute I'm not tracking down these bastards puts Ellie and the other children in danger."

"Legion needs them too much to harm them. They're being well taken care of,

❖

LaShaun," Pauline said, eyes closed. "That's as much as I can see for now."

"Are you kidding me? They've ripped kids away from everyone they know. Those kids are probably traumatized. We don't know what kind of grisly rituals they've got planned." LaShaun gathered up her things as she spoke.

"True, but they're also doing everything possible to make them feel comfortable. But what I know is too damn limited." Pauline struck a thigh with one hand.

Justine moved to her side quickly and placed an arm around her shoulders. "Calm yourself, sister." Then she turned to Miss Rose. "We need Daniel and any other remote viewers close by."

"On it," Miss Rose replied. She stepped to her laptop. Moments later, she'd sent an email.

LaShaun looked at her phone and saw a message from the veterinary hospital. "Beau is out of surgery. He's bad, but there's a fifty-fifty chance he'll make it through the night. They took out two bullets."

"Mèsi Bondje," Miss Rose said, thanking God in old Creole French.

"Mathieu is there," Justine said quietly, referring to the breeder who had raised Beau until LaShaun got him. "More than medical skill saved that wonderfully brave creature."

Pauline looked at LaShaun "Cher, listen to me..."

"I'm going to Matamoros. Help or get out of my way." LaShaun pulled out her .380, loaded it and then put it back into her cross-body bag. She checked the antique silver knife that had served her well. Tucked neatly into a leather sheath, she'd clip it to her waistband later.

Pauline held up her tablet computer. Five serious faces gazed back at them all from the open video conference app. "Meet members of the TEA ready to be your team when you get to Brownsville."

Chapter 12

Two hours later MJ stood with LaShaun in the check-in line at the Lafayette Regional Airport, both wearing sunglasses. The flight to Brownsville would take just under three hours. The line moved efficiently, but still LaShaun could not shut out the loud tick-tock in her head. Every second that went by felt like forever. The longer she was separated from Ellie, the more the ache in her belly grew. Nausea had become her constant companion. Smiles and laughter from families boarding for happy trips only made the ache more intense.

"Sure you don't want to check in with Chase before…"

⚜

"You've been texting him updates on me, right?" LaShaun raised an eyebrow at her friend.

"No. Well emails. Only two. Just to say you were okay. I'm not telling him you're going into rugged Mexico where vicious drug lords rule. Oh hell no," MJ said with force. "I'm leaving that bit of news for *you* to break."

"Chicken. Besides, the way we left it a few hours ago I doubt he gives a damn." LaShaun winced at the hurt from hearing a hard truth spoken aloud.

"I don't believe that, and neither do you."

"You weren't there. He blames me, MJ. I'm not sure I can forgive him for the things he said." LaShaun hitched the carry-on bag over her shoulder.

MJ bit her lower lip. "Damn, I've seen this kind of thing before. Families break up under the stress of a crime investigation. I can't stand the thought of you becoming a statistic."

"It's on Chase as far as I'm concerned. I didn't turn on him. Guess he's been listening to his mother more than I thought." LaShaun grimaced as she recalled the vitriol Mrs. Broussard spewed in her direction.

"No way. He's too much his own man," MJ said promptly.

"Family bonds and blood run deep, girl. We both know it." LaShaun sighed and turned to MJ. "Look, I can't say I hold it against Chase. She's his mother for God's sake. Of course being on the outs with her is tough. Puts a strain on the whole Broussard family, 'cause they were tight-knit before me."

"Don't beat yourself up with guilt about them or Ellie," MJ said, her voice strained with quiet force.

"I know for damn sure I didn't cause those..." LaShaun swallowed the curse word that almost came out of her mouth. "No worries. I've had time to process everything, so I don't blame myself. They want Ellie because of her inherited abilities. I'm no mistake, and neither is my child. If Chase thinks so, then he can get the hell out of our lives."

"Chase isn't going anywhere, and not just because of Ellie. I mean, please. Get serious." MJ frowned behind the sunglasses. "He's never been happier than the past four years since he met and married you, and y'all had Ellie. He told me his world was complete with you. Not his mother, or even the rest of the Broussard clan, but you and Ellie."

"Yeah, well, I'll say it again. You didn't hear him, see the look in his eyes. Not just last night after Ellie was snatched. I think his second thoughts about me have been simmering for a while. I was just too dizzy with happiness, playing house mommy and wife, to see it."

"LaShaun, I think you're taking it way too far," MJ replied. She put a hand on LaShaun's shoulder then withdrew it.

"I can't worry about Chase's feelings about me or my family background right now, MJ. Ellie comes first. I have to stop whatever they have in mind for her and for those other children." LaShaun shivered thinking about the unspeakable possibilities.

"I know but—"

"If you really want to help, tell me what you know about the Brownsville connection," LaShaun broke in to head off more well-intentioned advice.

MJ sighed. "Okay. Well, we've got reason to think the Menards have moved up in the criminal world. There's a gang operating in Tamaulipas calling themselves El Duro. They're connected to the Chapo Cartel. Seems some members of El Duro gang have paid a visit to Lafayette. Dylan, his two brothers and a cousin entered a business relationship with a couple of them."

"Dirty birds of a feather," LaShaun said, quoting her late grandmother.

"For sure. Thugs coming together to form a Drugs-R-Us chain of stores with the occasional illegal gun running thrown in. Some of these folks specialize in stealing weapons from military bases." MJ lowered her voice as she spoke.

"Which makes them even more dangerous. Chase once told me about the problem of the Army alone missing inventory." LaShaun looked at MJ.

"Yeah. Anyway, the worst part is their growing business in human trafficking." MJ passed a hand over her forehead. "I hate the ways people find to destroy others."

⚜

"We'll stop them, MJ." LaShaun had to believe the words or she'd fall apart. "I figure Chase told at least you about the Legion compound."

MJ nodded. "I had my guys check it out. The company has been around for a while. They manufacture cheap clothes shipped to the US to discount stores and a few boutiques. Been in Mexico for a good fifteen years, called Sierra Apparel C.V. They've got housing for some of the workers, improved the infrastructure in some little towns nearby. Making lots of friends with local politicians as you can imagine. Seems like a legitimate business. No ties to the cartel or El Duro." MJ frowned at her. "So why the interest?"

"Some friends of mine thought maybe it could be a cover for illegal activity," LaShaun said.

She had a flash of insight so sharp she could mentally see Chase talking to MJ. He hadn't told her about Legion. Yet MJ's sharp law enforcer instinct couldn't' be fooled. She glanced around, moved closer to LaShaun, and peered over her dark sunglasses.

"Oh yeah? I'm guessing the compound is connected to supernatural badassery," MJ whispered.

LaShaun laughed out loud, causing a few people in line to glance at them. "I needed some comic relief, girl. Thanks for coming through."

MJ grinned at her. "So I'm right. Chase knows that stuff freaks me out, but I could tell he left something out. Serial killers, drug dealing thugs, robbers I can handle. But spirits and demons? Uh-uh, give me human crooks any day of the week." She shook her shoulders.

"C'mon. You'd totally kick butt as a ghostbuster," LaShaun wisecracked.

"No ma'am. Old fashion crime busting is good enough for me." MJ's smile faded. "You think they have Ellie?"

"And other kids. Seven to be exact but not confirmed." LaShaun blinked to stave off tears that threatened spill down her cheeks.

"You're not going it alone. Chase told me about Miss Rose and the Dupart twins, your psychic sweet tea ladies." MJ looked around to make sure no one paid too close attention to them.

"See, that's why you're Sheriff Dave's HBIC. You got brains." LaShaun sidestepped giving MJ too many details.

"Okay, give me deniability. I can honestly tell our boss you didn't tell me everything." MJ gave a grunt. Then she frowned at LaShaun. "Hey wait a minute. HBIC?"

"Head Badass In Charge," LaShaun quipped and gave her a wink. She nodded toward the ticket counter. "My turn."

"Be careful. Text me if you need advice or to talk. And for God's sake, keep me updated." MJ gave LaShaun a hug.

After a solemn promise to let MJ know what was happening, LaShaun boarded the plane. The flight took her to Dallas for a con-

⚜

nection. LaShaun read the TEA intel files on her Android tablet. By the time she arrived at the airport in Brownsville, LaShaun could quote pages from memory. She walked to the entrance marked for ground transportation as instructed. She recognized the woman walking toward her as one member of the TEA team. Shoulder length dark hair swept back from her round face. She wore a blue sweater over a tan cotton peasant-style blouse, blue jeans, and cowboy boots. LaShaun estimated the heels gave the young woman a few inches, but in socks, she probably stood just under five foot three.

"Hello, Mrs. Broussard. I'm Valentina Valenznuela. Call me Val. This way, if you please." Val reached out to carry her bag then smiled when LaShaun refused. "I hope your flight was smooth."

"Fine. Let's get started," LaShaun said. Then she took a breath in and let it out. "I'm sorry. That was rude."

Val led her to a white Chevy S-10 truck. She clicked open the locks using a remote and then faced LaShaun. "Understandable. Your child is missing. We're going to get her back."

LaShaun felt at least a measure of the tension in every muscle release. Val's expression of determination made the slender short woman look formidable. Not interested in the landscape just yet, LaShaun spent the ride to TEA's local office reading the files. Miss Rose and Pauline had sent over more information. They arrived on Naranjo Boulevard fifteen minutes later. A business with a red and black sign that read Tech Innovation, LLC blended in with other nondescript gray and brown break buildings in the area. Val led her through the lobby. A couple of young people spoke to customers. They took no notice as Val directed LaShaun through a set of swinging double doors. They passed through a room with computers, some taken apart.

"We make and sell affordable computers, but we also recycle them. We've set up computer stations at ten community centers, including four just across the border."

Val gestured to the equipment and parts spread on large tables as they walked through another room. A tall man with red hair waved at them then went back to working.

"That's nice," LaShaun murmured.

"We can't exist on charitable gifts alone. Though we do have a few generous donors. We have multiple streams of income," Val said as they arrived at a door with a keypad next to it.

"I didn't realize."

"Well, we can't host a fundraiser to fight demons, can we?" Val smiled at her. Then she entered a series of codes with light taps. Beeps sounded between at least four sequences.

"Impressive security." LaShaun walked ahead of her when the heavy steel door swung inward.

⚜

"Less likely for anyone to crack it, unlike a simple four, five, or even six number cipher. This is the nerve center, as I like to call it."

Despite the name, the offices did not buzz with noise. In fact, anyone entering would take the place as just another busy office. The people, dressed in business casual style, looked like any ordinary employees. They could have been selling office products or answering customer service.

"This way. The team is waiting in the conference room."

LaShaun blinked when they entered to find more people around a round table. Pastries and coffee sat on another table in one corner. A fifty-inch television mounted on the wall was hooked up to video conference equipment and a computer tower.

"Mrs. Broussard—"

"LaShaun, please." LaShaun nodded to the people in the room. A chorus of "hellos" greeted her.

Val swept a hand around the room as she introduced them. "LaShaun, this is Ernesto Gonzalez, Abril Brown, Jennifer Evans, and Carla Cuevas. We call her Cee-Cee."

"For obvious reasons," Cee-Cee joked with a wide smile. She crossed the room.

"Nice to meet you all, though..." LaShaun shared a brief handshake with her.

"Yes, the reason we're getting acquainted is anything but," Cee-Cee said. Without asking, she poured coffee into a mug for LaShaun and put it on the table in front of an empty chair.

"Thanks." LaShaun sat.

"Here's what we know. Sierra Apparel C.V. is legit on the face of it. In fact, the town officials love them. They pay decent wages, have paid for paved streets, and even helped finance a water treatment plant." Ernesto tapped a wireless keyboard as he talked. An image popped up on the big screen television. "Here's one of their commercials. A very laudable, and it seems, profitable outfit."

"Helping the local economy, treats the employees with respect, like family," Jennifer added in a dry tone.

"And yet..." LaShaun frowned at the innocent looking attractive building that Legion showed to the public.

Val studied the image under discussion. "We suspect they're working with drug gangs to finance their efforts. So they accomplish two goals: spread chaos via drugs and illegal guns to thugs and the profits are used to fund their war against The Creator."

The woman named Jennifer rose and walked to the wide screen. "This might be their plant, but we know of at least two other locations. Outposts if you will."

"Taking them farther from the scrutiny of border patrol and other law enforcement into the more uncontrolled and lawless areas of Mexico," Cee-Cee added. The other young team members nodded.

⚜

"Legion is working with blood-thirsty gangs, no surprise there," LaShaun said.

"Yes, one of several unholy alliances," Ernesto replied. "Literally. Of course the gangs don't care about religion or philosophy even. They just want money and power." He sat straight when the conference door opened.

"So where do we start?" LaShaun's entire body shook with the need to take action.

An older man, tall with iron gray hair and a mustache, came in. He had the look of a retired military officer, lean and strong despite his age. Another man with brown hair mixed with gray followed him and quietly shut the door. He carried a leather messenger bag and seemed more of a business CEO type. LaShaun felt the atmosphere contract with increased tension. She studied the two men, both dressed in casual clothes like the younger team, but with an air of authority. The second man spoke first.

"Zachary   Desmond,   Mrs.   Rousselle-Broussard. Honored to meet you. I'm a member of the High Protectorate Council. My job as Secretary General is to implement field operations, determine strategy based on data."

"Frank Miles here. Glad you could come," the tall man said, though his impassive expression didn't indicate he was happy to see LaShaun.

She shook both their hands in turn, giving her more information. Both gazed at her. Of course. They knew she'd pick up on their auras. "Hello."

⚜

"To answer your question, we should gather more information. Legion, and its Juridicus chapter if you will, are tough to crack. Their members are extremely cautious. We've been quite successful in thwarting several of their plans. One with your help I believe." Zachary Desmond dipped his head to her with a slight smile that vanished into a grave expression again.

"My recommendation to the full council," Frank Miles broke in with a sharp look at Desmond, "is that we use the intel we have and initiate a foray into the main compound. We have solid evidence the missing children are there."

"Except we don't know for sure, Frank. If history is any indication, the latest recruits have been moved to a more isolated location for training," Zachary said. He lifted his chin and didn't look at Miles.

"We've done enough studying, research, and talking about strategy. Groups like Juridicus are spreading like fire ants while we have committee meetings," Frank shot back. The heat in his tone matched the jut of his square jaw.

"I don't think we can go blundering around blindly, Frank."

"You gotta be joking. Look around at the tools we have; the data we've gathered for decades. *Decades*, Zachary. Geez, your faction would have us sitting on our hands while Legion increases its influence. We're letting them

⚜

get too far ahead. They'll outgun and out-pace us at this rate."

"Are you suggesting that we can't triumph over evil forces? I didn't realize your faith had faltered so much," Zachary retorted.

"My faith is strong, but faith without works is dead. Don't question me." Frank tightened one hand into a fist as he glared at Zachary.

"Enough," a deep voice boomed from the speakers set up.

LaShaun started as she spun to look at the television. A distinguished looking man with ebony skin in a dark suit and tie had spoken. Bald, he had gray eyebrows and a neat goatee. Beside him sat an older woman, the lines of her porcelain face giving her an air of wisdom. She wore a crisp white shirt beneath a navy jacket and a gold and silver brooch on one shoulder. Her deep auburn hair, obviously colored, made her look like a former supermodel. Her thin lips pressed together in a look of disapproval.

"This isn't the time or place for squabbling. Not to mention it's undignified," she sniffed. Her upper-class British accent made the admonishment sound even more severe.

"President Truman, General Churchill-Soames." Zachary snapped to attention like a soldier in front of his military superiors.

Frank remained relaxed, but his expression melded from a scowl into one of respect. He nodded to them. "Mr. President, General."

"The High Cabinet met overnight to discuss recommendations from both your teams as presented by your leaders. We agree that careful strategy is the right defense since Legion has become more and more sophisticated." President Truman frowned, but not at them. He seemed to be looking into the distance at their future battles.

"Hold on one damn minute," LaShaun broke in. She walked over and faced the television screen, hands on her hips. "I don't give a crap about your internal politics or struggles for power. My child is at risk. So you best believe I'll be taking action with or without your strategies. I'm sure as hell not waiting around for more committee meetings. I'll recruit my own team if you won't let these people help."

"Oh, we'll help," Cee-Cee said with force and stood. Her declaration earned her a grimace from Secretary General Desmond. She cleared her throat, but tossed him a defiant glance before she looked away.

President Truman pursed his lips and waited before he replied. "May I continue?"

"Umm, yes sir," Cee-Cee replied, her tone softer.

"Frank is right, Zachary." President Truman raised a palm when Desmond's mouth flew open. "We can't justify leaving lives at imminent risk."

"Most importantly children's lives," General Churchill-Soames clipped.

"Yes, making them even more defenseless." President Truman's thick brows pulled together.

❦

"Sir, Mr. President, Madame General, with all due respect, we have data that shows the new recruits are not powerless," Zachary said.

LaShaun whirled around to confront him. "Stop calling them 'recruits' like they signed up for duty in Satan's army. They're kidnap victims, vulnerable children at risk for exploitation and great harm as the president said."

"Poor choice of words given you haven't been part of earlier discussions," Zach said, though his expression didn't quite succeed in being apologetic.

"What's he talking about?" LaShaun said, looking to TEA's local team.

Ernesto tapped the keyboard a couple of times. The screen split to show the leaders and Legion's main Mexican compound. "All of the kids they've taken have paranormal abilities, old news I know. But we, meaning our local Southwest division, managed to get someone on the inside as an employee. Mariela has been working for Sierra Apparel for just shy of two years. Long story short, she got a glimpse of some of the children. She believes they're advanced."

Val leaned forward with an eager expression. "They were selected because they not only have strong abilities, but they're aware of and in control of them."

"Even more exciting, it appears that the children developed mastery early by masking their gifts. They knew normal family members and others would see them as threats or freaks." Jennifer rose and paced as she spoke. "They're not only gifted, but smart, resourceful and take initiative."

"All reasons that make them dangerous weapons in the hands of our enemy," Zachary rumbled.

"Human beings, damn it. *Not weapons*," LaShaun hissed at him.

He looked back at her without flinching. "We know that most, if not all, of the children willingly followed Legion members. The two teenagers signed pledges in Bat's Blood Ink, with their blood mixed in. You realize the implications?"

"Of course the older kids would find such radical rebellion appealing. They had already gone very far to break rules, even drifting toward illegal behavior. That doesn't make them willing members of the Legion's forces. They're kids for Lord's sake," Cee-Cee said with fervor. Noticing the stiff mask Desmond wore, she added, "Sir."

"Unpredictable and emotionally unstable kids who have formed a bond with forces that threaten humanity in the present and future," Zachary shot back. He spun to face the two leaders, who frowned back from the television screen. "I call for a full council meeting before we launch such a risky operation. The consequences could be catastrophic to the long-term goals of TEA."

"Request denied," President Truman replied evenly. Then his taut frown eased. "Secretary

❖

General Desmond, the full council has considered all actions and the possible consequences.
The decision has been made. We urge you to
put aside your feelings on this matter and assist Frank. Can the TEA count on you?"

Zachary's eyes flashed blue fire as he raised
his chin. "Of course."

"Good. Now we must disconnect. Another
urgent situation has been reported in Iran."
President Truman gave a curt nod.

"I expect hourly updates until preparations
are complete for the foray. You must submit
any plans for non-standard weapons or attack
methods to me before use. Understood?" General Churchill Soames was already on her
smartphone reading messages.

"Yes, ma'am," Frank replied, with a sharp
glance at Desmond. "Okay, team. Let's get moving."

He smiled as the younger members slapped
hands and high-fived in celebration of the decision. LaShaun only felt an overwhelming rush
of relief that she wouldn't have to fight the
TEA and Legion at the same time.

****

For the next two hours, the team made
preparations for approaching the Legion compound. Almost one hour of that time was spent
in reviewing data and nailing down the details
of their strategy. LaShaun joined Val and Cee-

Cee in a warehouse that housed heavy equipment, including a modified Range Rover. She immediately noticed that the color of the SUV blended into the scenery. The camo paint was an almost exact match to vegetation, sand, and soil of the Mexican landscape.

"Yeah, helps it kind of disappear once we set out on foot. Harder to see. Notice the trim is painted," Cee-Cee nodded to the hummer as she strapped on a khaki vest. Then she looked at LaShaun. "Here, we got one to fit you. Lots of pockets."

"Should I pack these?" Val held up a hard case full of stun guns.

"Hell yeah. I can't believe you got hold of 'em so fast." Cee-Cee stroked the case lovingly as if it was a favorite pet.

"Hmm, well... having them handy isn't against regulations, just using them." Val grinned.

"You heard the general, get authorization. Prayers going up she approves. I don't like 'em, but in this case..." Jennifer appeared and frowned at the case.

Val nodded. "Not my first choice either, but we'll use every advantage we can get our hands on. Okay, I'm going to check on the rest of the guys. Then we'll head out."

LaShaun watched the young woman march off, purpose in each solid step with Jennifer following. "Why the big deal about stun guns? Cops and the military use them all the time."

⚜

"Our Weapons Section modified these stun guns. They not only deliver a larger electrical shot than normal, but the charge neutralizes psychic ability. Not maybe ten to fifteen minutes. Just enough to get you past your opponent. But it does make them slower even after they recover. It disrupts the neural activity in a way we don't quite understand. The effect is individual though. Some are more affected than others." Cee-Cee slipped one of the stun guns into a holster pocket on the inside of her vest. Then she gave it a satisfied pat.

"I don't get their objection though." LaShaun matched her actions. She slipped her knife and derringer into pockets that fitted them perfectly.

"Like I said, individual results vary. At least six deaths were reported over the last fifteen years or so," Cee-Cee replied.

"We're trying to stop people who serve demons, and they don't mind killing as many as possible. In fact, it's considered a job perk to them." LaShaun eyed a pair of boots on a shelf built into one wall.

"The TEA is very sensitive that we don't become like our enemy." Cee-Cee gave her body a pat down. She appeared satisfied. "Not weighed down but ready for action."

"And the political jockeying I just witnessed?" LaShaun pulled her thick hair back into a ponytail.

"Zachary Desmond is ambitious. It's common knowledge he intends to run for president.

❖

At forty, most members consider him a bit too unseasoned for such a heavy job. President Truman has served six terms already. Rumors are he's planning to retire sometime soon but of course be part of the Emeriti Council. Past presidents and high level generals continue in an advisory capacity."

"Damn. Even psychics have political and election drama," LaShaun mumbled.

"Hey, we're still human with all the flaws that go along with it."

As she waited for Cee-Cee to finish her preparations, LaShaun examined more of the inventory. "So 'non-standard' methods mean..."

"Lethal results, possible or certain." Cee-Cee pointed to the boots. "Yeah, switch out what you're wearing for those. You can change back when we're through. Size seven, right? Those are not only waterproof, but resists snake bites and scorpion stingers. Handy in this part of the world."

"Oh yeah, I want some of those." LaShaun changed in minutes. She put her boots in place of the ones she put on. "You wouldn't happen to have any children's sizes?"

Cee-Cee wore an expression of shock. "Girl, we don't usually include sprouts in martial operations."

"Legion isn't above using children for evil. Why not enlist them to fight for good?" LaShaun gazed back at her. "Criminal gangs use the sense of belonging to appeal to young people. Except for Ellie, the kids taken were

❧

rebels, not cared for at some level, and even abandoned."

"Instead of merely keeping a database, we should recruit? Hmm, might not go over so well with a lot of members." Cee-Cee's eyebrows arched.

Val walked in. "True. We have a strong aversion to anything that smacks of us acting like a cult. But LaShaun offers a valid argument. Naturally we'd need to craft guidelines."

"Politics and bureaucracy. Here I thought TEA would be different." LaShaun glanced at the two women.

Val smiled. "Don't be too disillusioned. Decisions are made fast and effectively. Not to mention members can and often do take independent action. The TEA doesn't stop us."

"Which is why Cee-Cee didn't mind saying she'd help me even if leadership followed Desmond's recommendation," LaShaun lifted an eyebrow at her. "I feel better knowing that."

"The TEA will even step in to help if things go sideways. Our biggest advantage is the lack of internal conflict throughout our hundred-plus-year history," Val said.

Cee-Cee glanced at Val. "Until the last ten years."

"Leadership has handled it well so far," Val said. She checked the time on her wristwatch. "Okay, we're going in at twilight. It's almost four o'clock now. Sunset will be at about six fifty-five."

⚜

"The drive to the main compound will take an hour. We start now, set up, and move." Cee-Cee packed gear into the Range Rover as she talked.

"Thank you all for being on my side," LaShaun said. She swallowed hard as Ernesto, Abril, and Jennifer strode in. She turned to Cee-Cee and hugged.

"Hey, soon as I hear kids are missing and in danger, I'm in, no discussion necessary," Cee-Cee replied with intensity. "I know what being held captive feels like. A gang killed my family and kept me for five years. The TEA rescued me when I was fourteen."

"You fought your way out. TEA members simply showed up following your psychic breadcrumbs." Abril walked by and gave Cee-Cee a collegial slap on the back.

"Y'all gotta tell me that story one day," LaShaun replied.

"Deal. Now time to saddle up," Val said.

"We'll be right behind you." Ernesto jerked a thumb toward the wide opening of the warehouse. A dark tan Hummer was parked outside.

"TEA foray teams always take back-up vehicles, even if there are only a few of us," Cee-Cee explained. She got behind the wheel of the Range Rover."

Jennifer waved. "I'm riding with Ernesto and Abril. See you guys in a bit."

The team exchanged information and last minute instructions. LaShaun was about to join

⚜

Cee-Cee and Val in the SUV when a steel gray Ford F-10 truck pulled up. The word Policia stood out in bold black letters on the hood. All four doors opened at once. Chase exited one from the rear behind the driver's side.

"Your husband gonna be a problem?" Val said as both she and Cee-Cee hopped to the concrete floor from the SUV.

"How did you... Right, the TEA has a full file on me along with photographs. You folks are starting to worry me," LaShaun mumbled. She faced Chase, who strode toward her. His expression behind the dark sunglasses was blank.

"Nope. My ability is to read thoughts and emotions," Val replied matter-of-factly. "This guy is pissed. He knows you didn't tell him everything. I recommend diplomacy sprinkled with a lot of 'I'm sorry, babe'."

"Humph." LaShaun didn't feel apologetic in the least and allowed her face to show it.

"I don't need to ask how you knew to come here, LaShaun." Chase's jaw worked as he tried to tamp down his fiery temper. He glanced around at the team members who observed. "This your squad? Looks like they're ready to defend you."

"I couldn't stay at home fretting while the big strong man took care of things. And do they need to defend me?" LaShaun glanced past him at the three Mexican police officers standing yards away.

⚜

"Don't pick a fight with me over this. We don't have time to waste," Chase shot back.

"Agreed. So y'all follow whatever legal procedures you have planned, and we'll be about our business." LaShaun turned to walk away, but his strong hand on her arm stopped her. When LaShaun spun to face Chase again, he let go.

He stepped close to her, his face only a couple of inches away. "We agreed to always be a team, to trust each other. This, this is against our promise."

"Trust. Nice word coming from the man who practically accused me of being the root of all evil. Sorry if I wrecked your white picket fence dream life. How long have you thought marrying me and having Ellie was a huge mistake, Chase?" Despite her efforts, LaShaun's voice broke.

The color drained from his face. Chase yanked the sunglasses from his face. The pain in his dark Cajun eyes struck LaShaun like a blow. She'd aimed to hurt him and now regretted it. But the question had hovered over them for weeks. LaShaun didn't feel like empathizing with the strain on his relationship with his mother. Let him work it out. Yet the longer she gazed at the man she'd married, the more she wanted to feel his arms around her. Miss Rose's wisdom rang in her mind. They needed to pull together. Maybe this test meant they couldn't.

"You and Ellie are my life. I'm not going to go through this world without either of you. My mother knows it." Chase breathed hard. When LaShaun didn't reply, he put the sunglasses back on. "We have a solid lead on where the children might be held. This local gang is vicious. They torture and decapitate anybody who crosses them. They traffic humans and drugs."

"El Duro, we know," LaShaun said.

"Your team looks like they graduated from high school last month."

"Yeah? Well looks can be deceiving." LaShaun glanced over her shoulder and at Chase again.

"Even the Mexican Federal Police won't go up against them at night. Look, they'll kill the kids if you guys go in blazing. They've done it before. Please, please, let us deal with it our way." Chase grabbed both of LaShaun's hands.

LaShaun flinched at the impact of his words. "You mentioned trust and being a team. Listen to me."

Ernesto stepped forward. "I don't think—"

"El Duro is a tool being used by the parent organization of Juridicus. You understand what I'm saying? You and the Mexican police will be facing more than guns. That clothing company is a front but not for the gang. The children taken all have powerful psychic ability." LaShaun spoke fast, ignoring the protests of the TEA team.

"They're going to make what we try to do even tougher, LaShaun," Abril blurted out.

❧

LaShaun looked at them. "No, Chase is right. We'll all do better if we combine efforts."

"One reason the local police in particular have left these guys alone is because of rumors about El Duro using witchcraft. Not that they'll admit it, but that's part of the reason they don't want to face these guys at night." Chase looked at them all in turn. "I'll tell them I want to spend some time with my wife."

"Let's move," Jennifer put in firmly, gazing at Ernesto for direction.

"Okay, if that's the only way to keep you guys from blocking us," Ernesto said.

"Let's make it even more believable," Chase said. He pulled LaShaun to him and kissed her.

Her objection was cut off when his mouth covered hers. Chase pressed hard until their bodies fused by the heat of his passion. Desire, love, and devotion flowed from him into LaShaun. When he pulled away, she gasped.

"Wow," Cee-Cee whispered.

"Time to roll out," Val cut in, her voice steady and practical.

Chase jogged over to the waiting Mexican police officers. After a short exchange, they seemed more than happy to accept his explanation. Two of them grinned and slapped him on the back. The officers gave LaShaun a friendly wave goodbye. Then they got into the truck and drove off.

Minutes later, Chase sat beside LaShaun in the rear seat of the Range Rover. She didn't pull away when he folded his large hand over

⚜

hers. Cee-Cee and Val discussed the terrain and other details without look back at or talking to them—their attempt to give them some measure of privacy.

"We still have to work out..." LaShaun gazed at him as her voice trailed away.

"I know, but right now we're team Broussard slash Rousselle, right?" Chase squeezed her hand.

LaShaun wrapped her arms around his neck. Pulling him close, she murmured, "Right."

"If I may interrupt the make-out session," Cee-Cee said with a smirk at them. "Ahem, I have news to report."

"Go," LaShaun replied as she and Chase broke apart.

"So we finally have a translation of the two messages left at the crime scenes in Louisiana. Just in via email from a Dr. Bakir who works in our Los Angeles group. They are written in the Jairo language, created by a 12th century philosopher who claimed he had visions from angels. Some dude named Randolphus Gywnek. He formed a cult based on these so-called divine visions that asserted that Satan had good cause to rebel, and the Creator is the true villain." Cee-Cee read from the android tablet in her lap.

"Bunch of bullshit," Val said flatly.

"The translation?" LaShaun leaned forward.

"So the first one says, 'Though they be young, yet they are wise beyond their years.

❧

Power flows from them. Rejoice at their join-ing." Cee-Cee frowned. "What?"

"Joining means wills and souls have com-mitted to the demonic mission to win the war between good and evil," Val explained.

"Left at the house of one of the kidnapped kids, the case that we're on," LaShaun replied. "Written in Bat's Blood Ink as part of the ritual to make the children part of Legion. And the other message?"

"So it is written, weaklings falter. The chaff shall be sloughed away from the wheat. That which serves not is destroyed." Cee-Cee contin-ued to scroll through more of the email.

"Murder scene," Val said, her voice grim.

"Yeah, how did you know?" Chase grabbed his vibrating cell phone.

"Similar inscriptions, usually on a wall or the floor, have been found with victims of Le-gion. Mostly in Europe. A few in North Africa. Written in other languages though. This Jairo is a new one to me." Val turned down a dirt road. "Okay, gonna be a bumpy ride for a bit."

"We're taking a back route. Our intel team says El Duro has informants watching the main drag that leads to the big compound. Plus, we'll pass one of their mini-outposts along the way." Cee-Cee checked the GPS of the Range Rover as she talked. The image changed to a photo.

"Image from one of our drones." Val nodded to the screen set into the Ranger Rover's dash-board.

⚜

"Damn, you people don't play. The local police could use some of this tech." Chase studied the images.

"Unfortunately, the cartel employ cops as well. Easier for us to operate behind a gray curtain than try to keep up with who's who," Val said. The woman couldn't have been over thirty, yet she sounded like a seasoned warrior.

Chase nodded. "Something American law enforcement takes into account, too. But I have to say the men and women I met seem dedicated. Of course the black magic angle doesn't thrill them."

"I'm not saying we've confirmed they're corrupt, but our team decided not to take the chance," Val said.

"We'll clear the outpost first. Ernesto and the others are approaching from the north. We'll meet up with them there. Maybe we'll get lucky and find the children there," Cee-Cee said.

"Not luck. Prayer," LaShaun said. She closed her eyes and asked for strength, wisdom, and guidance straight to Ellie.

⚜

Chapter 13

Ernesto, Jennifer, and Abril stood waiting for them outside a house along a neat but unpaved road. Several other houses were scattered across the mostly flat landscape. Congregación Chivos, according to the team, was a small residential settlement. The employee working on the inside for the TEA lived there with her family. But they didn't go to her house. Instead they met at the home of a friend a mile away from where she lived.

"Mariela isn't here. We can't afford to blow her cover, too risky. Some of her co-workers might mention she had visitors," Ernesto explained. "Small town conversation could get her killed."

Chase scanned the neighborhood. "Isn't that true for the guy who lives here?"

"Everyone knows Reynaldo is in prison. His house is always full of squatters, most of them his buddies. The neighbors are used to it and prefer not to notice who comes and goes," Abril replied.

She unlocked the door and led the way inside. Cee-Cee stayed outside. She leaned against the Range Rover drinking a bottle of soda. The others crowded into the compact living room. Sparsely furnished, the interior still managed to look cozy and lived in. Ernesto went to the kitchen and took a cold bottle of cola from the fridge. Val took out her iPhone and a compact projector. She moved with efficiency.

"And you trust Reynaldo because…" Chase raised an eyebrow.

"Rey is a member of our team. He grew up around here, had his own gang at one point. We enlisted him about six years ago. Actually he found us," Ernesto said. He leaned against the counter.

"But he's in prison." Chase frowned at them.

"Yeah, umm, we set up a crime for him to commit. His 'victim' was another TEA operative. That's all I can say." Ernesto swallowed more soda. He looked back at Chase with a closed expression.

"I feel like I'm surrounded by members of the US Army Special Forces. Operating in the black, infiltration, the works." Chase crossed his arms.

⚜

"Sorry, can't share details. That's how it is. Bother you?" Ernesto wore an impassive expression.

"I'm feeling much better about y'all the more I see and hear," Chase said with a curt nod. "What we got?"

Val tapped her phone and the display was projected onto a blank wall. "Here's the outpost. Now this is supposed to be a community center with bingo night, dances, and other services. It's also a safe haven for orphaned street kids. Their cover for having living quarters. Notice three guards."

"Humph, lots of muscle to guard the bingo kitty," Jennifer said.

Chase walked to the wall and pointed to a figure. "And they're armed. Those look like rifles they're carrying. I doubt they're alone, especially if the kids are on site and as valuable to them as we think."

"We're prepared." Jennifer opened a case she'd brought in with her. She handed out automatic pistols. "But using firepower is a last resort. Let's get set up."

Abril, Ernesto, and Jennifer placed a long thin black box with other items on the table. Val joined them at the table. Ernesto plugged a cable into a USB port on the device and then into a wall socket. A string of blue and green lights blinked on.

Cee-Cee came in and shut the door gently. "I set up the cameras. Chase, we need you to watch for anyone."

❧

"Okay." He accepted her tablet computer. A gray image showed the area around the house.

"We're going to attempt a connection." Jennifer nodded to LaShaun as she reached out a hand. The other team members joined hands as well.

LaShaun joined the others around the table. "Good."

Chase glanced up from the tablet. "What?"

"I've heard about this, but never been part of one. A psychic circle combines our paranormal energies to increase our reach. The children might be able to feel us and respond." LaShaun felt a glimmer of hope that they weren't just stumbling in the dark.

"LaShaun's emotional bond with your little girl will help. And if Ellie Broussard is as strong as the reports indicate..." Val whistled.

"When this is over, we will talk about you folks keeping files on my family," Chase rumbled.

"The intel TEA gathered got us close," Cee-Cee replied with a crooked smile. "Don't knock it."

"Humph." Chase went back to studying the video display.

Everyone grew silent. All closed their eyes at some point. A charged atmosphere filled the room. LaShaun got the impression that the team members drew each breath in sync. Her anxiety grew in the void of any kind of psychic vibrations coming from outside their circle. Then Jennifer let go of Cee-Cee and Val's

❖

hands. She pressed palms to the side of her head. Dropping to her knees, Jennifer uttered a muted cry of distress. Then LaShaun heard a voice... Ellie's voice... and another child's as well.

"Take her hands again," Abril whispered. "Now. Don't break the circle."

Cee-Cee helped Jennifer to her feet. "Come on. It's okay, chica. We got you."

"I hear voices. I..." LaShaun broke off when Ellie called out to her, with another child speaking rapidly. "I can't make out what they're saying.

"Center yourself, LaShaun. Reach out with your thoughts. Try to get details, maybe one of the older kids can answer."

"Right, right."

LaShaun squeezed her eyes closed tightly as if that might help. She mentally repeated reassurances to Ellie and anyone else who could hear. She let images of Chase and Beau form, things Ellie would recognize.

"They're close. At the outpost," Jennifer blurted out suddenly. Her knees buckled again, but Cee-Cee and Val supported her. "I can see Jonah. He's in a room with the boys. The girls are in a separate room. Damn it, he cut me off."

"Enough. Jennifer can't take much more. Besides, we've got what we need." Ernesto freed both his hands. He went to the device on the table.

"What the hell just happened?" Chase whispered to LaShaun.

❖

"A group of psychics just confirmed that the children are close by. Meaning they're—"

"At Legion's outpost about ten minutes from here. Got that. But how?" Chase glanced at the rest of the team members.

"There's a body of science behind the whole phenomena of psychic abilities. One day, under less urgent circumstances, we might explain it. Right now, let's go." Ernesto packed away the device on the table. He disappeared to another part of the house. He came back checking his Baretta. "Everybody ready?"

"Hell yes. Let's get our daughter," Chase said to LaShaun.

The two SUVs drove over paved roads. They arrived at their target in just over fifteen minutes. Even though Chase chafed against their progress, he agreed that speeding would likely attract unwanted attention.

"So that box on the table amps up super-natural energy or something?" Chase glanced around at the night time landscape as he talked.

LaShaun placed a hand on his thigh. She could feel the rush of adrenaline coursing through him. His entire body strummed with pent up force. She knew asking questions helped him steady his nerves. Chase put his hand on hers, but kept staring through the vehicle window.

"Nah, that was a Wi-Fi hotspot. TEA got updates, and they monitored the results of our circle," Cee-Cee replied. She put her tablet in the center console and locked it. "Ernesto plugged it in only to conserve the battery life."

"Praise the Creator," Val breathed. She pointed to a lively bar with cars parked around it. "Perfect cover."

"Yeah. The Range Rover won't stick out. Serious party going down. Can we hope the guards neglect their duties to join the fun?" Cee-Cee looked at the crowd standing outside a dilapidated looking juke joint. Booming music from inside leaked out into the night.

"Not likely," Val said with a grunt. "Split up once we get out. LaShaun and Chase, look like a couple enjoying a night out. Cee-Cee, we'll fade into the shadows fast. On the south side of the club is the street that leads to our site. Ernesto just messaged me that it's all clear. Looks like a lot of people are celebrating."

Without any more conversation, they all got out of the Range Rover and started walking toward the night club. Chase looped an arm around LaShaun's waist. He pretended to nuzzle her neck, his hands roaming over her backside.

"Let's go around the side like we want to make out," he whispered.

"Good idea." LaShaun walked beside him. She forced a casual pace even though she wanted to rush the community center.

They moved fast before anyone could notice they weren't local. A lack of outdoor lighting helped. Chase pretended to pin LaShaun against the wall and kiss her in case anyone

⚜

happened by. After a few seconds, they moved on. About six minutes of walking, keeping to the shadows, brought them within twenty yards of the long building owned by Legion. LaShaun gasped as she rubbed her arms.

Chase stopped. He pulled her against his side. "You okay?"

"Yeah. I've never been so happy to feel those tingly needles before. She's close, Chase." LaShaun forced her breathing to slow down. "We can't charge in though. Keep to the plan."

"I..."

Chase broke off when a shadow moved to their left. He took out his pistol. LaShaun slipped her own gun from the inside pocket of her vest. Both exhaled when a familiar voice whispered.

Ernesto, flat against the wall of a vacant shack, held up both palms. "I took out two of the guards. They'll be unconscious for a couple of hours at least."

"By yourself? Damn." Chase glanced around, checking their perimeter.

"Top of my class in hand to hand combat. Plus, my handy-dandy modified stun gun did most of the work." Ernesto cupped his hand around his smartphone as he talked. "Jennifer took care of the last guard. But there's probably at least one adult inside. Okay, they're in."

LaShaun followed, and Chase brought up the rear as they walked to the front entrance. The name of the community center, Los Brazo Abiertos, was painted in orange and green letters spread across one wall. Wide double doors served as the entrance. One stood slightly open. The three of them slipped in. Jennifer and Abril stood speaking rapid Spanish to two terrified women. A short older woman's head bobbed frantically as she babbled.

"That one is claiming they don't know anything about Legion or kidnappings," Ernesto said. Loud voices cut off his next sentence.

"Children," LaShaun said.

She sprinted away from them in the direction of the sound. A long hallway stretched with two doorways on either side. She went through one. A tall gangly teenage boy confronted her. LaShaun tussled with him.

"Calm down. We're here to rescue you and the other children," LaShaun panted. He almost matched her for strength, but she had the advantage of experience. She twisted his left arm behind his back.

"Get the hell off me." The boy grunted and swung at her head with his right hand. He went still when LaShaun pressed the stun gun into his side.

"Don't make me use this. Where are the girls?" LaShaun whispered. She pulled him out into the hallway, worried that more boys might surround them.

"The other dorm. Should've done your homework," the boy snapped.

"Come on." LaShaun wrestled with the urge to let him go and race through the rest of the building to find Ellie.

"Like I have a damn choice. You do know our guardians will kick your ass for this, right?"

"Just walk, son." LaShaun's heart hammered at the sound of girls talking fast, some in Spanish.

Moments later she pulled him along as more children filled the hallway. Val, Cee-Cee, and Jennifer herded the sleepy brood to the large common area. Ernesto and Abril continued to pepper the two women with questions. Cee-Cee spoke Spanish to calm some of the children.

"I count seventeen, including the tall one you've got," Val said.

LaShaun let him go and waded in among the smaller children. "Oh God, I don't see Ellie. All this way and I haven't found her."

"LaShaun..."

She spun around and grabbed the teen. "Did they take her somewhere? She's only three years old. Tell me!" LaShaun shook him hard.

"Yo no hablo Inglés señora." He smirked back at her.

"Don't play with me, kid." LaShaun dug her fingers into his flesh.

He winced, but gave a scornful snort. "Some rescuers alright. Yanks us out of bed, scare little kids half to death, and threaten us. Yeah, I feel so much safer now."

Cee-Cee stepped beside LaShaun. She spoke close to her ear. "We'll figure it out. C'mon now."

❧

"Wait a minute." Abril waved at them. Then she continued speaking gently to a little girl of about ten. "LaShaun, this way."

"We've got this. Go," Ernesto said, and stood in front of the teen who looked like the oldest of the group. He gazed at him with a taut expression. The boy studied the brawny man and swallowed hard.

LaShaun followed Abril down the hallway they'd just exited. "I thought you cleared the rooms. Let's not waste time. If there's another location I want to—"

"The little girl says that a kid named Grace took a baby and hid in a closet," Abril replied over her shoulder. "You take that end of the room. I'll check to see if they went out a back door."

LaShaun sprinted into the girls' room. She flipped a switch. Harsh white fluorescent lighting blinked on. She didn't see a closet, only the unbroken bland light green painted cinder block walls around her. A sob escaped before LaShaun could stop it. Hysteria flooded her entire body until she shook. She'd put a world of hope into the search. The thought of failure dropped despair on her like a bomb.

"Ellie, it's mama. Answer me, baby. It's okay. I don't see a closet," LaShaun murmured as she turned in a circle. "I don't see…"

Then she noticed handles in the wall. A set of floor to ceiling built-in closets the same shade of green sat to her left. The structures blended in perfectly. Even the handles had been painted. LaShaun held her breath and walked slowly to the doors.

"You're safe. No one is going to hurt you. Just come out."

When she pulled open a door, her heart felt as if it had exploded. A twelve-year-old girl cradled Ellie protectively in her arms. She stared at LaShaun wide-eyed.

"No, they'll punish me if I let her go," the child whimpered. She shrank back as if trying to push through the solid surface to escape.

Ellie, by contrast, didn't seem scared at first. Her eyes were squeezed shut. When she opened them and looked at LaShaun, Ellie started to wail, reaching for her. LaShaun took her when the girl released her hold on Ellie. She kissed the mass of brown curls on the top of Ellie's head that were so like Chase's. A single tear of joyous relief slipped down one cheek.

"I'm Ellie's mama. See? She knows me."

Chase entered the room and rushed to them. He wrapped them both in a tight hug, his breathing ragged. The girl pushed farther back into the closet. She clawed the masonry as though trying to dig a way out. When LaShaun glanced at her, her blonde pigtails bounced as she swung her head from side to side. Her small lips mouthing the word "No" repeatedly in English and Spanish.

Jennifer entered the room and took over. "You two take a minute to soothe the baby and your own nerves. I'll talk to her. Honey, it's okay."

⚜

Chase and LaShaun continued murmuring words of love and comfort to Ellie. They took turns holding her, both planting kisses on her smooth cheeks. After a time, Ellie gave a big yawn and rested her head on her daddy's chest. They went to the common room again. When the women saw them with Ellie, both looked even more terrified. The taller woman wrung her hands, speaking so fast even Abril appeared baffled. Her companion talked as well. She appeared to be pleading with Ernesto. LaShaun walked over to them.

"What do we know so far?" LaShaun gave the shorter woman a stony glance, which caused her to shut up.

Ernesto heaved a long-suffering sigh. "Between the denials and calling on God to save them, not much. These two were hired to look after the children. Val and Cee-Cee have missing kids from our database. The rest are local orphans or staying here because their parents are going through a tough time supporting them."

"They masked their agenda with a real center that helps local kids and families. Devious, but effective." LaShaun squinted at the women. "So it's possible these ladies are simply employees who don't know anything."

Ernesto put a hand on one hip. "Or they're putting on a masterful act of innocence. We've got ways of finding out which is true."

Both women's eyes got big. The taller one blurted out, "Señor, that's all I know. I swear.

❖

Consuela is the supervisor. Ask her what the leader told her."

The short woman shook a fist at her and let loose with a flood of angry Spanish. Ernesto blocked her from slapping the woman who'd tossed her under the bus. "Cortalo!"

Val marched over to the short woman, named Lupe, and pulled her to the side. "The quicker you answer my questions the easier things will go for you."

"Take the children to the dorm rooms. We can pack a few things for each, but move fast." Cee-Cee nodded to Abril and Jennifer.

"Okay, here's the plan. We return kids who have families around here. The others will stay with LaShaun and her little girl," Jennifer replied. "I suggest... Hey, where the hell is she going?"

The taller woman sprinted for the exit. She slammed against the door full force, but it didn't budge. She beat the solid surface in vain. "Let me out. Let me out."

"Good thinking, locking the door," Ernesto said with a smile. He went over to the agitated woman. He dragged her from the door, and then tried to open it. "Who left?"

LaShaun glanced around the room. "We're all in here."

Ernesto turned to face them with a frown. "Then how..."

"Welcome to Mexico my friends." A female voice boomed.

❧

Chase handed Ellie to LaShaun. He glanced around, and then pointed to a speaker attached near the ceiling in a corner. "There."

"We don't often get visitors, so we hope you've enjoyed your stay so far. Usually Legion doesn't like people dropping in, but in your case we're thrilled. Thank you for being so predictable." The woman's cheerful tone held an edge of menace. "You'll be unpleasantly surprised to know we were expecting you. What a wonderful bonus to have the daughter and the mother of such a powerful lineage join us."

Val pushed away the whimpering woman she'd been about to interrogate. "Do you see cameras?"

"Only in the dorms," the tall woman said between hiccupping sobs, "to make sure the children didn't get up to mischief."

"Yeah, silly stuff like trying to escape their captors," Cee-Cee snarled and took a step toward her.

"Calm down. What about microphones," Ernesto whispered. He moved around the large open area as he spoke.

"Yes, Ernesto," the voice answered, "at the desk, though ripping it out won't help you. May I direct your attention to the air vents, please." Her tone, like a tour guide enjoying her job, grated. "Soon you'll all take a nap. Sadly, we don't have much use for the rest of you. The two ladies who have Third Sight will be coming with us. The more, um, problematic adults must be disposed of, but only after we get the information we want naturally."

"You're going to harm a group of innocent children? You shouldn't wonder why we intend to eradicate you like the vermin you are," Val shouted.

"Legion is true to the right world order fools," the woman shot back, the playfulness gone. "I suggest you arrange yourselves in a comfortable position on the floor, or even a bed. That way you won't get hurt when you hit the concrete, which will happen in about five minutes. Good night to all, goodbye to some." There was a click, and the voice stopped.

"Look." the teenager, Jonah, pointed to one of the two vents set in the wall. A blue-gray mist curled from the opening. "They've used it before."

"Cee-Cee, you checked on a rear door," LaShaun said.

"Yeah, and it's locked, got a chain and pad-lock through the push bar handle," Cee-Cee replied.

Chase spun around to face the two Spanish women. "Tools, and make it quick. Sounds like your employers will get rid of you, too."

"Uh, uh. There's the locked cabinet with a hammer, a-and some other things." The taller woman fumbled with a set of keys. She cried out when Val strode over and yanked them from her hands.

"Which one?" Val went to the metal cabinet in a corner of the room. "This one?"

❖

"No, no, the brass one with a number marked on it," the shorter woman blurted out. "Hurry, hurry. I don't want to die here. My children need me."

"Like anybody cares," Jonah shot back and laughed. Then he turned to five of the children. "We're leaving. Marissa, you know what to do."

A petite brunette gazed back at him, nodded, and closed her eyes. "I know."

"What are they doing?" Chase said, glancing at LaShaun.

"I have no idea." LaShaun held Ellie tight as the toddler squirmed.

"Mama, no." Ellie pressed her chubby fists against LaShaun's chest to get free.

"You're safe, baby. Mama and daddy…"

"No, no."

Suddenly LaShaun felt dizzy. She coughed as the air seemed to thicken around her. "The mist is starting to get to me."

Jennifer rushed around handing something to everyone one. "Cover your mouth and nose, everyone. Help the younger ones, kids. Once we get the back door open, we'll crawl out. That drug or whatever will fill the place from the top down."

"Sure, scurry around breathing hard like trapped mice. Your efforts will only help speed up the effects. Best reality TV ever." Laughter floated from the speaker.

"Hold onto her, LaShaun," Chase shouted. He pulled out the Baretta and spun in a circle looking for an enemy.

⚜

"You can't shoot, the children." LaShaun fought to keep her eyes open as Jennifer tied part of a torn pillow case around her face.

"Go help Ernesto and Cee-Cee get that damn door open." Jennifer jerked a thumb in the direction of the rear ext. "You two, help us line up the kids or I'll shoot you myself right here."

"Let go, mama." Ellie, a determined frown on her face, stared at LaShaun.

"Don't..."

LaShaun's voice faded, then she blinked hard in the effort stay conscious. Her legs buckled as if the bones had turned to liquid. Then she looked at Ellie. Determination and intention glowed in Ellie's gaze. The realization that Ellie had a purpose stunned her more than the effects of the drug. When LaShaun sank to her knees, Ellie easily scrambled free of her weakened hold. She joined the now seven children who stood in a circle holding hands. They quickly made room for Ellie. Their voices joined together, the words melting into a continuous hum that seemed to expand like an invisible balloon until it filled the room. Through a haze, LaShaun heard loud cracks she thought might be gunfire.

"Don't shoot, the children," she gasped.

Her muffled voice came out as a raspy sound drowned out by the hum, terrified screams, and more popping noises. LaShaun had the sensation of a great weight holding her down. The entire scene around her played out

⚜

like a movie set in slow motion. Smoke coiled above. Not smoke. No smell of burning. LaShaun fought to reason through the events unfolding around her. She spotted Ellie standing what looked like so far away. She tried to reach for her, but her arms felt resistance.

"Come to me, Ellie. Please, you don't understand…" LaShaun swallowed hard.

Images flashed in the room. Glyphs, pictures of an ocean, a lush garden filled the room and then vanished. People dressed in flowing garments appeared like old photographs, yet some moved. These faded, replaced by scenes of brick huts, caves, and tall stone jars.

"Stop from happening." LaShaun's throat hurt from the attempt to speak louder.

"Concentrate," a male voice rang out.

Then more shots, rapid popping around. LaShaun's heart hammered with fear for Ellie and the other children. Her mind fought to process all of the sensory input. Whatever Legion had pumped into the room blunted her paranormal abilities. LaShaun sobbed as she once more tried to control something, anything, and failed. Her mother's face floated above her as she collapsed onto her back to the floor.

"Don't resist, cher. Fighting what will happen next is making Ellie's task harder. Give in and she'll reach you. Yes, that's it. Let her flow into your being."

Francine's voice continued, and then combined eerily with her grandmother's deeper contralto voice. Then both faded into whispers,

⚜

then they transformed into what sounded like wind rustling through leaves. Ellie played in the backyard with Beau leaping around her, both so happy. Sunshine painted the scene yellow, then it melted to dusk. LaShaun tried to call out to them to come into the house. Something malevolent crept in with the dark. Then nothing.

Bright white assaulted her closed eyelids. On reflex, LaShaun opened her eyes. Faces above hers. She struggled to recognize them but couldn't. The pure white lights flashed overhead. She was moving. But how?

"No visible bruising or wounds. We're taking her up to radiology for scans and x-rays to rule out internal injuries," a male voice said briskly.

"Wha..." LaShaun's lips felt stiff as she tried to ask a question. Then she lost the thread of what she was about to say. Her eyes closed against the glare against her will.

"Sure, got it." A woman said. Then she continued lower. "Let's tell her about Chase when she's stable. Not now."

⚜

Chapter 14

She woke up and sat straight in the bed. Then winced at the pain that shot through her neck and shoulders. LaShaun, at first, thought she had straps around her body. Voices filtered through the haze that filled her brain. Hands pushed her gently back. She settled on two pillows behind her. Then she felt woozy and gasped from the nausea that twisted her stomach.

"Take it easy. You took some hits back there," Cee-Cee said.

"Yeah, no sudden moves," Val added.

Recognition of their voices helped center LaShaun. She shivered as another set of hands extended something to her. A small tablet in foil. She glanced up to see a nurse holding the medicine in one hand and a small cup in the other.

"Señora, you take. For the sickness in your tummy. Sí? It melts. Very easy. You'll feel better." The nurse smiled at Cee-Cee and Val, who stood aside for her. Then she waited patiently as LaShaun followed her instructions.

"Thanks," LaShaun managed to get out. A cool mint flavor coated her tongue as the tablet dissolved. The nurse bustled out, a satisfied look on her face, and LaShaun looked at Cee-Cee first and then Val. "Where am I? What happened? Where's Chase?"

"Slow down," Val replied in a calm voice. She smoothed the hospital bed linens.

LaShaun strained forward, ready to leap from the bed, get dressed, and get her own answers. "You're stalling for time. Something horrible has happened to my family. Tell me."

Val pushed LaShaun back and held her in the bed. "Limping around in a hospital gown won't help. Chase is here, he took a bullet."

"Oh my God. Ellie..." LaShaun panted as tears slid down her face.

"Listen," Val said firmly, her strong hands still keeping LaShaun in place. "He was shot in the shoulder. The bullet missed bone, so it's a flesh would. He was in surgery and they got it out. He's going to recover."

"Where is 'here'?" LaShaun broke in.

"Hospital San Charbel in Matamoros. Excellent medical care," Cee-Cee added with a nod. When tears slipped down LaShaun's

❖

cheeks, she cleared her throat. "Not that we wanted to sample the services of course."

LaShaun worked against the rising terror as she tried to form the most frightening question. She swallowed hard, and then forced out the words. "And Ellie?"

Cee-Cee exchanged a quick glace with Val. "Gone. At some point the doors opened, Legion members stormed us. We were outnumbered, drugged." She rubbed her forehead.

"The drug didn't take affect quite as they'd expected. Or maybe getting the back door open helped vent some of it," Val added.

"One of the caretakers made it to a window and opened it. I think that increased cross flow." Cee-Cee nodded.

"Then why couldn't we fight back? We should have stopped them from taking Ellie." LaShaun glared at them both through tears of outrage. Her voice rose until she was shouting. "The TEA should have anticipated we'd walk into a trap. Why didn't they? And don't give me that bullshit about strategy!"

A short woman came in wearing a white lab coat. "I'm Dr. Mendoza, and I think this visit is a bit too much for my patient. You should go now, please."

"Listen, doctor, we'll be careful," Cee-Cee began, but stopped short when Dr. Mendoza waved a hand at her.

"I don't think so," Dr. Mendoza said. She frowned at them all.

⚜

LaShaun inhaled and exhaled slowly to get control. "Wait, wait. I'm okay."

Dr. Mendoza took the clipboard in a file holder attached to the wall near LaShaun's bed. "Señora Broussard, really what you need is rest. I'll have the nurse bring you something so you can relax, get some sleep."

"No!" LaShaun blurted out with such force, Dr. Mendoza glanced at her sharply. "I mean, no more drugs. I need to find out what is happening to my husband and about efforts to find my child. Please. I don't want to be knocked out while they're both in danger, not knowing how my family is doing."

The doctor made a brief note on the chart and replaced it. "I realize these are extraordinary circumstances. Follow my nurse's instructions and stay in bed until I say otherwise."

"Yes. Thank you," LaShaun replied.

"And you," Dr. Mendoza looked at Val and Cee-Cee, "keep disturbances to a minimum. I want to be informed if there are developments."

"Got it," Val said promptly.

"I'll check on you later this evening." Dr. Mendoza smiled at LaShaun and left.

"By 'developments' she means if you have to break bad news that will upset me."

"We don't expect more bad news, LaShaun. Well, worse news I mean," Cee-Cee added when LaShaun sniffed.

"Really poor job of encouraging her, Cee-Cee," Val said dryly. Then she took LaShaun's right hand, cupping it in both hers. "We know

Legion values Ellie. In fact, it appears that she's the focal point of their entire operation."

"Which means they won't hurt her. Everything we found at the building where they kept the kids indicates they took good care of them. The two women confirm that the children were treated well. The little girl that hid with Ellie really seems to have bonded with her," Cee-Cee said.

"Great. TEA is doing a fabulous job of getting facts after a gigantic screw-up." LaShaun shook her hands free from Val's attempt to console her.

"Hey, that's not quite fair to us," Val began.

"She's right," Frank Miles cut in before Val could continue. "We should have had a back-up team, maybe even two, in place. Legion keeps getting the upper hand on us. Desmond is driving home his I-told-you-so point every chance he gets."

"That guy spends his days kissing butt and taking credit for the work of his staff," Val replied and gave a snort. "Tell Secretary General Desmond to zip it unless he's got something useful to contribute."

"I don't give a damn about your bullshit politics, okay? All I want to hear is the next move to find my child," LaShaun shot back. Her heated scowl silenced them. "And it better be one freaking good plan. Otherwise, I'll tell you all to go to hell and do it myself."

"Look, everybody get some chill," Cee-Cee said. "LaShaun, we made the best decision we possibly could based on the facts we had and the possible consequences of waiting. It would have taken days to get more boots on the ground."

"I saw plenty of people at your place," LaShaun shot back.

"They're computer geeks and communications specialists. They know how to handle tools and build programs, not weapons. None of them have field training or experience," Cee-Cee countered.

"We also know Legion has at least one private plane here. They could have even taken the kids out of Mexico. The longer we delayed, the greater the chances Legion would have known we were coming," Val said.

"So have they taken them out of the country?" LaShaun looked at Val.

"Not by air. The plane hasn't left their hangar at the airport. We're monitoring it, and the airwaves. Not that they would file a flight plan, or even have to," Val replied. '

"We still might have an edge. Legion doesn't know the extent of our resources. After last night, they think we can't match their set up," Cee-Cee said.

"They're not far wrong," LaShaun snapped back. Then she closed her eyes as she rubbed her forehead. "Sorry, it's just…"

"Forget it. You're showing restraint. If my kid was missing, I'd be ripping everybody within the sound of my voice to pieces." Cee-Cee sighed.

⚜

"For real," Val said and gave LaShaun a look of sympathy, "we should apologize for not coming through for you guys."

Jennifer came in holding a floral arrangement. She set them down on the table. "Morning everyone. Hope you're feeling better, LaShaun."

LaShaun accepted a brief hug. "At least I'm not hurt so bad I can't go after the bastards."

"Better not let Dr. Mendoza hear you. She'll slip some strong meds in your food to keep you here," Cee-Cee quipped.

"So I've got intriguing info. We picked up some chatter on the Deep Web. Seems Legion doesn't know where the kids have gone," Jennifer said. She glanced around the room with a wide grin. "They don't have them."

"What the hell?" Cee-Cee's mouth fell open.

"I don't get it. Legion attacked the community center, shot it full of a drug fog, and then..." LaShaun glanced at Val and Cee-Cee in turn.

"We all blacked out for short periods. The sequence of what happened, how, and when is mixed up for all of us. We met first thing today to piece together what we remember, but there are gaps," Val said.

"Yeah, nothing like a meeting at five in the morning after a night of getting your butt kicked and handed to you," Cee-Cee muttered. She shrugged when Val shot her a heated look. "The coffee and donuts tasted good though."

⚜

"We haven't earned sleeping late, not even close," Val cracked back at her. "Jennifer, what else?"

"So according to sources, Legion is sort of in high alert mode. They aren't sure that we didn't take the kids." Jennifer grinned.

"Good, this is good," Frank put in. He paced in a small circle as he talked. "Let's take steps to keep them off balance. We won't say we have the kids. In fact, we shouldn't say anything. Let our 'silence' on the Dark Web imply we have the upper hand. Buy time while we find out where they are now."

"Sounds great, but where do we start?" Cee-Cee frowned. She raked fingers through her short boyish haircut. "We have no suspects. With no suspects, we can't check out possible hang-outs or known associates."

"We can search houses nearby, including a couple of cantinas. There's one tiny store in the area," Jennifer said.

"Then we'd tip off Legion that we don't have the kids," Frank replied, shaking his head slowly. "Let's slow down a minute and think this through."

"Could one or both of the women who worked at the center have them?" LaShaun sat forward, the fatigue and pain fading as she saw a glimmer of hope.

"No, we have them secured," Val replied. "TEA Communications Section is monitoring mobile phone transmissions and the regular web, especially social media."

❧

"The TEA is holding them? Is that legal?" LaShaun glanced from Val to Frank.

"We questioned them for a couple of hours before handing them over to the police. Let's just say we have a working relationship with local law enforcement." Val, back in team leader mode, kept her expression neutral. "

"Damn, you've been busy in the last few hours. Thanks for getting right back to it. Did anybody from the team get sleep?" LaShaun felt a prick of guilt at being so hard on them.

"We took turns. Ernesto and Abril turned in right after our meeting. Hey, we'll take a vacation when we have Ellie back safe." Val wore a resolute expression that implied she would work her team hard.

"When we have all of the children back safe, not just Ellie," LaShaun countered. "I intend to get them out of whatever sick plan Legion has for them."

"Damn right, girl," Cee-Cee said with force.

"Okay, so I've never heard of the Deep Web." LaShaun blinked at Jennifer.

"Geeks in the know don't call it that. It's a group of servers and databases that allow users to browse without having their identity or origin tracked," Val said.

"Yeah, but Deep Web is way cooler to say, right?" Jennifer gave her a crooked grin.

"If it makes you happy," Val said in a dry tone. "Back to finding the kids."

"Cool would be if the Deep Web told us where they are," Cee-Cee said.

❦

Jennifer sighed. "Unfortunately, we're not that lucky."

LaShaun stared into space without speaking for a short time. "Let's review what we know. The eight kids taken have paranormal abilities. All of them are aware of what they can do. Even more, they can control their gifts."

"Right." Frank's brow furrowed as he gave her a puzzled look. "Go on."

"If they have some control, that means they don't just have raw abilities. They've honed them into skills they use with purpose, to get what they want." LaShaun looked at him.

Val stepped forward, her thick ponytail bounced as she nodded agreement. "Another thing, they take initiative. The little girl put a plan in action to protect Ellie. Jonah, the oldest one, gathered the children in a circle to do... something."

"So they have formed a bond, maybe because they share the experience of being kidnapped?" Cee-Cee frowned at them all.

"The older teens joined up, Jonah and his fifteen-year old girlfriend Marissa. But you're right, they seem to have become a cohesive subgroup. So you're thinking the children came up with their own plan? Fascinating. No wonder Legion wants them so bad. Think what kind of potential they represent." Frank crossed his arms as he lapsed into thought.

"Yeah, and the danger if they're seduced into believing Legion's agenda is the right one,"

❧

Jennifer said. "I think Grace has grown close to Ellie for sure. She's a sweet caring child."

"You talk like you know her." LaShaun raised an eyebrow at her.

"I do. Kris is my cousin. I've only met her adopted children once or twice when they were young. She kept them away from the family mostly. But I sensed they possibly had paranormal abilities early on." Jennifer said.

"Jennifer Evans! I didn't make the connection. Oh my God." LaShaun gazed at her steadily.

"I'm not a double agent. TEA has vetted me from here to heaven and back. Literally." Jennifer wore a brief grin that faded fast into a grave frown. "As for my cousin, I only met her a few times at family gatherings. We didn't have many. I won't go into our long history of dysfunction. Anyway, about the time my faith journey deepened, she slipped into the world of the occult. She's always been drawn to the occult, got involved in Goth role play games and freaky music."

"The Lord works in mysterious ways indeed. You're here to give us added insight into your cousin's motives." Frank's deep voice made him sound like a prophet sharing his vision into a profound mystery.

"Amen," Val and Cee-Cee said in unison.

LaShaun felt the familiar tingle, but as a lovely comforting sensation. Hope. The word popped into her mind like a pure ray of light. The dread that had settled into her core eased

⚜

into a calm feeling. An image of the older girl tickling Ellie, caring for her, played before her like a video on a small camera screen. Tears came down. This time of relief. LaShaun started to get out of the bed.

"Whoa, none of that," Cee-Cee said quickly. She stepped forward to block LaShaun from sliding to the floor.

"I have to see Chase, tell him Ellie isn't in immediate danger. That at least one child is her protector. He's probably beating himself up about not being able to save her." LaShaun swung her legs down, but the hospital bed was tall enough that her feet didn't touch the floor. Then she realized the team members were exchanging significant glances.

"He's recovering from surgery, LaShaun. So he's still out of it, you know." Cee-Cee stammered over the words.

"You said he would be fine, that his wounds aren't serious. There's something you're not telling me." LaShaun gripped Cee-Cee's forearm hard.

"He won't wake up," Cee-Cee blurted out.

"Smooth Cee-Cee," Val hissed. She yanked Cee-Cee hard enough to break LaShaun's weak hold on her.

"Sorry. I-I, she wanted to know. Aw hell, LaShaun deserves to know what's going on with her own husband," Cee-Cee said.

Val stood over LaShaun, both hands on her shoulders. "The surgery wasn't all that complicated, like we said. They expected him out of the anesthesia, of course still feeling the effects. But he's in a deep... but not because of the drugs."

"He's in a coma. A brain injury," LaShaun whispered.

"They're doing tests. If you're up to it, the doctor can explain the results." Val gazed at her in silence for a second or two. "That's all we know."

"We're not next of kin, so of course they won't tell us more. I'm happy Dr. Mendoza revealed that much." Frank Miles stepped closer to stand next to Val. "Honestly, we don't think his unconscious state has a medical source. The initial exam showed no visible signs of a head injury. He was talking right before the surgery."

"There could be internal bleeding that they'll only see on a scan or x-ray." LaShaun lay back, all the fight drained from her.

Frank glanced sideways at Val, then back to LaShaun. "True, but our medical team doesn't think so. We've seen this kind of deep sleep before. Has Chase had an encounter with a malicious spirit in the past?"

"Oh God. This is my fault." LaShaun covered her face with both hands.

Jennifer took over. "I know this is rough after all you've been through, that you're still going through, but focus. Tell us what happened."

LaShaun dropped her hands. "About four years ago, right before we got married, a demon called Abiku possessed him. But we were able to fight it. Chase has been fine since then."

"He's one of the stronger imps," Jennifer said.

"How you keep them all straight is a mystery to me. They multiply like flies hatching on a corpse," Cee-Cee grimaced.

"The king demon only selects a handful to dwell among us on a semi-permanent basis. Turned humans carry out most of his evil," Val said to LaShaun.

"I don't understand. We freed Chase from that... thing. Abiku never succeeded in taking full control of him anyway," LaShaun said.

"Even with successful demonic extractions residual effects of possession can leave the victim vulnerable to attack later." Frank huffed in frustration. "But only when someone has called the demon to earth and willingly used them for some selfish purpose. Chase has never been a member of a cult, or taken part in a calling forth ritual, right?"

LaShaun closed her eyes for a second, then opened them again. She twisted her hands together. "No, but I did. I used my psychic abilities for selfish gain or just because I liked screwing with other people. I performed a ritual which provided an opening for the demon in. Pretty much an invitation to our world. I didn't realize you can't simply undo such a thing. Not that it would have stopped me at the time."

"Don't blame yourself, LaShaun. Your experience is common among us and the reason the

❧

TEA steps in to guide young people with paranormal gifts." Frank nodded when LaShaun blinked at him in shock. "Discovering you have 'super powers' can be intoxicating at any age."

"Yeah, I can tell you stories. There was the time I tossed a bunch of pencils at my math teacher's head while I was sitting at the back of the class." Cee-Cee shrugged. "Yeah, I move objects. Anyway, we can swap stories later. How can we fix Chase?"

"Abril is coordinating with two TEA members who can help. You know them. Justine and Pauline Dupart. They're close by and can get here fast." Frank took his vibrating cell phone from a jacket pocket. "I need to take this."

He walked out, and the three women all moved in to be close to LaShaun. Cee-Cee sat at the foot of the bed. Val kept one hand on LaShaun's shoulder as though trying to give her strength. Jennifer took one of LaShaun's hands.

"I didn't know either of them were traiteurs," LaShaun murmured.

"Huh?" Cee-Cee blinked at her companions with a puzzled frown.

"The Cajun and Creole term for faith healers. They use prayer and herbal medicine to treat illnesses of the body and spirit. The power to heal comes from God alone. True traiteurs never claim they have the ability to heal. The most gifted can perform psychic surgery, but that's extremely rare," Jennifer explained.

"Ah, got it. We call them la curandera here." Cee-Cee sighed. "At least we know help is on the way."

"They should be here this afternoon. I believe another friend insisted on coming with them. Rose Fontenot. Very strong willed." Val's eyes narrowed.

"You tried to convince her to stay home, and she wasn't having it, right?" LaShaun glanced at the stern take-charge woman.

"I could feel her stubborn drive push through during the video conference like a bulldozer," Val muttered.

"In other words, you couldn't order her around," Cee-Cee retorted with an impish grin.

"Our local team has a solid plan and good data to guide us," Val replied. She shot a stony look at Cee-Cee and Jennifer.

"Neither the Council nor anyone else has criticized your leadership in this foray, Val," Jennifer said.

"To my face," Val mumbled.

"Look, I'm sorry for dumping on y'all about what happened at Legion's community center. I didn't want to wait around for more planning either. Hell, I'm to blame for all of this. If I hadn't been such a greedy, power hungry..." LaShaun chewed her lower lip.

"Girl, you didn't single-handedly set loose evil on the world. Besides, you're forgiven. We all are." Cee-Cee wore a serene smile. She pointed to the ceiling. "The Big Boss says so."

"Amen," Jennifer and Val chimed in.

⚜

LaShaun wiped tears from her cheeks with the back of one hand. She accepted a tissue from Val. She blew her nose and sniffed one last time. "Amen. Enough with the self-pity. We'll start working to find the children. Include me in all meetings, video chat or using the speaker on my cell phone. But first, I need to be with Chase."

****

An hour later LaShaun engaged in a power struggle. While the others had left, Cee-Cee elected to stay longer and offer LaShaun moral support. Still, Dr. Mendoza was unmovable on her decision. The doctor didn't want her to get sick from the strain of seeing Chase. Instead she gave her a full report, even brought her a picture of him on her cell phone.

"In the morning after he's stabilized a few more hours and you've had a night of rest," Dr. Mendoza said crisply. She looked at the nurse.

"Yes, ma'am. Understood." The nurse gave LaShaun a look of empathy. "It's for the best, señora. We're taking good care of him."

"I'll check on you early tomorrow and we'll arrange for a wheelchair. Good night." Dr. Mendoza turned to leave, but LaShaun's voice stopped her.

"No wheelchair," LaShaun protested. "You said I have minor bruises and scrapes."

"I don't have all the results form radiology just yet. Besides, you're still prone to dizziness. Nurse, a wheelchair." Dr. Mendoza gave the pretty nurse a pointed look. She seemed to sense the nurse might give in out of sympathy.

"Of course doctor." The nurse gave LaShaun a smile, then followed the doctor out.

Cee-Cee waited until both were gone and the door whisked shut. She spun to face LaShaun, a finger to her lips. Then she lowered the bed railing. "Let's go. I know the room number and location."

"My new best friend," LaShaun replied. She swung her legs over the edge of the bed. She braced herself on Cee-Cee's offered arm but panted when the room swirled and zig-zagged around as if she was on a fast merry-go-round.

"Whoa, take it easy," Cee-Cee said, and supported her. "Maybe the doc is right, and this is a bad idea. I could go and report back on—"

"No, no." LaShaun started to shake her head, but stopped fast when the spinning sensation intensified.

"LaShaun, really. I don't think you should try to walk." Cee-Cee frowned at her, her dark gaze filled with trepidation.

"I'll crawl on my own if I have to, Cee-Cee. Together we fight and win. Always. Chase needs me." LaShaun exhaled and pushed her hand away. "If you're too scared of breaking the rules, then go."

⚜

"Oh hell no with that weak attempt to mind game me," Cee-Cee retorted. "Fine. But your stubborn ass needs a wheelchair."

"Yeah. Not much help if I pass out before we get there."

LaShaun took deep breaths while Cee-Cee darted out. Minutes ticked by. LaShaun began to think Cee-Cee had changed her mind. She put her feet on the floor and slowly stood. When the room didn't spin she smiled.

"What the hell?" Cee-Cee whispered and looked over her shoulder. She came in pushing a wheelchair.

"I almost started without you," LaShaun quipped. Then she eased into the wheelchair. "I'm not as sore as I thought."

"Let me check the hall first." Cee-Cee went to the door and stuck her head out.

After a few seconds, Cee-Cee came back and they set off. LaShaun tensed when they passed two hospital employees, but they weren't challenged. Neither of them glanced up from the medical chart they were discussing. After a nerve racking trip down to the elevator and through two hallways on the third floor, they found Chase's room. LaShaun put a fist to her mouth to keep from crying out. A layer of clean white bandages crisscrossed his chest. Purplish blue bruising on his right arm made her wince. Pain shot through LaShaun's right arm the longer she looked at him.

Cee-Cee wheeled LaShaun close to the bed. "Don't connect to him or you'll suffer the same pains, even faint. Our empaths trained us, so I know. In your case, the emotional and spiritual union you two have has the same effect."

LaShaun glanced at her in surprise. "Well, well."

"Hey, Jennifer ain't the only one able to drop knowledge," Cee-Cee clipped. "I'll make sure nobody interrupts you. Go chat up the nursing staff for more info."

Her gaze on Chase, LaShaun waved a hand to signal she understood. She hardly noticed when Cee-Cee left. All of her attention switched to her husband. His chest rose and fell with each breath. LaShaun tried to find comfort in watching that sign of life. Taking her time, LaShaun put her feet on the floor and stood. Then she leaned over him.

"Honey, I'm here. Try to open your eyes. Chase, can you hear me? Picture my face and then me standing in front of you. Imagine we're walking toward each other, like when we got married."

LaShaun continued to whisper softly for several minutes. When he didn't move, she started a prayer. At some point, she wasn't sure when, LaShaun sat down again. Minutes slipped into over an hour. Her eyes shut as she lay her head on the bed, both hands clasped around his arm. The rest of the world slid away. Images of them played out in her mind like a full color video: LaShaun and Chase dating before they got married. Going fishing together. A trip to Jamaica. Chase looking tan

❖

and gorgeous on the beach walking toward her. His arms around her as they lay in bed watching an ocean breeze move the curtains. Another hospital, this time with pure joy as Chase held Ellie for the first time.

"Sweetie, come back to us," a gentle voice urged.

"Hmm, what?" LaShaun's eyes popped open. She blinked hard in an effort to focus.

"Ah, cher. We are here."

Miss Rose smiled down at LaShaun. Justine and Pauline stood with her. All wore loving smiles that offered hope. Their hands on her shoulders and back transferred warmth that spread through her. LaShaun cried with relief at the sight of her three friends.

"I feel better already," LaShaun said through sniffles.

"Oui. There is strength in unity," Pauline replied softly.

"Can you help him?" LaShaun felt a shadow creep back into the room. She lifted Chase's right hand to her lips. "He feels far away."

"The enemy tries to drive us apart with lies. They are trying to break the link between you, Chase, and Ellie. They can't take control of him, but they can pull him into another realm. Make him believe all is lost." Justine crossed to stand on the opposite side of the hospital bed.

"God no!" LaShaun gripped his arm tighter.

"Don't give in to fear and doubt. That only makes their dirty work easier," Miss Rose admonished. She transformed into a stern mater-

nal figure. "Falling into despair is what the enemy counts on."

"And that includes feeling guilt and regret,"
Pauline added. She nodded when LaShaun
looked at her. "You must be as forgiving of
yourself as you are of others."

"His Word says so," Justine said.

"Blessed be His name." Miss Rose bowed
her head. Her prayer in Creole French seemed
to glide from her lips and hover in the room.
"Amen."

"We begin." Pauline nodded to the other two
older women.

"Hurry, please. Dr. Mendoza gave instructions that I should stay in bed. I'll bet she has
the staff checking on Chase to make sure he
doesn't get visitors." LaShaun glanced at the
door anxiously.

Miss Rose chuckled softly. "TEA has things
in hand. We have members on staff. They'll
making sure we're not disturbed."

"Dr. Mendoza is at her private practice clinic until she makes rounds at seven this evening." Pauline glanced at her wristwatch. "It's
only a bit before noon. Plenty of time."

LaShaun studied Chase's face. She brushed
his tousled dark hair away from his forehead.
"Please, go on."

Justine nodded, closed her eyes, and placed
her hands lightly on Chase's chest. Pauline
murmured along with her, offering pleas to
have their prayers heard. Tranquility settled
over LaShaun after a time, like soothing balm

⚜

over a wound. Thirty minutes slipped into an hour, and into two hours. The middle-aged women seemed untiring, though they took turns sitting at different points.

A hand on her shoulder startled LaShaun. She realized Val had come into the room. Val nodded toward the door. She blinked in surprise when LaShaun got up without help. They walked into the hallway where Frank and Ernesto waited. The men's eyes widened when they looked at her.

"You look... refreshed." Ernesto stared at her.

"Renewed," Frank added. He smiled at her. "Traiteurs, you call them in Louisiana. Remarkable. The Creator chooses sparingly when it comes to the gift of faith healing. Despite what a lot of fake 'preachers' would have us believe."

"I can tell they prayed for you, too?" Ernesto asked.

"Probably, or maybe I feel the healing effects of their love and support." LaShaun felt lighter without the load of guilt weighing on her soul. She stood straight. "Tell me you have solid leads on the location of the children."

"Not where, but we've found out information that sounds promising," Frank replied with a curt nod. He glanced at Ernesto.

"From interviews with the two women who worked at the community center, and a few other sources, we know the kids have rebelled. Which isn't surprising. Jonah and his girlfriend made bucking authority their favorite hobby," Ernesto said.

"So that fits with them taking off on their own. Jonah acted like the leader." LaShaun flashed on the memory of the eight children forming a circle at his command.

"Teenagers challenging adults. Hell, that's their job description. I have three of 'em at home. I suggest you space out offspring by the way."

LaShaun laughed. "I'll remember your wise advice."

Frank gave a grunt. "For the first time, I'm happy to deal with disobedient adolescents."

"These kids are smart. What move would they likely make? I mean, Legion has infiltrated the area. Drug gangs all around. Who could they trust?" LaShaun looked at Ernesto for the answers.

Ernesto rubbed the stubble on his chin. "Despite his wise-ass, scruffy appearance, Jonah is a brilliant kid. He doesn't just stumble into his next move based on a whim."

"Reminds me of you at that age," Frank said with a twinkle in his green eyes. "So think. What would seventeen-year-old Ernesto do?"

"Hmm." Ernesto continued to think. His nut brown brow furrowed.

"I know a thing or two about being a smart, conniving teenager. I'd look for people willing to help me. He doesn't have cash to pay bribes or offer incentives in this poor region though."

⚜

LaShaun sighed. Then she snapped her fingers. "But they have psychic gifts."

"And the local people are both religious and superstitious," Ernesto agreed.

"What about your TEA insider working at Legion's clothing factory?" LaShaun turned to Frank.

"Ah yes, Mariela. She's helped build a select group who know Legion is dedicated to the fallen angel, Diablo." Frank's eyes brightened. "We don't contact her often to avoid suspicion. Yes, he could have met others through her."

"Jonah has charisma, even at his age. Not just with other kids." LaShaun nodded. "They've cultivated their own squad of allies."

Ernesto clapped a hand on his forehead. "Mind blown."

Miss Rose walked out to join them. She pulled the hospital room door closed behind her. LaShaun's heart froze as she searched the older woman's face for signs. Miss Rose turned to the set of expectant gazes with an impassive expression.

"Praise God from whom all blessings flow," she said, her contralto voice resonant though quiet.

"Thank you," LaShaun whispered. Val supported her as she sagged from weakness. This time with relief.

⚜

Chapter 15

That evening, Dr. Mendoza relented and allowed LaShaun to sit with Chase. Dressed in a comfortable sweat suit Cee-Cee had brought for her, she sat in a comfortable chair at his bedside. Luckily, she didn't know LaShaun had already defied her orders with Cee-Cee's help. LaShaun only felt a short tinge of guilt at the doctor's kindness. Cee-Cee glared at Val when she cleared her throat loudly as Dr. Mendoza praised them for following instructions.

"You see. The extra rest has done you much good." Dr. Mendoza beamed at them all. "Now, not too many visitors. I know Mr. Broussard's aunts insisted on seeing him, but we don't want to overdo it. Agreed?"

❖

Cee-Cee raised a hand like she was in grade school. "Hey doc, I was about to leave anyway."

"His aunts are resting at their hotel, so they won't be back. We'll be sure to keep the crowd manageable," LaShaun replied.

"Excellent. Being surrounded by such love is good medicine, so we won't be too strict." Dr. Mendoza's softer side shone through as she nodded at them. Then she left.

"Don't lecture," Cee-Cee blurted out, cutting off Val when she opened her mouth.

Val pointed to them both in turn. "You two are trouble together."

"Thanks." Cee-Cee smirked when Val rolled her eyes.

LaShaun kissed Chase's forehead and sat down again. "If he'd just open his eyes..."

"Don't get discouraged, girl. Healing takes time. He's not super human." Cee-Cee put a hand on her shoulder.

"I know, but." LaShaun pushed against the wave of doubt rushing toward her like a tsunami.

"That's how demons work," Val put in. "They don't only commit their evil deeds, but they strike us mentally and emotionally. Despair is an effective weapon."

LaShaun continued to gaze at Chase. His expression, once stiff, had relaxed into the image of a man sleeping peacefully. Then she brushed a hand across her eyes and sat straight. She would undo the wonderful efforts of the twins if she sank into hopelessness.

⚜

"What's our next move?" LaShaun said. She forced her gaze away from her husband to look at the team leader.

"I've been thinking for the past few hours. These SOBs attacked your husband spiritually, which leaves traces of... energy. No, that's not the best word. Sort of like a stream of smoke in the ether. Surprisingly durable in fact." Val raised an eyebrow at LaShaun.

"Like when one of those military jets flies across the sky. Which means we can follow it like a trail," LaShaun replied.

"Yeah, but it's not easy. I brought along a little something to help. It feeds data back to our system." Val held up what looked like a white finger clip monitor with a digital screen.

"How?" LaShaun blinked at the device.

"Wireless. I set up a modified router so the signal can get past all the medical equipment in here. Fortunately, he's not in ICU." Val tilted her head toward Chase.

"Please, go on," LaShaun said.

"So that's why you got him in a room facing east. Gives a clear line to our office. I love my people so damn much." Cee-Cee gave a little dance. "I'll watch the door. Don't want a nurse wandering in here and asking what the hell."

"You mean the TEA had Chase put in this room?" LaShaun stood to observe Val's movements.

"Our people on staff, yeah. Never know when we'll need medical attention. The TEA was building up to a direct confrontation with

❧

Legion. Their use of this site heated up in the last year or so. Only a matter of time before we had to take some decisive action. Your case just pushed that ahead. At least some thought so." Val talked as she worked. She placed the monitor on the tip of Chase's left ring finger. Then she stared at the digital read out for several minutes.

"The debate between Frank and Zack Desmond about waiting versus making moves," LaShaun replied.

"Complicated and fueled by individual ambitions. The TEA doesn't want to become an organization bogged down by bureaucracy or politics." Val positioned Chase's hand and arm. "Okay, that should do it."

LaShaun went around the bed to study the device. A series of numbers and symbols scrolled across the tiny screen. "Just when I think the TEA can't amaze me anymore."

"I know right?" Cee-Cee said from her station at the door.

"We literally stay up nights thinking of ways to beat Legion and spoil their grand plans." Val gave a grunt of satisfaction. "Now we need the monitor to stay in place for the next four hours at least. Longer is even better."

"The nurse will find it when they check on his IV and vital signs." LaShaun glanced up from the indecipherable codes to look at Val.

"The male nurse working the night shift is one of ours." Val checked the smart wrist watch on her right arm.

⚜

"Damn. No wonder you're in charge," LaShaun murmured.

"It takes a village, trust me. After that disaster last night, we better fix our screw-ups." Val frowned, then her expression relaxed. "Excellent signal getting through. It's not strong but good enough."

"Dr. Mendoza might be watching. She knows we're not the usual set of patients." LaShaun let out a long sigh. "I'd of been happy with her attention and firmness under different circumstances. She doesn't miss much."

"Yeah, she's not a TEA member. Firmly grounded in science despite her strict Catholic upbringing. But you'll be here to keep her occupied." Val took out her cell phone and tapped a message.

"No, I won't." LaShaun went to the closet and took out her street clothes.

"LaShaun, you were the one who insisted you needed to be with your husband," Cee-Cee burst out. She left the door and crossed to LaShaun. As LaShaun tried to pull off the top part of her sweat suit, Cee-Cee pulled the shirt back down.

"Okay, this is craziness, Cee-Cee," LaShaun hissed. She shooed her away, pushing Cee-Cee by the shoulders. "Don't make me whip your butt in here."

"I'm younger, faster, stronger. Take a shot. Listen, to me, girl. You need to rest. Not to mention you should be here when Chase wakes up," Cee-Cee argued.

⚜

Her last sentence stopped LaShaun in her tracks. She let go of Cee-Cee. "You're right."

"Thank you." Cee-Cee straightened her sweater.

LaShaun walked back to stand close to Chase's bed. She brushed her fingers along his right arm, then gripped his hand. "Why can't I see the spiritual tug of war going on inside him? My psychic skills are useless with him."

Val looked at Chase as well. "You know the answer, too close. We're not psychic robots with an on and off switch."

Cee-Cee joined them. "We have solid information on where the kids might have gone. Legion is scrambling to find them as well. TEA staff are sorting through a lot of coded messages flying back and forth via the Dark Web. My point is, we're close. Add in our local contacts embedded in the community and... LaShaun, our analytics tell us we're a few days away from finding them."

"That includes the clairvoyants on the team. They have a seventy-nine percent accuracy rating," Val added. When LaShaun glanced at her, she grinned. "Yes, we track data on everything we do."

"Seventy-nine percent," LaShaun repeated and sighed. "When lives are involved..."

Val grew serious. "Factors like the actions and choices of others, even the weather, affect outcomes. Only God knows the future perfectly."

⚜

"Our gifts help us know more than ninety-eight point five percent of the population," Cee-Cee added.

"You have data on that as well I guess." LaShaun tucked a corner of the sheets to make Chase's bed linens neat.

"Of course. Anyway, I agree with Cee-Cee. Your husband will expect to see you when he wakes up." Val faced LaShaun. "He'll be confused, anxious. Having you close will reassure him."

LaShaun continued to stare at Chase. She knew every angle of his handsome face. Every corner and curve of his muscular body. Together they had faced dangers seen and unseen. She could close her eyes and hear his voice, see familiar gestures and facial expressions. LaShaun leaned down, her face close to his. His warm breath caressed her skin. She lovingly touched her cheek to his. Eyes closed, she savored the fierce link they had. Then she stood straight. Val and Cee-Cee moved away like the force of LaShaun's resolve had pushed them.

"When Chase wakes, have a team member with the knowledge of every step taken give him details," LaShaun said firmly.

Val pressed her lips together for a second, then spoke up. "You're coming with us."

"Chase would make the same decision if I was in that bed. Tell him I'm going to get Ellie back. Give me five minutes to dress." LaShaun returned to the closet.

Without another word of protest, Cee-Cee and Val left the room. LaShaun noticed that her jeans, shirt, jacket, even her socks and underwear, had been laundered. They felt soft and clean as she put them on. Her TEA issue boots had been spit polished. She smiled to herself. They'd predicted she'd rejoin the search with one hundred percent accuracy.

One full hour later, LaShaun walked out of the hospital. Dr. Mendoza had put forth a valiant effort to prevent her leaving, yet she finally resigned herself that this patient was impatient to be gone. LaShaun's release papers had "AMA" in bold letters at the bottom, Against Medical Advice. The nurse who had looked in on her most frequently followed them out and hugged LaShaun before she left.

"Don't worry, señora. I will take good care of your husband. So will two others," she whispered.

"Thank you." LaShaun squeezed her hand.

After the fifteen minute trip, they arrived at the staging point once more. The atmosphere in the warehouse was charged. Additional members of the local Matamoros team packed equipment in the Range Rover and Hummer. Ernesto and Frank Miles strode among them giving instructions.

Jennifer approached LaShaun and gave her a hug. Then Cee-Cee came up. She handed LaShaun three items.

"A modified stun gun, your own little Glock. That's a G43, sweetest 9mm on market in my humble opinion. And finally a sword of Damascus." Cee-Cee pointed to a plain looking knife. Brown leather covered the handle.

LaShaun raised both eyebrows at her. She tucked the weapons into various pockets of her vest. "Sword of Damascus?"

"Made from steel in the ancient city of Damascus. So I named any knife we have made from Damascus steel a sword. TEA has King David's sword from the battle where he captured Damascus. I think it was 1010 BC. Or was it 830 BC?" Cee-Cee strapped on a shoulder holster as she talked. "I didn't pay much attention during history lessons at the TEA school."

"The date is debated among scholars," Jennifer put in. "But you should have studied harder."

"Yeah, yeah. Knowing the exact number of millennia won't help if some Legion chump tries to jump me." Cee-Cee waved to another team member, then jogged off to talk to him.

"Is she joking? TEA has King David's sword?" LaShaun followed Jennifer to the Range Rover.

"In one of several vaults. We don't keep all sacred items in one place for security reasons. Below a certain level, TEA members don't know what is even in those vaults. Much less where they're located."

"God," LaShaun breathed and stared at her wide-eyes.

⚜

"Basically," Jennifer replied with a wide smile. Then she grew serious again. "We're going to get Ellie back. Trust and believe."

LaShaun gazed around at the buzz of preparation activity in the warehouse. "I do. This is one time I wish I had the gift of bilocation, being in two places at once."

"Hey, I happen to agree with your decision to come with us. The maternal bond with a child is powerful. Grace came to live with my aunt for about six months five years ago. Kris had relapsed on drugs. I had Aunt Helen send me one of Grace's toys she'd kept in the attic. I'm hoping that gives us an extrasensory breadcrumb to follow." Jennifer hopped behind the wheel. She checked instruments on the dashboard.

"I don't get why Kris Evans wanted to be tied down to kids," LaShaun said.

"Kris was always a planner. Being a single mother gave her a sympathetic cover. She was with the con artist boyfriend, one of several. I think they used Grace in their scams," Jennifer replied with a grimace.

"She dabbled in the occult from the time she was a teenager. I suspect either Juridicus or Legion steered her to the children. Urged her to adopt them. Wheels within wheels as the twins would say." LaShaun went around to the back of the Range Rover.

"I didn't think Kris would slide into real evil. I just thought it was all part of her sex, drugs, and heavy metal phase. But your guess could be right." Jennifer hopped out of the SUV again. She walked around it, kicking the tires

"Not a guess. My friends and I did our homework on Juridicus. They created a charitable non-profit that includes supposedly helping at-risk kids. Your cousin spent time in New Orleans volunteering for them." LaShaun turned just as Val and Cee-Cee joined them again.

"Using Legion members to target and indoctrinate psychic kids. Ominous," Val said with a scowl.

"I recommend the TEA review its policy on merely observing children it identifies. Especially if they're in unstable families, foster care or orphanages. Legion exploits those places to further their schemes." LaShaun crossed her arms. "I'm ready to get started."

"We're meeting in the conference room," Val said. She walked off toward a glass enclosed office in one corner of the warehouse.

"Another damn committee meeting? Unbelievable. You people told me you had solid leads on which direction we need to go," LaShaun shouted after her.

Val spun around and marched back to LaShaun. "The stakes for us and Legion have jumped up by a hundred percent. We can't go charging across the countryside without attracting a lot of attention."

"News flash, Val. They know we're here looking for the kids. Sounds like you've bought into Zack Desmond's wait and see philosophy," LaShaun shot back.

"We're trying to delay Legion figuring out we know more than them. The longer we can keep them off our tails, the better. If we make a beeline to the trail we think the kids took, we'll lead the bastards straight to them. We have a plan, a damn good one." Val blew out a puff of air. "I know this is frustrating for you. Just please, hear us out."

LaShaun had paced in a circle while Val made her case. Then she stopped. "I'm used to being on my own. Gets in the way sometimes. Lead on."

Val gave a curt nod. She spun around and started toward TEA's version of a war room in the warehouse. Val gestured to two other team members, who followed as well. LaShaun heeded the slight tingle spreading up her arms. Confirmation that she'd made the right choice to hear Val and the others out.

Once everyone stood or sat around the table, Frank began. He pointed to a map on the screen that took up a wall. "Here's where we think they went. Or at least where they're headed. Monterrey."

Ernesto whistled low. "Over three hundred kilometers. Does the kid even have a driver's license?" He glanced around at Abril.

"Jonah's an American teenager. Of course he has one, not that it would do him any good. They don't have a car," Abril said.

❖

"Remember he's brilliant and resourceful" Frank replied.

"They all are, even baby girl." Ernesto smiled at LaShaun.

"Exactly. Jonah has either found a way to get his hands on a car, or found other means of transportation. They're obviously not on foot. A group of kids have managed to get the tools needed, or the means, to slip away from Legion. Impressive." Frank stared at the map.

"Why Monterrey?" LaShaun walked closer to the screen to study it.

"Large city, pretty good standard of living. Easier for them to blend in than staying in small rural towns," Jennifer put in.

"Great points. Big tourist destination. Foreigners speaking English won't stand out," Cee-Cee added.

"Even more important it's where El Obispado is located." LaShaun spoke low, but those nearby turned to her.

"Excuse me, I didn't hear you." Frank glanced at LaShaun with a baffled expression.

"The Bishop's Palace. It was built in the 1700's. Obviously for Catholic Bishops. It's a museum now. That's all I know." Jennifer shrugged, and looked at LaShaun.

"It sits on a hill. Here's what you won't read in history books. During the Mexican-American war, some of the US soldiers decided to loot the palace of gold and silver sacred objects." LaShaun touched her vest as if she expected to find a familiar object in one of the pockets. Of course she didn't. She couldn't risk having it confiscated by the TSA screeners. "I inherited a knife, made of ninety-nine percent pure silver, made strong by the Holy Spirit. Family journals claim it was used by ancient Mayans to kill demons. But there were other objects at El Obispado."

"Wait, wait." Abril raised a palm. She hurried over to the laptop set up in the room. "Just give me a minute."

"What the hell, girl. We ain't got time for one of your geek moments." Cee-Cee rolled her eyes.

"A few seconds. This is important. C'mon." Abril bounced in the chair, impatient with the speed of the computer. "Got it. The TEA has objects from that site. It's on the list for excavation by our archeology division."

"I would be so fascinated with knowing this stuff any other time," Cee-Cee said, her tone drenched in sarcasm. Then she tapped her wristwatch. "But tick-tock."

"During the Mexican-American war, a couple of trenches were dug by soldiers around the site for defensive purposes. They found gold coins that convinced them more riches could be found in the Bishop's Palace. They were more right than they knew." Abril stood up. "Legion didn't choose Mexico simply to exploit the chaos caused by cartels."

"Okay, let's start with a radical reassessment of what they're up to in Matamoros."

⚜

Frank's eyes went wide. He took off his reading glasses. "Game changer."

"Somebody clue me in," Cee-Cee blurted out in frustration.

"Not just you," Ernesto added as he glanced around. Other members of the team nodded.

"We know many major biblical figures visited the area. The Spaniards looted sacred objects from North Africa. When they returned to Spain, many of these relics were donated to the Catholic Archbishops and Cardinals of their country who then doled them out to other churches." Abril waved her arms around as if frustrated they didn't understand.

"And?" Cee-Cee finally said, voicing the question it seemed they all had.

"The TEA must have reason to believe something is still at El Obispado." LaShaun looked from Abril to Frank.

Frank shrugged. "It's always been nothing more than a theory. I mean it could be in any of a number of places. Mexico is such a long shot."

"My family stories tell of battles against evil being fought here. Something of huge importance must be at stake. This is the part where you can fill us in, Frank." Ernesto gestured to the regional leader.

"What I'm about to tell you can't be repeated. No one who's not in the room can be told." Frank jabbed a finger in the air.

"Yeah, yeah. We got it. Now spill," Cee-Cee said.

⚜

"I'm sure you all know the story about Jesus feeding the five thousand?" Frank rubbed a large hand over his face. "Well, we have accounts that the descendants of the boy who supplied the fish and bread kept his basket. It's been passed around, ended up in a Coptic church in Tunisia. The priests there became the guardians, but during a war, it disappeared. I'm giving you the short version. The history is way more complicated than that."

LaShaun broke the stunned silence of the room. "So you think a Spanish Bishop was given it as a gift for his service, and he brought it to El Obispado."

"All just talk between archeologists and historians. Gossip over drinks at conferences. We have our own legends and share of wild theories. Like the ancient alien fanatics." Frank gave a snort to indicate what he thought of them. "Anyway, most believe having something so amazing end up here is about as plausible."

"I don't get what Legion wants with the basket. The power wasn't in what our Savior used," Jennifer said. "Right?"

"His use changes ordinary earthly items. One thing the ancient Christians understood. We don't worship the relics of course, but..." Frank trailed off.

"The supernatural can and does affect physical objects. Call it physics, or molecular dynamics, or whatever for the scientists among you. All I know is we don't want Legion to get their hands on it." Val picked up her backpack

❧

from a chair. "Let's go. We have two people in Monterrey already.

"There are three popular youth hostels in and around the city. We've jammed signals that would tip off Legion where we're headed. No using cell phones for calls. Texts only until we're at least an hour out of Matamoros," Cee-Cee added. Her usually joking demeanor switched to all business mode.

Two hours of driving gave LaShaun way too much time to worry. Soft music played on the SUV's sound system, but didn't help calm her nerves. The TEA staff person at the hospital sent encrypted text updates to Val on Chase's condition. Miss Rose and the twins took turns keeping watch at his bedside. His physical wounds were healing as expected. The spiritual attack however had been more dangerous. Chase was responding slowly, which made LaShaun's insides twist with guilt. She had no control over her family history and the para-normal abilities she'd inherited. Her behavior was another matter.

"None of what's happened is your fault," Val said. She never took her eyes off the road ahead.

LaShaun glanced at her before staring out of the passenger side window of the Range Rover again. "You don't know…"

"That you were a badass once upon a time and used your skills to do some shady crap," Cee-Cee put in her two cents. She continued to check her automatic pistol and other weapons. "Yeah, we do actually."

"I'm going to propose changes to TEA snooping policies," LaShaun muttered.

"We didn't have to snoop to find out. You're not unique when it comes to having a past you're not too proud," Cee-Cee said.

"We can swap war stories about shit we stirred up back in the day to pass the time." Val wore a crooked grin.

"Like when you tried to get a cute teacher you had a crush on in middle school to notice you. She dabbled in a love potion. Or was it an incantation?" Cee-Cee glanced at Val, but didn't allow her to answer before she plowed on. "Anyway, things didn't go to plan. The guy's libido kicked up. Women couldn't resist him thanks to Val. He started humping every female teacher with a pulse, including the sixty-year-old vice principal. The girls' basketball coach found them going at it in the sports equipment room. Get this, while she was leading three school board members on a tour of the new athletic facilities."

"Oh. My. God." LaShaun burst out laughing at the vivid image that flashed in her head.

"Hey, I'll be the one to decide if and when I share my own list of scandalous deeds," Val protested. Then she joined them in giggling. "What a mess. I was broken-hearted for months."

"I needed that laugh. Thanks." LaShaun wiped tears from her eyes.

⚜

Val's smile faded. "Of course the conse-quences weren't so funny. Both their careers suffered. Mrs. Madison's husband left her, and she was demoted. My teacher transferred to another school. His ambitions to become a school principal went down the toilet."

LaShaun grew somber as well. "But nobody died."

They rode in silence for fifteen minutes when Val spoke up. "Who is the most revered saint in the Catholic faith, and the most revered apostle in the protestant church?"

"St. Paul," LaShaun and Cee-Cee answered at the same time, and exchanged a glance.

"Before he became Paul, he was Saul. He persecuted Christians, killed them by the doz-ens. Not only that, but he loved hunting them down. Yet he was totally transformed on the road to Damascus. I'm gonna just let that mar-inate in your minds for a minute." Val wheeled the Range Rover expertly around a sharp curve as she spoke. Then she read the screen display on the dashboard in a code only she knew.

Cee-Cee leaned forward from the back seat to whisper, "She's right. Forgive yourself or it will mess up your relationships. Clouds your thinking. And in this fight, we gotta stay sharp."

"Miss Rose and the twins keep saying the same thing. I'm working on it." LaShaun sighed.

"Lots of us in TEA have the same issue, wrestling with things we've done in the past.

Some of their stories have no punchline. I'm talking true evil unleashed. You're not alone." Cee-Cee gave her shoulder a quick pat before she eased back onto the seat again.

Val kept the speed at seventy-five miles an hour. The trip seemed too slow, but at least LaShaun felt better. She didn't have the luxury of fighting herself. The real enemy lay ahead of them. The lives and souls of eight children were at stake. Ellie needed her focus to stay on the right target.

When they arrived in Monterrey, Val headed straight for the most popular hostel on the list the TEA had provided. LaShaun's heart beat kicked into high gear with hope. But the kids weren't there. They went to the other two with the same result.

"Okay, so now we've been to the nice ones. I had hoped they wouldn't resort to some of the rougher areas, but..." Val tapped her fingers on the steering wheel.

"Jonah is no fool. His girlfriend, what's her name?" Cee-Cee snapped her fingers a couple of times.

"Marissa," Val replied. "She's fifteen, but dressed older to blend in with Jonah's crowd."

"Yeah, whatever. Anyway, they figure Legion will look in those places. But they don't have money." Cee-Cee glanced around the neighborhood as they talked.

"I'm betting they do. Look, these kids have managed to slip out of a very determined, paranoid group's grasp. Let's give them more cred-

❦

it. I'll bet Jonah and Marissa have managed to get their hands on money. They need to melt into a crowd." LaShaun gazed ahead as well. "Too bad we don't know this city all that well."

"But we know people who do," Val said. She spoke into her blue tooth headset. "Got it."

Seconds later she nosed the Range Rover down several streets of a busy neighborhood. Like any big city, a mixture of heavy pedestrian traffic combined with lots of cars. A few side-walk vendors sold food. Finally, Val pulled up to a historic building away from the center of the action.

"Looks nice enough." Cee-Cee peered up at the colonial architecture, one elbow hanging out of the open window.

"I'm going in." LaShaun started to open the door, but Val stopped her.

"They were here, but they've left. Like we said, they're smart enough to keep on the move. This is a nice boutique hotel. Which means Jo-nah has more than a little cash to spend. Let's just hope he isn't taking chances to earn it." Val nodded and then got out.

LaShaun joined her on the sidewalk. "Why waste time if we know they've moved on?"

"He's running from us, too. Remember? Let's see if we can find out something helpful from the staff." Val went through the front door before LaShaun could respond.

"We're along for the ride, honey. Relax. Val has hella good instincts." Cee-Cee motioned for LaShaun to follow. "Let her do the talking."

A slender young man the color of nutmeg greeted them with a warm smile. Val asked for the manager, and moments later a taller man emerged from a door that must have led to his office. He had the polished good looks of a Latin pop star. He beckoned for Val to come with him. She signaled for LaShaun and Cee-Cee to wait for her. Fifteen minutes went by. Cee-Cee strolled around the lobby, flipped through magazines, and even flirted with the desk clerk. LaShaun was about to charge the manager's office when Val came back alone.

"Paolo has it arranged so they can't run. The older kids are definitely in charge. Somehow Jonah got his hands on a decent amount of cash. He and Marissa are pretending Ellie's their baby. The other four kids are with different families. Paolo is working on getting them back to their countries. He's a good man." Val wore a soft smile. She put on her sunglasses.

"Paolo, huh?" Cee-Cee nudged LaShaun. "You two got a thing going on?"

"You're stuck in high school up here." Val tapped her temple with a forefinger. "Let's go. They're at an apartment in San Pedro Garza Garcia. Not a far drive. Upscale neighborhoods. I wouldn't have guessed they'd end up there."

"Let's hope Legion is making the same mistake and following dead-ends, too," Cee-Cee replied. "I'll drive to give you a break."

Fifteen minutes later they drove into San Pedro Garza Garcia. The modern city had clean wide streets and lovely neighborhoods.

⚜

LaShaun gazed around in surprise. "This is not the Mexico you see on the news back home."

Val grunted. "Don't get me started on the US media and the narratives they love to push."

"Amen," Cee-Cee added. She gave a low whistle at the apartment complex she finally found. "Wow, pretty fancy. This is a pricey place to live."

"A lot of American and UK ex-pats in the area. Which means our TEA member fits right in. He transferred here with his company." Val tapped in updates to Ernesto, Abril, and Jennifer. "The others are nearby. Ernesto says they're sure they haven't been followed. If they pick up funny vibes, they'll lead them away from us. We have two other decoy teams pretending to search Monterrey."

LaShaun was about to express admiration of TEA team planning when childish screams cut through the air. LaShaun leaped out of the SUV and ran to the front door. She slapped the surface in rage because it was locked.

"LaShaun," Val called out to her.

"That's Ellie." LaShaun raced through a neat flower bed. Petals scattered around her boots as she searched for an opening.

"Listen to me." Val ran after her.

"I know my child's voice," LaShaun shouted without looking around.

Her boots pounded along a paved walkway that led to a courtyard. LaShaun rounded corners down more paths following the sounds.

⚜

Her head pounded at the rush of adrenaline pushing her forward. Val and Cee-Cee sprinted to catch her. All three skidded to a halt at the scene before them. Ellie and the other youngsters wore bathing suits. They played in the community pool of clear blue green water. Grace cradled Ellie in her lap as the toddler happily splashed water from the shallow end. Jonah and Marissa sat with tall glasses of something cold, slices of fruit on the rim. Jonah saw them first. He jumped to his feet and reached for something beneath a beach towel.

Ellie waved happily at LaShaun. She acted as though nothing more serious had happened than she'd been away at summer camp. She pointed, and clapped her hands with excitement.

"Mama's here. Yay!"

❧

Chapter 16

Jonah sprang from the patio lounge chair. He stood around six feet tall. A thick lock of brunette hair fell across his forehead as he glared at them. His azure blue eyes widened with anger. Marissa, her dark blonde hair still wet from the pool, jumped behind him. She darted a look of panic at Grace and Ellie in the pool. They looked like regular kids on spring break except for the automatic pistol Jonah held and the knife Marissa pulled from a picnic basket.

"Okay, relax kids." Cee-Cee held up both hands as a sign they'd come in peace. "We're the good guys, well women. You know what I mean."

"As if any adults are 'good guys'," Jonah said with perfect teenage disdain. He squinted

⚜

at them. But still Ellie's reaction seemed to blunt his fight response. He was still on guard with the gun pointed to the ground.

"You'll soon be one. Let's see how you do," Cee-Cee retorted.

"Cee-Cee, we want to make friends," Val muttered low. Then she looked at Jonah, arms held out wide. "We're with the TEA."

"We know who you are," Jonah snapped, his fight ready stance unchanged.

LaShaun took a cautious step closer to Ellie. "Then you know I'm Ellie's mother. Her father came as well to get her back."

"He's the cop," Marissa said to Jonah. She wore a worried frown.

"Ellie's daddy didn't come to arrest you. We only want to take our little girl home." LaShaun's voice broke. She darted a glance at Ellie. The toddler pushed away from Grace's attempts to hold her.

"Mama."

Ellie gave Grace a frown as if scolding her. When the older child didn't attempt to grab her again, Ellie ran to LaShaun. Her little legs pumped as she scampered across the pavement. LaShaun didn't even try to hold back the tears as she scooped Ellie into her arms.

"Mama and daddy have been looking all over for you, sweet baby. We love you so very much." LaShaun forgot about the others as she enjoyed the relief of having her child once more.

❧

"I took good care of Ellie. We all did," Grace said defensively. She stood, a picture of twelve-year-old wrath in a neon pink bathing suit. "You shouldn't have let them take her. She's just a baby. What kind of mother are you any-way?"

"The same kind all of us had," Marissa said. She grimaced as she stared at LaShaun.

"Oh get a clue. Does she look like she will-ingly handed over her kid? Legion stole Ellie at gun point." Cee-Cee lowered her voice and add-ed, "Her father was shot the other night by some of their crew."

"You won't get your hands on the other kids," Jonah said after a few moments.

"Paolo is a friend of ours, Jonah. He's going to make sure they're sent home." Val kept her eyes on the gun in his hand.

"Another old guy sold us out. Figures." Jo-nah's eyes flashed fire.

"Slow down. We're not going to use them the way Legion wanted to, I promise," Val re-plied.

"Of course you won't. Yeah right. You'll use them in *your* way. Then you'll tell us how that's going to be so much better. Gee, thanks. How about we don't want to be used by any of you. And don't give me the we're-the-good-guys speech." Jonah gazed at Ellie and LaShaun.

"Do you know why Legion is so keen to have you?" Val's abrupt shift seemed to throw the older teens off balance.

⚜

Marissa beckoned to Grace, who quickly moved to stand next to her with Jonah. "Doesn't matter. We decided not to play."

"Why don't you tell us what they were up to, since you're on our side," Jonah countered.

"Okay" Val wore an impassive expression.

Cee-Cee glanced at Val then at Jonah "Val, I don't think—"

Val raised a palm to cut her off. "They're smart enough to have gotten this far, away from both Legion and us. I think they should know. Legion wants to use your paranormal abilities to conquer mankind. Not all at once. In stages. We also have good reason to believe Legion is after a powerful sacred relic. They believe it will enhance your powers."

LaShaun stood still holding Ellie as Cee-Cee joined her. She whispered, "Cee-Cee?"

"I don't think she's making it up. The kid's psychic, remember? He'd see right through any kind of lie. Frank must have filled her in on some top level intel he didn't share with us. Damn," Cee-Cee whispered back quickly.

"Yeah, Palcio del Obispado. I figured there was a good reason they brought us here instead of somewhere else. I looked up information about sacred places of Mexico. Internet cafés are the best." Jonah wore a crooked grin. Then he grew serious again. "So tell us what exactly is worth them kidnapping us and shooting up police officers?"

⚜

Val glanced at Cee-Cee and LaShaun, then at Jonah. "One of the baskets given back to Jesus after he fed the five thousand."

Jonah looked at Marissa. "Huh?"

"Matthew 14 in the Bible," Marissa said. She huffed in annoyance. "Didn't you pay attention to anything in Sunday school?"

"Get serious. My parents haven't been in a church since they got married. They couldn't have dragged me to Sunday school even if they wanted to, and they didn't." Jonah shrugged.

"Since we're pulled into the *war with God thing*, you need to look up this stuff," Marissa shot back.

"Yeah, yeah." Jonah gave Marissa a scowl but looked abashed all the same.

"Jesus multiplied five loaves of bread and two fishes to feed thousands who had come to him for healing and to hear him speak. Twelve basketfuls, carried by each of the twelve disciples, held the leftovers," Marissa explained. "That's the short version."

"Very good." Cee-Cee grinned at the girl, who blushed and looked away.

"So at least one of these baskets used by Jesus to perform a miracle survived and is at the museum. Okay, so how did something made of straw survive for over two thousand years? Come on." Jonah snorted.

"Duh, miracle from God." Marissa glared at him.

When Ellie giggled and Grace rolled her eyes, LaShaun figured the two teens regularly bickered. LaShaun smiled at them. "She has a point."

"I don't buy the God bit. Every day science explains things people used to think were magic," Jonah replied.

"We have the same debates at some TEA conferences. I say..." Cee-Cee stopped when Val held up her smartphone.

"I'm getting a message." Val scrolled down a string of text. "Damn, the other team had an... incident."

"Stop talking in code. We're not idiots. You mean Legion knows you're here, which also means they could be on their way." Jonah held up the pistol pointing it at Val. "We're leaving."

"I won't let you take Ellie." LaShaun moved a few feet farther from him.

Marissa studied LaShaun. "She's just a baby, Jonah. I don't think her mother is like the others."

"You sure?" Grace looked up at Marissa and then at LaShaun. When Marissa nodded, she seemed satisfied.

"Fine. You leave and we'll take care of ourselves." Jonah gestured with the pistol.

"Don't talk crazy. We can protect you," Val argued.

"We've got bigger and better weapons, too. I'll bet you can't do this," Cee-Cee added before Val could go on. She gazed at a decorative stone garden statue of a woman holding a bowl. Seconds later, it toppled over. The right arm broke off.

⚜

"Whoa." Grace did a double take between the statute and Cee-Cee.

When Val hissed and frowned at her, Cee-Cee cleared her throat. "I'll send them a check later. Promise."

"The point being you're better off sticking with us," LaShaun said.

Jonah raised the pistol. Marissa hefted the knife in her hand. Gracie ducked behind a hedge and emerged again holding a machete. LaShaun, Val, and Cee-Cee shouted at them. While the other two adults looked for cover, LaShaun raced behind a column as she shielded Ellie from harm. That's when she heard the sound of running feet and the pop of gunfire. Val and Cee-Cee needed her help, but she couldn't leave Ellie. Then silence. LaShaun risked a quick look from behind the stone column.

"Good shot," Cee-Cee said. "LaShaun, you can come out. We need to leave, like now."

"Yeah. Mexican prison is not where you want to be," Val said to Jonah. She knelt down over a prone figure and turned the man over.

"Is he..." LaShaun tried to keep Ellie from looking. The toddler buried her face against LaShaun's shoulder.

"He's alive. Let's let him deal with why he's someplace he doesn't live with a bullet wound." Val gestured. "No arguments."

Jonah glanced around at the two girls. "Yeah, right."

⚜

A man wearing green shorts and a yellow polo shirt appeared on a second floor balcony. He spoke a rapid stream of Spanish, then switched to English. Sirens keened in the distance. "I took care of the other one. I'll tell the policía that he tried to break in and I shot him. Now go!"

"Don't have to tell me twice," Cee-Cee huffed. She waved an arm at the teenagers, who hustled behind her.

Seconds later they all piled into the Range Rover. Val hit the gas pedal, taking them down the street. She hooked a right and drove as fast as she dared through a series of turns and twists. The sirens sounded more distant with each city block they traveled.

"Where exactly are we going?" Jonah eyed their surroundings.

"We have a temporary staging location to meet up with the others. First they had to get medical attention for Ernesto," Val replied.

"What the hell, Val. You didn't say a word. How bad is he?" Cee-Cee pressed a palm to her forehead.

"Wasn't the time back there, okay?" Val took in a deep breath and exhaled. "They were ambushed in a little town outside Monterrey. Ernesto was shot, in the chest. He's in critical condition. Two of the attackers were neutralized. One got away."

"You mean your dudes killed two people. Golly, what good guys." Jonah squinted at the adults in turn.

⚜

"They were attacked and defended them-selves you little moron," Cee-Cee yelled. She twisted around in the front passenger seat to face him. "Our friend got shot protecting your ungrateful—"

"Cee-Cee, don't." LaShaun put a hand on her shoulder. Cee-Cee glared at him, her eyes shiny with unshed tears, but she finally faced forward again. "I don't have time to rundown a list of Legion's dirty rap sheet to convince you. Point blank, TEA has known about you and the other kids for some years now. They didn't mess with you. Legion kidnapped the younger kids, including my baby. You and Marissa real-ized they'd lied to you after joining, right?"

Jonah's jaw muscles clenched. He wore a stony expression, but when Marissa hooked an arm through his, Jonah nodded. "Yeah, so now what?"

Val darted a quick glance of gratitude at LaShaun in the rearview mirror, then looked at the street ahead. "We have to push on. Legion can't get their hands on the basket, or any sa-cred object for that matter. And they still need you, all of you."

"Ellie most of all," Grace blurted out. She turned bright pink when Jonah and Marissa scowled at her. "Well, her mom needs to know."

"Gracie," Jonah hissed at her and rolled his eyes. "Kids."

"I'm not that much younger than Marissa," Grace snapped. She tossed her hair. Arms crossed, she turned to LaShaun. "They can't

⚜

use the sacred items because they're all like dirty."

"They've pledged to serve the cause of evil, so they have the mark of Satan on their souls," Marissa added. She glanced at her boyfriend. "Ellie's mom is right, Jonah. Pick a side. At least for now."

"Which means simply getting a sacred object is pointless. They need the faithful to make them powerful," Cee-Cee frowned. "Wait a minute, something's missing."

"As in Jonah doesn't believe in God. Still, I'm guessing the other children have been baptized." LaShaun looked at the two older teens.

Marissa nodded. "Donnie, the thirteen-year-old from Indiana, is Pentecostal. His preacher father used to beat him up. Said Donnie had a demon in him because he could predict things, mostly bad."

"He'll get a choice whether or not to go home," Val replied. "TEA will work with child welfare authorities in Indiana. Hopefully, he'll tell them about his treatment."

"His folks handed him over to Legion. Donnie says two Legion women pretended to be from Pentecostal headquarters. They told his folks they were going to cleanse Donnie. His parents were happy to get him out of their house," Marissa said.

"Geez, Marissa. Tell them our life story while you're at it," Jonah muttered.

❧

"They need to know so they can protect Donnie. Him and the other three kids will be okay, won't they?" Marissa looked at LaShaun.

"Okay, Mari," Ellie burbled before LaShaun could answer. She grabbed a lock of the teenager's blonde hair and tugged on it.

Marissa tickled Ellie's cheek. "You little scamp. That's what my grandmother used to call me when I was little."

"What did Grace mean about Ellie being most important to Legion?" LaShaun's arms tingled. Ellie wiggled as if she felt it, too.

Jonah and Marissa exchanged a glance. After heaving a sigh, Jonah spoke up. "Ellie is still young, but her powers of perception and knowing are strong. They figure as she grows up, she'll be among the most powerful gifted in the world."

"If not the most powerful. Something about her ancestry, repentance or something. We didn't get the whole story." Marissa looked at Grace.

"I listened in on some conversations. They let me wander a bit since I'm Kris's daughter. I pretended to like them." Grace's hazel eyes sparkled with triumph.

"Damn. They formed a mini-rebel team inside Legion." Cee-Cee looked at Val.

"No way, Cee-Cee," Val said and cocked an eyebrow at her.

"I haven't even laid out a complete strategy yet," Cee-Cee protested.

⚜

"We're not sending kids undercover into that nest of snakes. The council would never agree to such a plan, and I don't blame them. Forget it." Val's tone of finality boomed like a bell tolling.

"Yeah, yeah." Cee-Cee huffed back to silence.

"Here's the address Abril sent me." Val parked in the lot of a strip mall.

Jonah gripped Marissa's hand in his as he looked around. "A lot of people. Any of them could be after us."

"TEA has cleared the area. Look, you can either sit in the SUV and wait for us or come in and hear every detail of what our local action team plans to do." Val cut the engine. She patted her vest to make sure all her weapons and tools were in her pockets.

Cee-Cee did the same, and then checked for updates on her smart phone. "Your move kid."

Jonah scowled at her. "Stop calling me 'kid'."

"Whatever," Cee-Cee retorted.

She brushed fingers through her short curly red hair. She swung the door open and hopped onto the pavement. When Marissa caught Jonah staring at Cee-Cee's khaki covered rear end, she jabbed him in the side with an elbow. He winced. Then scrambled out of the Range Rover after her.

"Hey, cut it out," Jonah called after Marissa as she marched ahead of him.

⚜

LaShaun and Val exchanged a look of amusement. LaShaun leaned forward to whisper, "I think Marissa's got some competition. Notice the way Jonah has been looking at Cee-Cee?"

"Lord help us. All we need, teenage love triangle drama."

Ten minutes later, the mood was anything but playful. They gathered with the rest of the original Matamoros team in the back of a spacious upscale beauty shop. A table, chairs, small refrigerator, and microwave oven filled the break room. The owner wasn't a member, but one of many sympathizers to the goals of TEA. She came in with one of her employees to hand out snacks, then she was gone. Ellie greedily slurped up applesauce, even though Grace declared they'd eaten that morning. LaShaun suppressed a grin when Ellie stuck her tongue out at her surrogate big sister. Then LaShaun grew somber when she glanced at the team. Frank, Abril, and Jennifer looked tired and stressed. Jennifer's eyes were red as if from crying heavily, her cheeks red. Cee-Cee pulled LaShaun aside.

"She and Ernesto have been a couple for almost a year," she whispered.

"I know how she feels," LaShaun said, thinking of Chase. She was about to ask about him when the door opened, and the twins came in. She blinked at them in shock. "Is Chase..."

"He's doing fine and dandy, cher. Strong one." Justine nodded.

Pauline smiled. "Oui. We had to practically sit on him to keep him from leaving the hospital to come with us. Stubborn."

"Speaking of which, before I forget," Justine pulled out a case from her cross-body bag, "TEA gave me this fabulous smart phone. And baby, is it smart!"

"Secure connections," Pauline put in. Then she looked at Ellie and held out her arms. "Hello, my sweet baby. Come say hello to Auntie Pauline." She continued to murmur to her once Ellie grabbed onto her.

Justine handed the phone to LaShaun. The sound of Chase's voice brought joy to her heart. His deep rumble complained of being left behind. Yet his irritation vanished when Ellie babbled into the phone. She seemed to be filling her daddy in on all her adventures. LaShaun laughed with Chase because her baby talk was totally undecipherable.

"Yes, we—" LaShaun glanced at the twins and shrugged. "I'll definitely update you as soon as I can. Right, I'll remember. Got my weapons. The twins are here and... yes, okay. Bye. I love you, too." She ended the connection.

"You got your instructions?" Pauline said.

"Oh yes. Makes him feel better, like he's part of the action. Though I'm sure he'll keep trying to join us." LaShaun gazed at the cell phone with interest. Ellie pawed at it with childish curiosity as well.

"Hmm, hand it back please. You can ask TEA to get you one." Justine held out a hand.

❧

LaShaun reluctantly gave it back. "Yes, ma'am. So touchy."

"Sister's new toy," Pauline teased.

Frank, Abril and Jennifer broke apart from the separate conversation they were having at the other end of the room. Two other men LaShaun hadn't seen before were seated at the table.

"This is Manuel and Naldo. They're from here, so they know the area well." Frank nodded to the two men, who both nodded to everyone as a greeting.

"Help us what?" Jonah said. He leaned against the wall, a bag of chips in one hand.

"Legion has a team in place to steal three items from the museum tonight. A silver cup, a jewel encrusted cross, and the basket," Naldo spoke up.

"The cup and cross are worth several million, both said to have been used by St. Francis of Assisi. They were gifts from a sultan who converted after hearing a sermon by St. Francis in 1220. But we know the basket is what they're really after." Manuel nodded.

"We didn't think Legion knew it even existed," Abril said. She continued to use the small tablet computer in her hand.

"Heck, TEA didn't know for sure like I said. Bringing the children here tipped us off. So now Legion knows we know. But, couldn't be helped. We had to rescue the kids," Frank replied with a grimace.

⚜

"Yeah, because you didn't want us to become more powerful than *either of you*. They don't care about us, just stopping Legion." Jonah spoke to Marissa and Grace.

"We're pretty good at multi-tasking, son. But I can assure you, your well-being trumps everything," Frank replied.

"Besides, they can't use the relics without any of you," Cee-Cee wisecracked. She winked at him. "So it's kinda a package deal—caring about you guys and sticking it to Legion's plan."

Jonah grinned back and blushed. When Marissa jabbed him in the side, he jumped. "Cut that out," he mumbled through gritted teeth.4092

"Back to our priority, stopping them from robbing the museum," Val said. She glared at Cee-Cee, who shrugged with a puzzled expression.

Frank, engrossed in the task ahead, plowed on without spotting the exchange. "Right. Only the museum director knows the true value of the basket. It's kept in a glass enclosed display case with other artifacts used by local priests in the 1700s."

"Hidden in plain sight," LaShaun said.

"Exactly, but the glass is reinforced with motion sensors underneath the pedestal the basket sits on. Also if the glass breaks, an alarm sounds. Only the electronic key to the case can open it without the security system going off," Naldo said. "And we have a key."

"*A* key? So there's more than one," LaShaun glanced from Naldo to Frank.

"Legion has one. They held the director's two children at gunpoint until he gave them a copy," Frank said. His heavy eyebrows pulled together. "I don't blame him. Legion has a suicide squad who would have gladly killed them even if the police or us had stormed the house."

"Damn, those dudes are coldblooded," Jonah murmured, a trace of admiration in his tone.

"Yeah, they're ruthless and have nothing to lose. They're minor demons. They won't die, simply return later. The evil one's servants aren't into noble sacrifice," Jennifer said with a grimace. The bitterness in her voice matched the look of pain she wore.

"So they've got a demon suicide squad, hostages, and a key to one of the most power relics on earth. Wonderful. Any more good news, boss?" Cee-Cee rolled her shoulders.

When Frank's frown deepened, LaShaun's heart thumped. "What else, Frank?"

Frank glanced at Jennifer. "Take the kids—"

"I'm not a kid, and I'm not going anywhere," Jonah stood straight. He crumpled the empty chip bag into a ball and tossed it into a nearby trash can.

Jennifer led Marissa, Grace, and Pauline holding Ellie to the door. "Ricardo says you girls can get your nails done for free."

⚜

"Cool," Grace blurted out, her eyes bright.

They left with Jennifer and Pauline trying to offer cheerful small talk. Marissa hesitated at the open door. She looked at Jonah, at Cee-Cee, and back to her boyfriend. He crossed the room and kissed her lightly on the lips. Her mood brightened at once. Jonah gently guided her out and closed the door.

"Go on." Jonah stood, legs apart and arms crossed.

"Our information indicates the local head of the police is a Legion recruit," Manuel said. A look of distaste twisted his mouth into a grimace.

After a few moments of grim silence, LaShaun pulled out her gun. She checked it and slipped it into a pocket again. "Fine, we know what we're up against. So let's get moving."

"Wait a minute. You don't need to go with us tonight. Your child needs you," Frank protested.

"They brought the fight to my home, took my child, and shot my husband. If that's not enough, they're a threat to the world my daughter will grow up in. I want to deliver some much deserved righteous payback. Besides, Chase is recovered and already on his way here. He'll be with Ellie while I'm kicking demon ass. Y'all coming or what?" LaShaun strode to the door without waiting for a reply.

⚜

Chapter 17

An hour later, they pulled up to the opulent eighteenth century building that was once a palace, the home of Catholic bishops and other prelates. The air felt charged, but LaShaun knew it wasn't because of the exalted human church officials who had lived there. She glanced at Val to her left. The team leader nodded as if signaling she felt it, too. Cee-Cee stared up at the imposing structure. All of their group paused as though to give a moment of respect to the place.

"This way," Naldo said quietly and gestured with a nod.

He walked to the east of the building instead of climbing the stone steps up to the front entrance. They went around to a ground floor door of ornate carved wood. Angels, clouds, and figures that were probably saints had been intricately illustrated by a craftsman with great artistry. As if by magic, the heavy door swung open smoothly without so much as a creak. A man with steel gray hair and a bitter scowl stood back as they filed in.

Manuel glanced from the man to the team again. "This is—"

"They do not need to know my name," the man broke in. "Time is short. This way."

"Man of few words," Cee-Cee muttered.

Frank raised both his thick eyebrows at Naldo, but the young man shrugged and gestured for them to follow. "He's a veteran of this work. His daughters are leading the team guarding the museum director and his family. Two demons were banished back to hell in the fight."

"Yet we know they'll return. Los bastardos malignos," the older man hissed into the darkness. He didn't slow his pace or look back at them.

"I kinda like him," Cee-Cee whispered and Jonah snickered.

"There were four in the suicide squad, so we're still facing a lot of danger," Manuel said over his shoulder.

"Cheery news," Val muttered. She held up her Glock, checked the magazine and held it to the side of her thigh.

"Beautiful. "Abril gazed around.

They walked down a dimly lit hallway with crosses and other stone figures carved into the walls. They emerged into a wide room dominated by even larger paintings of bishops from the past three hundred years.

"The next floor up has more paintings of the most prominent bishops since the palace was built. Then there is a room with their vestments." Naldo spoke quietly, his tone reverent. He continued on without pausing to look at the items he obviously admired.

"Being from the south, I haven't traveled here before. I'll take the complete tour when this is over," Abril said.

"If we survive, you mean," Cee-Cee retorted.

"Hey, not in front of..." Val gave a slight nod toward Jonah, who walked ahead of their guide.

"I'm not a kid, and I'd be an idiot not to have figured out one or all of us might not make it out alive," Jonah said in a cool voice. Still he started at every sound.

"Wrong attitude. We go into every foray not only determined that everyone will make it out, but with strong faith that we will," Cee-Cee replied. Her usual playful tone gave way to an earnest one.

"Amen," Abril breathed.

Jonah nodded, his blue eyes gazing at Cee-Cee with way too much intensity. LaShaun and Val exchanged a glance. Val heaved a sigh. LaShaun grinned back at the annoyed team leader. Dealing with a school boy crush most certainly hadn't been part of her war with evil training. Suddenly the older man came to a full stop. He held up a hand, his back to them. Then he turned around to face the group.

"We're coming to the inner chamber. My men moved the glass case down here, but I'm afraid it didn't escape notice," the older man rumbled.

"Hell, I'd be shocked if Legion didn't have eyes on the relics." Cee-Cee paced in a circle as though looking for someone hiding in the shadows.

"Stay here while I check." The man didn't wait for comment, but bounded up a flight of stone steps.

The group members all paced around nervously as minutes ticked by. No one spoke, but the silence didn't reassure anyone. All of them drew their weapons as time passed. When footfalls echoed on the stone, Val and Cee-Cee aimed at the archway opening. When the man appeared again they relaxed, but only briefly. He panted, sweat rolling down his face, and he leaned against the wall.

"It's them," he gasped, then he sagged to his knees.

LaShaun rushed to his side and pulled back the jacket he wore over a shirt. Blood soaked one side of the chest pocket, the circle growing. "He's been shot or stabbed."

"We didn't hear gunfire though." Cee-Cee went up the steps before Val could stop her. Seconds later she came back. "I don't see anyone."

❦

"My men, not sure they're okay," the man got out between sucking in air. "Come, I show you."

"You need medical attention. Abril, get him out of here," Val ordered.

"But..."

"We need Naldo and Manuel to lead us through the maze of passages in this place. We'll distract the Legion operatives." Val gave a curt gesture with her hand to indicate she wouldn't debate further.

Abril gave a sigh. "Okay."

But the older man shook his head with vigor. "No, my duty is stay and protect La Reliquia Sagrada. I will not leave my task unfinished."

"The what?" Jonah blinked at him.

"The Sacred Relic. Three families have guarded it, mine included. For five generations we kept La Reliquia Sagrada away from the evil ones.

"I wouldn't waste time arguing with him," Naldo said. He nodded. "See what I mean?"

Indeed, the older man had already gotten to his feet and started up the stairs. He did at least acquiesce when Cee-Cee insisted on going first. Two small recessed lights illuminated the stone stairwell. They climbed up three flights to another hallway. Several yards away, they emerged into a grand central room. Two levels of balconies lined the walls. Massive oil paintings depicting biblical scenes and Mexican history surrounded them. Yet this time, no one, including Abril, stopped to appreciate their

⚜

beauty. Instead they focused on the scene near what LaShaun thought must have been an altar at one point. Six men stood around a glass case, each holding automatic rifles. A seventh man, at least six feet seven inches tall, took center stage. His shaved bald head, tanned a tawny color by the sun, shone beneath modern lights overhead. He strode toward them unhurried, a smile on his face that scared LaShaun more than if he'd been scowling. The man appeared confident, pleased even to see them. Not an encouraging sign at all.

"Welcome to you all and especially to the latest descendant of a great line of seers." The man swept hands out as if greeting them for a cocktail party. "But then you're not the youngest great one. Your daughter, now she is truly a rare jewel. I had high hopes she would join us."

LaShaun pulled the Glock from one pocket, and a silver knife Cee-Cee had provided from another. She planted her boots firmly on the polished stone surface of the floor. "Like hell."

"Funny you should mention it, but no time to dwell on pleasantries." The big man's smile cracked wider.

The older man who'd led them in gasped. He made the sign of the cross and murmured, "Santos nos protegen."

"Aside from the big guy and big guns, I'm guessing even worse news," Cee-Cee said quietly.

Naldo swallowed hard. "That's Barbatos, an earl of hell. He rules thirty legions of demons.

❖

He can locate treasures hidden by supernatural means."

"He's also a fighter of great power," Manuel added.

"Oh yeah, well he's gonna make one helluva boom when we bring his ass down," Cee-Cee said. She took aim at the demon's head.

"The bastard who led Legion scum to my child is mine." LaShaun pushed past Cee-Cee and pointed her Glock to the spot between his reptilian like eyes.

"Now, now ladies. Is that anyway to treat your gracious host? Besides, I look forward to enjoying both of you. There's enough of me to go around." The big man grabbed the prominent bulge at his crotch.

"Keep your funky junk covered or I'll shoot it off," Cee-Cee shouted.

Barbatos heaved a melodramatic sigh. "I see we're not going to play nice. Well, at least I can say I tried."

"On the bright side, we're not facing Satanchia tonight." Manuel wore a grim expression as he hefted his own short automatic rifle.

"Who?" Cee-Cee circled a few steps. Her gaze, like her gun, still trained on the big demon solider.

"He's the commander-in-chief of Satan's army. Barbatos's boss, and the leader of all other legions." Manuel aimed for one of the fierce looking warriors standing around their general. Two were women.

"I'll take out the three at nine, ten, and eleven o'clock," Cee-Cee murmured.

"Three by yourself, eh?" Manuel gave a humorless chuckle. "Leave some action for me."

"We all know how this is going to end, my friends," Barbatos said with unsettling calm. He slipped a leather bound book into a pocket of his field jacket.

"Yeah, we do," LaShaun yelled back.

Barbatos held up a palm. "Before you do anything ill-advised..."

"His fake old world charm act is getting on my damn nerves," Cee-Cee blurted out.

"Please note." The demon snapped his fingers. One of the two females pulled out a slim laptop and opened it. The screen images sprang to life as a hologram projection. Gunfire popped as dark figures raced toward a building.

"That's the safe house where we took your people," Naldo said, and he muttered curses in Spanish.

"You mean Ellie..." LaShaun stood rooted to the spot, staring at the scene in horror.

"Yes, your husband and child are within. My people were nice enough to wait for them to arrive. You see, Deputy Broussard didn't trust leaving his precious daughter behind, and needed to fight by your side. This is not the touching family reunion you'd hoped for, but I'm afraid it will have to do. My soldiers should bring them here shortly. Though I must compliment the TEA's team for putting up a valiant fight."

⚜

"I'm going to enjoy sending you back to hell," LaShaun spat. "You'll have even more scars on that ugly hide."

Barbatos waved a hand as if swatting away her words like annoying gnats. "Since we're at the end, you might as well know how much you helped us. Observe."

The hologram image changed to show LaShaun and Dina in the field. Dina hugged LaShaun as if grateful to be found. Yet the image zoomed to her face. A faint evil smile marred her childlike features. The picture changed again, to the team leaving the TEA building in Matamoros. LaShaun detected movement out of the corner of her eye. She darted quick glances in that direction as Frank and Cee-Cee moved in close to her. All the others gazed at the hologram in fascination.

"Someone in our team has been turned. No other way they would know so much," Cee-Cee spoke before Frank could. He nodded grimly in agreement.

"So I have no idea which one of you to trust. Damn it." LaShaun looked around at the faces she'd counted on for days. Then she fanned the spark of rage that came from betrayal. The heat roared in her chest, spread to hear arms, and through her body. "Doesn't matter. Cut off the head of the snake."

"We never wanted the child." Barbatos paused and snapped his fingers twice. "Oh what is the urchin's name?"

"Dina something or other," one of his lieu‑tenants replied gruffly.

"Yes, yes. Dina. We knew you'd follow the trail, drop your guard just enough until the time was right to take Ellie. But we needed you together. Such a strong bloodline right here with the basket to focus its power. My soldiers are bringing her closer. Can you feel it? Ah, yes, I see you understand." Barbatos clapped his hands as if applauding a performance.

Suddenly the hologram flickered and faded. The soldier holding the laptop grimaced at the device. He tapped the keys and then shook it hard. The lieutenant who had spoken up growled at the woman. She stepped close to her and stared at the device.

"Don't be a fool. Shaking a high tech in‑strument like that won't work." He entered var‑ious keystrokes while the soldier still held the laptop. "Sir, something is blocking our wireless transmission."

"Could be you've underestimated us, again," Frank called out. Then he muttered, "Let's hope."

Barbatos shrugged, though his sharp edged features twisted into a frown. "No matter. The odds are still very much against you."

"We have to protect Ellie," Abril called out, so desperate she didn't care if the Legion sol‑diers heard.

"Too little and much too late." Barbatos nodded to the lieutenant.

❖

The big man made a chopping motion with his left hand. Police officers entered the wide room at a trot, like warriors circling for battle. They formed a ring around the TEA team. Proof that the local police commander worked for Legion. Naldo whispered a short prayer in Spanish. Manuel glared at his countrymen with sincere disgust.

Barbatos smiled at them, then turned to LaShaun. "Very efficient, yes?"

A female soldier took out a cell phone and put it to her ear. Then she grinned as she ended the call. "Commander, channels are open again. The signals are getting through. There's static, but good enough to get messages. They're almost here."

Barbatos slapped his massive hands together. The sound echoed in the large chamber. "Our mission is complete. We can draw on your power and reverse the effect of the basket. Your weakling God used it to feed the hungry and convert simpletons to a false religion. We'll use it to free millions who will hear our message."

Then he turned his back on LaShaun and the TEA team as if they no longer concerned him. He conferred with his squad. Two soldiers ordered them to line up out of the way. Police officers trained their guns on them as if the team needed a reminder they were trapped.

"Can he do what he says?" Naldo looked at Frank, who could only shake his head.

Abril squinted at the demon and his men. "It's possible. Once an object becomes powerful,

⚜

that power can be directed for the wrong reasons. We haven't tested that theory for obvious reasons."

"Experiments on holy relics. Seriously?" LaShaun studied their surroundings. Her mind raced with alternatives, consequences, actions to take next.

"Of course. Most of the relics are simply symbols. Stories passed down tend to grow in exaggeration as you can imagine. Then there are those few genuine Holy items, like the staff of Moses," Frank said quietly. "Only a handful know where it's kept."

LaShaun felt an electric shock go through her body. "What?"

"We could sure use that bad boy right now," Cee-Cee said. "You know, they're sloppy mercenaries. They haven't taken our weapons."

A female soldier seemed to appear out of nowhere as she pushed aside two police officers roughly. "That's because your weapons are worthless. Our leader has a put a shield around all of us. Go ahead. Test your gun."

"Sure as hell will," Cee-Cee shot back. Before Frank could grab her arm or LaShaun could speak, she'd pulled out her Glock 19 Gen4 and pulled the trigger. Nothing happened.

"His power disrupts opposing forces." The woman smirked at them, then sauntered off.

"Can't be," Cee-Cee shouted. She kept clicking away. Nothing. "Damn, damn, damn."

"Now you're finally getting the idea. Welcome to the Army of the Damned. Victory!" The

⚜

female soldier's voice rang out. She stretched her arms wide.

Cee-Cee spun around and yelled a battle cry. She lunged for the nearest soldier. LaShaun, shaken from her daze of despair, grabbed the enraged woman and dragged her back. Cee-Cee fought to get loose, but Manuel and Abril joined to help LaShaun restrain her.

"I'm going to scrape that grin off her face with my fingernails," Cee-Cee barked.

Frank stepped close until his nose was inches from Cee-Cee's. "We need our energy to fight smart. Don't make us waste it dealing with you."

He spoke low, but his words took effect. Cee-Cee panted a few seconds longer, blinked hard and then exhaled. "Sorry, sir."

Abril yanked Cee-Cee against her body. "No, no, keep going like you're still pissed."

"Huh?" Cee-Cee gave her a baffled look.

"Just do it," Abril muttered close to Cee-Cee's ear.

"Easy," Cee-Cee rasped back. She spun to face Manuel. "Get out my face, chump. I take orders from TEA commanders!"

Manuel's eyes narrowed to slits. "Typical arrogant American females."

LaShaun glanced from them to Abril and mouthed, "What the hell?"

The police officers and a soldier nearby smiled at the scene before them. The lieutenant and her soldiers broke into something Barbatos was saying to point over to them. All laughed and continued conferring.

"Barbatos isn't all powerful like they want us to believe. Remember the tools of demons: lies and killing hope," Abril said.

"Right. You think maybe they don't have Ellie and the others?" LaShaun's heart fluttered at the chance they were safe.

"Sorry." Abril put a hand on LaShaun's forearm to console her. "I mean he can't disrupt our weapons without disrupting *all* weapons near us. Barbatos doesn't have that kind of power. No demon does. Only the Creator is omnipotent over all things."

The others went quiet at her words. Cee-Cee and Manuel continued their fake bickering. Naldo paced around them nervously. Yet he shot knowing glances at them. LaShaun felt a connection to all of the team members, except the older man who had led them in. He stood aside with one burly Mexican police captain.

"So he's the traitor," LaShaun muttered.

"Forget about him," Val said without looking around. "Explain more, Abril."

"Demons can influence men, even use a few supernatural powers. But they have limits. Fear and despair lead humans to believe they have more power than they in fact do."

"You'll be happy to know your family is near, Mrs. Broussard," the lieutenant called out from across the grand room. His fellow soldiers laughed.

⚜

Barbatos didn't join in though. Instead, he glowered at them with a grim and resolute expression. Then he spun around when two Mexican police officers entered from behind the altar. Each held one end of an ornately carved wooden box.

"Screw you and the demon horse you rode in on," Cee-Cee yelled back.

"You're out of control," Manuel snapped. They went back to exchanging insults in English and Spanish.

"If we fight, he'll have to release his control in order for their guns to fire or knives to cut. His ability to maintain the so-called shield is temporary at best," Abril whispered.

"And we'll get shot up." Frank frowned at Abril.

They gazed at each other in silence, then he looked at Cee-Cee. In response, she pretended to finally get herself under control. Manuel still gripped her left arm as if he didn't trust her. When the others formed a loose circle around him, LaShaun felt another shock. She knew and opened her mouth to protest. Frank raised a palm to silence her.

"Protect LaShaun," Frank said quietly.

Cee-Cee lifted her chin to glare at Barbatos and his men. "At all cost."

"No, I can't let you—"

"You and Chase must survive for Ellie's sake." Val stood straight.

⚜

"Agreed. Team?" Frank glanced around quickly at the rest of his TEA members, and all nodded assent.

LaShaun shuddered at the mention of Ellie and Chase. "We can't start a fire fight with the children here."

"Trust your husband and the team to get Ellie somewhere safe," Frank whispered. He glanced around the room.

LaShaun watched him assess the room. Naldo and Manuel followed his lead. Cee-Cee resumed her act of looking pissed off with the rest of them. Abril stood with her eyes closed. LaShaun wondered what she was doing, but didn't ask. Barbatos stood across from them as if listening to his men. Yet his reptilian gaze bore into LaShaun. She felt a wave of malevolence wash over her. His almost lipless mouth moved. Though he stood almost ten yards away, she heard him. All of the TEA team stopped at once and turned toward him.

"Your plans are dead. No amount of conspiring will help. But all is not lost for you. Join us." Barbatos walked toward as he talked, his voice like the first rumble of a thunderstorm.

His men objected, but he dismissed them with a wave of one massive hand. He smiled at LaShaun. Cee-Cee moved to stand shoulder to shoulder with LaShaun. The impotent Glock in one hand, a modified stun gun in the other. Naldo dropped to one knee. Frank faced the big demon with his arms folded across his chest.

✤

LaShaun ignored their whispered warnings and took a few steps to meet him. "Our plans have just begun." Then LaShaun lifted her arms high and spoke in ancient Hebrew. She recited Isaiah 54:17, "No weapon that is formed against thee shall prosper; and every tongue that shall rise against thee in judgement thou shalt condemn. This is the heritage of the servants of the Lord, and their righteousness is of me, saith the Lord."

Barbatos flinched, as did his soldiers. At each word of the scripture, Barbatos took a forced step back. A few times his huge feet slid on the floor as he tried to gain some purchase. A single large drop of sweat rolled down his forehead. He angrily swiped it away. His men muttered in frustration. LaShaun observed it all as if from a distance. Her surroundings took on a hazy quality. She felt part of the scene yet at the same time strangely outside of it.

"How is she..." Manuel's voice trailed off. He darted a glance at his cohorts.

"Damn," Cee-Cee breathed.

"Now you see why Legion went to so much trouble. I don't think even the TEA realizes." Frank cut off.

Barbatos roared with frustration. The police officers standing around fidgeted. A few exchanged nervous looks at each other, muttering in Spanish. Then the wooden box holding the basket used to feed the five thousand moved. Several whoops of shock came from the crowd. Others gaped at the box. When it moved a sec-

⚜

ond time, several of the local police officers fled. Barbatos' lieutenant roused when he saw them.

"Come back fools," he shouted at them. He raised his 50 caliber pistol, teeth bared as he aimed at the police officers too slow to take flight. "They'll die later. Run like cowards and you die now."

The crackle of a walkie-talkie cut through the chaos. "We've arrived, secured the perimeter. Captured some police running away. Awaiting instructions."

Everyone froze, but Barbatos. His frown transformed into an ugly smile. "If you don't want me to slaughter your loved ones, stand down."

LaShaun mentally unclenched the ball of concentration she'd formed as she quoted the scripture. Barbatos gave a grunt of satisfaction. Then he spun around and strode to a decorative archway leading to the outer courtyard at the front of El Obispado. His men spread out to aim their weapons at LaShaun and the other TEA team members. A tense thirty seconds went by in silence. No one, including the local police officers, moved. The lieutenant and his men visibly relaxed, sure they'd gained control once more.

"Do we have a plan?" Manuel murmured aside to Frank, his lips barely moving.

"We have to play out this situation by ear. Too many unknowns. Connect with our folks when they get close enough. Use your gifts, push to the limits." Frank swallowed hard.

⚜

Cee-Cee's gaze darted around the room. "Hey, where the hell is Jonah? Holy shit. Either they've got him or..."

"Barbatos would be parading him out here to gloat even more," Val whispered. "They're not searching for him. Which means they don't realize we're missing somebody. He's slipped off."

"A wild card we can use?" Frank looked at LaShaun.

"Let's hope and pray so," she replied softly.

With her head lowered, LaShaun concentrated again. The soldiers maintained their confident stances. None of them, including the lieutenant, noticed a shift in the atmosphere. Apparently only Barbatos could detect her aura. Frank moved closer and put an arm around her shoulders as if to comfort LaShaun. Then LaShaun looked up to the domed ceiling, a faint smile on her face.

Frank leaned in close to her right ear. "What?"

"And a little child shall lead them all," LaShaun   murmured.

❧

Chapter 18

All of the electric lighting winked off. A collective gasp went up when shadowed darkness dropped over them like a heavy blanket. Several of the police officers yelped when flames of huge torches set into the walls flared to life. Soon the smoky scent of Sulphur mixed with lime filled the air. LaShaun looked at Frank who gave a slight shake of his head.

"No clue," he said softly. He continued to frown, a blank look in his eyes.

LaShaun could almost hear his mind working as he lined up alternatives, evaluated consequences. She looked at the police officers, and then the soldiers. "Frank, they're all human."

Frank blinked back from his intense mental strategizing. "Which means..."

⚜

He didn't finish the thought as the sound of multiple footsteps on stone grew louder. Moments later, cowed police officers, still looking shaken, marched Chase, Jennifer, and the salon owner into the room. LaShaun's heart froze with dread when she saw Ellie in Chase's arms. One chubby arm circled her father's neck. She glanced around the crowd until her little brown gaze settled on LaShaun. Ellie waved a tiny hand at her, yet didn't call out. LaShaun started toward them, but the lieutenant closed the few feet between them in seconds. He pressed the muzzle of his heavy pistol against her neck.

"Any clever moves and we'll put an end to this bullshit right now," he barked.

"Seriously, dude. You ain't foolin' nobody. Your boss will skin you if anything happens to her," Cee-Cee replied. She punctuated her words with a snort.

"True." The lieutenant swung the pistol around to Cee-Cee's chest. He smiled when Cee-Cee stepped back. "Your friends will miss you, but the general won't give a crap. Let's see how much they care about you."

"Take it easy, Cee-Cee," LaShaun said softly. "Do not be afraid of them; I have given them into your hand. Not one of them will be able to withstand you."

"What in hell is she talking about?" A tall female soldier shot a quick glance at LaShaun, and then at the lieutenant for guidance.

He bared his crooked gray teeth in what passed for a smile, gaze still on Cee-Cee.

❧

"Speaking in riddles under pressure. Religious idiots."

"If she's talking in Holy Scriptures, we should know what it is. Maybe she's getting a message from..." The woman looked up at the ceiling.

"Don't be a stupid cow," the lieutenant snapped. He didn't react when the fierce woman hissed at him. "Their so-called Supreme Being doesn't care about them. They die by the millions without their precious deity lifting a finger."

Cee-Cee guffawed. "You should've gone to Sunday School, bitch."

"See?" The female soldier glared at him. "She's right to call you a fool. Knowing your enemy is the first rule of engagement Barbatos teaches us. Otherwise your enemy has advantages you don't even know exist."

"Humph. Good for you, girl," Cee-Cee replied with a tight grin. Her gaze never left the lieutenant. "Sounds to me like y'all need a change of leadership up in here."

"Mighty smartass for someone with a .50 caliber bullet aimed at her heart," the lieutenant snarled. "Now shut your fu..."

"Well, well now. Seems like someone is eager to get the party started without me," Barbatos called out from across the wide room. His booming voice bounced off the walls.

"This one seems eager to die," his lieutenant snarled. He aimed at LaShaun again, nudging the muzzle against her neck hard.

⚜

Barbatos settled his menacing gaze on his second-in-command. "Kill her too soon and there will be consequences."

"Sir, she..." The big man's voice petered when he saw the expression on his commander's face.

"Should I put someone else in charge who understands what must be done?" Barbatos didn't raise his voice as he stared at the lieutenant. The unspoken threat sparkled in his eyes.

"See? Like I was sayin'," Cee-Cee muttered to the disgruntled female soldier. The woman shot a heated glance at Cee-Cee, but didn't reply.

The lieutenant, his gaze still on Barbatos, pulled the gun away from LaShaun. Then he took care to take a few stiff steps away from her. LaShaun smelled anxiety seeping from his pores. She glanced at Cee-Cee, who gave a slight nod. Yet LaShaun couldn't sense Cee-Cee's intent. Emotions and paranormal energy crackled in the air around her, causing havoc with LaShaun's psychic gift. Still something didn't fit. Then she felt it. Tingling in the soles of her feet. Encouraged, LaShaun closed her eyes. Nothing. She gathered the familiar electric force within. A deep voice reached into her mind.

"You need to accept that your god cannot rule here," Barbatos rumbled.

LaShaun's eyes snapped open. The demon continued a mocking diatribe. His lips, curved into a horrid smile, never moved. His head jerked a fraction when she smiled back. Then she whispered a prayer aloud while conjuring the image of a shining cross in her mind. She mentally pictured the stipe of the cross as a sword.

The big demon rocked back on his heels. "You cannot stand against us."

"And the gates of hell shall not prevail against it," LaShaun shouted back at him. The cross materialized, a blade of golden radiance that plunged from the ceiling.

"We've cleansed this so-called 'holy' place." Barbatos drew himself up to stand ramrod straight. He lifted his arms, or tried to. He grunted like a weight lifter attempting to lift a barbell.

LaShaun walked toward him. "You're a thing from hell, so of course you don't understand. This is merely a building, meaningless stone and wood. The church's power is in the faith of His people."

"LaShaun don't," Chase called out.

He handed Ellie to Jennifer, then shoved aside the police officer next to him. Caught off guard, the man fell. The salon owner seemed to transform in a blink from a petite girly-girl into a warrior. She kick-boxed her way through the remaining two policemen, and left them crumpled in pain on the marble floor. But other officers rushed in. Automatic rifles surrounded Chase before he could race to LaShaun's side. Another officer shot the salon owner, and she dropped to her knees. The man then slammed the butt of his rifle into her head, and she fell over. A policeman wrestled Chase to the floor when he tried to go to her aid.

Barbatos's roar cut through the bedlam. "Enough. Look how we triumph!"

He pointed to Jennifer holding Ellie, one hand closed around her neck. Chase tried to get up again, but the officer stabbed the rifles into him. Barbatos strolled over to Jennifer while everyone else stood as if paralyzed.

"Move and I'll blow you into a thousand pieces. We don't need you at all," the lieutenant yelled at Chase, his bravado restored.

"We have the girl. You know..." Barbatos stopped speaking. He paused a few feet away from Ellie and Jennifer. Then he slowly turned to face LaShaun again. "We could just end this foolish back and forth right now. Take our prize, be done with you annoying vermin."

"I like that idea a lot, sir." The lieutenant glowered at Chase then LaShaun.

Barbatos looked up at the cross. It hovered a good ten feet overhead. "Hmm. A nice magic trick, but nothing more. Thank you, Sergeant Evans, you've done very well indeed."

"But we investigated you," Frank blurted out. "Covered every aspect of your life. How—"

"You found what I wanted the TEA to find," Jennifer broke in. She darted a quick glance at Barbatos. "I look forward to a promotion, sir."

"You'll have it my dear. A change of plans. We'll take the child. Dispose of the rest. Unfor-

✤

tunate for you, but ah well. Into each life some rain must fall," Barbatos said to Jennifer and his lieutenant.

"Yes, sir," the lieutenant barked back.

Barbatos faced LaShaun, Frank and Cee-Cee. "The child is young, raw clay ready to be molded in the hands of our skilled artists of wickedness. She'll grow up knowing the true nature of man, and how the world should be. In due time, she'll lead her own army. An epic battle against her own mother. What do you humans say? Ah, yes. Now that's something I would pay to see. But of course I won't have to. I'll have a front row seat."

"I won't let you take my daughter," Chase shouted. He batted away one rifle pointed at him.

"Chase, no!" LaShaun started to run to him, but Frank and Val yanked her back.

"They'll kill you both while Ellie watches," Val said.

"She's absolutely right you know," Jennifer said, her mouth twisted into a smile.

Barbatos brushed off the front of his uniform as if preparing for a parade or television interview. "This has been an entertaining exercise if nothing else. However..."

"Sir?" The female soldier blinked hard, her head tilted to the ceiling.

"Don't interrupt me," Barbatos snapped without looking at her. He started to go on, but then his ugly mouth hung open. The leathery skin of his forehead creased as he frowned. At

⚜

the sound of a rumble that seemed to come from the walls, he glanced at his lieutenant. "I see you called for more soldiers. Not necessary since we outplayed these humans with such ease."

"Uh, I didn't bring in more troops, sir." The lieutenant looked around at the other members of their squad. All shook their heads no.

Barbatos snorted. "Then I'll personally deal with any TEA members insane enough to think—"

A loud boom made the floor beneath their feet vibrate. LaShaun's mind swirled with confusion for several seconds. Then she realized the force came from outside her efforts. She'd been too distracted by terror for her family to concentrate.

"Look!" A police officer pointed up.

The cross glowed brighter by the second. Artifacts on display rattled when thunder rolled as if a mighty storm brewed. Two huge oak doors blew open with a crash. Chase stood, his frightened gaze glued to Ellie. LaShaun held her breath when he pushed past one officer. But none of them moved. All seemed unable to look away from the cross, despite the dazzling light that became painful. Some cried out as they struggled to move, but couldn't.

"Don't." Jennifer reached into a pocket of her jeans, and pulled a knife. She put it to Ellie's throat.

"Chase, she won't hurt Ellie. They need her too much," LaShaun yelled, but another deafening clap of thunder drowned out her voice.

Barbatos grabbed the nearest soldier. He shoved the brawny man as if he weighed nothing. "Get out there and stop whatever is happening. Move you idiots!"

The ambitious female soldier took up the call. "You heard him. Go, go."

LaShaun fought to stay on her feet as the entire museum seemed to sway. Chase stumbled until he fell on all fours. Still he crawled with great effort toward Ellie and Jennifer. Ellie looked oddly placid amid the upheaval boiling around her. She placed a tiny palm on Jennifer's forehead. Seeing the lieutenant distracted, LaShaun ran to Chase. She crouched and put her mouth to his right ear.

"Move only on my signal." LaShaun squeezed his shoulder hard to make sure she got his attention.

Chase managed to tear his relentless gaze away from their daughter. "You know what's happening?"

With a nod, LaShaun put as much reassurance as possible into her gaze. Though in truth LaShaun didn't fully understand, but rather felt a shift of the balance of forces in play. Then she glanced back at the demon general. His massive head swung from them to Ellie. His snake-like eyes widened with what would pass for alarm in a human. His slash of a mouth formed a wide circle as he tried to warn Jennifer. Too late.

Jennifer's mouth worked, but LaShaun couldn't hear her over the bedlam. The Mexican policemen's shrieks did come through. LaShaun turned to find them shaking violently, blood flowed from their eyes. Some attempted to pray for mercy. Then they suddenly jerked into movement, as though released from invisible ropes that had bound them. The men crashed into each other in a mad dash for the doors. They skidded to a halt. When LaShaun whirled to the double doors, her breath caught. Jonah stood at the apex of a triangle of others lined up behind him. All seven youngsters lured in or taken by Legion followed him, their smooth faces as grim as battle-ready adults. Jonah stopped. He stared at LaShaun. Her mind opened up and images flashed. Calm certainty engulfed her. She raised her arms to the sky. First Jonah, and then the other children followed her lead. The cross transformed into a spinning star.

"Stop the bitch!" The female soldier screamed as she pointed at LaShaun.

Another soldier lifted his rifle. Everything, everyone around her, moved in stop action sequences. Sound became muffled as if cotton had been stuffed in both her ears. LaShaun watched the big man lift the rifle and train it at her head. A Colt Close Quarters Battle Receiver, she mused. She turned her head to watch Chase. Still on his knees, he reached out an arm as if that would bring Ellie to him. LaShaun's gaze slowly traveled along his arm to Ellie. Their daughter's hand seemed attached to Jennifer's forehead. A glow surrounded it. The woman's mouth worked, eyes wide in a silent scream. LaShaun felt a smile inside without knowing why. Then something snapped and the noise came back. The slow action movie sped up.

Chase blinked as if coming out of a daze. He rolled across the marble, sprang to his feet and raced to a Mexican police officer. The man seemed unhinged by fear, shooting wildly. Chase brought him down from behind with a choke hold then with a sharp jerk twisted the man's head. The policeman went limp in Chase's arms. Gun in hand, Chase swung to the left and pulled the trigger just as the soldier fired. LaShaun felt as though a powerful fist had punched her. She spun around, stumbled and then felt rage. Violated. Her child, her husband, her friends, her world. Her mind pushed hard until a tongue of white hot energy shot out like a laser. She ran to the female soldier. The woman tried to shoot, but screeched. Smoke came from the big pistol. The woman shook hard, desperate to drop the source of her agony. LaShaun helped her by slapping the gun away. Flesh from the soldier's hand still clung to the metal. Then LaShaun jumped high, kicked the woman in the chest. Once down, the female soldier scrunched into a half conscious ball.

⚜

Barbatos roared in rage across the room. All of El Obispado Museum shook as he took giant steps toward LaShaun across the once sacred space. He batted one of his own soldiers out of the way, tore the head off another man in his path. Jonah and the children stopped fighting. They formed a circle, hands clasped. The remaining soldier tossed away his weapon and ran away. A snake-like rope popped out of nowhere and wrapped around his legs. The man wailed when he fell, and the rope slithered up his body until he couldn't move.

The star gleaming over their heads formed into a cross again and started a rapid descent. Barbatos skidded to a halt. His size seventeen boots squeaked as he tried to avoid the symbol of redemption. His huge mouth stretched into a wide circle, the dark interior resembling a pit of hell.

"St. Michael the Archangel, defend us in the day of battle," LaShaun shouted.

"Be our safeguard against the wickedness and the snares of the devil," Abril added.

"Cast this demon into Hell, and with him all the evil spirits who came to spread their foulness across the world," Frank shouted.

"Into Hell," the children chanted. "Into Hell. Into Hell. Into Hell."

"Amen." Ellie's childish voice cut through the air.

An earsplitting clap, like two gigantic hands coming together, shook the world. Barbatos squawked "No" once. Blazing white light blind-

❧

ed them, and everyone covered their eyes. The demon's voice echoed then faded away. When LaShaun dropped her hands, only the enormous boots remained. A wisp of muddy brown mist drifted from them but disappeared seconds later.

LaShaun whirled around and looked for Ellie. She gasped when she saw her little girl. Ellie stood next to Chase, who raised his head slowly. When he saw Ellie standing before him, he cried for joy and gathered her in a tight embrace. Ellie giggled as if they'd just gone through an exciting carnival ride.

"Honey, your baby girl is amazing," Cee-Cee said over LaShaun's shoulder. "What the hell did she do to Jennifer though?"

"What?" LaShaun could only see her child and husband safe. Everything else had faded out of focus.

Abril and Frank stood next to Cee-Cee. All pointed at the same time. LaShaun glanced in that direction to see Jennifer standing stiff. Her eyes looked glazed, unseeing anything. She blinked slowly.

"Whatever it was, she deserved it," LaShaun replied and joined her family.

****

Chase went into panic mode again when he saw bloodstains on LaShaun's field vest. Only then did the pain in her arm set in. For the next three hours, Frank directed his team to clean up the museum. Local TEA operatives made quick work of clearing the area. Manuel and Naldo gave orders in Spanish. A cadre of uncorrupt police arrived soon after. LaShaun allowed an emergency medical tech to examine her wound. Ellie sat close by, her dark eyes clouded with fear. Between reassuring her child, and assuring a worried Chase that she would survive, LaShaun missed most of the action around her. Then she was taken to a local hospital.

The next day, Cee-Cee visited LaShaun. She walked in with a vase full of marigolds. "Girl, you one tough b..." She broke off and glanced at Ellie perched in Chase's lap.

LaShaun laughed. "I accept the compliment, and thanks for the beautiful flowers."

"Hey, yellow in honor of the golden symbol that saved all our... all of us," Cee-Cee finished with a grin. She put the flowers on a table. "How are you feeling today?"

"Like I've been fighting demons all night," LaShaun quipped. Then they both laughed. "How are you?"

"Every inch of me is sore, but I'll be fine. Nothing some protein and exercise won't cure."

"What about the others? I don't remember seeing Val, but so much hell had broken loose." LaShaun's smile faded at the sudden change on Cee-Cee's face.

"Umm." Cee-Cee cleared her throat.

⚜

Chase stood up when Cee-Cee looked at him, Ellie perched in the crook of his left arm. "Let's go get you a snack, sweet girl."

They crossed to both plant kisses on LaShaun's cheek. LaShaun gave Ellie a wink, and watched them leave. Then she pushed the button that raised her hospital bed. Cee-Cee turned away. When she faced LaShaun again, she swiped her cheeks with a tissue.

"LaShaun, Val didn't make it out. But she went down fighting." Cee-Cee choked up. Then she recovered. "She was the best pain-in-the-ass boss ever."

LaShaun ignored the pain and stiffness to reach out to Cee-Cee with her uninjured arm. They clasped hands. "I agree, honey. A tough loss. Ernesto?"

Cee-Cee cleared her throat. "He's coming along fine. Complaining that he'll be on medical leave for a while, but he's doing good all things considered. I broke it to him about Jennifer."

"Maybe you should have waited?" LaShaun said.

"I had to. Ernesto kept asking about her, and then... we're all psychics. Said he couldn't feel her presence and freaked out thinking she'd been killed. So I told him. Not about Val though. When he's stronger."

"What did you say about Jennifer? I'm not clear on what's happened to her.

"Girl, it's weird. Okay, we're psychics in a secret organization fighting supernatural bad guys, yada yada. But even vets in TEA have

⚜

never seen anything like what happened with Ellie. Jennifer is like a wind-up doll with a drained battery. What did your baby girl *do* to her?" Cee-Cee blinked at LaShaun with an expression of wonder.

"Before all this, I would have said Ellie was your typical toddler. I figured she'd be at least a few years older before there'd be signs of paranormal traits."

"Yeah, some say it's really unusual for a kid that young to use paranormal abilities with a goal in mind. She knew what to do, when to do it, and why. Like the old saying, she's born with an old soul." Cee-Cee shook her head.

"Yeah, exactly," LaShaun murmured. A flash image of Monmon Odette, wearing an impish grin appeared in her mind. Then LaShaun dismissed the fanciful notion. "So tell me what's up with Jennifer."

"I wanted to whip her ass, but Abril stopped me. Can't have no fun." Cee-Cee faked a pout. "Anyway, whatever whammy Ellie put on her has Jennifer's brain more than a bit scrambled. But she's talking. Seems she was closer to Kris Evans than she let on. Legion recruited her two years after TEA had done all the background screening. She was slick enough to stay far away from Legion members."

"Damn, a sleeper," LaShaun said.

"You can guess that has our R&D team working long hours," Cee-Cee replied.

"Right. TEA will have to come up with new screening protocols and look at all members

❖

again. Learn from how Jennifer pulled it off."
LaShaun rested against the pillows again.

Cee-Cee stood straight. "We'll get it done.
We always do. Val didn't die for nothing. Ernesto will recover in body and spirit. The fight
will go on."

"The Lord said to Joshua, 'Do not be afraid
of them; I have given them into your hand. Not
one of them will be able to withstand you,"
LaShaun murmured.

"Amen. Not that I went to church on a regular basis, much less Sunday school." Cee-Cee
shrugged when LaShaun looked at her.

"Girl, please," LaShaun joked.

"Oh, I go now. Well, not every Sunday."
Cee-Cee's shapely brows went up, a twinkle in
her eyes. "Okay, not most Sundays."

"He can use even the backsliders to do
good."

LaShaun laughed when Cee-Cee winced
and grabbed her chest as if in agony. Then they
laughed together. The sensation and sound
provided healing for them both. They spoke of
faith, and Val. Of loyalty and betrayal. Two
soldiers in arms who knew more battles lay
ahead.

****

Two days of recovery went by fast. Chase
moved around like he hadn't been shot only a
few days before. Doctors attributed his quick

recovery to youth and how healthy he was before getting shot. LaShaun knew the real reason, healing prayers offered up by the twins. They visited her on their way to the airport.

"Honey, you sure livened up my life for a minute," Justine said. She fussed about LaShaun's hospital room, straightening up.

"Lots of action. I'm gonna need a few weeks of doing nothing in between long naps to get over all this drama," Pauline added. She sat in a chair, her feet propped on the small sofa along one wall. "Where's your hubby and the sprout?"

"Chase is showing Ellie some of the local culture. You know, art, music, and fun. Since we're done fighting demons, might as well be tourists," LaShaun quipped. She wiggled around in the bed to relieve stiffness.

"Let's get you up and walking." Pauline said. The retired nurse shifted into professional mode. "Exercise helps blood flow. Even at your age, staying in bed too long isn't good. Blood clots."

Minutes later, both women walked on either side of LaShaun down the hallway past other hospital rooms. Both kept a watchful eye to make sure she wouldn't get dizzy. They kept up a steady stream of gossip while LaShaun concentrated on taking each careful step.

They walked through a bright visiting room and onto a small balcony. At Pauline's instruction, they made a circuit. The view of the city spread out three stories below. A warm breeze

⚜

blew, and sunshine lit up the scene before them. It was hard to believe they'd faced the ultimate source of depravity in such a place. Yet evil oozed into even the most idyllic settings. Pauline ordered LaShaun to rest a minute on a nearby bench. She sat next to her. Justine continued to feed her compulsion to check messages on her phone.

Most of her life, LaShaun had felt isolated, an outsider. Worse, shunned. No one to lean on for support but her grandmother. Coming home four years before to bury Monmon Odette had done the opposite of making her alone in the world. LaShaun wondered if her grandmother had instructed the twins and Miss Rose to be her maternal stand-ins. When Pauline spoke, it seemed she'd followed LaShaun's train of thought.

"We knew of the famous Odette Rousselle, but we never met her. I'm sure she would be so proud of the woman you've become." Pauline nodded as she looked ahead, one hand on LaShaun's back.

"Yeah, according to Rose, you kick ass and take names just like she did." Justine never took her gaze from the smartphone she held. She scrolled through texts and occasionally tapped responses.

LaShaun laughed. "Thank you, ma'am. Sorry I didn't get to say bye to Miss Rose before she flew home. I was on so much medication that I hardly remember our conversation when she visited me a few days ago. I miss her already."

"I don't know how. She's called every hour since her plane touched the runway in Lafayette," Justine retorted. "Humph, here's a text right now from her."

"The ultimate mother hen." Pauline grinned. "She had to get back to her babysitter duties. Her daughter and son-in-law left for a business trip."

"Return to life as usual. All the routine stuff like running errands, pulling weeds in the garden, wiping baby bottoms and such. Sounds so wonderful," LaShaun replied and heaved a deep sigh.

"Yeah." Pauline nodded in agreement.

"Only until the next time the TEA sends out an alert."

"Or one of us sniffs supernatural skullduggery in the air," Justine replied.

LaShaun turned to Pauline and stage whispered, "Did she just say supernatural *skullduggery?*"

"It's those damn word game apps," Pauline stage-whispered back.

"Yeah, that's exactly what I said. And of course I can hear you." Pauline turned to face them. She stopped looking at her phone. "My point being, we're only taking a break from creepy for now. Y'all know the Devil stay busy."

"At least we knocked Legion back on their heels. Rose checked in with the TEA. Chatter on the Dark Web has it that our little skirmish blew their minds. Giving Satan a migraine is so much fun." Pauline smiled as if enjoying the image that conjured.

"Yeah, Frank told Chase the local Legion operation is in disarray. The municipal government came down on their clothing company. They've been hit with all kinds of inspections. Plus, Barbatos is gone." LaShaun felt an involuntary shudder merely saying his name out loud. The memory of him beheading his own follower with his bare hands would haunt her for a long time.

"They tell me y'all prayed his repulsive butt right back to hell. High five, cher." Justine shared a gentle palm slap with LaShaun.

Pauline didn't share their enthusiasm. She continued to wear a sober expression. "He'll be back, or maybe one even worse than him."

After a few seconds of all three women engaging in grim introspection, Justine blew out a huff of air. She smiled at them. "Hell, let's celebrate any damn way. Not today Satan."

"Not today," Pauline repeated, a small grin on her otherwise serious face.

"Not today," LaShaun agreed.

Then every vestige of gloom vanished. Chase walked toward them holding Ellie's hand. Ellie wore a purple top with flowers and a purple skort. Her matching sneakers had her favorite cartoon characters on them. She waved at LaShaun with her free hand as they got closer.

⚜

"Now that makes me miss my own kids." Pauline beamed at them.

"Speaking of which, we need to get to the airport, sister." Justine tapped the clock display on the screen of her smartphone.

The twins said their goodbyes to Chase and Ellie. They took turns showering Ellie with compliments about her outfit, her cute hairstyle, and her bravery. Observers would never guess the remarkable series of events their little group had gone through. They looked like a family sharing an ordinary reunion. Once the twins were gone, Chase and LaShaun decided to stay on the balcony for a while longer. Toys and child-sized furniture in a corner captured Ellie's attention. She made friends with two other children, a boy and girl. The fact that they jabbered in different languages didn't dampen their play one bit.

"She seems okay," LaShaun said. "But..."

"The nightmares, I know. We'll move her bed into our room for a while when we get home. We'll make it, darlin'. We'll make it," Chase said quietly and put an arm around LaShaun.

LaShaun gripped his hand. "Did you find out about the other children?"

"Don't worry. I talked to Cee-Cee and Abril. The younger kids will be in foster homes, all of them TEA members or supporters. How did they manage to pull that off?"

⚜

"They've got connections in several state child welfare agencies. I was shocked Jonah agreed to foster care."

"He didn't. Jonah took off without Marissa. But then she didn't want to go. Seems she's pissed off about him crushing on Cee-Cee." Chase grinned. "Oh yeah, I noticed. Hard not to the way he follows her around. Though he tried to keep it low key. Marissa went home, says her parents aren't that bad."

"I'll bet she's got a new perspective after being shot at and chased by a ginormous demon," LaShaun replied in a droll tone.

"Abril promised her TEA would offer her shelter if she needed it. Amazing how TEA has people strategically placed in so many locations."

"Like state and local child welfare agencies. They started it some years back because gifted children were being abandoned or worse— abused. People fear what they don't understand even if it's their own flesh and blood," LaShaun said.

Chase pulled LaShaun against his body, his gaze on a laughing Ellie a few feet away. "LaShaun, I worry about what the future holds for Ellie. But don't ever doubt that I cherish her."

"I know." LaShaun studied his profile and then looked away.

"And you. I love my mother, but nothing she has said or can ever say will change what I feel for you. I may stumble 'cause the magic stuff is tough to swallow sometimes." Chase broke off.

"Yeah, for a boots-firmly-on- the-ground Cajun officer of the law." LaShaun brushed her fingers through his dark hair with affection.

Chase looked at her. "I love you."

"And I love you more," LaShaun replied.

"Not possible." Chase gave her a tender kiss then drew back. They both sighed, and he went on. "Hey, we got some lagniappe—drug arrests. So Dave and MJ are happy even though they complained about me being gone so long. The Policía here broke up a ring as well. So much for Legion's alliance with local gangs. Several of the Bradford and Menard family members are in jail back in Louisiana."

"So Legion has been hit hard from all directions. Good. Speaking of the Bradfords, what about Dina? Is she back with her mother?"

"She's been removed by DCFS, but her mother and grandmother didn't fight it this time. They're scared of her. Sherry and Arliss claim she's possessed or some nonsense." Chase's eyebrows pulled together and he gazed at LaShaun. "Or is it?"

LaShaun bit her lip as she considered the possibility. "No. Dina came under evil influence not of this world. I'm guessing TEA will step in."

"Legion will re-group and come up with some other dirt to throw at the world. They're like regular criminals and roaches. You can

❧

clear 'em out for a while, but they always come back."

"Only a thousand times more disgusting," LaShaun added.

"What happened with Ellie at El Obispado." Chase's voice trailed off as if he couldn't articulate what he'd observed. "The other children, including Jonah, looked at her as somehow more than... I mean, like she's extra special. The TEA members did, too. What does it mean, honey?"

LaShaun followed his gaze to Ellie. She giggled with the other children while they took turns tossing a colorful ball between them. A fourth child joined them, and Ellie welcomed him like a long lost friend. Then Ellie turned to look at her parents. Her knowing smile made her look far wiser than a typical almost four-year old. LaShaun felt a warm reassuring flow of energy. The words, "Happy mama, safe mama" popped into her head. Then Ellie flapped a hand at her gaily before turning her attention back to the mini-ball game.

"We'll keep her safe," LaShaun murmured, a sense of wonder shaking her to the core.

Then she felt the tension leave Chase's body. When she looked at him, a tranquil smile had spread across his face. Ellie wore an intent expression as she gazed at her father, then she went back to playing.

"Hey, what am I worried about? She's got an amazing mother, and her daddy carries a gun. Ellie's gonna be just fine. No, better. She's going to be great." Chase waved at Ellie.

"Of course," LaShaun smiled back at him.

LaShaun thought back to Ellie's hand on Jennifer's forehead, immobilizing an adult psychic. Then her tiny voice pronouncing "Amen" with such conviction that it vanquished a powerful demon. Her daughter, her first born, would be in future battles. LaShaun tightened her hold on Chase as he enjoyed watching their child have fun. They would face the future together, and that enough gave her reason to feel hopeful. Whatever the future might bring.

Then LaShaun noticed something odd. All of the children deferred to Ellie, giving her the most interesting toys. Ellie touched each child playing with an item she wanted. After a brief refusal, each child relented seconds later and Ellie smiled with contentment.

We're going to have a serious talk soon, young lady. LaShaun gave a mental push. The thought sailed out like a tiny boat sliding on the glassy surface of an invisible pond. Ellie looked up. She blinked at her mother with an innocent "Who me?" expression on her pert face. Yes, very soon. LaShaun heaved a sigh and rested her head on Chase's shoulder.

⚜

More
LaShaun Rousselle Mysteries

A Darker Shade of Midnight
A demon is on a kill spree, and LaShaun is next on its list. Suddenly being a murder suspect is the least of her worries.

Between Dusk and Dawn
Whispers of rougarou begin as the dead bodies start to pile up in Vermilion Parish. LaShaun goes after both human and supernatural killers.

Only By Moonlight
The man she loves is changing, and not for the better. LaShaun figures out the cause, he's possessed. Will she have to kill him to save his eternal soul?

❖

About the Author

Lynn Emery's novels explore Louisiana's exciting contemporary culture and exotic history. From the big cities to the stunningly beautiful and mysterious swamps, stories of intrigue, secrets and murder play out on the pages. A native of the state, her knowledge of folklore, the uniquely colorful politics and crime combine to spice up each tale. For a complete list of Lynn's novels and to read more about her visit:

www.lynnemery.com

Printed in Great Britain
by Amazon